T
COLDEST CLUES

An absolutely gripping crime mystery you won't be able to put down

A.J. CROSS

Dr Kate Hanson Mysteries Book 2

Originally published as *Art of Deception*

JOFFE BOOKS

Revised edition 2023
Joffe Books, London
www.joffebooks.com

First published by Orion in 2013 as *Art of Deception*

This paperback edition was first published
in Great Britain in 2023

This book is a work of fiction. Names, characters, businesses, organizations, places and events are either the product of the author's imagination or are used fictitiously. Any resemblance to actual persons, living or dead, events or locales is entirely coincidental.
The spelling used is British English except where fidelity to the author's rendering of accent or dialect supersedes this.

Cover art by Nebojša Zorić

ISBN: 978-1-83526-062-3

NOVEMBER 1993

I've been hit and I'm so cold it's hard to think straight . . . scared. I can't see a way out. Funny . . . I remember all the times as I grew up when you told me how clever I was, how 'aware'. You wouldn't say that if you could see me. I'm here because I heard something terrible and then did something really stupid. Maybe I haven't been thinking straight for a while? I know what's going to happen. Must happen. Because he won't believe me, even if I promise. Because I'll talk. Someone has to—

I thought I just heard something . . . I'm trying to stay calm. My mind keeps drifting over . . . everything. Maybe you'll catch my thoughts? You know — that bond we've got? I'm hoping that you'll get it, that you'll realise . . . Say 'sorry' for me, would you? Say that I wanted to be there. I would have been if I could—

I did hear something . . .

Mom, I'm finished.

CHAPTER ONE

He took a single, quiet step in the failing afternoon light, watching the solitary figure raise its arm and point two joined fingers at the glossy rooks and large-beaked raven across the water. Hearing the single '*Bam!*', he saw the birds rise as one, then continued on, soundless despite his heavy build — so close now he could almost touch the back of the pale grey Stingray ski jacket. Another silent step and he reached out, gripped the shoulder. '*Yar!*'

The figure in the ski jacket spun on mud. 'What you playing at, you fat *idiot*?!'

Bradley Harper grinned and pointed. 'Look up there, Stuey. Look at that!'

Stuey ignored the directive. He'd seen it. He didn't need another look at the low-roofed structure squatting on its foundations, flanked by trees, the gnarled trunks twisting away. He was intent now on scraping his muddied trainer soles against the coarse grass. 'These cost a hundred and fifty quid, you *moron*.' He pointed at a nearby sapling. 'Break off a couple of those thin branches so we can set some snares.'

Harper gave the sapling a reluctant glance. He was well aware of his companion's interest in wildlife. And the not-so-wild. Teachers at their school still didn't know all that had happened to the three guinea pigs that used to live in the science block but Harper knew: Stuey had happened. Persisting with his own agenda, he pointed again. 'It's one of them summer houses. My mom told me there used to be some big old houses around here before they turned the land into a conservation area. It probably belonged to one of them.'

But Stuey was on the move, mercurial mood darkened by this further reference to the brooding structure and now the arrival of sudden heavy raindrops. 'Yeah, and your old lady's a fat slag and her bloke's an on-the-rob thicko,' he called over his shoulder.

'No she's — Where're you going?'

'Catch me hanging about here in the cold *and* rain. I'm off. If *you* want to stop here till it's dark and the nonces come out to play, suit yourself.' He turned to deliver a parting sneer: 'Maybe *that's* your scene.'

Harper's round pale face flushed as he stared after the departing back. 'That was ages ago.'

Stuey was continuing to put distance between them. 'They come anywhere near *me* they'll be wearing their balls for earrings. They'll—'

Tuning out sentiments he'd heard many times before, Harper gazed after the pricey trainers and jacket, deciding to play to Stuey's fine-tuned acquisitiveness. '*Think* about it, yeah?' he shouted. 'There might be stuff inside there that we could—' Without warning the raindrops increased to a sudden torrent. Pulling his hood over his unkempt blond hair Harper turned and ran, scrabbling the incline towards the small structure. Pounding up the steps to the doors, he grabbed the handles with a rough push-pull movement then whirled, breathless. 'It's locked! Come on! Give us a hand.'

Shed or summer house, it was shelter and Stuey was already retracing his steps. Clawing his way upwards he arrived at the doors to deliver a practised shoulder-shove. Hinges shrieked as the outward-opening doors quivered then wavered inwards.

They stepped inside where Harper broke the silence, whispered words drifting on cloudy breath. 'This is great, Stu. It's dry. Nobody will know where we are and—'

Stuey mooched across the floor, blowing on his hands. 'It's *effing* cold and there's nothing here.' Belligerence was replaced by quick craftiness. He turned. 'Know what it needs?'

'. . . No, what?'

The smooth face beneath the neat dark hair split into a grin, the words slow and deliberate. 'A — nice — warm — fire.'

Harper shot his friend a quick glance. He slowed his words. 'Leave it out, yeah? Just . . . calm down a bit. I *know*—'

'Shut the fuck up. You know nothing.'

'Okay . . . okay,' soothed Harper, plump hands batting the tense space between them, watching the restless prowl start up again, guessing the lack of medication. 'We stop in here for a bit, yeah? Nice and quiet. Have a coupla fags and then the rain'll — *No*, Stu, *don't*!'

The expensive trainer made destructive contact with the drab wall. 'Fires need wood. See that? Dry as anything.'

'*Leave* it, Stu. I don't—'

Halting the sudden vandalism, Stuey fixed his companion with a look. 'What? You don't *what*?' Without warning he lunged at Harper and both fell to the floor, a mass of flailing limbs halted by the harsh crack of fracturing wood as a heavy boot made contact. They sat up, eyes converging on an area of flooring close to the wooden wall. 'Look at what you've done!' Stuey crowed.

Catching his breath, Harper looked to where Stuey was pointing: a newly created hole near the crumbling skirting. He watched as Stuey went to it, dropping to one knee to grab and pull at the damaged floorboards. Harper was tired now. He felt cold. He didn't want more trouble. He'd had enough of Stuey and he didn't want to be here any more. He wanted to go home. When he got back he'd ask his mom to put some chips on. 'You're right. Let's go. You know what?' He glanced over his shoulder towards the darkening windows. 'I thought I heard something.'

Stuey was still occupied with the hole, running his fingers along the ruined wood, showing the fixed concentration which always provoked nervousness in Harper, and anyone else in close proximity. 'This stuff's dead dry. Come on! Let's rip up some more.' He seized another of the broken boards which gave a high-pitched screech then split. He clicked his fingers. 'Give us that torch your old man nicked.'

Harper struggled to his feet, anticipating trouble. '*No.* He said not to take it out of the house. He's coming round to see my mom tonight so I've got to put it—' He watched as Stuey approached him, blue eyes unwavering, felt the small torch being lifted from his back pocket, knowing resistance was pointless.

He watched as Stuey returned to the hole, placed the torch on the floor and pulled at more boards. As another resisted with a piercing screech Stuey glared at him. 'You gawping or helping?'

Reluctant, he moved closer, grasped one of the floorboards then let it go again. 'What if somebody comes? What if . . .'

Stuey shook his head. 'You're such a *wanker*.'

Harper allowed himself to be pushed to one side and watched as Stuey seized one of the longer boards, releasing it almost immediately — '*Shit!*' — saw the finger and the red bloom on its tip go into Stuey's mouth.

Within minutes and with no assistance from Harper the hole had grown to over a metre at its widest point. Harper watched as Stuey kicked broken flooring to one side then lay down and lowered his head into the hole's dark mouth. He edged closer, thinking of a likely deflection, a motivational carrot. 'How about the community centre, Stu? We could go there, have a laugh, a game of pool, shake things up a bit. How about it?'

He heard the soft click of the torch, followed by Stuey's voice. 'There's something . . . I can . . . almost . . . *reach* . . .'

His words were cut short by a ragged intake of breath and the wild gyration of all four of his limbs as Stuey reared, propelling himself backwards across the floor, torch still clamped in his hand. He halted, eyes stretched, breath rasping.

Harper looked from him to the hole and back. 'What's up? What's in there?' Uncertain, he watched as Stuey, ashen-faced, wiped his mouth on his sleeve and got quickly to his feet, the forgotten torch falling from his hand. Slow to act, Harper saw it hit the floor, marked its steady progress towards the raw, broken edge where it teetered then disappeared. He moved too late. 'Oh, man, I'm *dead*. When my dad—' He whirled round. 'Where're you *going*?' He watched Stuey make a rapid exit through the doors and away in the fast-diminishing light, listened to the sound of his retreating feet. And something else? He frowned, listening hard. No. Nothing. Only silence.

With Stuey's departure the lake house felt calm. '*Tosser!*' yelled Harper, confident now in the distance Stuey was putting between them. He took a tentative step to peer into the void. It wasn't about to give up its secrets easily. That's *if* it had any. Stuey was just trying to spook him. Stuey was a dickhead. Everybody said so, although not to his face. Harper got down onto his broad knees, head low, trying to discern something within the blackness. Stuey was a liar. You couldn't count on anything he said. Stuey was a head case. Everybody said that as well. He sat up, eyes still on the pool of blackness. His dad's torch was somewhere down there. He had to get it back.

Lying down he extended an arm, playing his fingers within the space, brushing against something smooth and leathery. Jerking his hand he reached to one side, the tendons in his arm screaming, locating the slender tube where it had settled. Light-headed with relief he grasped it. Now his old man couldn't get on his case. All he had to do was get home before him.

Lifting out the torch he hesitated then pressed. The soft click delivered a dim, puttering light. Directing it downwards he moved it steadily, his eyes following the tiny beam as it moved over the uneven, sandy floor and onwards to a tiny object which glinted in the meagre light. Excitement surging, he peered at the small—

His lifted his head and he looked towards the doors. 'Stuey?' Silence. He called again, louder this time. 'That *you*, Stu?' More silence. Earlier talk of the area's after-dark clientele surged into his head. Harper responded as he did to most troublesome information which came his way. He closed a mental door on it. As a shadow drifted past the windows his head was back inside the hole, lower this time, to reapply the failing torch, trying to relocate what he'd seen. If he could reach it . . .

He shot upright, emulating Stuey's earlier backwards scrabble across the floor, stopping several feet away, heart pounding. Now he knew what Stuey had seen. Waiting for the blood thud in his ears to stop, he stared at the black void, his head full of the conflict of wanting something yet fearful of getting it. It could be worth a few quid. He might even keep it. To do that he had to go back to the hole, reach down inside. Brow creasing, he thought of the time he'd walked with his mom to visit his nan. He remembered his mom swapping the flowers she was carrying to her other hand, putting her arm around his shoulders, telling him dead people couldn't hurt you.

With a single-minded determination not displayed in any area of his sixteen years to date, Harper returned to the void, activated the dying torch and lowered his head into the hole, gaze averted. No way he wanted to see that again. Locating what he was seeking, he stretched until his fingers closed on it.

Pulling himself upright, sweat coursing, breath coming in harsh gasps, he held it, small and cold against his palm, then moved across the floor and sat, hand fisted, his eyes on the pool of blackness. People had to know. The police. He frowned. He didn't want more trouble. No. He wouldn't tell anybody. Ever. Wouldn't even tell Stuey he'd seen it.

Opening his hand he looked at the item in the torch's minimal light. He brushed sand from it. Nice. Maybe he could get it to—

His head whipped round. 'Who's there?' he whispered, eyes on the doors. Had to be Stuey, come back for another look. Come back for *this*. Unzipping the concealed pocket of his parka he placed it inside, rezipped it then ran his fingers over the coat's surface. Confident now, he called again, louder this time. 'How about it, then? The community centre, yeah?'

Fractured hinges squealed as dank mist and cold air drifted inwards. He got to his feet, eyes wide, and started to back away, hearing a voice unrecognisable as his own, a tremulous quaver at panic's edge. 'I didn't do nothing . . .'

In the minutes that followed, wings flapped and the mist, the trees and the smooth, dark water absorbed all sound from the lake house.

CHAPTER TWO

'*Here*, boys!' The man in the Barbour clicked his tongue, looping the plaited-leather dog leads over one arm to clap his hands. He got only muffled barks in response. Where the *hell* were they? He pulled back his sleeve to look at his watch: six fifty a.m. Tuesday was always a busy day at work. To have any chance of getting to the office on time he needed to be back home, showered, breakfasted and ready to leave the house by eight thirty at the latest. He scanned the area, intense cold filming his eyes. Irritated now, he headed in the direction of the barks, calling again. 'Barney! Zac! *Here*. Now!'

He reached the lake where he'd half expected to see them, hoping he wouldn't. He didn't have time to dry them off. They weren't in the water. Nor were they anywhere else in sight. He listened. Their barks were coming from inside an elevated wooden building on the other side of the lake. Picking up speed he walked towards it, wondering how they'd managed to get inside. He scrutinised the doors as he neared, one of them half open, both showing evidence of damage. Reaching the top of the small flight of steps he pushed on the half-open door. It resisted. A second push and he walked inside.

Barney and Zac were poised over an area of wooden flooring, their compact bodies quivering, tongues lolling, tails up. He moved towards them, watching them execute little leaps on their front paws. He recognised the behaviour, knew what it meant: extreme frustration. '*Here*, boys. Come *on*.' They remained where they were. Going down on one knee he rubbed and patted Zac's shoulders and Barney's flank. 'Hey, hey, what're you two up to? What's got you so hot and bothered?'

His eyes drifted over the area of wooden floor immediately in front of them. A small piece of it was missing. He guessed that the dogs' frustrated pawing had loosened it, causing it to fall beneath the floor. Curiosity piqued, he leaned towards the hole and the dogs' excitement spiralled as another, larger piece of flooring disappeared. Hooking a finger he raised a section of board, pulling it to one side as both animals whimpered and circled on either side of him.

He gazed into the small hole, unable to discern anything in the blackness. Straightening, he pushed a hand into one of the Barbour's pockets, drew out his torch then leaned forward to apply it. It took him some seconds to process what he was seeing as the dogs bobbed and whined. '. . . Easy . . . easy, you two. It's . . . okay . . . okay,' he soothed, knowing that it wasn't.

Pulling air into his chest he switched off the torch and swapped it for his phone. The early-shift operator responded almost instantly. 'Emergency. Which service do you require?'

'Hello?'

'*Emergency*. Which service do you require?'

He shushed the dogs, passing a hand over his damp forehead. 'I wouldn't describe it as an emergency exactly . . .'

The operator's weary voice persisted. 'What's the nature of your situation, caller?'

'My dogs . . .' He sensed impatience on the line, imagined the operator's lips thinning. She was probably fed up of people calling to report some cat stuck up a tree. 'They've found . . . I think . . . I think they've found a body.'

* * *

The sound, followed by the significant mass of Chief Superintendent Gander coming at speed through the door, got Detective Sergeant Bernard Watts's immediate and undivided attention. Eyebrows climbing towards greying hair, Bernie glanced across the table to Lieutenant Joe Corrigan, his colleague on secondment to Rose Road's Headquarters from Boston, Massachusetts.

'Where's Kate?' Not waiting for a response Gander ploughed on. 'A body's been found at Woodgate Country Park. Near the lake.'

Bernie gave Gander a speculative look. 'And it's one for us? For UCU?'

'Initial reports suggest it's been there a while. It could be connected to one of half a dozen cold cases on the system. Get to the scene. Pathology and SOCOs are already out there. Find out what they know.' He was on the move again but turned, surprisingly quick on his feet, finger pointing for emphasis. 'Contact Kate. If she's available I want her down there as well.'

Bernie seized the phone as the chief's massive bulk disappeared through the door.

* * *

Kate Hanson was in deep water, that first day of a new term in a new year. Scent from a nearby candle joined steam wisping upwards to the ceiling and the humming extractor fan. Immersed to her shoulders, thick, dark-red hair secured on top of her head, she lifted the sponge and watched the water's hypnotic fall, ambushed by a sudden memory of her ex-husband Kevin's nine p.m. phone call on Christmas Eve. Citing overwork and an imminent departure for Paris, Kevin wondered if Kate would *please* give Maisie money on his behalf? With a sigh she'd hung up on the sounds of airport announcements and a soft female laugh, gone to her bag, got cash, placed it inside a card, mimicked his signature and his love and sealed it all inside an envelope on which she'd written their daughter's name.

Releasing the sponge into the water Kate took a deep breath, switching her focus to the day ahead: a gentle segue into the university's new term, beginning with a morning of admin. Her first lecture wasn't until — *Relax. New year; new me . . . All of my responsibilities well-organised—*

There was a urgent knock on the bathroom door and one of those responsibilities spoke. 'Mom?'

—well-managed, and to hell with Kevin and his—

'Mom!'

Kate sat up, sending a bow-wave of water to the end of the bath where it swelled then cascaded to the floor. 'Stop shouting, Maisie.'

'Phone! For *you*.'

She sank back into wet warmth. 'It's too early. Tell whoever it is to ring back.'

'It's *Bernie*. He wants to talk to you. He said it's important.' Kate heard quick feet scampering away.

'Oh, for—' She stood and seized a towel. Wrapping herself inside it and stepping out of the bath she thrust her feet into the pink slippers Maisie had given her for Christmas. Pulling open the bathroom door, Kate padded across the landing and downstairs to lift the hall phone. '*What*?'

'Happy new year, Doc!'

'Same. What do you want?'

'You got anything on this morning?' Clutching her towel, gooseflesh forming on her bare shoulders and arms, she gazed upwards. 'Me and Corrigan are on our way to a scene. Goosey wants all three of us there.'

Kate was on immediate high alert. 'I'll be there. Where is it? What—'

'The lake at Woodgate Country Park. Know it?'

'I'll find it. What do you know?'

'Nothing beyond Goosey saying it's a likely cold case.'

Back in the bathroom she applied a quick slick of body moisturiser, smoothing in extra to the healing ten-centimetre scar running up one thigh, a souvenir of too-close contact with razor wire during the Unsolved Crime Unit's previous case. The scar responded with a twinge. Taking a couple of swipes at her hair with a wide-toothed comb she acknowledged defeat, snapping a band around the heavy mass to secure it. Hurrying to her bedroom she dragged a pair of warm tweed trousers and an overcoat from the wardrobe, aware of a desultory movement on the landing. 'Maisie?' Reprising the scant details of the telephone conversation, she took out her leather boots, put them in a bag, then pulled on glossy black Hunters. 'Maisie!'

Maisie was on the landing, still in pyjamas, cross-legged on the low wooden chest, cereal bowl in hand, ears stopped by her iPod, head nodding beneath the chaos of deep red curls. Kate tugged.

'*Hey!* Oh.'

'I'm in a hurry and *you* should be dressed by now.'

'I haven't had a chance because I've been rushing around taking *your* phone calls and—'

Pointing to the bedroom Kate was now on the move, talking as she went. 'I'm phoning Chelsey's mother to say we'll be at their house in — seven minutes, *max*.' Maisie peered through staircase spindles to watch her mother's urgent downward progress. Putting the bowl on the floor she ambled to her room as Mugger shot across the landing and began opportunistically lapping at the remains of the milk.

* * *

Ten minutes into the journey, Maisie and her friend Chelsey were communicating in squeals inside the small car, causing Kate's scalp to tighten. She took the opportunity for a quick glance at the smooth-skinned picture of health in the passenger seat beside her. It was almost a different story last year when Chelsey was abducted by the man Kate and her police colleagues in the Unsolved Crime Unit had been pursuing. Harry Creed.

She refocused her attention. If the traffic kept moving she would reach her colleagues within twenty minutes. Her attention on the road ahead, she thought of Birmingham-born Detective Sergeant Bernard Watts. Tall and heavy, he spoke as straight as he thought. Often, too straight. Coming from academe, a southerner by birth, Kate's initial impression of him was of a full-on loudmouth and politically incorrect nightmare. Now she recognised his strengths as a long-serving officer, and his loyalty, although his resistance to psychological theory still annoyed her.

Kate dropped both girls at the school doors before following the drive back onto Edgbaston Park Road. Bypassing the main gate into the university, her usual destination, Kate's thoughts drifted to Lieutenant Joe Corrigan. His main role at Rose Road was that of firearms trainer: a stark indication of the change in British policing over the last decade. He was tall like Bernie but dark-haired and in his early forties. Joe Corrigan. His name was almost a byword for calm. She grinned. Calmness hadn't been the response of females in the workforce at Rose Road when he'd first arrived.

The traffic had slowed and she tapped the steering wheel, impatient to be moving as she activated the satnav, voice clear and authoritative: 'Woodgate Country Park.'

CHAPTER THREE

Kate drove into the makeshift parking area and slid into a space next to the Range Rover parked among several official police vehicles, including a black estate car with tinted windows. Turning off the ignition she studied the low-lying area as it fell away beyond her. The lake was partially obscured by early mist, white-suited figures moving methodically around it and another focal point: a dark green wooden structure on higher ground set amid bare trees and thick evergreens.

She got out, picking up barely discernible voices drifting upwards, plus another subtle sound: the hum of heavy commuter traffic from the nearby M5. Reaching the edge of the parking area she gazed downwards, seeing the expanse of Bernie's broad back emphasised by his quilted jacket as he walked with the tall, dark-haired figure in the navy overcoat. She started down the slope.

* * *

'Bloody hell, it's cold.' Bernie Watts's hands were thrust deep inside his pockets, his words billowing ahead of him. He nodded towards the diminutive, white-clad figure just visible through the open doors of the small wooden building. 'Hope

Connie's got her thermals on.' He glanced back the way they had come. 'The Doc's arrived.' Joe turned to see Kate as they continued onwards. They approached the steps leading up to the small structure and the figure inside gave them a latexed wave. 'All right if we come on up?' asked Bernie, running a hand over his hair, particularly the bit that tended to stick up if left to its own devices.

He got a nod from the Hong Kong Chinese pathologist. 'You're fine. The external area's been processed.' They climbed the steps and went inside, arms folded to avoid inadvertent contact, and on to where Dr Connie Chong was on her knees beside a cavernous hole in the wood floor. They all looked down at it as she spoke. 'A man walking his dogs phoned it in this morning. Ah, here's your forensic psychologist. Hi, Katie.'

Kate came inside, acknowledging Connie with a wave and nodding to each of her male colleagues. She saw Joe's eyes drift downwards, saw his grin at the trousers tucked inside the Hunters. 'Hope I haven't missed anything.'

'I was about to get into it,' said the pathologist. 'Dog walker was out here around six thirty a.m. According to the brief statement he gave PC Whittaker, this place was already open and his unleashed dogs came inside.' She held out both hands above the mid-section of the wide hole. 'The dogs started worrying this area and they wouldn't be persuaded to leave. So he came to take a look. The floor was more or less intact when he entered except for a small piece his dogs had dislodged, which I've retrieved, along with another piece from down there.' She pointed inside the hole. 'Curiosity appears to have got the better of the dog owner and he wanted to know why his dogs were fussing. So he lifted a short length of floorboard and, being a sensible type equipped with a torch, he took a look. Saw enough to phone it in.' She sat on her heels gazing up at them. 'When I arrived with SOCOs at seven thirty we lifted more boards and' — she stretched for a cardboard carton and held it out to them — 'if you put these on I'll show you what it was he saw.'

Each taking a pair of blue latex gloves, they crouched at the hole's edge, craning as Connie angled a lamp squarely into the hole and switched it on. They waited for their eyes to adjust to the stark light.

Bernie veered away. 'Bloody *hell*,' he said for the second time that morning.

Supporting herself on her hands Kate lowered her upper body closer to the hole. The shocking visual assault caused her to draw back. She met Joe's eyes as he straightened, saw him shake his head.

Connie was speaking. 'Awful, yes. And pitiful.' Kate waited as the pathologist fixed each of them with a direct look. 'I can't give a time estimate yet so don't ask but we can all see that it's been here a while.' She transferred her gaze back to the hole. 'I'll have more for you once we get it back to Rose Road but my *guess* is young and male.'

They were silent, their eyes still on the hole. Kate watched Bernie, his heavy shoulders hunched against the cold as he moved away to survey the remainder of the floor. Joe stood and went to examine the damage to the doors that Kate had noted on her arrival.

As they returned Connie continued. 'What else can I tell you? Ah, yes. The floor itself. Now *that's* very interesting. Want to know why?' This got three nods. 'I suspect these floorboards had previously been taken up and replaced prior to the dogs' visit this morning. I'd go so far as to say that *that* happened very recently, probably within the last few days, after which it was reconstructed. Like a jigsaw puzzle. Which is essentially what dogs and owner found when they got here this morning.'

Kate looked from the hole to the pathologist. 'You're saying that someone else was here recently and removed this area of flooring and then replaced it?'

'That's what I suspect. Take a look at those.' She indicated pieces of flooring of various sizes laid in neat order to one side of the void.

They moved towards them, Kate picking up one then another, running her fingers over the raw edges before replacing them and looking at Connie. 'What we've seen — down there. It's been there years?'

'Certainly has.'

'Got any guesses how long?' asked Bernie.

'I knew you'd push,' said Connie with a head-shake. 'No. I haven't.'

Kate's full attention was on the flooring, face intent. 'I'm trying to get a sense of what's happened here from what you've said and what we've seen so far.' She stretched her arms, hands spread. 'What you're saying is that all of *this* area of flooring was taken up at some point in the past so that someone could leave it — him? The floor was then replaced and remained undisturbed for years — until it was taken up *again* a few days ago then put back together again. And this morning, the dogs arrived and started the process again.' Kate took a few short steps, her attention fixed on the hole. 'And here we are.'

The pathologist looked up at her. 'That pretty much sums it up.'

Kate paced the area around the hole. 'Why would whoever placed the body under the floor come back only a few days ago and take the floor up again?'

Bernie glanced at her. 'Who said it was the same person?'

'If it wasn't, why take the time and trouble to reconstruct the floor and keep what was underneath hidden?'

That earned her an exasperated look. 'Whoever pulled up the floorboards has probably got nothing to do with what we've just seen. It was probably the usual witless vandalism.'

She looked at him. 'And your "witless" vandal has a tidiness fetish?' She watched his eyes roll upwards and shook her head. 'Vandalism tends to be a young crime, I doubt the casual young vandal would have either the patience or the motivation to reassemble this floor.'

He sent her a sidelong glance. 'You're pulling it all apart a bit quick, even for you. How about waiting till we know more about what we've got here before you start on the theories?'

She sat back looking up at him. 'But this *is* UCU's next case?'

'From what Goosey said this morning and the speed he was going when he said it.'

Connie looked up at them with a grin. 'Much as I like to see enthusiasm in the workplace, right now this case is *mine*. A lot more of this floor has to come up so we can remove what we have.' They all turned at the sound of approaching footsteps. 'And that's Forensics, come to assist me.' She leaned towards the doors. 'Good morning, Adam! Come on in.'

Adam Jamison, the serious-faced head of the Forensic Service at Rose Road, came inside with a waved acknowledgement to Kate and her colleagues, speaking directly to Connie. 'How extensive do you need the hole to be?'

Connie got to her feet with a suppressed wince. 'Nobody warns you how hard pathology can be on the knees. Give me a minute and I'll mark it up.' Reaching into a metal carry case she brought out a reel of acid-yellow and black striped adhesive tape and bent to her task, gloved hand patting tape onto wood as she went.

Adam watched her progress then nodded. 'I'll go and fetch the tools. You'll be snapping it all before we remove the floor?' Connie nodded, intent on her task. 'I'll still bring the SOCO camera and recording schedules.' With a wave he was gone.

Joe had been gazing into the void during the exchange. He turned to Connie. 'There's something else down there. Looks like a flashlight.'

'Which is exactly what it is, Joseph.'

He moved to one side as Kate approached to take another look. 'Right there. See?'

She leaned at the void's edge, breathing in a pleasant mix of soap and subtle aftershave. She gazed downwards, eyes drifting over the pale, sandy surface until they came to the small cylindrical shape. She looked up at him. 'The killer dropped it?' She returned her gaze to the hole for another look at the remains, her attention snagged by a tiny, well-illuminated and heart-rending detail. Dark, curving sweeps. Eyelashes. Kate straightened and walked to the door, arms around herself, to stare out at the flat, black lake. Somebody had once loved him. Missed him still? She sighed. *Focus on the job.*

Turning from the door she went back to examine the several pieces of broken flooring. On her knees she lifted and turned each piece, arranging then rearranging, interrogating each for meaning, identifying their fit. After a few minutes she stood, brushing at her trousers. 'My working theory is that whoever took up and then replaced this flooring within the last few days already knew what was beneath it and wanted to ensure that it remained hidden.'

Bernie looked down at her, rubbing a hand over his jowls. 'My money's still on the usual type of idiot who was up for a bit of vandalism, got more than he bargained for and hopped it.'

She shook her head. 'He didn't "hop it" did he? He stayed, took time to reconstruct the floor, to conceal what was there. Why bother to do that unless he was the person who put the body there originally?' She paced the area around the hole, voice low. 'He assembled a jigsaw of broken wood. That would require certain specific aptitudes: visual discrimination, hand–eye coordination, good fine-motor skills.' She looked up at Bernie then Joe. 'A patient, methodical type of person, good with his — or her — hands.'

They turned at the sound of more footsteps heading inside and watched as Igor, Connie's post-mortem suite assistant, entered lugging a large metallic case, breathing heavily, long hair restrained in a ponytail, his plump face flushed with exertion.

Bernie returned his attention to Connie, now lying on her side, her head below floor level. He crouched at the side of the hole. 'When will you know more?'

She reached out a hand for the camera Igor was holding towards her. 'In my experience UCU's enthusiasm invariably turns to pushiness. Right now I need to snap what we've got down here and then give some thought as to how best to free it. I'll ring you.'

The three left the lake house and walked the steep incline back to their vehicles, Bernie gasping words. 'Right, Corrigan, how about when we get back you and me pull the male MISPER cold cases going back . . . what d'you think? Five, six years?'

'Based on what we've seen, I'd say ten,' Kate interjected.

Joe turned to her. 'How's life treating you, Red?'

She grinned as they reached the makeshift parking area. 'About the same as it was when I last saw you two. Busy. Which is how I like it. When Bernie phoned this morning I was rationalising my new year approach to life and work.'

Bernie gave her a sideways look. 'And this was before breakfast?'

She looked down at the ground around her feet. 'And now there are people connected to what we've just seen who have started their new year oblivious to the bad news heading their way.'

Bernie shook his head. 'If you want my opinion, Doc, that's too much thinking too early in anybody's day.'

CHAPTER FOUR

Kate's Audi followed the sweeping curve of Chancellor's Court, passed the wide, red-brick frontage of the Aston Webb building and carried on to the limited parking in front of the nearby School of Psychology. Securing the car, briefcase in hand, she hurried up the steps, returning the greetings of a few early students inside the cavernous hall, and took the lift to the third floor. *Another cold case.* She opened the door of her room, impatient to consult her diary, identify blocks of time when she could be available to—

She stopped. The desk lamp was already switched on and a glowing halogen heater was turning from side to side, the high-ceilinged room already pleasantly warm. Bemused, she walked inside, dropping her belongings onto the elderly armchair. Opening the briefcase she took out two cartons of skimmed milk, senses on alert. Skirting the massive desk she pushed open the leaded window and deposited the cartons to one side on the small external ledge. '*Hel-lo*, boys,' she murmured to the two small stone grotesques perched there, muscled bodies straining outwards, mouths stretched, fangs bared.

Closing the window on cold air she turned back into the room to see a slender young woman with spiky blond hair, her lips and fingernails neon red, wearing a short skirt and heavy-duty black tights, standing at the room's communicating door. 'Dr Hanson?' Kate nodded. 'Crystal Devine.'

Kate's eyes narrowed, then, 'Of course! Human Resources told me you were starting in the new year.' She'd also received a memo from the vice chancellor: in recognition of her dual workload at the university and at Police Headquarters, she was being given additional administrative help. She walked, hand outstretched, to the young woman a head taller than herself. 'I'm sorry but I won't be able to give you much guidance today. From midday—'

Crystal nodded. 'I know. You have tutorials. I've word processed a list of the names from the sign-up sheet on the door and I'll set the phone to divert until two thirty, including a thirty-minute lunch break at one. From what I've heard, you probably don't need the students' records, but I got them out anyway.' She beamed. 'So you can put your notes inside each one as you tut them.'

Kate stared at her. *So efficient . . . And exactly what have you heard about me? 'Tut'*? 'Thank you, Crystal. That's really helpful but I don't expect you to—'

The young woman smiled again as she turned back towards the small adjoining office. 'I've only done bits and pieces. Tell me if you need anything else? It can't be easy doing all you do here and with the police *and* being a single mom.' And with that she was gone, leaving Kate gazing at the empty doorway, feeling invaded. *Damn the rumour mill in this place!*

Taking a deep breath Kate walked to the adjoining office. 'Crystal, I think it might help if you and I get something straight. This place is a hive of gossip but I don't like—'

'*Tell* me about it.' The spiky blond head nodded vigorously. 'You don't need to worry. Whatever work I do for you, I *know* it's confidential. Trust me.' She beamed up at Kate. 'Was there something else?'

Feeling wrong-footed Kate ran a hand through her hair. 'No. *Yes*. If a Detective Sergeant Watts rings or a Lieutenant Corrigan—'

‘I’ll let you know immediately.’ She nodded, giving Kate an earnest look.

Kate returned to her own room to sit at her desk. Putting Crystal’s comments from her mind she took a student assignment from the neat stack she’d left in readiness at the end of last term and selected two marker pens from several lined up and waiting. Her new admin assistant’s style might feel intrusive but her efficiency suggested that she could be a godsend. Particularly if what Kate and her colleagues had seen earlier that morning *was* UCU’s next cold case.

CHAPTER FIVE

Later that afternoon Kate's study group of first-year students was sitting in a receptive semicircle inside her room, the halogen heater doing its job to a comfortable degree. Kate gave a silent acknowledgement to Maslow's Hierarchy of Needs. Nineteen forties' psychology, yet she knew it had its truths: if they're comfortable they'll focus.

Perched on the edge of her desk she looked along the row of faces. 'Last term we began our exploration of visual perception. For those of you planning careers in criminology, eyewitness testimony has its uses *and* its limitations. Seeing is not as reliable as we like to think because the human memory isn't a recording machine. We store *constructions* of what we see, including features we *assume* are there, all influenced by our emotional state at the time.'

She turned and reached across her desk for the sheets she'd prepared. 'I've got some research references here, plus a couple of case examples of the kinds of difficulties associated with eyewitness testimony.' She handed them to the student at one end of the line, waited till each of them had a copy, then continued, voice brisk. 'Page two. Case example: fourteen-year-old girl abducted from her bedroom in Utah. No matter. The theory is universal. She shared the room with her nine-year-old sister who observed the abduction unfold and described the kidnapper as a man aged between thirty and forty, wearing light-coloured clothing and a hat. Subsequent investigation confirmed the man's clothes were black, he was hatless and almost fifty.' She regarded the silent students. 'Why the disparity?'

A hand shot up. 'She was only nine. Little kids don't make good eyewitnesses.'

Kate shook her head. 'It's true that children can have difficulty with age estimates but research indicates that they can be as effective as adults in the witness role.' She looked along the row again. 'Other ideas?'

'It was night-time so there wouldn't have been much light?'

'Valid point.' She nodded to another student. 'Yes?'

'Like you said before, emotion? The little sister would've been frightened.'

Kate nodded. 'Emotion compromising perception. Yes, Ashley?' she said to a young woman sitting in the middle of the row of students.

'Did they find her? The girl who was kidnapped?'

Kate nodded. 'My apologies for not making it clear. They did, after months of committed investigation. A salutary lesson for anyone contemplating a law-enforcement career. *Never* give up on cases.' The students exchanged quick glances, aware of Kate's work with the police.

She stood, giving each of them a direct look. 'I've given you a reading list. You know the motto of this establishment: *per ardua ad alta*. Very loosely translated it means "Put your backs into it". In other words, get reading.'

As they packed away she checked her diary. 'I see I have the pleasure of your company tomorrow. That lecture now starts at *four* thirty, remember. I *know* — but I'm not responsible for the shortage of lecture space. It's what you get for applying to a prime university. *Don't* be late.'

She was still in her room an hour later when her desk phone clamoured. She lifted it. 'Kate Hanson.'

It was Bernie. 'I'm at Rose Road. How're you fixed?'

She picked up the urgency behind his casual words. 'I'll be there in twenty minutes.'

* * *

Igor squeaked across the tiles to open the frosted-glass door, then pointed to the wall dispensers. Kate and her colleagues came inside to be met by a chemical onslaught and an extraction system running at maximum. Masked and gloved they approached Connie Chong who was working in plastic face shield, latex and pale green coveralls. She spoke, voice low, eyes on the examination table in front of her. 'Good afternoon, UCU. No bright young psychology student?' she queried, referring to Julian Devenish, Kate's student trainee helper, one-time hacker into the university's confidential records and soon-to-be graduate.

'He's at the university,' responded Kate as Bernie ran a restless hand over his hair, eyes adrift of the occupant of the examination table.

Connie gazed at them through the clear plastic. 'We had a full house down here earlier today but things are looking up: I've been sent a locum. For a whole week.' She made a small gesture with her scalpel at the remains. 'So I've dedicated my entire day to him.' She eyed each of them. 'It is a "he" and we've been getting better acquainted. Now I can tell you who he is, or *was*, rather, and that I know he died around two decades ago.' Not hiding her surprise, Kate's eyes drifted over the dried, nut-brown remains, teeth exposed in the vast, primeval scream they'd seen the previous day, the dark, fanned eyelashes evident now. 'I know what you're all thinking: "How's he managing to look so dandy after all this time?"' Kate frowned. 'Dandy' was one word to describe what they were seeing. Connie surveyed the body from head to feet. 'His good condition is due to his being mummified. For those two decades he's lain on a nice thick layer of fine sand. That, plus the elevation of the lake house and its brick foundations, kept him comparatively warm, dry and protected from animal predation. Want the detailed tour?' Not waiting for responses she pointed at the head. 'His tendons have dried out and shortened, which is why he's so conveniently displaying excellent dentition. A minor cue that he was young when he died. Young enough to benefit from fluoridation.' She nodded towards a nearby table covered in heavy-duty cartridge paper. 'That's the remains of his hair. Dark brown. The longest measures thirty-five centimetres.' She pointed to other items laid out alongside. 'And his clothes: Converse All-stars, size nine and a half, grey socks, ditto. Nirvana T-shirt, legend nicely preserved. Boxer-style underwear, good old M and S, dark blue. Denim jeans, a little mouldy but I've consulted the Rivet Book for thoroughness. They're Levi 501s.'

In the following silence they returned their attention to the remains. 'No other clothing?' asked Joe. Connie shook her head. 'How did you identify him? Dental records?'

She nodded. 'Few individuals approach the end of their teens without *some* minimal attention from a dentist. Our boy took good care of his teeth but he had one tiny filling.' She hooked a finger, moving closer to the yawning jaws. 'Come and have a look.' Joe and Kate took up the invitation, leaning closer as the pathologist pointed out the almost imperceptible repair. 'I checked the dental records on MISPERS. One hit. Which is all we need.'

She straightened and looked at each of them. 'So, UCU, allow me to introduce to you Master Nathan Troy.' She looked from Bernie to Joe. 'Did I see recognition at the name?'

Bernie nodded. 'We searched for young, male MISPERS. Went back as far as 1990. He's on the shortlist we ended up with. His disappearance was investigated during the last months of 1993.'

Connie looked back at the remains. 'He would have celebrated his twentieth birthday if he'd lived a further three months.'

'Any news on the cause of death?' asked Bernie.

There was a small shake of Connie's neat dark head. '*Bernard*.' The soft reproof brought some colour back to his jowls. 'And we were doing *so* well.' She became brisk again, picked up a clipboard, her eyes on highlighted words. 'I can't confirm that yet. The only thing I *can* add, in case you don't already know, is that at the time of his disappearance Nathan Troy was a second-year student at the Birmingham Institute of Art and Design. More specifically, Woolner College in Bournville.' Kate looked down at Nathan Troy. He'd been tall in life. Young and tall with everything still in the future. Until death came for him and he no longer had one.

In the lingering silence Connie drew a green sheet over the remains and they watched Igor's progress towards the door in response to a faint tapping sound. 'Adam said he'd drop in with any results they've obtained. That's probably him.'

Adam came inside, halting some distance from the examination table, a single sheet of A4 in hand. 'Can't stop. Here's what Forensics has so far: the soft ground below the lake house steps bore several footprints, mostly overlapping and indistinct but we managed to get a complete cast of one.' He grinned at Joe. 'I searched the prints in our "Soul Database", as you call it. It was made by a classic Adidas Originals ZX 750 trainer. Size ten and a half. That excludes the dog walker, by the way. His were walking boots. A nine.'

Bernie nodded towards the post-mortem table. 'How about the torch that was with him?'

'It isn't contemporary with the remains. The make is fairly recent, no more than a couple of years old. There's a date stamp on the batteries, almost indecipherable but we're working on it. We found plenty of very poor prints on the outer casing, none of any use, but we did manage to isolate a tiny blood sample.'

Kate's head and those of her colleagues snapped upwards.

'When do we get the results?' asked Joe.

Adam held up both hands. '*Whoa*. It's not that easy with such a small sample.' He gave each of them a mild look. 'Just think how lucky you are still to have us here.' They understood what he was saying. The Forensic Science Service had undergone massive change over previous months, from a government-owned company to one which was now contracted out. Rose Road had been ahead of its time with its in-house forensic team, which was being retained despite the recent changes.

'For once we're on the right side of this "progress" we're always hearing about,' said Bernie. 'Any road up, got anything else for us?'

'Nothing from the marks on the interior floor but we did a full series of photos at various stages of its removal. You know the floorboards were removed and replaced very recently prior to discovery of the remains.'

Kate watched Joe tap a speculative index finger against his lips. 'Suggesting a weird combination of impulsiveness and patience?'

Adam grinned at him with a brief shake of his head. 'Can't comment. My speciality is the silent evidence, the traces left behind. I don't get into people's heads or behaviour although I'm betting one member of UCU has a view on it.' He gave Kate a grin and a brows-up glance.

She smiled. 'I might have.'

Adam held out his report to Bernie, turned and went to the door. 'I'll let you know about results on the blood smear, if and when there are any.' With that he was gone.

Shortly afterwards they also left. Back in UCU, Joe broke the short silence. 'We need the original files.'

'And Nathan Troy's got a family that needs telling,' added Bernie with a glance across the table at Kate. 'When's young Devenish in?'

'Tomorrow afternoon.'

He stood and headed for the door. 'In that case I'll get Whittaker to go down to the basement for the files and boxes relating to the Troy investigation.'

Joe turned on his chair to look up at Kate as she also stood. 'You got an idea how you'd like to approach the case, Red?'

She lifted her hair free of her coat and reached for her bag and keys. 'I have. We need to learn as much as we can about Nathan Troy's life to begin to understand his death. How about you?'

'I want to know what he was doing at that place. But then I guess everybody has to be somewhere, yeah?'

CHAPTER SIX

In the subdued lighting of the lecture theatre Kate's eyes swept over the seated audience comprising all of her first year study groups. Five thirty and she was nearly done. She smiled. 'Okay. Enough Perception Theory. How about a little exercise in *not* seeing?' She tapped a key of the laptop next to her on the raised platform and the image of Holbein's *The Ambassadors* lit up the vast screen behind her. She glanced up at the painting's two young male subjects, depicted flanking an array of objects displayed on two shelves, the artist's visual puzzle in the foreground between them. She considered it for some seconds then turned back to them, voice low. 'Tell me what you see.'

After some seconds several hands were raised. Kate nodded to a student near the back.

'Two well-off-looking types? The one on the left looks a bit like Henry the Eighth.'

'All that stuff on the table between them — they're clever men, early scientists,' suggested his neighbour.

Another voice drifted down to her. 'How about they're musicians — or they could be explorers?'

Following several more ideas Kate gave a directional nudge, pointing the red laser pen at the long, narrow shape in the foreground. 'What about this? What is it?'

There was another brief silence then more hands appeared. 'Some kind of carving?'

Another voice: 'It's a type of shell.'

'Is it . . . an oar?'

Kate nodded at the last suggestion. 'I can see why you'd think that but, no.'

'It's a *shell*.'

She waited for the hum of voices to subside then surveyed the puzzled faces. 'Art always has meaning but in this painting Holbein used artistic technique to conceal it. The solution lies in what we know of the *whole* picture.' Seeing continuing puzzlement she tapped the laptop's keyboard and they watched in silence as the huge artwork on the screen executed a slow half-turn. She approached the screen, raising a hand to the side-on picture. 'This is *purposeful* distortion we're looking at. Holbein's intention appears to have been for this painting to be approached from an oblique angle, perhaps hung on a staircase.' She looked out across the small auditorium. 'Understanding what it means is *all* to do with viewpoint. See how the "oar", the "shell", has shortened?' Hearing a further hum of comment she came to the front of the platform, searching the nearest row for a specific student. 'What has your "oar" morphed into, James?'

'A *skull*. Clever.'

Kate returned to stand beside the screen. 'Holbein didn't employ the technique simply because he could. He used it to convey his message, his view of life: young and wealthy as these two men are the possibility of death is always present.' She returned to the front of the platform. 'Right. That's it. Thank you for your attentiveness today. Have a good weekend, everybody.'

They'd loaded their backpacks and were heading for the exit when her phone rang. 'Kate Hanson.'

'Hey, Red.' It was Joe. 'What're you up to?'

She picked up her file of notes and slid it into her briefcase. 'Just finished a lecture and going home. How about you?'

'We've got the Troy investigation files out of storage. His parents still live at the same address. I've contacted them and now I've got a proposition for you. How about you and me visit? Ask some questions.'

'I've had better invitations in my time.'

'Bet you have, Red. I suggested Monday to give them time to absorb the news of their son being found but they insisted on tomorrow morning. Guess they've waited long enough. Pick you up at eight?'

* * *

Kate was assembling a hurried dinner, distracted by what she knew of the case thus far. *Maybe the flooring was taken up by someone who was trying to move Nathan Troy from his two-decade-long resting place? If so, why? He'd lain undiscovered, undisturbed for . . .*

Maisie was well into her theme. 'So *then*, I go, "If we use the substitution x equals two minus — Mom!' Kate looked up, face guilty. 'You're not *listening*.'

'*Sorry*. My mind was on something else. Carry on.'

Maisie's eyes narrowed. 'You're thinking about that body that's been found at Woodgate Country Park.'

Kate stopped what she was doing to stare at her. 'How do you know about that?'

'There was a bit on the local radio. They said he was nineteen and a student and he'd been there, like, ages. What happened to him?'

'That isn't something you need to be concerned about,' said Kate, ruffling her daughter's hair, despite knowing it infuriated her. 'Carry on telling me about Professor Dallow.' Maisie was currently one of three maths-precocious students from her school who crossed the road to participate in once-weekly lectures with the professor at the university.

Maisie huffed. 'He admitted I was right but told me off for "looking ahead at the syllabus". I *told* him I hadn't, that I just *knew* it, but he didn't believe me, I could tell. Have you seen the body? Did he drown in the big lake?'

Kate removed garlic bread from the oven and gave it a critical look. 'I'm not discussing it, Maisie. Move those books off the table, please.'

'*Think* about it. I might be planning to follow in your footsteps, work-wise, in which case anything you tell me could be useful to my chosen career.'

'I thought you'd decided to be an engineer? And my careers advice is "stop being so patently manipulative".' She returned the garlic bread to the oven then turned, her face flushed, a single word of Maisie's in her head. *Drown*. 'What did you say just now? About the park?'

'Wha'?'

'What you just said. About the lake in the park. You sounded as though you're familiar with it.'

Maisie's blue eyes rolled. 'No I *didn't*. Well, I *do* know of it, kind of, and anyway, since when's that a crime?'

'Stop backchatting and lay the table please.' She watched Maisie fetch linen placemats and cutlery with bad grace. 'You don't go to that area *ever*, do you hear me?'

'Mom, it's *miles* away and the only people I know who do go there are Beatrice and Violet Miller—'

'So *now* you know two girls who frequent the place?'

Maisie snorted. 'They're the spooky twins so they don't really count as *two* and I never said they *frequented*.'

Feeling under siege Kate yanked the oven open and pulled out the garlic bread again. 'I *mean* it. Don't go there.'

'I'm not!' Maisie flounced from the kitchen leaving Kate hot and rattled.

* * *

Walking upstairs much later, Kate heard a soft call. Pushing open Maisie's bedroom door, she found her sitting cross-legged on her bed, Mugger curled beside her. 'Look at this, Mom.'

She went and examined the intricately constructed pattern of small chains worked in fine pink yarn. 'That's lovely! I didn't know you could crochet. Where did you learn?'

'Old Mrs Hetherington showed me,' replied Maisie, referring to their neighbour.

'That was kind of her . . . but I think "Mrs Hetherington" is sufficient . . .'

'Okay, but she *is* like *really* old. Have you noticed how sometimes old people's mouths look like Mugger's bottom?' The cat opened an eye.

Weary, Kate lifted the pink and white duvet. 'Get into bed, minx.' She leaned over and kissed the mass of red curls. 'Love you, sweetie.'

'Love you too, Mom.'

Lifting the dissembling cat she carried him from the room, recalling what Maisie had said about two girls from her school going to Woodgate Park. She'd reinforce her warning.

CHAPTER SEVEN

Kate was upstairs on the phone when the doorbell rang at eight a.m. She glanced at her watch. 'Candice, I have to go but now we're agreed I'll tell Maisie. Okay, bye.'

As she walked from her room to the landing she heard the front door open, followed by Joe's deep voice inside the hall. 'Hi, Cat's-whiskers. You teaching school today?'

'Now *that* would be *really* good. For starters I'd get rid of boring stuff like Personal Social Health.'

'That you would. Where's your mamma?'

'Upstairs, messing with her hair probably.'

Kate rolled her eyes and started down the stairs. 'Hi, Joe. I'm ready for the Troys, but I need a word with—'

'What's "the Troys"?'

'That's nothing for you to be concerned with. Remember what I said to you last night? You don't even *think* of going to Woodgate Park.'

Maisie's eyes rolled. 'Wha'ever.'

'I've had a word with Candice and we're agreed: you and Chelsey can go to and from school by bus from today. We'll *see* how it goes.'

Maisie scowled her way to the stairs. 'We're almost thirteen, *Mother*. Don't make out it's some massive deal.'

Choosing to ignore the words Kate glanced at Joe. 'Shall we get going?'

'Anything you say, Red.'

Maisie's voice drifted down to them from the upper floor. 'Don't let her be in charge, Joe.'

Shrugging into her coat and lifting her bag, Kate directed her voice upwards. 'Your bus arrives at the end of the avenue in exactly twenty minutes and there'll be no one to take you if you miss it.' She listened, hearing a muted 'Yeah, yeah'.

A key turned in the lock of the wide oak front door and Phyllis appeared, knitted hat pulled well down. 'Morning, both.'

'Hi, Phyllis, we're just leaving and I'd be really grateful if you could make sure that Maisie is out of the house no later than eight twenty.'

'Will do.'

As Kate got into Joe's car she saw his look. 'What?'

He shrugged. 'None of my business, but that seems like tough stuff you're pulling with Maisie.'

'You mean the bus thing?' She shook her head. 'No it isn't. You weren't in the UK in 2002. A girl not much older than Maisie disappeared. She was on her way home from school by public transport, followed by a short walk. Safe area. Daylight.' Fastening her seat belt Kate looked up at him. 'She did everything right but she never reached home. Don't say it: bad stuff happens. I know that Maisie needs some freedom to come and go but *I* need to know that she can handle it.'

'It's your call, Red. Let's go see Mr and Mrs Troy.'

* * *

Joe drove steadily, Ray-bans blocking the morning sun, following the satnav route as the bulk of traffic filed slowly past on the opposite side, into the city. Low music filled the car. Not for the first time Kate thought how relaxed she felt with him. That is, when his attention wasn't fully on her.

She switched her thoughts to their imminent meeting with Nathan Troy's parents.

By the time they pulled up on a road lined with small, modern houses in Castle Vale she'd formulated a clear idea of what they needed from Nathan Troy's parents. She gave Joe a quick outline. 'What do you think?'

'Agreed. We'll work it together.' He glanced through the window. 'It's the row house with the grey front door,' he said, pointing to the small dwelling beyond the grass verge and pavement. He looked back to Kate. 'That's "terraced", right?'

She grinned at him. 'You know, you're *really* picking up the language now.'

'Doin' my best, ma'am.'

They exited the car and walked across verge and pavement then down a short path. As Kate pressed the bell a cacophony of hysterical barks erupted inside, accompanied by the tic-tic of claws on hard flooring. Admonishment from a male voice was followed by silence and the door was opened by a man somewhere in his late fifties.

'Mr Troy? William Troy?' The man barely nodded as Joe showed identification. 'Lieutenant Joe Corrigan from Police Headquarters, Rose Road, Harborne. We spoke on the phone yesterday. This is my colleague Dr Kate Hanson.'

'Come on in. Mind the dog,' he said, turning away to deliver a '*Stay*, Flossie' to one side of the hallway. Kate stepped over the threshold, apprehensive about the initiator of the bark-and-claw. A small Yorkshire terrier was on the stairs displaying two rows of needle-sharp teeth between parted lips. 'Don't touch her,' he advised. 'The wife's the only one that does anything with her. She's at the church at the end of the road. She'll be back soon. I'm in the garden.'

They followed him down the hall, through a small kitchen and outside. Even in January there were no errant leaves clustered in corners, no weeds encroaching on slabs. The garden was dominated by a roomy shed and they followed him to it; inside, Kate noted its warmth, saw other evidence of domestic comfort including an old armchair and an electric jug. She took a subtle look around, knowing that this was no mere shed. It was a bolthole. Nathan Troy's disappearance would have wrought its own havoc in his parents' lives and they were still dealing with it in their own various ways two decades on. She watched as Mr Troy went to the workbench to resume his task without looking directly at either of them, intuiting that he found non-engagement as good a way as any to avoid difficult emotion.

Still without a look in their direction he spoke. 'You want to know about our Nathan.'

Joe responded. 'We're very sorry about the recent news of your son and your loss, sir. We're also grateful to you and your wife for agreeing to our visit. We need your help.'

Still engrossed in his task Bill Troy gave a slow head-shake. '"Help." That's something my son doesn't need any more, wouldn't you say?' He applied a screwdriver to the metal object he was holding.

Kate and Joe exchanged looks and she spoke. 'We need to ask about Nathan's . . . situation at the time he disappeared, Mr Troy,' she said, editing out the word 'life'. 'Can you tell us about that?'

'Not much, no. We didn't see him all that often once he started at that college.' Now he turned to them and they saw anguish in his face, heard it in the harsh tone. 'I can tell you what my son was like if you're interested: he was a quick learner, *clever*, good with his hands and . . . full of *life*!' The word burst from him, hitting the walls, the chair and the rest of the illusory comforts he'd brought inside his space. His pale face had darkened. 'He could've done . . . *anything* he put his mind to. He could've had an apprenticeship if he'd listened to *me*. But no. He was hell-bent on that art college.' He turned his face away, shoulders rigid.

Kate was aware of a string of frantic barks drifting from the house. She didn't want to press him but knew she must. 'You didn't agree with his choice?'

'Makes no difference now, does it? But I never saw the attraction of that place for him. I still don't get it.' He turned to look at them. 'Not my world, you see. All I know is that he could've learned a good trade. They were willing to take him on at Jaguar Land Rover with me—'

'But it wasn't what Nathan wanted, Bill.' They each turned towards the quiet voice. A dark-haired woman of similar age to Bill Troy was standing in the doorway, hands in the pockets of her long black coat, face pale in the harsh outdoor light. She gave them a friendly nod. 'Come into the house. I've put the kettle on.'

As she disappeared her husband's concentration was back on what he'd been doing when they arrived. 'Do as she says. It's easier.'

They followed the path back to the house and into the small kitchen. Flossie was nowhere in sight. Mrs Troy was putting a plate of biscuits on the table. 'Tea or coffee? It's only instant.' She turned to a small neat pile of papers on a nearby work surface then back, holding out a large photograph to them. Kate took it. 'I got this out for you. It's similar to the one the police had when he . . . went. We want to do anything we can to help the new investigation.' She looked at the photograph in Kate's hand. 'I'd like it back eventually, please.'

Kate studied the head-and-shoulders photograph of Nathan Troy. He dark hair was to his shoulders, his eyes clear and candid, a smile on his full mouth. He was well beyond that stage of development when the male face has a soft genderless beauty, but Kate thought she could still detect a semblance of it. Mrs Troy put her head on one side. 'He was eighteen there. About to start at Woolner.' Kate nodded, knowing now from where Nathan Troy had inherited his dark good looks, his sweeping lashes. She handed the photograph to Joe.

Mrs Troy was removing her coat. 'Please — sit down.' She went across the kitchen to make their coffee then brought it in bright red mugs to the table. 'You're the lieutenant who rang. The name's Rachel, by the way.' She gave Kate a brief glance.

Joe nodded. 'This is Dr Kate Hanson, a colleague in the Unsolved Crime Unit, Rose Road. We'd appreciate hearing anything you and Mr Troy can tell us about Nathan to help us build a picture of what was happening to him around the time he disappeared.'

Rachel took a seat and gazed at them for a few seconds before she spoke. 'You'll get a different picture from me, compared to what Bill would say. He still struggles with it. We both do but — well, you've met him. He's angry that he's lost him. He needs somebody to blame. He wanted Nathan with him. In industry. He thinks if Nathan had done that, opted for an apprenticeship, he'd still be here.' She looked down at the table. 'They made Bill redundant at the age of fifty-seven and he hasn't worked since.' She paused then spoke in a firm voice, chin up. 'The other difference between Bill and me is that he thinks *we're* also the victims here. I tell him we're not. I tell him we're witnesses to Nathan's life, to the fact that he was here.' She took a sip of coffee. 'Is there anything in particular you want to know?' she asked into the silence.

Joe replied, 'Yes, ma'am. We have the files of the original investigation. We know that Nathan shared a house with three other students during the time he was at Woolner. Can you tell us anything about them?'

Rachel Troy got up and went to a nearby dresser, reaching for a box. As Joe stood she turned to him. 'It's okay, I can manage. It isn't heavy.' She carried it, large and glossy black, to the table. 'The police took Nathan's main belongings from the house and held onto them for a while.' Her hands rested on the dust-free lid and then she lifted it off. 'These are the few small things that were still in his room. The police looked through them and I asked if we could have them. They said yes.'

Kate and Joe gazed inside at layers of small sketches executed on quality paper. Rachel Troy did the same. 'Nathan had *real* artistic talent. I think he got that from me but he was *so* good at drawing and painting from when he was just a little boy. He was our only child,' she added, removing two skilful, subtle, life studies and placing them gently on the table. They listened as she told them that she'd had copies made and professionally mounted which had been exhibited at the local library and the church hall in the months following Nathan's disappearance. 'A couple of the exhibitions were featured on local television.' She looked up at them. 'We did all we could back then to keep Nathan's disappearance in people's minds.' She pointed to the two drawings. 'These are what I wanted to show you. Two of the boys Nathan shared the house with.' She lifted one and handed it to Kate. 'That's Alastair Buchanan. He was from Edinburgh.' Kate looked down at a brown-haired young man, the heavy, arched eyebrows adding an imperious quality to his rounded face.

'Was this Buchanan a particular friend of Nathan's?' asked Joe.

Rachel Troy shook her head. 'I don't think so. I can't remember anything specific that Nathan said about him. I met him once after they'd all moved into the house.' She outlined the impression she'd gained of Buchanan at that time: a bit posh. A bit pompous. She pointed to the other sketch. 'That's Joel Smythe. He seemed really nice. He came here. Nathan and he were friends for a while.'

They looked down at the mild-faced, fair-haired youth, Kate thinking that he looked young for what, eighteen? 'They didn't remain friends?'

Rachel Troy gave her a surprised look. 'Oh, I see what you mean. They hung around together quite a lot in their first year but not so much afterwards. Sometimes when Nathan came here during his first year he brought Joel with him. After the start of their second year that changed. We didn't see Joel but Nathan never said why.' She shrugged. 'And at that age you don't ask, do you?'

'What about the other student Nathan shared with?' asked Kate.

Reaching inside the box again she sifted among the papers. 'He's here somewhere . . . Ah, here it is.' She brought out a third sketch and offered it to Kate. 'That's Matthew Johnson. Nathan got on okay with him as far as I know. They were on the same fine arts course. The other two I told you about were doing something else, "Art in Archaeology", or something like that. I don't think Matthew and Nathan were particular friends. Matthew was in some kind of theatre group, "Am-dram", Nathan called it, and he also belonged to a choir. Those kinds of things didn't interest Nathan.'

'How did it go, these four young guys sharing?' enquired Joe.

Rachel Troy laughed, describing how she'd found the small house fairly chaotic on the few occasions she'd gone there to leave laundry for Nathan. 'There was one time I tidied it up and he wasn't very pleased so I didn't do it again.'

Asked by Kate if Nathan appeared to be enjoying his fine arts course she confirmed it with a firm nod and a smile. 'He *loved* it. His first year met all of his expectations and he was looking forward to the next.' The wall clock ticked on in the ensuing silence. 'Such a long time ago, isn't it? Nineteen ninety-three.'

'What about the faculty at Woolner? How did Nathan get on with them?' This from Joe.

Rachel Troy's face brightened. 'Very well. I met the two main ones at an open day. His tutor, Dr Wellan, was a nice man. Down to earth. Very kind, he was. He came here, you know, after Nathan . . . went. Just the once, to say he was sorry Nathan had left.' She looked at each of them. 'Everybody back then, including the police, believed that Nathan had *decided* to leave.' She shook her head. 'We . . . I knew he hadn't. He *wouldn't.* We were very close, Nathan and me. He wouldn't have done that. Not to me. Nor his dad.' There was another brief silence, then: 'What was I saying? Oh, yes. The other lecturer. He was more senior than Dr Wellan and a much older man. Like a professor. He never came here and his name escapes me but I know Nathan liked him.'

Joe nodded. 'Did Nathan date at all?'

Rachel Troy smiled. 'He was *nineteen*. Of course he did. He mentioned one or two specific girls to me. He was very open about that side of his life. That's how I know he was keen on one or two of the female students at Woolner and he was friends with a couple of others, one in particular.'

'Can you recall any names?' asked Joe.

'That one, I can. The one he was particularly friendly with. I remember it because it was unusual: Cassandra.'

Kate looked up from her note-taking. 'Did he say anything about her?'

Mrs Troy gave a small head-shake. 'Not that much. I remember him saying that they talked a lot and that she had some sort of problem. I got the idea it was a health issue. Now I come to think about it, Bill actually met her once.'

Kate made swift notes. 'So as far as you were aware Nathan had no problems or difficulties at the time he disappeared?'

'Not that I know of.' She glanced at Joe then back to Kate. 'He mentioned another student who irritated him but it didn't sound like it was serious. At odd times when he came home he'd say, "Oh, that Rod's been hanging around again, being a pain." Or something like that. It didn't strike me that it was a serious problem for him. More like Nathan regarded him as a pest.' She looked down at her hands clasped round the bright coffee mug. 'When somebody's part of your family you take it for granted they always will be. Maybe I didn't listen as well as I should have.' She glanced away from them to the chill garden beyond the window. A single tear slid down her cheek.

Kate spoke softly. 'You never met him? That student?'

'No,' she said, her hand brushing her face.

Joe gazed at Rachel Troy. 'You've been told where Nathan was found, ma'am?'

She nodded. 'We don't actually know it. We thought we might go and see it but . . .' Her voice faded and she ended with a small shrug. 'Is it . . . nice there?'

Joe nodded, augmenting his words with small gestures of his hands. 'It's not a small, suburban green space. It's a big spread of open land with paths for walkers, jogging and cycling tracks. Woods. A lake. Can you think of a reason why Nathan would have gone there? In November?'

She frowned. 'Nathan wasn't a jogger. He didn't have a bike. Maybe he went there to draw, but it doesn't sound that likely in November, does it?' She shrugged. 'Maybe they were told to do winter sketches or something?'

Kate listened as Joe chose his words. 'The park's a nice place in daylight, especially in summer, but at other times its character can change. Parts of it become a meeting point for some problematic types involved in drug-taking and—'

Rachel Troy responded, voice quiet but firm. 'Nathan didn't take drugs, if that's what you're wondering. He had no time for anything like that. He was your straightforward nineteen- almost twenty-year-old. In fact I'd go as far as to say he was a bit "moral" for his age. He was the type who'd take a stand against things he didn't like or disapproved of. Drugs was one of them.'

The kitchen door opened and Mr Troy walked inside. Joe provided a quick resumé of the conversation for him. 'Is there anything you'd like to add or tell us, sir?'

They waited as he crossed to the sink, washed his hands and began drying them on kitchen paper. 'Me and Nathan weren't that close back then. We both tried but . . . Just before he went he asked me to go to London for the day with him. Wanted to show me a couple of the big galleries: The National and some other place. I knew what he was thinking: if I understood art a bit more we'd have that in common. So I said yes and bought the train tickets.' He raised his head and gazed out of the window. 'But it never happened. Maybe he decided he had something better to do that day.' His wife reached out and laid a hand on his arm. He glanced down at her. 'What did Father O'Ryan have to say?'

'He listened.'

'May I?' asked Kate. Getting a nod from Rachel Troy, Kate reached into the box. 'Who's this?' she asked, holding up a fine pen-and-watercolour of a young woman, blonde, ethereal and extraordinarily beautiful.

Rachel tilted her head to look. '*That's* the girl I mentioned. Cassandra.' She took the drawing and held it up to her husband. 'That's her, isn't it, Bill?'

'Mm. A strange one.'

'Why do you say that, Mr Troy?'

He turned to Kate. 'I met her once when I went to the house. They'd got trouble with the electrics so I went over. She was there.' He lapsed into silence.

'You described this young woman as "strange"?' prompted Joe.

'Don't know how else to say it. She was there but . . . not there, if you know what I mean. The others said hello, but not her. To be honest, I thought she was a bit above herself at first but then I got a different idea. My impression was that she was on something. That's how she looked to me.'

Kate directed her next question to both parents. 'Would you have any objections to our taking this box and keeping it whilst our investigation is ongoing? You have our word we'll take good care of it and return it to you intact.'

They exchanged brief glances and Rachel Troy spoke for both: 'That's fine if it helps you to do your job.'

As Joe picked up the box and they prepared to leave Kate felt a rush of sympathy for both parents. 'Look, we'll do a thorough job and we'll keep *on* doing it until we know what happened to Nathan,' she said, closing that part of her mind into which Inspector Roger Furman, manager of the Unsolved Crime Unit, had slithered. Known throughout Rose Road as 'the Arse', Furman and Kate had never gelled, partly because of his unremitting emphasis on fast results with minimum financial outlay and his keenness to close reinvestigations down without a second thought if those results didn't happen quickly enough for him. Tensions had reached a head in UCU's previous case when Kate had had a couple of stand-up rows with him. She frowned, feeling Joe's eyes on her, aware that she was making a promise to Bill and Rachel Troy which UCU might not be able to deliver.

Rachel Troy was holding out her hand and Kate took it in hers. 'Having met you both I think you'll do your best for our Nathan. Don't you, Bill?' He gave an almost imperceptible nod. 'Anything you want to know, anything we can help with, just call us.' She walked them to the door. 'It's not right for anybody's child to die before them, is it? We're grateful he's been found and in time we'll have somewhere to go . . . to visit him, but what really matters to us right now is that you're working on his case again.'

* * *

As the Volvo rolled smoothly along the wide carriageway Kate's eyes were fixed on the road disappearing beneath it, feeling Joe's intermittent gaze on her. 'How the hell are they managing? Coping with what they know?' she murmured to herself, then glanced across at him. 'What do you think of their characterisation of Nathan?'

He kept his eyes on the road. 'A talented, likeable youngster with a clear moral compass. Maybe it's what parents say in their situation.'

She gave him a surprised look. 'You don't believe it?'

'Didn't say that, Red. We'll be talking to other people who knew him. What they say could give us a rounded picture.'

Kate leaned back, somebody's description of children as 'hostages to fortune' drifting into her head. She gazed through glass as Joe negotiated the Five Ways island then drove on past Edgbaston's Georgian architecture and leafless trees. After several minutes the Volvo slowed to enter her drive so she could pick up her car en route to the university. *Most of us willingly accept the responsibility and the risk involved in being parents. Wouldn't have it any other way. Ask Bill and Rachel Troy.*

CHAPTER EIGHT

Inside UCU the following morning Inspector Roger Furman was fully occupied with flexing his management muscle. 'You need *real* evidence. *Physical* evidence. You need *facts*. When you've got them I want to know, and I want them *soon*.'

Kate was watching him, head propped on one hand. *What an arse*. She looked away to gaze out of the window, ears stopped. *What was it that got you killed, Nathan? Was it a stranger who brought you death? Or was it someone you knew? Rachel had told them that he had girlfriends. Maybe his death was about a girl?*

She heard the continuing drone of Furman's voice, knowing much of it was aimed at her. 'Murder investigations don't run on airy-fairy theories . . .' She knew about Furman's restricted view of what constituted a thorough murder investigation. *As if you'd know*. '. . . What you need is facts, evidence. *Solid* leads.' She felt his glance, heard his clenched fist punctuate his words with a thump of the large glass screen which dominated the room. She turned to the screen. Nathan Troy's photograph was now up there.

She looked at Furman, not for the first time wondering how Chief Superintendent Gander tolerated him. *Probably has no choice*. 'We have some real evidence, some facts already,' she said, nodding at the screen. 'A torch found with the body and some very interesting treatment of the floor at the scene. Plus we have several names to follow up who will probably provide information.' She saw his mouth curve downwards and wanted to smack it.

'Glad to hear you've found something "interesting",' he murmured, not looking at her directly, his attention switching from Bernie to Joe. 'We've got the media onside for now and they're limiting their news reports to the discovery of the body and not much else until we have incontrovertible evidence that it is murder.'

Eyes widening, lips parting, Kate stared up at him, hardly believing what she was hearing. 'Evidence that it's — What *else* could it be? He didn't commit suicide, lie down and reconstruct the floor over himself.' She snapped shut her notebook, suspecting that he hadn't read all of the available information.

She heard Joe's voice. 'We're waiting on Dr Chong for a cause of death but Kate's right. It looks to be murder.'

Furman was gathering papers together, eyes on Joe as he responded. 'Follow up the names you've got ASAP.' He reached the door, turning with a parting shot they all recognised was intended for Kate. 'If it is murder, police work is about solid leads, not speculation and woolly, academic theories. Work the leads. Get the facts. I want to know about them by the end of the week.' He stalked towards the door and was gone.

Lowering his fingers Bernie passed a single A4 sheet to Kate. 'It's best to just let him run on. Brief report from Connie — cause of death still unconfirmed but foul play likely.'

She studied it. 'Like I said, people don't place themselves under floors, die and then cover themselves over. What's Furman talking about?'

'Ignore him. The guy's all about costs,' said Joe. 'He's hoping to delay any real expenditure until it's unavoidable. How about the visits to be done? Any preferences?' he asked, looking at each of them.

Bernie was frowning at the information on the screen. 'Them three names who shared the house with him need seeing but we've got no current location details. We need Sherlock to track 'em down. Where's he got to?'

'He's here, somewhere,' said Kate, thinking of Julian Devenish, the tall, gangling student and how he and the most senior member of UCU related to each other: mostly it involved sarcasm and quips from Bernie which she recognised as Force practice, particularly with the young. For his part Julian dealt with it well, at times giving as good as Bernie gave him. She opened her notebook. 'I know one of those names Rachel Troy mentioned.'

Bernie nodded, large head supported on a hefty fist. 'Am I surprised? Which one?'

'John Wellan. He's still a part of Woolner's faculty. When I say I know him, my direct contact with him has been limited to the occasional reception at Staff House at the university, you know the kind of thing.'

'Yeah. I'm a regular at them shindigs.'

She flipped the pages of her diary, giving him a look. 'Your *chip* is showing again. I'll phone him and agree a visit.'

'So, where's this institute place fit in, that Connie mentioned?'

The door opened and Julian walked inside looking harassed, sorting papers on the move. Hearing Bernie's query he flapped a couple of sheets in the air then placed them on the table in front of him. 'It's all here. Birmingham Institute of Art and Design. There's three sites: Margaret Street in the city centre, another in Aston, and the main Woolner campus on Linden Road, Bournville.'

Bernie studied the sheets. 'Good work, Sherlock.'

'Any contact details for the students Troy shared with?' asked Joe.

Julian was now holding up a clutch of photocopied sheets. 'Still looking, but I found an envelope of old newspaper cuttings about the disappearance so I photocopied them.' He handed them across the table.

Joe took the cuttings and walked to the glass screen. 'How about I extract the *facts* that Furman loves.'

Kate grinned then glanced across the table at Bernie's belligerent face. 'What's the matter with you? You seem a little . . . mardy,' she ended, using the colloquialism he often directed at her.

He pointed to the ceiling. 'There's a meeting going on Upstairs. The brass and Human Remains.' She recognised his name for the Force's Human Resources Department. 'They're drawing up a redundancy list and I can see my name being on it, but I'm telling you straight — listening to the Arse's yapping this morning I'm thinking it might be no bad thing if I was.' She nodded, having heard similar sentiments from him in the past, wondering not for the first time why police officers had nicknames for everything. And everyone. She decided not to speculate on the name he probably had for her.

Julian came to the table and sat, a single sheet remaining in his hand. 'Have a look at *this*, Kate.'

Bernie looked ceilingward. '*Doctor* Hanson. How many more times?'

She glanced at the map of Woodgate Park in Julian's hand and the delineation to which he was now pointing. 'The M5? I know it's close to the park. I could hear it when we were there.' Kate studied the thick line snaking across the map. Her attention halted at a particular point. 'And there's an exit fairly near it too.'

'Your point, Devenish?' demanded Bernie on his return from switching on the kettle in the 'refreshment centre', a corner of UCU equipped with a sink and a kettle.

Julian looked up at him, face keen. 'Whoever killed this student, maybe it was a stranger, a *Repeater* with wheels who could've travelled miles to the park.' His face fell. 'Although . . . *twenty* years. Whoever did it is probably dead now.'

Bernie sent him a sideways look. 'Two decades isn't that long.'

'It is for older people,' responded Julian, his eyes drifting over Bernie's face.

Kate was considering what Julian had said. Given her own forensic experience and the place in which the body had been left, murder-by-stranger was as plausible as Troy being killed by someone he knew. 'We'll keep both possibilities in mind: murder-by-stranger and by known individual.'

'And I'm suffering from dehydration here. Kettle's on. *Three* sugars when you're ready, Devenish.'

As Julian left the table Kate looked at her watch. She needed to be at the university in forty-five minutes. Searching the information Joe had added to the glass screen she found John Wellan's number and lifted the phone as PC Whittaker hurtled through the door, three thick files balanced on one arm. He reached the table and let them drop with a thump.

'Hold *up*. What's all *this*?' demanded Bernie, eyeing them then glaring up at him.

Whittaker was already quitting the room. 'Files on the Nathan Troy investigation of 1993 you asked me to find.'

'*Now* where're you—'

'Back downstairs. There's two more.'

As Kate's call was picked up Bernie's voice drifted across to her. '*Bloody* hell. How you fixed to start looking through this lot, Corrigan?'

CHAPTER NINE

Breath visible on the cold air, Kate hurried up the steps of Woolner College on Monday morning, passing students bundled inside parkas amid the chimes of the nearby carillon flowing from beneath their domed cupola. Entering the huge low-lit reception area she crossed the wide expanse of parquet and climbed the three flights of stairs as instructed by Wellan on the phone the previous day. She located his room at the end of a long, shadowed corridor. His name-plate bore the words: *Dr John Wellan. Senior Lecturer. Fine Arts.* Raising her hand to the door she knocked, reviewing what she knew of him from the few times they'd previously met. *One of the Awkward Squad.*

Five minutes later she was inside his studio, her eyes drifting over white-painted brick walls and wide lantern roof, the old wood floor splotched with colour, charcoal-coloured protective suits hanging from hooks on a nearby wall above a white-edged watermark. Kate absorbed the atmosphere, breathed the air, eyes closed. Oil paint . . . turpentine . . . chocolate—

'Here you go. Come over here and have a seat.'

She took the mug Wellan was offering, conducting a covert evaluation as she followed him to a desk piled with sketches, assorted art materials and what looked to be student papers. At fifty-plus years old John Wellan looked as if he'd lived most of them to the full. A gossiped whisper of historical hard drinking slipped into her head, along with a couple of opinions on him: institutional malcontent or disappointed loser, depending on whose opinion it was. She knew that he was a keen runner. Her eyes moved to the block of pale granite nearby. Running and hammering stone were keeping him fit. Today his tall, wiry frame was inside a black sweater topped by an elderly fleece and baggy jeans of similar vintage, feet in newish black Vans. She guessed his students rated him. She also guessed he didn't give a damn what they thought.

He took a seat opposite Kate, following her gaze to the far corner of the studio. 'I'm offering the kids an opportunity to experiment with spray paint. Look what I had to provide.' He pointed to the protective clothing and face masks. '*That's* the cold, bony hand of Health and Safety. What can I do for you?'

'As I said when I rang, I work with the Unsolved Crime Unit at Police Headquarters. UCU is investigating a murder case. Do you know Woodgate Country Park?'

'*Hhrrumph!*'

Startled, Kate looked behind her to see a tan and white basset hound sitting on a cushion close to the wall, face mournful, ears hanging.

'*Quiet*, Rupe.' Wellan looked at Kate. 'I try to avoid "w" words. He loves to be outside, dashing around. Yes, I know it. A few of us run there in good . . .' he mouthed the word 'weather'.

'It's where the body was found.'

'There's been rumours for years of dodgy goings-on down there.'

'This wasn't a substance abuser needing to score or somebody without a home. It was someone young whom you knew years ago—'

'Don't tell me. Nathan Troy?'

'Good guess — or did you get it from the newspapers, the TV news?'

'I ignore the *mediah*. Load of bollocks.' He shook his head and turned to churn the detritus on his desk. She eyed it then watched him reach for a small metal box, open it, and begin to construct a roll-up. Evidently Health and Safety wasn't allowed to intrude into John Wellan's personal behaviour at work. 'I guessed it was Troy because he's the only youngster I ever knew who disappeared. Autumn term of ninety three — or four?'

'Ninety-three.'

'Where, exactly?' Glancing at Rupe, who now appeared to be napping, Kate gave general details of the location of the remains and watched Wellan light the thin roll-up, eyes narrowing against smoke. 'Poor kid.'

'What can you tell me about him?' She watched his face, thinking he looked morose at the news she'd delivered, although it was difficult to judge. On the few occasions they'd met previously he'd looked similarly dour.

'Excellent student. Talented. Determined to do well and make the most of his time here.' He inhaled deeply.

'You were his main tutor. Did he have any problems at Woolner as far as you were aware?'

She watched him shrug and inhale more smoke. 'Not that I know of. Soaked up the course like a sponge.'

'What about his life outside Woolner?'

He shook his head. 'All I know is he shared a house with two or three other kids from here on one of the roads bordering Cadbury's-As-Was.'

'And that arrangement was working out?'

He shrugged again. 'Haven't got a clue. My interest is in what they do when they're here with me. What they do out there is their own affair.'

Kate eyed him, translating what he was saying to shorthand strokes. 'So you weren't aware of Troy having *any* difficulties?'

'No. If he'd mentioned anything I would have listened, obviously, but Troy was mature for his age. If he'd had any he'd have sorted them out himself.' He drew on the thin roll-up again.

Kate nodded, glancing at her itemised list to a question to which she already knew the answer. She gave a mental shrug. She'd ask it anyway. 'His family was local?'

With a brief nod he leaned towards a green metal filing cabinet to one side of the desk, pulled open the lower drawer and lifted out a dusty box file. 'Parents lived in . . . here it is: Castle Vale. Still do, for all I know. He house-shared because getting from there to here on public transport in the rush hour would've been no joke.'

She nodded then looked up at him. 'Know anything about his background?'

He shook his head. 'Not a lot. His mother came here for an open day before he started. Pleasant woman. Thrilled that he'd been accepted.'

Kate's pen sped. 'What about the father?'

Wellan was leaning back on his chair gazing up at the lantern roof. 'Mm . . . Negative about art in general, I'd say, and Woolner in particular although that's only an impression I got from the mother. I think the father had worked in the car industry all his life so it's hardly surprising. A traditional Birmingham bloke who knew how things worked and took it for granted that work meant you got your hands dirty. I picked that up because it's similar to my own background, just a different location.' He looked across at her and grinned. She'd known from his accent that he came from the north. 'Men from that social clique are inclined to consider art a dilettante occupation. Or effete.'

Kate's brows rose at the last word but she continued with her next question. 'Had Troy made friends here? Did he mention any names?'

'I'm sure he would have done, although I can't recall any. In my lectures and workshops he was fine with the other students.'

Kate gazed at what she'd written. Much as she disliked Furman's investigative approach she found herself wanting more facts. 'What about the students he lived with? Anything to say about them?'

Wellan propelled himself upright with a glance at his watch. 'Don't even remember their names. If you leave it with me I'll see what I can find from my records and I'll let you know.'

She wrote her number on the back of a UCU card and passed it to him, eyes skimming her list. 'Tell me about the last time you saw Nathan Troy prior to his disappearance.'

He was on his feet, delving among the layers of papers on the desk. 'Hold on a sec while I find some stuff for my next workshop.' He located a folder then turned to Kate. 'I don't recall the exact day he disappeared ever being established. Everybody assumed he'd just taken off, including the police. It happens. You probably know that from your own experience. He was almost twenty. Old enough to make his own choices.'

She frowned up at him. 'But he was a good student. You said he liked it here. Why would he do that?'

'That's a question for you and your "comrades" on the Force. As to the last time I saw him . . .' He raised his shoulders. 'I'm trying to think back. It's hard to remember.' She saw his brow crease and waited. 'I think I saw him last in a tutorial. If I'm right I should have a note of it somewhere.' He reached down to retrieve the box file from its drawer and leafed its contents, then: 'No. Can't see anything. Again, leave it with me and I'll have a proper look.'

'Can you make a guess as to when in the November you would have seen him for that tutorial?'

He looked upwards again then back to Kate. 'Somewhere between the start and the middle of the month.'

She had another thought. 'Any reason you can think of why Troy would have gone to the Country Park?'

'None that makes sense.'

She gave him a direct look. 'How about some that don't?'

He glanced at her then laughed. 'Before you arrived I had this picture of you from before as very determined.' His face became serious. 'Maybe he was down there partying? Kids have been known to go there to smoke weed.'

'Was Nathan Troy into that?'

'I didn't get the impression that he was but' — he shrugged — 'you know what kids are like. Never bet on anything you *think* you know about them.'

She sat back, closing her notebook. She'd covered her list. Her eyes moved to the long work surface against a nearby wall and the various objects it was supporting: paint tubes, soft new brushes, cold chrome, then on to the crowded wall above. She pointed to a print of *The Ambassadors*. 'I used that in a lecture recently. As an example of distorted perspective.' She turned back to him. 'There was another member of the faculty here who would have been involved with Troy and his student group.'

Wellan grinned. 'Henry Levitte, our esteemed leader at the time. He's emeritus professor now. Wafts in and out as the mood takes him. Do you know him?'

'I know *of* him,' nodded Kate, deciding to be economical.

'Then you'll probably also know what an awful old tart he is.' From his cushion the dog gave a wide yawn followed by a whine. 'Hang on, Rupe. I haven't forgotten.'

Kate was thinking along the lines of a couple of birds and a single stone: 'Is Levitte here today?'

He grimaced. 'Haven't seen him and I doubt he'll be any help to you.' He glanced at Kate. 'Okay, maybe I'm being a bit harsh. He's in his seventies now so he's entitled to do as he likes — and he does. But even back then, when Troy was here, Henry was never that involved with any of the students. I doubt he'll even recall him.'

Aware of voices in the corridor beyond the door, Wellan straightened, glancing at his watch. Realising he now had students waiting Kate pulled on her coat, collected her other belongings and headed towards the door with him, past an unframed portrait on a nearby wall of a young, dark-haired woman, olive-skinned, holding an infant in one arm.

'Sorry to cut your visit short,' he said.

She turned to him. 'Thank you for your time. You won't forget to let us have any information you find?'

'I won't.'

She walked out of the room and through the cluster of waiting students. As she walked away Wellan's voice followed her down the corridor. 'Come on in, you bunch of ne'er-do-wells. Nicki? Start mixing *hot* colours. Attwood! Take Rupe outside for five minutes. *Walk*.'

'Wwmph!'

At her car, Kate stowed her bag in the boot, got in and turned on the ignition. Waiting for warm air to clear the windscreen, she checked her phone. There was a text waiting: *No heat in UCU. Meet at uni.* Thoughts still on her conversation with John Wellan she gazed through cold glass to the misted scene beyond, wondering about her own recall of students from years before. She thought back to the beginning of the decade, which was as far back as she was able to go in her lecturing experience. Closing her eyes she tried to bring to mind her first ever student group. The odd name or two surfaced, along with a couple of faces. She gave a small headshake. Difficult. Although it would have been an easier task if she could link the group to a significant occurrence back then, like disappearance and murder, for example.

She put the car into gear and released the handbrake as her mind settled on a single word: *effete*.

CHAPTER TEN

Kate was seated at her desk inside her room at the university, Bernie's words flowing towards her. 'UCU's like a fridge and he's already got a cold.' He jabbed a thumb at Julian who gave her a bleary grin. 'So we've left Maintenance to it. Nice and warm in here.' Listening, she squared the textbooks on one side of the wide desk, straightened pens and did a quick scan of her to-do list: *Contact details for 3 housemates. Phone H. Levitte.* Looking up she saw Crystal walking towards them with a tray of coffee. Opening a drawer, she took out a 'Psychology is all in the head' coaster and placed it on the desk.

Bernie continued. 'So I went down to the park and had another look around . . . Ah, thanks, love. You're a good girl.' Kate's eyes rolled.

Crystal smiled. 'That's what my dad says. Just as well he doesn't know the half of what I get up to.'

Bernie grinned at her then looked across at Kate. 'That's what's needed round here. Somebody with a sense of humour who's in touch with the real world.' He saw Kate's facial expression. 'Present company excepted.'

'What's it like at the park that time in the evening?' she asked.

'You don't want to know, Doc.'

'I *do*. That's why I'm *asking*.'

He raised his brows to Joe then looked back at her. 'Black as a witch's knickers at seven o'clock last night.' She heard Julian titter. 'Drifting mist and *dead* quiet except for odd rustlings. I tell you, I was glad when Corrigan showed up.'

She looked at Joe. 'You went too?'

Joe stretched his arms to clasp his hands behind his head. 'Uh-huh. Like Bernie said, it was useful to see it, given the likelihood that Troy was murdered under cover of darkness.'

Julian gave a quick nod. 'I was thinking—'

Taking a slurp of his drink Bernie groaned. 'Ay-up. Now we're in trouble.'

'—how useful it is for UCU that it's investigating Troy's death *now*. At this time of the year. We can get an idea of the scene pretty much as it was in November when he was killed.'

Kate gave a nod. 'Well said.' She glanced at her senior colleagues. 'Anything else gleaned from the park, other than dark and creepy?'

'Hang on, I hadn't finished. Like Sherlock said the other day, it's close to the M5. You can really hear it at that time of an evening. If this is murder-by-stranger it makes sense to think that the killer came and went by the M5.'

'Or we could stay focussed on what we're doing for now?' suggested Kate as she stood and walked to the front of the desk. 'I've told you what I got from John Wellan, which wasn't much, although he confirmed Bill Troy's negative attitude to Nathan's choice of an art course. We need to contact Professor Henry Levitte. See what he has to say about Troy, if anything.' She paced, changing tack. 'Remember what I said the other day. About the lake-house floor?'

Bernie tracked her. 'About it being fitted back together?'

'I think that floor is really important. Reassembling it took skill and patience. I keep coming back to the fact that whoever took it up and replaced it shortly before the dog walker's visit had to know that Troy was concealed beneath it. The obvious implication is that *that* was the same person who put Troy there in 1993.' She sat on the edge of the desk. 'And then there's the torch. Exactly how did it get there?'

Julian looked excited. 'How about the person who put Troy there brought it with him to search for something? Something he left behind all those years ago?'

'Even vandals like to see what they're doing,' muttered Bernie, still pursuing his own theory.

'I agree with Julian. As I can't come up with a single plausible reason why the torch would have been *placed* there, the alternative is that it was left by mistake or dropped, maybe because its owner was in a hurry or under stress.'

'As he would've been if he'd seen the remains,' suggested Joe.

Arms folded across his wide chest, Bernie regarded Kate. 'Any answer as to why the doer waits all that time to come back? And why bother? As you said, Doc, the body had been well concealed for twenty years. If there was something else there, it could've stopped another twenty without anybody being the wiser.'

Joe looked from one to the other. 'We need to ask Mr and Mrs Troy if any of Nathan's personal items weren't recovered. If they confirm that all of his belongings were accounted for then if there was something there with him it probably belonged to his killer.' He glanced across to Bernie. 'But as you say, why would the killer bother to go and look? Why disturb what's been secure this last two decades?'

'We're all ideas and no real information. Either of you heard from Connie?' She got two head-shakes.

Joe sent a sideways glance to Bernie. 'Tell Kate how much you favour the M5 theory.'

Bernie caught her facial expression. 'All right, Corrigan. I was waiting for the right time. I'm thinking that Troy was killed by somebody he didn't know. If we can agree on that we can get our show on the road. Check out if there's been any other similar cases.'

'What's the basis for your theory?' queried Kate.

His brows lowered. 'My *basis* is the closeness of the M5 to the scene, like I said. In police work you get a feel for cases and it makes more sense to me than one of his arty pals done him in.'

She shook her head as she returned to her desk. 'We can't say "stranger" yet, surely? It's too early to decide on an investigative direction.' She narrowed her eyes. 'You muttered?'

'I *said* that just because you don't fancy the idea of a stranger-murder, *meaning* another Repeater, it don't mean this isn't one.'

She leaned forward on the desk, eyes on him. 'It has nothing to do with what I might like or not like. I'm *theory*-driven. Right now we don't have enough information to start to develop one for this case.'

Bernie refolded his arms. '*Civilians.* All I'm doing is flaggin' it up.' He tapped the arm of the chair with a thick forefinger. 'Putting it on a low light to cook, so to speak. Here, Devenish. Go and ask Lady Gaga for some more coffee.' Julian took the mug and sighed his way to the connecting door.

Kate leaned back in her chair, gazing out of the window at the icy campus. 'What we need is information about Nathan Troy and his life from the people who knew him at the time he disappeared. Which *might* point to his being killed by someone known to him. It could point us in another direction.' She looked from Bernie's vexed face to the relaxed occupant of the armchair. 'That's *my* view. What's yours, Joe?'

He gave her a mild glance. 'That there's room for both approaches and I enjoy working in a feisty atmosphere.'

She looked down at her notes. 'Apparently, the specific day on which Nathan disappeared was never established.'

Joe shook his head. 'Now *there's* something I don't get. That should've been easy to do. He shared a house. He had a lecture time-table.'

'Loads of students skip lectures.' This from Julian returning with coffee, adding a hasty, 'Not *yours*, Kate.'

'*Doctor* Hanson,' muttered Bernie.

She nodded her agreement of Julian's words. 'Attendance isn't registered on a daily basis and there's always a proportion of students who take a casual approach to lectures, although from what John Wellan said it's unlikely that Nathan Troy took that line. I'll contact Woolner College for any data it's got on attendances for—'

'Already done it, Doc. Records computerised in ninety-five. That's Year Zero as far as records go.'

Kate dropped back in her chair. 'Why do I ever expect easy?' She pointed to her notes. 'At the time Troy disappeared Professor Henry Levitte was the departmental head. We need to speak to him as soon as we can.'

'And you know him as well, I suppose?' said Bernie.

'I met him once, years ago. I'll fix a date to see him. Wellan said he'd send details of the current contact details of Troy's housemates if he could find anything—'

Julian sat up as if cattle-prodded. 'Hang on! Furman handed me some stuff about that as I was leaving.' They watched as he pulled crumpled sheets from his backpack.

She reached for them and scanned details, thinking that Furman had his uses. It was here. The names of the housemates: Alastair Buchanan, Joel Smythe and Matthew Johnson, along with contact details, except for Smythe. Kate looked up at her colleagues. 'How about *that*? It says here that Matthew Johnson is now *Professor* of Fine Arts at Woolner. Presumably Levitte's replacement. The boy done good.' She glanced at the sheet again then at Joe. 'Remember what Rachel Troy told us, about a student called "Rod"? He's not down here. We need to establish who he was and where he is now.'

She stood and went to sit on the edge of her desk. 'I don't give a damn what Furman says about leads and evidence, I'm saying that once we really *know* Nathan Troy as an individual, the person he was, how the people who knew him felt about him, we'll know why he was killed.'

Julian rummaged inside his backpack again and dragged out a manila folder. 'This is the last of the files that Whittaker fetched from the evidence store. How about I stay here and search through it for—?'

Kate held out a hand. 'Pass it to me, please.' She took it from him, turned and dropped it into the wastepaper bin.

Bernie lurched forward. 'Hang on!' Joe grinned and slow-handclapped.

Kate pointed to the bin. 'That stuff didn't help in 1993. It won't help us now. It's *police*-style information.'

'And *this* is a police-*style* investigation in case you've forgot! We've been through the others.'

She watched as Bernie, red-faced, retrieved the file from the bin. 'And did you find anything useful in them?'

'Too early to say,' he snapped.

Joe came and sat next to her on the edge of the desk, giving her a direct, blue look. She ignored a sudden rush of warmth. 'Have to say it. Murder-by-stranger makes a lot of sense, Red.'

The phone on her desk rang. Distracted, she turned to reach for it. 'Kate Hanson.'

'Hi, Katie. If you and the Three Musketeers drop by Rose Road in the next half-hour I can tell you a little more about Nathan Troy.'

She put down the phone. 'Connie.' They all stood except for Julian. She turned and glanced at him. 'Coming?'

He was first out of the door.

CHAPTER ELEVEN

They stood either side of Connie as she reviewed her written notes. 'Nathan Troy was strangled.'

Bernie gave the leather-textured neck a sideways glance then looked at Connie. 'To me, strangling says male-to-female. If it was male-to-male it could be there was a sex angle. Both of 'em gay and something goes wrong.'

Kate gave an eye-roll, catching sight of the keen interest on Julian's face. He'd matured a lot in the last year or so. They needed to include him more. She listened as he now spoke. 'If it was male-to-male, how about he was knocked out to begin with?'

'Calm down, Devenish. Listen and learn.'

Joe looked up from the examination table. 'We've had male-on-male cases of strangulation back home — the I-70 Strangler: eight-plus male victims, another operating in Florida, one in Georgia. All three killers were heterosexual. Another in Indiana killed two males. He *was* gay. His victims weren't. In Troy's case we can't assume that gender orientation is relevant.'

Hearing the litany of repeaters Kate's mood sunk. *Maybe what Bernie said is true: I don't want another Repeater case.*

'Could Nathan Troy have been gay?' queried Bernie, not about to give up on his theory.

She shrugged. 'As Joe just said, we can't extrapolate from the method of killing that Troy's murder was sexually motivated. A killer may strangle a victim due to extreme anger, not pausing to select a weapon, which may suggest a degree of relationship between them. On the other hand strangling might be chosen because it gives total control over a victim who is viewed as an impersonal object by the murderer.' Kate's mood slid further as she reviewed her own words. *A pretty good definition of how a Repeater might operate*. 'Sorry, Connie.'

'Want the detail?' They nodded. 'It was strangulation by ligature not hands. Strangulation is almost always murder. However, use of a ligature can indicate another scenario: death as a result of auto-erotic asphyxia — otherwise known as "Bound-for-Glory", or "Dying-For-A-Good-Time", and one or two other terms I won't say. Given the concealment of *this* body, we can assume murder.' She pointed to a specific area of the neck. 'That's a ligature furrow which I noted during my preliminary examination but I had to be certain it wasn't a crease due to the position his body had been in for so long, or possibly an artefact of the mummification process. Now—'

'Troy was young and he would've been strong.'

'I hear what Bernie's saying,' said Kate. 'Strangling does seem more likely from a male to a female because of the power to weight ratio.'

She saw Connie's nod. 'Unlikely, isn't it, that a healthy young male would stand around whilst another male placed a ligature around his neck and pulled it tight?' Connie turned and pointed towards one of Nathan Troy's shrunken arms. 'I've examined both of his hands: the nails are in good condition. No debris under them, in terms of blood, tissue or hair belonging to another person, so there's zero indication of Troy attempting to defend himself.'

As Kate processed this information Joe glanced down at the withered hands. 'You're saying Troy *did* stand around while somebody put something around his neck?'

Connie grinned. 'I can't *help* it. I love the unfolding process with UCU. How about a couple of intervening factors?'

She lifted a clipboard, turning it to show the information attached.

Kate read the top line: *Screen for Alcohol/Acid/Alkaline/Narcotic*. 'You've tested for the possibility that he was *compliant* when he was killed due to substance use?'

Connie nodded. 'I won't burden you with detail. The useful bit is that although analysis couldn't confirm or otherwise the presence of alcohol in the tissue it *was* informative for drugs: Lithane, to be precise. Which could have slowed him, maybe rendered him somewhat sleepy, more so if alcohol *was* taken. Depending on Troy's level of compliance, it's not possible to rule out that he died at female hands.'

Bernie was looking nettled. 'What's this Lithane stuff?'

Connie glanced towards Kate who answered, 'Lithane is a brand name for lithium.'

He gave the ceiling a quick once-over. 'And *lithium* being . . . ?'

'Medication commonly used to treat episodes associated with mood disorder.'

His brows shot upwards. 'This Troy was a head case?'

'Neither his parents nor John Wellan mentioned any such difficulties.' Kate looked down at the remains. 'We don't even know that it was his medication.'

'How about he was a bit high-strung, seeing as he was one of your arty types?'

Exasperated, Kate turned to Connie. 'So Nathan Troy ingested lithium and *possibly* alcohol, around the time he died, making him sufficiently compliant for a female to strangle him.'

Connie raised cautionary hands. 'If both substances were involved it's *possible*. But there's a second intervening factor. One your youngest colleague has already mentioned.' She beckoned to them and they followed, Julian open-mouthed, to stand around the mummified head. Connie pointed a latexed finger to an area of darkened surface. 'See? Just there?' She re-angled the overhead light. 'Now do you see it?' They stared at the circular indentation. 'Lateral blunt-force trauma to the right side of the head sustained by Nathan Troy around the time he died.'

Joe leaned forward, his eyes drifting over the head injury. He looked up at Connie. 'He *was* knocked unconscious prior to being strangled?'

'Can't be that categorical, Joseph. It could merely have disabled him temporarily.'

'Caused by?' he asked.

'A hard object with an approximately four- to five-centimetre diameter, a flat, *very* smooth surface and a well-defined but equally smooth edge.' Connie pointed to the mark on the skull and they looked again. 'With magnification you can see the clear imprint. However, it isn't uniform. When it hit him, it was at an angle. He was struck on his right side, like *this*.' She made a sudden sideways movement with her hand. 'It seems likely that he was in a seated position, his killer to one side and at a similar level. The limited force of the blow reduced the damage. The lack of debris within the wound leads me to surmise that the weapon, instrument, whatever it was, was metal.'

'So, what're we talking about?' asked Bernie. 'Something like a hammer?'

'Possible. I can't be more robust than that.' There was silence. 'Resisting *slight* feelings of inadequacy born of *CSI*, do you have any other questions to which I might be able to supply a *categorical* answer?' In the following silence she drew the green sheet over the remains as Igor appeared.

Watching him wheel away Nathan Troy a query surfaced inside Kate's head. She turned to Connie. 'Was Troy murdered where he was found? Inside the lake house?'

Connie shook her head. 'That's a can't-say. No evidence either way.' She waved a hand. 'Come and see the torch Joe spotted when we were at the scene.'

They followed her to a nearby table where the small item sat alone on thick, white cartridge paper. His broad middle against the table Bernie eyed the black plastic cylinder. 'We can discount that as the weapon?'

Connie nodded. 'Not heavy enough.'

A thought occurred to Kate. 'There wasn't anything inside it, apart from batteries?'

'No, and they were long past their best. Remember Adam mentioned that they had an expiration date stamped on them, more or less illegible? Forensics have managed to enhance it: July 2010, which confirms that it went under the floor years after Troy did.' She looked up at Kate. 'And nicely confirms what you were saying about the floor being raised recently.'

'At which time the flashlight fell into the hole,' added Joe.

'UCU, at times your attention to detail makes me want to cheer. How about I give you another?' She caught Bernie's eye and smiled, pointing at the small torch, its cylindrical shape constructed of black ribbed rubber, each end a smooth, metallic grey. 'It's pretty ordinary, although not the kind of thing you'd pick up in a pound shop. But, *this* is where it gets *really* interesting.' Kate watched as Connie indicated the ribbed section. 'Just around here, within these grooves, is where Forensics found the tiniest of blood smears.' She raised her head, face impish. 'And we *all* know what *blood* means, don't we?'

'DNA,' whispered Julian.

Connie grinned. 'As you know, samples are run through CODIS for a match. You *also* know that a match depends on whoever left a sample having had his DNA taken previously as a consequence of a prior arrest. Want to know whose DNA it is?' They stared at the small oval face, topped by short black hair. 'His name is Stuart Butts.'

'*Yes*.' Kate watched as Bernie punched the air, turning to Joe to high-five, then back to Connie, face beaming. 'Did I ever tell you you're the *best* pathologist we've had here?'

She gave him a sidelong glance. 'No, you didn't. You're usually less than impressed when I won't confirm what you want when you want it.'

'Yeah, well — we've been on Troy's case no time and we've got a breakthrough. We've got the murderer! After nearly *twenty* years! Anything else you can tell us about this Butts bloke before we have him in?'

She nodded. 'He's local.' Seeing his broad grin she gave him a sympathetic glance. 'Sorry, but the next bit of information won't please you at all. He's not long celebrated his sixteenth birthday.'

* * *

They were inside UCU in their coats, the heat from the radiators barely enough to move mercury. Stuart Butts's family had been visited by two officers from Upstairs at Bernie's request. He wasn't at home and his parents were unable to provide any information as to his whereabouts beyond a vague reference to his staying with some cousins and that they had no concerns about him.

Bernie was summing up the implications of what they knew about the teenager and the situation. 'There's nothing else we can do. He's not been reported missing by his family. Until that happens we can't make a case to Goosey for a search. It's obvious that at sixteen he can't have murdered Troy. The fact that a torch with his DNA on it was down there with Troy's body don't necessarily mean that it was Butts who left it. He could've lost it, give it away, or it was pinched, who knows?'

Kate turned from the window and went to the glass screen as Julian began to fill his backpack with textbooks. 'When he reappears we'll interview him and establish what connection he has to the park.'

Bernie nodded. 'It's going to be vandalism, like I said.'

'Why?' demanded Kate. She watched the heavy face settle into its bulldog-with-a-gripe expression.

'What d'you mean "why"?' He tapped the Police National Computer printout relating to Stuart Butts with a forefinger. 'We know his form: he's sixteen and he's already been done for theft and violence. Just the type to vandalise stuff because he's bored, hanging around the streets, the *parks*.'

She pointed a finger at him despite knowing it riled him. 'We don't *know* anything about him yet: was he even at the park? If he *was*, was he alone? If he wasn't alone, who was there with him?' She frowned. 'If he was there with someone, is it possible that it was Nathan Troy's murderer from twenty years ago?'

'Doc, that's a lot of questions and we won't know no answers till we have him in here.' Kate watched him reach for a paper bag and open it with delicate movements of forefingers and thumbs to reveal a jam doughnut.

She turned to look at Joe, his chair set to 'recline'. 'We've got Detective Sergeant Nightmare's view.' She heard a tutting sound. 'How do *you* think we should progress this?'

'Until Stuart Butts is located and in here we continue what we're doing, which is talking to the names we've got and following any potential leads we get.'

She sat, looking pent up. 'It is annoying, not knowing if this Stuart Butts is at all relevant.'

She saw even, white teeth as he smiled. '*Relax*, Red. All in good time.'

Bernie licked his fingers. 'Didn't get where you are today by relaxin', did you, Doc?'

'I'm merely frustrated because of a possible lead we can't follow up,' she snapped. Her eyes were on the middle distance. 'What if Troy's body was an accidental discovery by Butts? . . . Maybe it *was* vandalism like you said.'

'*Thank* you.'

'And he saw the body.'

Bernie looked at her 'And according to you he never legged it like any normal person would've done but hung about and covered it up again?'

She gave him an aggrieved glance. 'I'm agreeing with what *you* said. That he's got nothing to do with Troy's murder. He's just a destructive type who came across it. If this Stuart Butts didn't spend time replacing the floor, who did?'

She paced back to the window to gaze out, the neurons in her central nervous system processing information, communicating it to thousands of others via as many synapses, flooding her head with questions. *Where was Nathan Troy when death came for him? Was the lithium his? Effete? Might that be construed as a hint about Troy's sexual orientation? There was nothing so far to suggest he was anything other than heterosexual. But what if someone thought he was gay? Might it have led to a fight? An unequal fight: medication and alcohol.*

She returned to the table as Joe reached for the phone, listened as Bernie left a message for Professor Matthew Johnson. Right now all they could do was follow up what contact names they already had. She sat, distracted, thinking of the clothes belonging to Nathan Troy which they'd seen downstairs in the post-mortem suite. *November. Surely he'd been wearing more than jeans and a T-shirt?*

She picked up her phone and dialled the home number of Professor Henry Levitte. No reply and no opportunity given to leave a message. She cut the call and dialled the number of the college, to be told what she already anticipated: that Professor Levitte had no set hours and wasn't there today.

* * *

An hour later Kate was in her hall, interrogating the thermostat with equal parts of doubt and suspicion as she waited for her call to be answered. She still felt chilled despite changing into a long-sleeved white top, faded sweatshirt and black workout pants tucked inside black Uggs. The thermostat continued to inform her that the house temperature was twenty degrees. 'That's *your* story. Come on, come on.'

'Professor Johnson's office.'

'This is Kate Hanson, Police Headquarters, Rose Road. A colleague of mine, D.S. Watts, left a request for a meeting with Professor Johnson but hasn't had a response. We need to see the Professor as soon as possible, please.'

'I'm sorry,' a female voice intoned. 'He doesn't have any availability this week.'

'This is urgent police business,' said Kate.

'Hm . . . Let me see . . . How about ten-thirty tomorrow morning? He has a thirty minute window.'

It was enough for an initial visit. Kate ended the call and rang to let her colleagues know the arrangement and that she had a couple of hours free.

Returning to the kitchen she switched on the kettle, aware of a soft rhythmic tapping. Going to the huge garden doors she released a bolt and pushed one of them outwards into darkness and bitter air. Mugger shot into the kitchen and skittered to a stop next to his empty food bowl, giving her a reproachful stare.

'Hungry, little cat?' She poured biscuits and stroked his chill coat, an image stealing into her head of Troy in T-shirt and jeans in November.

Maisie padded into the kitchen carrying a plate. 'Mm . . . that toasted cheese was de-*licious*. Can I have another?'

'Of course you can.' Kate washed her hands then crossed to the fridge-freezer to fetch cheese.

'Mom?'

'Mm?'

'Cheese is good nutrition, right?'

She glanced at her across the kitchen. 'You know it is.'

'We had boring old Home Economics today.' Kate sighed, knowing that Maisie's keenness for matters mathematical did not extend to some of her other lessons. 'And Mrs Rodder was going on about good nutrition being a main contributor to bodybuilding.' She swept a critical eye over her mother. 'You're always going on about having a good diet and stuff but . . .'

'But what?' she asked, bringing the cheese to the table and starting to slice it.

'Face it, Mom, you're not exactly "built", are you?'

She stopped slicing and looked at the young face across the table. 'Maisie, could you provide me with a *hint* as to what we're talking about?'

Maisie looked piqued. 'I'm *talking* about me still being in my *first* bra that you got for me last year! *That's* what I'm talking about. Have you *seen* Chelsey?'

Kate had. Now she understood. She crossed to where Maisie was standing and slipped an arm round the small shoulders. 'You're *twelve* years old. You won't stop growing — *developing* — for years. Stop being in such a hurry.'

Seeing Maisie pull at the neck of her jersey to peer inside she shook her head and returned to slice the bodybuilding cheese. 'You *do* want this?'

'Course I do. I'm hungry. The thing is, though, what if I don't get built?'

Kate stopped slicing. 'Maisie, we've talked about puberty, haven't we? Young people develop at different rates. As I've said, you've got years of development still to come. You'll get taller and . . . lots of other things will change.' She resumed slicing. 'You'll be whatever you're going to be and *that* will be absolutely fine.'

Maisie came to stand next to her mother at the counter. 'Okay. But just in case, make that *two* slices . . . Why are you smiling?'

CHAPTER TWELVE

They were en route to Woolner College in the Range Rover next morning, Bernie having declined a lift in Kate's car. 'That thing puts me back out.' Now he was thrusting papers in her direction. 'Have a read. Got some of it from a Google search of the college's site and the rest out of the original *police files*.'

She sped through the sheets. 'It says on this one that Matthew Johnson was a "surprise appointment" as Henry Levitte's successor given his comparative youth.' She looked ahead doing quick computations. 'He's around forty now so he was only thirty . . . thirty-*two* when he made prof.'

'That good?'

'Practically unheard of where I work. I'm surprised John Wellan didn't mention it, given that it means he was effectively passed over for somebody easily ten-plus years younger. He wouldn't have liked that, surely?' She reprised her conversation with him. 'Although, it's possible he didn't care.' She returned to the printed pages. 'Nothing much about Johnson the man apart from one or two very brief mentions of his name during the original investigation. Seems he didn't contribute anything useful to it.' She passed them back. 'We need details, facts from Johnson and anything else he's got to offer, and we've got half an hour to do it.'

Minutes later they were being shown inside a large wood-panelled room, the professor waving them inside from where he was standing behind his desk, framed by a huge mullioned window looking out over Woolner's gardens to the mellow old building housing the campus's carillon bells some distance away, his attention on a phone call. 'Yes, I know. Yes, I understand. As I said, leave it with me.' Kate took in the expensive jeans, the shirt and Johnson himself, tall, in good shape and lightly tanned. He looked like someone who took regular, outdoor exercise. Maybe be was a runner like Wellan?

Phone call ended he gestured them to chairs as Bernie made introductions. Kate saw Johnson's easy smile, noted the well-modulated voice. 'Unfortunately I have to begin with an apology. My admin assistant was misguided when she suggested this meeting. I have to be away from here in' — he consulted his watch — 'ten minutes at most.'

Bernie nodded. 'That's all right, Professor. We'll cover what we can and what we don't get to you can come to Rose Road to finish off.' Ignoring the surprised look his words had caused he continued. 'Nathan Troy. Body found at the Country Park down in Woodgate. Tell us what you know about him.'

'I only heard about it this morning. John Wellan mentioned it in Briefing.' He pointed to the *Birmingham Mail* on his desk. 'There's a bit in there, although it doesn't mention Nathan by name. What a tragedy.' He shook his head, his eyes on each of them in turn. 'What can I tell you about him? Not much, I'm afraid.'

Kate gave an encouraging nod. 'You both shared a house as students.'

'Yes we did but we moved in completely different circles and had different—'

'Tell us about them "circles" you was both moving in, Professor.'

Johnson stared at Bernie for some seconds then back to Kate. 'I was very involved with the Woolner Choral Society and I was part of the Woolner Players. Still am, as a matter of fact.' He gave an engaging grin. 'Both took up a lot of my time back then. I don't know what Nathan was involved with. We weren't friends, you see.' He frowned, raising quick hands. 'By that I mean that we were mere *acquaintances*. The house arrangement was merely a practical—'

'We know that. We're waiting for you to expand on anything you do remember about him, "acquaintance" or otherwise,' prompted Bernie.

Kate watched the merest hint of colour rise above Johnson's gleaming white shirt collar. He shook his head. 'I'm sorry. I can't tell you what I don't know and I'm being brief and to the point in the interests of efficiency.' He glanced at his watch again.

Bernie nodded. 'Most people speak to us in the interests of being helpful and open, Professor.'

There was a short silence and Kate watched Johnson take a breath. 'Look, we've obviously got off on *slightly* the wrong foot here.'

'Perhaps you can help us understand your seeming lack of knowledge of Nathan Troy's life back then?' she suggested.

He shrugged. 'Like I said, we had different interests and it was such a long time ago, wasn't it?'

She nodded. 'To his family it feels as raw as if it were yesterday.'

She watched him look down at his desk, face set. 'Nathan and I didn't socialise much but on those rare times when we *did* have contact it was perfectly pleasant. As far as I remember he was doing okay here.' He lifted his shoulders, spreading both hands. 'Wellan's the person you need to speak to about that.'

'You and Nathan were taking the same course? Fine Arts?'

'Yes. But we followed our own inclinations. I was into oils whereas he liked watercolour and pen sketching. We shared the same college environment but that was about it.'

'And you shared a syllabus,' Kate reminded him.

He regarded her in silence. 'We both had lectures but opted for different workshops.'

'The workshops would have been with John Wellan?' He gave a terse nod. 'Did you and Nathan enjoy those?'

'I can't speak for Nathan,' he snapped. 'If it's relevant, I found Dr Wellan's workshops and lectures enjoyable—' He stopped, face disapproving. 'But given that you're a fellow academic and that Wellan is still part of the faculty here I find your enquiry a little questionable.'

Kate was unfazed. She was thinking back to the discussion she and Joe had had with Troy's parents. 'Do you remember any names of fellow students of yours and Nathan's?' Johnson made no response. 'What about Joel Smythe?'

He shrugged. 'What about him? He was on a different course.'

'Alastair Buchanan?'

Johnson was beginning to look disengaged. She saw him take another quick glance towards his left wrist. 'So was he.'

Kate gave a slow nod. 'Can you tell us anything about a young female student who was a particular friend of Nathan's? Her name was Cassandra.'

Face hardening, he got to his feet. 'I can't see what I can contribute about Nathan for reasons I've explained and I *don't* see the point of your going through a roll-call of names from years ago—'

Bernie gave him a look. 'You could volunteer information to save us having to prod for it. Starting with any students *you* was friends with? I'm assuming you had some?'

Eyes on Johnson's face Kate saw that he was annoyed. She watched his hands clasp each other, a gold band on the left catching the light as he massaged them together. There was a quick knock and the door opened, a woman's face appearing round it.

'Time you were leaving.' She disappeared.

Johnson lifted a briefcase onto the desk. 'I've answered your questions as well as I can and I'm afraid that's all the time I can give you.' He gestured towards the door.

Bernie gave him a mild look. 'We'll be calling again, Professor. How about next time we see you away from your work pressures?'

'I assure you that no matter where you see me there's nothing else I can add.'

As Bernie followed Kate through the door he stopped and turned. 'We often find that people remember more on a second visit. Next time we see you, how about we make it Rose Road? Or maybe where you live? More relaxed, yeah?' It was evident from the look on Johnson's face that neither was a welcome option. Bernie was still looking at him, an eyebrow raised. 'Your wife — was *she* a student here?'

Johnson's reply, when it came, was terse. 'No.'

* * *

The Range Rover hummed along the dual carriageway. Kate listened to Bernie giving his take on the meeting as the suburban scene flashed past. 'He started out pleasant enough. *Then* he got defensive. Didn't want to talk about the good old student days at Woolner, did he? Why's that, do you think?'

She grinned. 'He's good looking. How about he was a bit of a player back then?'

'Exactly. Comes across as up himself but I'm thinking he was probably sociable with a lot of pals back then. Although according to *him* Troy wasn't one of them. To the point that Troy barely existed for him, if we accept what he said.' He glanced at her. 'What's on *your* mind?'

'He wasn't keen on us seeing him at his home, was he?' asked Kate.

He grinned. 'Maybe he don't want his wife hearing what he got up to in the nineties. He wants anything he got up to at Woolner to stop there.'

* * *

He stood, his back to the massive leaded window, thinking over the events of the past few minutes, then reached for the phone. When his call was answered he spoke, keeping his voice low. 'You have a problem.'

'Do I? Who says?'

'*I* do. Their questions were very direct.'

'That's what the police *do*.'

'And being vague was no help at all. They'll be back. They won't give up. Especially her. This has got nothing whatsoever to do with me and—'

'You're an ungrateful bastard with too short a memory. We'll talk again.' His call was ended.

CHAPTER THIRTEEN

They returned to Rose Road as Joe was bringing a phone call to a close. He looked at Kate and mouthed, 'Alastair Buchanan.' The other phone rang and Kate lifted it. 'UCU. Kate Hanson.' She listened then covered the receiver with a hand, holding it towards Bernie. 'For you. Woman returning your call from this morning. She wouldn't give her name.'

'I know who that is. Got an old number from the files.' He took the phone, switched it to speaker and replaced the receiver. 'Detective Sergeant Bernard Watts, West Midlands Police. Thanks for ringing me back. I'm trying to trace somebody by the name of Joel Smythe. S-m-y-t-h-e.' Silence drifted across the room. Bernie looked at each of his colleagues. '*Hello?*'

The voice came, faint and uncertain. 'What you're asking . . . I'm not sure I can help you . . .'

'This is the number of Joel Smythe's family?' After a further lengthening silence and some irritable tutting from Bernie the diffident voice was replaced by another with a firm tone. 'Who *is* this?'

'Detective Sergeant Watts, Police Headquarters, Birmingham.'

'What do you want?'

He frowned at the instrument. 'I want Joel Smythe's current contact details.'

'I'm sorry. We can't help you.'

His face set. 'And you would be?'

Her voice rang out across the room. 'His sister. That was my mother you spoke to and now she's upset.'

Hands on hips, Bernie glared down at the phone. 'Sorry to hear it but we're conducting an investigation here and we think your brother might be able to help—'

The voice cut him off. 'Joel hasn't lived here since he was eighteen. We lost touch with him completely in 2004.'

'You're saying you've got no idea as to his current whereabouts?'

'If we did we'd tell his ex-wife. My brother walked out on his family years ago and never made contact again, apart from a phone call six months afterwards. That's all I can tell you.'

Bernie ended the call then looked at his colleagues. 'That's that then. Smythe upped sticks and left his job, his wife, his *life*. No use looking in that direction for any help.'

Joe turned from the screen. 'Why would a guy in his thirties choose to leave his family and disappear? How about Force records?'

Bernie turned as Julian came into UCU. 'Job for you, Devenish. Do a full search of missing persons' reports for 2004: name of Joel Smythe, with a Y. Last known location: Surrey.' He watched him settle at the computer. 'You ever share a house, Sherlock?'

Julian clattered keys, looking morose. 'Part of my contract with the vice chancellor after that problem—' Kate heard the routine euphemism for his hacking history, '—was that I stay living in halls. I don't like it there. It's too noisy. Now he's saying I can move out and rent a place but I can't afford to because it's too expensive.'

'All right, Goldilocks, calm down. Something'll turn up.' He turned to Kate. 'None of these students who lived together in ninety-three seem to have bothered to keep in touch with each other.'

Kate provided a quick overview of the workings of students' shared accommodation. 'I know what you're saying. I'm still in contact with two or three friends from my student days but for many they can be friendships of convenience. You finish your degree, apply for jobs and you're gone, often to another part of the country and new friendships.'

He huffed. 'Looks like Smythe got into the habit and carried it on even after he was married.'

Julian lifted his backpack onto the desk. 'I'll have to come back to the search. I've got my six-monthly interview with the VC in half an hour.'

Kate was aware of the vice chancellor's continued focus on Julian, which had originally led to his being assigned to her as a student-helper with a part-time placement with Rose Road's forensics team. Two ways for her to keep an eye on him. It would have been accurate to describe Julian as underwhelmed by the arrangement at the time but he'd taken to it quickly and well. She stood. 'I'm going into the university. I'll give you a lift. Bernie? Would you phone Henry Levitte on his home number and arrange a visit. I can do Thursday or Friday afternoon. I'll be back later.'

* * *

In the fast-fading afternoon light inside UCU, Julian turned from the screen to his senior colleagues. '*Found* him. Housemate number three. Joel Smythe is an official MISPER. His wife filed a missing report on him in 2004 when he'd been gone a month.'

Kate approached the screen to look over his shoulder, skimming details. 'Where was he living at the time?'

'Farnham, Surrey, with his wife and two children. He left home telling her he was going on a short business trip. See?' He pointed at a specific line. 'He was taking architectural drawings he'd prepared to a client in London. At least, that's what he told *her*. He'd actually withdrawn eighteen thousand pounds from their bank account without her knowledge. She initially contacted the police when she was unable to make contact with him during the following week. After a further three weeks she made an official missing report. She had one phone call from him after six months to say . . .' Julian tracked a forefinger across the details on the screen, '—he "wanted a different life . . . couldn't stay married". Police already knew about the eighteen grand. His phone call spelt the end of their involvement. As far as they were concerned he disappeared by choice.'

Bernie settled back in his chair, fingers laced together. 'I've got a nose for what that'll be about: "Shershay-la-*fem*."'

Kate returned to her seat. 'That's in addition to your unflagging nose for a coincidence?'

'I'm not seeing no coincidences here. He was at Woolner and he knew Troy but we're talking *years* down the line when Smythe done his disappearing act. There's nothing to suggest a connection between him and what happened to Troy. It's obvious. He cleared off to another woman.'

Amid the silence Joe glanced at Bernie. 'I know a housemate of Troy's we *can* see. Alastair Buchanan. He's available tomorrow morning from eleven.'

'Where?'

'Worcester.'

Bernie shook his head. 'I want to be around here in case that Stuey Butts is located.'

'How're you fixed, Red?' She looked up from her diary with a nod. 'Good. I'll pick you up between nine-thirty and ten.'

CHAPTER FOURTEEN

The Volvo moved smoothly along in the bright Wednesday morning sunshine, a melodic male voice drifting from the CD player. '*Love is the sweetest . . .*' Joe focused on the road ahead, following the route being provided by the silent satnav.

'Who's this?' Kate asked.

'Al Bowlly and the Ray Noble Orchestra. Recorded in 1932.'

'American?'

'Uh-uh. British. Worked in New York way back in the thirties. My grandmother was a fan and the family still played his stuff while I was growing up.' She absorbed the detail. Joe almost never talked of his family. Except once, following the ending of their last case, when he'd told her that he was divorced and had a daughter in her early twenties back in Boston.

'What happened to him?'

'Came back to England as the Second World War started. Killed by a parachute bomb, courtesy of the Luftwaffe.' The car slowed and he looked out of the window. 'We're here.'

Kate turned. They were outside the middle dwelling of a graceful curve of white-painted stone houses, elegant sash windows on the ground floor. A well-dressed man was standing in front of one of them, watching as they got out of the car. '*Very* nice,' said Kate, barely moving her lips.

'Real toney,' responded Joe in similar mode, knowing she was referring to the house. They crunched gravel. 'Mr Buchanan? Alastair Buchanan?'

He nodded. 'Come on in.'

They followed him inside, along a wide passageway running through the middle of the house and on to a massive kitchen. Joe made introductions as Kate covertly absorbed the dark green Aga, glossy cabinets and long, central counter over which were suspended metal light fittings hanging from chains attached to the high ceiling.

Buchanan gave each of them an enquiring glance. 'Since you rang I've been wondering what this is all about. Coffee?'

Kate nodded. 'Please.' Aware of Joe walking casually across the kitchen to look out of one of the windows, she watched Buchanan assemble china cups then eyed the extensive paraphernalia of the earnest cook. No small metal hammer. She gave Buchanan a bright smile, running a light hand over the smooth mahogany of the counter. 'You have a lovely home, Mr Buchanan.'

'The kitchen alone took months to come together.' He tapped the counter. 'This came from an old chemist's shop in western France.'

Kate responded with a quick nod and another pass of her hand over the rich wooden surface. 'It fits in beautifully. It must have been a lot of hard work.' She'd already conducted a physical evaluation of him: early forties; not tall; dark-haired still, possibly a little grey above the ears, receding a little at the temples. He was good-looking, or would have been if he smiled, and evidently a man with a taste for the select, the exclusive, plus the means to afford it. Kate's attention dropped to his mid-section. He wasn't a large man, but he would need to watch his diet as the years rolled by.

'Sugar? Milk or cream?' Kate indicated milk only for herself and Joe who was still at the window, his back to them but doubtless listening. 'This whole terrace was falling apart fifteen or so years ago but the company salvaged it, replaced the period features and now it's "Home Sweet Home".' Carrying a laden tray Buchanan nodded them towards a long beechwood table.

They sat and Joe made a start. 'When I phoned I said that we needed to speak with you about a cold case the Unsolved Crime Unit is investigating.'

Buchanan nodded. 'Mm . . . *Very* intriguing.'

'We're investigating a murder, Mr Buchanan,' said Kate, her eyes on the smooth, fleshy face. She saw no facial response but sensed a sudden tension in his upper body. Had their case made it into newspapers as far afield as Worcester? 'The victim was someone you knew: Nathan Troy.' As he replaced his cup on its saucer he lowered his eyes, but not soon enough. She had seen his pupils dilate. 'We're hoping that you might be able to provide us with information about him. You and Nathan Troy were students together at Woolner College around twenty years ago?'

He nodded. 'Poor Nathan. Unbelievable. And so long ago. Makes you wonder where your life's gone.' He glanced at Kate. 'Actually, what you just said is a little inaccurate. We weren't students *together*. We were on different courses. I was at the School of Architecture, he was doing something else. I can't remember what.' Following the rush of words he lapsed into silence.

She waited. When nothing further came: 'You and Nathan Troy shared a house.'

He gave a brief nod. 'For a few months.'

'An academic year-plus, is our understanding,' said Joe. 'Tell us about him.'

He puffed his cheeks. 'Well . . . as I said, this *is* a shock . . . and unfortunately, knowing the distance you've come, there's not much I *can* tell you. He lived on the first floor of the house a few of us rented back then. I was on the ground floor.'

Kate decided to stick with the patient approach. For now. 'Yes we know. There were four of you: Nathan Troy, Matthew Johnson, Joel Smythe. And you.'

'That's right. Have you spoken to the others?'

She raised her brows. 'Why do you ask?'

He shrugged. 'Because Matthew Johnson was on the same course as Nathan so he'd probably be able to tell you about him. As I said I hardly knew—'

'You're starting to recall information just fine now,' Joe soothed. Buchanan compressed his lips, his eyes shifting to the window.

Deciding that a little encouragement might help Kate sent him a smile. 'Tell us whatever you recall about Nathan Troy, no matter how incidental it might appear. We'd be very grateful for any information you can provide.' She waited, giving him only peripheral glances which were enough to tell her that he was now very busy thinking. *What has he got to think about?* She gave an inward sigh and decided to be fair to him. They *were* asking about events a long time ago.

'The reason I can't tell you anything is that he was hardly ever around.'

She gave him a surprised look. 'Why not?' asked Joe.

'He was out most of the time.'

'Where'd he get to?'

'Haven't a clue.'

Kate experienced the first small ripple of irritation. 'Mr Buchanan, all four of you would have interacted on a daily basis to some degree.' He made no response so she continued, emphasising words with a light finger-tap on the table. 'You were all at the same college. You all shared a house. You ate there. Used the same kitchen, bathroom. Your paths *couldn't* have failed to cross fairly regularly.'

'And as *I* said, Nathan and I were pursuing different courses and I had little contact with him otherwise because he wasn't often around. He'd come back late.'

Kate's patience was starting to wear thin. She fixed him with a look. 'In *my* experience that's typical of the student lifestyle.' He looked away from her.

Joe changed tack. 'How about your impression of him as an individual?'

The seconds slid by and she saw that Buchanan was beginning to look stressed. 'I don't know what you want from me. I *really* don't know what to say. He was young . . . weren't we all? He was rarely around.'

'We've already gathered that,' said Kate. 'Tell us what he was like on those seemingly rare occasions when you and he *were* together.' She stared at him across the table, determined to get an answer to a reasonable question.

Leaning on folded arms, he looked from her to Joe. 'Okay, this is going to sound bad but you're asking, so here it is. Nathan wasn't popular. He wasn't a likeable person.' They waited, Kate's head thrown into confusion. 'Not wanting to speak ill of the dead and all that but Nathan Troy was an *oik*, if you understand what I mean.'

Kate saw Joe frown and she looked at Buchanan. 'No. I want to know *exactly* what you're saying.'

He gave her an appraising glance then grinned, directing his next words to Joe. 'I like a woman who knows what she wants. How about you, Lieutenant?'

Kate's mouth set. 'Tell us about Nathan Troy being an "oik" and everything else you remember about him,' she demanded, not bothering now to conceal her irritation.

He'd regained some equilibrium in the last few seconds. Now he leaned back in his chair. Having found his theme he was warming to it. 'Nate Troy was a comprehensive-educated specimen of the under-class. He didn't fit in at Woolner and he *knew* it.' He paused and Kate saw the superciliousness she'd picked up from the sketch of him which Rachel Troy had shown them. He delivered his next words in a clipped style. 'He took drugs. He partied. He was *a thief*.' Seeing the shock on Kate's face his own took on a look of satisfaction. He lifted his cup and drank.

She gazed at him. 'That's a lot of information about someone you hardly knew.'

He stared at her then replaced the cup. 'Someone I *chose* not to know.'

'What drugs did he take? What did he steal?'

Buchanan looked impatient. '*I* don't know. I had nothing to do with him. I heard he went to raves back then. Took E's.' Kate waited. 'Can't remember what he stole . . . I suspect he took a watch of mine.'

'Did you report the theft?' asked Joe.

He looked surprised. 'What? No. It was only a Rotary: present from the parents when I got my place at Woolner.'

'What makes you think it was Nathan Troy who stole it?' pursued Kate, seeing arrogance in his eyes and on the curve of his mouth, thinking how fortunate he was that it wasn't Bernie who had come here with his Geiger-counter vigilance for snobbery and condescension.

'I've already told you what he was — a working class misfit.'

'We've been told he was an excellent student,' said Kate softly.

'Can't comment, unfortunately. I wasn't on the same—'

'*That* was from his tutor, Dr Wellan.'

'Johnny Wellan?' Buchanan sneered. 'He had a reputation for seeing artistic talent where there was none.'

She regarded him coolly. 'Would you care to speculate as to *why* Nathan Troy was killed?'

Buchanan's dark brows shot upwards. '*Me?* Not really. God only knows. Maybe he went out that night and met up with somebody equally unpleasant.'

Joe gave him a steady look. 'Which night would that have been?'

'*Whichever* night he went out and didn't come back,' Buchanan countered, not missing a beat.

Joe's attention was still on him. 'You're assuming he was killed at the time he disappeared in 1993?'

His eyes flicked from Joe to Kate and back again. 'You said—'

Joe shook his head. 'We didn't specify *when* Troy died. He could have reappeared after 1993 and been murdered at some later date.'

Kate also watched Buchanan. He was looking guarded. 'You *said* you had a *cold* case . . . that a body had been found. Okay, maybe I was assuming he died shortly after he disappeared. That'd be a reasonable assumption, wouldn't it?' Kate counted fifteen seconds of silence before he broke it to ask where Nathan Troy's body had been found.

She told him. 'Do you know Woodgate Country Park?'

'No. I've hardly been back to Birmingham since I left. Not my kind of place.'

She nodded. 'But you know it's in Birmingham?'

'I *lived* there for three years, remember?'

'Tell us what you recall of the original police investigation into Nathan Troy's disappearance,' invited Kate.

Buchanan took a mouthful of cooled coffee then gave a brief account of the police visiting the student house after Troy disappeared. According to him none of the housemates could offer any assistance.

Kate changed tack. 'Tell us about a friend of Troy's back then. A female student. Cassandra.'

She saw dismissiveness on his face as he described Cassandra: a 'Woolner drop-out' who continued to hang around the campus.

'How well did you know her?' asked Joe.

'I didn't. She'd turn up at the house occasionally. We put up with her. She was off the wall. For her, any man . . .' He sat back, face closed.

Kate gave a verbal nudge. 'Any man . . . ?'

'Nobody bothered with her. That's all I can say.'

Kate was now following her own agenda, convinced that Buchanan had been about to impute promiscuity to the girl. 'Did you and the other housemates have steady girlfriends at that time?'

He sent a conspirator's grin to Joe. 'At eighteen, nineteen? Hardly!'

'So how were you meeting your sexual needs?'

He looked shocked but made a quick recovery with another glance at Joe. 'That's conversationally blunt, Dr Hanson.'

'This isn't a conversation, Mr Buchanan.'

He looked at her then away. 'There were one or two . . . casual girls.'

'Names?'

'Don't recall,' he said, matching her abruptness.

She left the topic, eyes drifting over the walls of the kitchen. 'This is a nice family home. Are you married?'

'No.' Aggression now edged his voice. 'Are *you*?'

She gave him a direct look. 'You don't appear to understand the situation here, Mr Buchanan. *You* are a potential witness in the case of unlawful death. Any questions we ask *you* to that end are legitimate whereas my personal status has *no* relevance.' He looked away.

'Earlier, you mentioned the company that renovated these houses,' said Joe. 'Which company would that be?'

Buchanan looked from him to Kate. 'If you must know and I don't see the relevance, it's my property company.'

Joe gave a slow nod. 'That how you make your living? Using your architectural design skills for renovation?'

He shrugged, eyes watchful. 'Partly. The practice I run also works with developers. When they start knocking down old stuff to start a new build and they find medieval walls or a Roman mosaic they come to us. My foundation course was in archaeology, before I switched to architecture. We help clients navigate their way through myriad regulations, negotiate any delays on their behalf.' Kate made quick shorthand strokes with her pen, listening to the steady flow of information. *How easily he talks when he's comfortable with the topic.*

'How about your pal Joel Smythe?' asked Joe. 'He get an archaeology job after he finished college?'

'No idea. I lost contact with him after Woolner.'

He glanced at a nearby clock on the wall as Joe put another question to him. 'Did Nathan Troy show any interest in females at the college?' She watched Buchanan's face, getting nothing from it.

'No idea.'

* * *

They were moving along the motorway back to Birmingham, Kate watching the rural landscape flowing past, listening to Joe's voice. 'In the year-plus that these young guys lived in the same house they must have gone to some of the same social events.'

Kate nodded. She also had issues about Buchanan that she wanted to raise. 'Did you notice how easily he spoke of anything not directly linked to Nathan Troy?' Her brow furrowed. 'And what he said about him as an individual *really* surprised me. I hadn't realised I'd formed such a strong impression of Nathan as a likeable person. My initial response was to disbelieve what Buchanan said but . . . I suppose it's possible that I've lost some objectivity.'

'Maybe you really liked his folks,' Joe suggested, changing lanes to pass a dawdling vehicle.

'What did *you* make of Buchanan?'

'Reluctant informant.'

'Very. To the point of avoidance. Like him?'

'Nope.'

She watched the scene beyond the windows again, thinking about Buchanan's reluctance to talk. And what he'd almost said about a young woman called Cassandra. Or did she get that wrong too?

* * *

Following an afternoon at the university Kate walked inside the house to a barrage of grouses from Maisie. 'Mom, you have to *do* something. The internet connection in this house is *rubbish*. It takes *hours* to get onto Google and me and Chel have got a history test on Monday.' She headed for the hall. 'I'm going to ring her and ask if I can go to hers later to revise.'

Kate shed her coat and went to the fridge, searching drawers for edibles. 'Before you do that, could you get two large potatoes from the laundry, please? And in my experience online access in this house is good.'

Maisie grumped her way into the laundry, returning with the potatoes. 'Mom, *trust* me, at your age you're, like, *grateful* for the net. You don't notice how long it takes.'

Kate examined the day's post stacked on the granite counter where Phyllis had placed it. 'Mm . . . That's because in the olden days we had to wait for our computer gas jets to fire to a critical level.'

'Gas?' She scowled. 'Daddy's *right*. You take refuge in sarcasm.'

'Oh, really.' She left the letters and began chopping fruit, pressing the pieces into the juicer in an overly firm manner. 'Internet access in this house is as speedy as it is at the university.' *More or less.*

She handed fresh juice to Maisie, who stomped out of the kitchen with it, plus some hair-tossing and a parting shot. 'And another thing. When am I allowed Facebook?'

'When you're at *least* thirteen,' responded Kate to an empty kitchen. She dropped her voice, 'But preferably when you're around thirty-five and on *my* terms. *No* profile picture and monitored *every* step of the way.'

'Didn't catch that,' said Phyllis as she came through the door.

'For my ears only.'

Five minutes later Phyllis had departed and Kate was alone in the kitchen reflecting on the meeting she and Joe had had that morning with Alastair Buchanan and his reluctance to engage with them. She gazed out of the darkening windows, acknowledging the possibility that his view of Nathan Troy was more accurate than that provided by Troy's parents. She reprised Buchanan's attitude towards her during the interview. Challenging. Overly assertive at times. She sighed. *Is it because I is a woman?*

As Kate's mind drifted over the entire exchange they'd had with him, a thought slid into her mind to do with an earlier discussion in UCU: about the proximity of the motorway to the Country Park. The M5 ran along one of Woodgate Park's boundaries before it continued south towards Worcester.

Worcester. Buchanan.

CHAPTER FIFTEEN

By Friday morning it was warmer inside Rose Road although three electricians continued to labour on hands and knees in the corridor, rear cleavages well displayed. Kate came into UCU at a quick pace to find her two colleagues already there.

'Bernie?'

'Blimey, here we go.'

'Have you managed to contact Henry Levitte yet?'

'Your underwear on fire or what, and I have, as a matter of fact. It's sorted.'

She dropped her belongings on the table. 'When?'

'This afternoon at two o'clock.'

'Don't forget I'm coming as well.'

'I know. I'm thrilled.'

He grinned as she went to the glass screen to read the details Joe was adding of their visit to Alastair Buchanan.

Joe turned to her. 'Anything you want to add, Red?'

She glanced at the photograph Nathan Troy's parents had provided. 'I've been thinking about the negative view Buchanan gave us of Troy. It was *so* contrary to what his parents and John Wellan said of him I'm inclined to disbelieve it.'

Bernie was also absorbing the notes. 'The parents would paint a good picture though, wouldn't they?'

Kate sat on the table facing the glass screen, eyes skimming words. 'What interested me as much as *what* Buchanan said was his behaviour when he said it.'

Bernie nodded at what Joe had written. 'I'm guessing this Buchanan's a smooth bastard?'

She considered his question. 'On the right lines. He presented as genial at the outset but became increasingly reluctant to give us anything and at one point he became verbally challenging.'

Bernie waited, brows up. 'Who was talking to him then?'

She gave him a sideways look. '*Don't* start.' She waved a hand as Julian appeared through the door. 'Buchanan was determined throughout to give as little as possible.'

'Maybe somebody tipped him off before you arrived?' suggested Bernie. 'Somebody who'd already been spoke to?'

Kate nodded. 'It's possible. It's twenty years since Buchanan was part of Woolner yet he still experienced an anxiety surge when Nathan Troy's name was first said.'

Joe spoke over one shoulder. 'Speaking as devil's advocate here, maybe what we saw was simple shock that somebody he knew when he was young was dead?'

She leaned on one hand, musing. 'Remember that hint that Nathan's friend Cassandra was promiscuous?' Joe nodded as he wrote. 'Yet, if that were true, he wanted us to believe that neither he nor the other housemates took advantage of what might have been on offer. Freely offered sex from a legal-age female to three healthy young males who don't respond?' Kate got down from the table. 'That I do *not* believe.'

Joe nodded. 'I'm with you there, having been a healthy young male in a previous life.'

Bernie pushed forward on his chair, index finger at the ready for Kate. 'Hold on. You're assuming "male" means sex-mad. Perhaps they *did* hold back. On account of this Cassandra being some sort of head case, like Troy's mom told you. Speaking personally—'

She took a seat and began writing. 'Wish you wouldn't, or keep it brief and completely lacking in detail.'

'—I remember years ago when quite a few girls was putting out feelers, making all the signs—'

Kate bowed her head. 'Somebody stop him.' Julian tittered.

'The point I'm making is our mother brought us up proper: respect for the other sex. That was her big thing, our mother. Respect the female.'

'Really?' said Kate, thinking of the politically incorrect nightmare he was at times.

Bernie was running on. 'Mind you, we seen the *other* side as well. With our sisters. Our mother would get the broom and knock 'em off the wall where they was sitting.'

She stared at him. 'Your sisters?'

He glared at her, riled. 'The dodgy blokes that was after 'em! You know, for a brainbox, you're a *real* disappointment sometimes.'

She gave him a discouraging look. 'Personal reminiscences aren't relevant.' Then grinned. 'In the days you're talking about piano legs were covered.'

'Oh, *very* droll. Listen, Clever Clogs, maybe Buchanan's problem is that he's not used to a woman who's pushy and *you've* got a lot of lip.'

Joe glanced from the screen. 'Mmm. Noticed that.'

Kate was up and pacing again. 'Buchanan was defensive *and* stressed. He exhibited fight-flight responses. He was uneasy from when Nathan Troy's name was first mentioned, *plus* he took an age to ask where Troy's body was found.' She frowned. 'I'll contact John Wellan and ask if he knows anything about Troy's alleged drug-use and light fingers. While we're on the subject, how about a search against Buchanan's name?'

'Jump to it, Sherlock,' instructed Bernie.

'I have. Nothing's come up.'

Turning to the glass Kate added a three-letter acronym in large letters and beneath it one name. 'I think Buchanan is a duplicitous type, so . . . what do you think? Alastair Buchanan. POI. Our *first* person of interest?'

'Funny how I've got this idea that it was *you* who said during our last case not to focus on anybody too quick.'

'Who's focusing? Buchanan's a *start*.'

CHAPTER SIXTEEN

Kate listened as Bernie drove them the few miles to Selly Park, the small residential enclave developed in the eighteenth century on the grounds of Selly Manor, bounded by Selly Oak, Moseley and the university campus. 'This visit could provide just what this case needs: *basic* answers to *basic* questions.'

Deciding not to specify her own preference for general questions followed by content analysis of responses, she nodded, giving him a sideways glance. He was wearing the old, multi-pocketed quilted jacket he invariably wore in cold weather, the wide tie flowing over the barrel chest and stomach. He was a long-serving police officer who knew his job well and she liked him a lot, despite his ability to irritate her to distraction. She sighed, thinking of his liking for Connie Chong. Everyone at Rose Road knew it. Bernie wasn't aware they knew and she seriously doubted his awareness that he might have to make some sartorial changes for progress to happen in *that* area.

He was speaking again. 'Troy was a student in this professor's department so *he'll* know about him if anybody does.'

'I'm not so sure about that, you know. John Wellan didn't seem to rate Professor Levitte as the type to take an interest in any of the students.'

He didn't reply, attending to the route displayed on the screen, bearing an address: 4 Hyde Road. 'Levitte told me it gets tricky around here. This house of his is tucked away . . . You said you met him once?'

'Years ago. Kevin and I were still married and he wanted to buy me one of Henry Levitte's paintings so we came here.' She caught the look he gave her. 'What? We were here an hour or so and I don't remember that much of the visit. I had to look up his details on the college website.' She did a quick mental inventory. 'Professor of the School of Fine Arts in the 1990s. Now in his seventies. More or less retired, married twice. One son, two daughters by his first wife. She's deceased. His children are a little older than Troy would be if he'd lived so I think we need to talk to each of them. I've already managed to contact the son. I'm seeing him late tomorrow.'

There was a sudden change in the level of light inside the vehicle as they turned into a curving drive made narrow by arched trees and vigorous bushes. Kate watched as the drive widened into an extensive area of land on which sat a single dwelling. Bernie blew air through his teeth. 'Blimey. Welcome to the House of Levitte. Big place. You'd never know it was here, would you? And where's numbers one to three?' The Georgian-style residence was still a few metres ahead of them, the trees flanking it far taller and denser than Kate recalled. 'Know what I'd do if this was my place?' Bernie pointed through the windscreen. 'I'd chop that lot down for a start. Too dark.'

She looked to where he was indicating. 'They're yews.' She transferred her attention to the house's wide facade, the two brick chimneys running upwards at either end of its frontage and thrusting through the eaves of the shallow roof, her memory stirring. They got out of the Range Rover and started in its direction, past a sporty dark blue Mercedes and a small tree growing in the middle of the open area in front.

'Daft place to stick a tree if you ask me,' muttered Bernie as they passed.

'It's a rowan. Allegedly it's the tree from which the devil hanged his mother.'

'Thanks for that. If you come up with anything else horticultural keep it to yourself.'

Within the open doorway stood a tall, elegant man with a full head of styled silver hair. His mouth widened and he gazed down his long patrician nose, massaging his hands together in the cold air as they approached. 'It is *Kate*, isn't it? Kate Osbourne, my *dear* girl! How perfectly *lovely* to see you again. I hadn't realised it was you whom the detective sergeant mentioned on the phone. Come inside. *Come, come.* It's *so* cold, isn't it?'

She continued up the wide steps and hands clasped her upper arms. Her face was kissed on both sides. Somewhat fazed, she looked up at the thick hair and weather-browned face. 'Thank you for seeing us, Professor Levitte.'

'Stop that right now. *Henry*,' he chided, tone avuncular as he turned to Bernie. 'And this must be Detective Sergeant Watts. Welcome to *you*. You had no trouble finding us?'

He ushered them into the high-ceilinged hall off which stairs curved to the upper floor. Kate's visit a decade or so before had done nothing to prepare her for what she now saw. All available wall space in the vast hall as far as she could see bore a spectacular, hand-painted mural, an Amazonian sweep of sturdy, brown-hued trees bearing leaves of all sizes, all shades of green from almost black to dark olive to palest yellow with small flashes of milky pistachio background and fleshy cream-pink magnolia-like blossoms. The whole verdant mass trailed and thrust towards the upper floor, its lushness and scale seeming to give off heat. She delivered a swift nudge to Bernie's mid-section. 'Close it.' Aware of the professor immediately behind her she continued in the direction he was indicating, Bernie following.

They were now inside a large, square sitting room, logs glowing in the fireplace. Henry Levitte waved them to a sofa against one wall. 'Would you like to meet my wife too?'

They exchanged glances. 'I don't think—' Bernie began.

'I'll tell her you're here, anyway. I'm sure she'd love to meet you, Kate.' He strode from the room, taller, straighter than many men half his age although she now thought he was thinner than she recalled. Frail, even.

Bernie dropped onto the sofa. 'I've never seen *nothing* like it! Talk about being dropped without warning into a bloody jungle! And why's he calling you by your married name?'

Kate walked across the room to what appeared to be an array of family photographs on a nearby wall. One in particular claimed her attention, the clothes dating it at least three decades earlier. A broad-shouldered Henry Levitte, his hair dark, his nose and jaw prominent, was sitting beside a slender, large-eyed woman wearing what looked to be a cheesecloth top. She was following his laughing gaze to three children sitting nearby: a studious-looking boy and two small girls, one holding what appeared to be a plush rabbit. A photograph next to it featured a heavy-faced woman with very black hair. Kate's attention drifted onwards to framed paintings further along the wall which she recognised from their intricate curves and striations as Henry Levitte's own, then downwards to polished metal tubes and fussy china—

'Viewing the Rogues' Gallery, I see.' Henry Levitte had reappeared and was striding to the drinks table. 'Theda will be down in a minute. What's your beverage of choice, Detective Sergeant Watts?'

Theda. Unusual name. German, perhaps?

Bernie eyed the assembled bottles. 'Bit early for me and I'm on duty. Thanks all the same.'

'I can't even interest you in a Hine Antique?'

Kate was now aware of a regular tapping sound coming across the hall towards the sitting room. They each looked towards the slowly opening door and the woman now standing there. The heavy-faced woman in the photograph on the wall.

'Theda, darling, let me introduce you to our visitors. This is Detective Sergeant Bernard Watts and *this* is Kate Osbourne whom I told you about.'

'*Really*, Henry. Our visitors don't want alcohol at this time of day.' She came into the room with a swish of shiny hose, plump feet squeezed inside high-heeled, sharp-toed shoes, the slight northern accent disproving Kate's theory of a German origin. She gave Bernie a closed-mouth smile. 'Detective Sergeant.' She nodded, the gold charms on her bracelet jangling as they shook hands. She moved towards Kate. 'And *Mrs* Osbourne, I can't tell you how pleased I am to meet you.' Kate felt the need to step back as she closed in. 'I do admire you young women these days, you know. Working, bringing up a family, often *single*-handed. Have a seat.' She held out a wide, capable hand to the sofa and Kate went to it and sat next to Bernie. '*There.* That's right.'

'As you say, dear, no alcohol. What do you suggest?'

'I'll go and tell Mrs Danes to make coffee.' She moved towards the door, glancing at Kate as she went. 'Do you have domestic help, Mrs Osbourne? Do I call you Kate?'

'Kate is fine and coffee would be nice but please don't go to any trouble. This is an official visit.'

'*Nonsense.*' She turned and walked from the room, heels clicking across the hall.

Professor Levitte's eyes were fixed on Kate. 'I remember when you came here with your husband to buy *Sun on Land*. How many years ago was that?' Surprised at his recalling the specific painting she said nothing, listening as his melodious voice rolled on. 'You brought a delightful child with you. Her hair had the same Titian tones as yours.' He raised an admonishing forefinger. 'You were *very* naughty when you refused to sit for me back then. You could have been my Lizzie Siddal, you know. How old is your daughter now? No, let me guess . . .'

Theda Levitte had returned with a laden tray and her husband rose and went to assist. Bernie filled the small silence. 'I was saying to the Doc, that hallway you've got—'

'Move those magazines off the table please, Henry,' directed Theda. He did as directed then sat with her on the sofa opposite them, their backs to a window overlooking the garden. A woman entered carrying a heavily gilded china teapot and plates which she placed on the table in front of the Levittes. Theda Levitte gave a brief nod as the woman left the room then turned to them with the closed-mouth smile. 'Ah yes, the hall! Henry's handiwork, isn't it, dear? His opus.' She busied herself with what was on the table before her. 'Isn't this pleasant? I decided on tea, which I hope suits you both. It's Harrods' Breakfast Blend. We don't have exotic tastes, do we, Henry?' As she laughed Kate noticed the overbite for the first time. 'Now, Detective Sergeant Watts, do you take sugar and milk? Would you like a slice of cake? How about you, Kate?'

Kate was feeling uncomfortable on several levels as Bernie began to make his presence felt. 'Like I said on the phone this is an official visit. We've got some questions about a case we're investigating.'

The professor nodded his elegant head. 'Of course, of course. Kate, you didn't meet Theda when you came here last?'

We've come here hoping to take the investigation further and now we're mired in a tea party. 'No,' she responded briefly.

Theda Levitte sent her a glance and a brief nod as she cut cake. 'I was probably shopping in London whenever it was you came. Do you live locally?'

Her husband gave Kate an indulgent smile. 'If my recall is correct you live in Harborne, don't you? My family lived there for many years, you know. They were lifelong members of St Peter's church congregation—'

Theda Levitte sent him a frown. 'I don't think Detective Sergeant Watts is here to listen to family history.'

'Of course not, dear.' He beamed at them. 'So! How might we assist the Force?'

Kate was relieved that they'd finally reached the purpose of their visit. 'We're hoping you can give us some information about one of your students in the early nineties. Nathan Troy.'

Henry Levitte sipped tea, considering what she'd said, his brows drawn together, head on one side. 'Troy . . . Troy

. . . Was that . . . no, I'm not sure I recall anyone of that name. Theda?'

The plump shoulders rose and fell. 'Woolner was *your* life, Henry, not mine.'

Bernie intervened. 'It might help if I tell you a bit about him. A local lad from Castle Vale. Tall. Dark hair. Dr Wellan was his tutor. This was back in—'

'Ah! There you are, you see,' said the professor, his face brightening. 'I possibly have a vague recollection of the boy but that is all, I'm afraid. If he was one of Wellan's students, you'd need to ask him. Any contact I might have had would have been minimal.'

Kate gave the long-case clock against the nearby wall a subtle glance. Wellan had been right. Professor Levitte wasn't about to provide anything helpful and now she wanted to be away as soon as possible. She heard Mrs Levitte speaking. 'Castle Vale, you said? Woolner doesn't attract many students from that side of the city, does it, Henry?' She lifted cake to her mouth again. 'So many young louts around wearing hoods these days, aren't there?'

Her husband delivered a gentle rebuking pat to the plump thigh. 'Now, Theda. We all need to keep a non-judgemental attitude.'

'Don't make me *laff*! They'd have your handbag as quick as look at you.'

Kate was impatient to move the process on. 'This is the second time that the police have taken an interest in Nathan Troy. The first time was when he disappeared in 1993 and now—'

Henry Levitte raised his elegant, long-fingered hand. '*Now* I recall him — well not *him*, exactly, but the event of his leaving.' He turned to his wife. 'Do you remember it, my dear? He left and then the police came—'

She broke in, voice sharp. 'It sounds very likely he left because he didn't fit in at Woolner.' More cake went inside the mouth.

Kate's thoughts flew to the Troy family. 'Nathan Troy *didn't* leave. As I said, he disappeared. Now we know why. He was murdered.'

The clock ticked on into silence. Theda Levitte stopped chewing and swallowed. 'How dreadful. Are you sure?' She turned. 'Henry! *Say* something.'

'We're sure,' said Bernie. 'His body was found a few days ago and it's been identified.'

'You do need to speak to John Wellan,' repeated Henry Levitte. 'He's the most likely person to remember details of the young man.'

Mrs Levitte made a dismissive sound and leaned towards Kate and Bernie. 'I'm not convinced *he'll* be much help. Do you know, the students call him "Johnny"? And he *lets* them!'

Kate felt Bernie's disapproving eyes on her. She switched her attention to the window and the misted garden beyond and froze. Pressed to the glass was a gaunt figure, hollow-eyed, the skin of the long face almost translucent. Kate stared at it, mind a wasteland, recognising it without knowing why, dimly aware of Bernie half rising, juggling hot tea and china. She watched as the figure raised thin white hands and began to beat the glass, shredding the quiet inside the room.

The Levittes struggled to their feet and turned to the window, all four transfixed as the beating hands slowed, slid down the glass and the apparition backed away to be absorbed by mist.

Henry Levitte ran an absent hand over his hair then looked across the room to them. 'I *do* apologise for this. That was—'

His wife took charge. 'Pour more tea, Henry.' She bustled past them to the door, frowning at Bernie as she went. 'That's a *Hereke* silk rug you're staining.' She disappeared and they heard her fractious voice: 'Mrs Danes? *Mrs Danes!*'

* * *

Following Mrs Danes's ministrations to the Hereke, Henry Levitte was the first to speak. 'I apologise for that little . . . display earlier.' He turned to his wife, voice low. 'Shall I . . . ?'

'I've already taken care of it,' she snapped.

Bernie shot a glance at Kate who was waiting for one or other Levitte to explain the scene beyond the window. Henry Levitte was looking across at them, smiling. 'More tea, Kate? Sergeant Watts? Some cake?'

Realising that no explanation was about to be volunteered, Kate knew she had to ask. 'Who was that at the window just now?'

'Well, *really*,' fumed Theda Levitte. 'It has absolutely *nothing* to do with the reason you've come here. In fact, Henry can't help you with that either so—'

Henry Levitte's hand patted the plump thigh again as he directed his words to Kate. 'That was my daughter,' he said and Kate caught a look of deep sadness cross his face. 'She's . . . fragile, like her mother, my first wife, was, but everything's under control. Theda has alerted her professional carers and asked that they send somebody to collect her.' He glanced at the clock. 'They'll be here shortly.'

Kate pushed to the edge of the sofa. 'In that case I think we should leave. There's nothing else you can tell us about Nathan Troy? As a person? His friends?'

Theda Levitte turned her heavy face towards Kate. 'Now I think of it, there were rumours about drug-taking among the students in the early nineties.' She prodded her husband. 'Tell them, Henry. He was probably involved in that.'

They looked at him and waited. He was silent for some seconds then, 'Theda's right. Woolner *did* have a problem around that time. It was a concern for some months.'

'What drugs are we talking about here, Professor?' asked Bernie.

He shrugged. 'Oh, you know — cocaine was popular in the city back then, and crack.'

Kate brows rose. 'Are you saying that you believe Nathan Troy may have been involved in *serious* drug use?'

Henry Levitte raised his hands. 'I'm merely advancing it as a possibility, given his sudden departure.'

Kate was trying to find the sense in what they were being told. 'I'm sorry but can I clarify that? Did you have any specific knowledge at that time about Nathan Troy using such substances?' The Levittes remained silent. 'Did you do anything about it if you did?'

He looked blank and his wife sent her a sharp look: 'What do you mean? How could Henry have known about it? Nathan wasn't his student. And what could Henry have done, anyway?' Kate frowned at her words, her head filled with the agreed actions by faculty members at her university for such situations. Theda Levitte laid her hand on her husband's sleeve, diamonds sparkling. 'This is dreadful news you've brought us about this student.' Kate looked at her, realising that she disliked the woman, not least because it was clear she couldn't be bothered to use Nathan Troy's name. 'We've told you all we know and you're aware that Henry is upset about . . . family matters. In fact, we're both too shocked and distressed to continue now.'

Bernie leaned forward. 'We might want to talk to you again, Professor.'

Theda Levitte sent Kate a fleeting glance, followed by a conspiratorial look for Bernie. 'I'm sure you'll understand when I say that I think it best that any future discussion happens elsewhere. You may have heard that Henry is anticipating a significant honour for his services to art and his charitable work. We don't want that compromised by even a peripheral involvement in something so . . . distressing as a *murder* investigation.' She turned. 'Do we, Henry?'

Henry Levitte covered his wife's hand with his. 'These two fine people have a job to do, my dear.'

Her mouth set. 'And I'm sure they understand what I'm saying.' She lapsed into silence, then: 'Have you seen this boy's parents?'

'Yes,' replied Kate.

'Well, if you see them again do pass on to them our condolences.'

She watched her husband stand, shoulders bowed as he moved across the room to a small writing desk. Taking an item from one of the drawers, he walked directly to Kate. 'Have these, my dear. Your family, your friends might like to use them. If you and the detective sergeant need to talk to me further about Troy I'm at the White Box Gallery every day from next Monday for the setting up of my Retrospective. Now, if you'll excuse us. We are both somewhat shocked by this news of one of Woolner's students, despite not knowing him well.'

Kate took the thick envelope from him and watched as he crossed the room to sit beside his wife. She and Bernie stood. 'I hope your daughter feels better soon, Professor,' said Bernie as they turned to leave.

Theda answered for him. 'I'm sure she will. This isn't such an unusual event. Despite what you've seen, Cassandra is resilient.'

Faces expressionless, they nodded their thanks and made their way from the sitting room, across the lush hall and out of the house.

Once inside the Range Rover they eyed each other. '*Cassandra*,' whispered Kate.

Bernie eased the vehicle down the narrow drive, both of them searching the heavy tree cover for any sign of the distressed young woman they now knew to be Cassandra Levitte.

* * *

The sitting room was silent except for the subtle swish of legs moving across the room towards the window overlooking the drive.

'Gone?' he asked.

'All gone.' She turned. 'You look as though you need a drink.' She left the window for the drinks table. Then, a glass of scotch in each hand, she came towards him. 'Stop looking so worried. What they've told us has nothing at all to do with you. How can it?' Her eyes glittered. 'And now, there are . . . *other* things to think about aren't there?' He watched her, his gaze moving upwards as she drew nearer, his eyes anticipatory as he took the drink she was offering. He poured it into his wide mouth and set down the glass. She did the same then grasped the hem of the tight wool dress, pulled it to her waist and straddled him. His hands went to the lacy borders of the stockings where they bit the heavy, dimpled thighs. Leaning into him she pushed her tongue between his open lips as they looked into each other's eyes, low laughter bubbling and drifting across the warm room.

CHAPTER SEVENTEEN

'I've seen her before. Cassandra,' said Kate turning from the glass screen.

Bernie stared up at her. 'How come? Don't tell me she's one of them types you sometimes interview in prison.'

She shook her head. 'Not actually her. There was a sketch of her in the box that Troy's parents gave Joe and me — although she's changed a lot over the years. We'll have to see Henry Levitte again and ask him about her. I doubt we'll be able to talk to Cassandra directly for some time, judging by what we saw earlier.' She came and sat facing him at the table. 'You do realise we have yet another view of Nathan Troy totally at odds with what we've got from his parents and John Wellan? The more I hear the less I think I know him.' She looked at what she'd written, then back to Bernie. What do *you* think about what they said? About Troy and drug taking?'

He shrugged. 'Hard to say. They weren't that clear and from what *she* said, she never had much to do with Woolner, so what does she know? Sounds like it was all rumour to me.'

'Mm, and they suggested they barely knew Troy anyway. If they weren't sure of the drug issue it wasn't a good thing to say about him, given what we know has happened to him.' She watched him examining a reddened area on his hand. 'I've got something in my bag to put on that.'

'No, you're all right,' he murmured, reaching for a printout lying on the table.

'What did you make of him? Henry Levitte?' she prompted.

'Seemed alright. Not stuck up. He was pleased to see *you*.'

Kate stood and returned to the glass screen, her eyes sliding over the detail there. 'What about *her*?'

He looked up. 'As you're up there add that *she's* the driving force in the relationship. She's a lot younger than him, isn't she? What would you say? In her fifties?'

Kate added the few words to the glass then came to sit on the table edge, reflecting on Theda Levitte. 'Probably. Do you know, if I'd tried to imagine his wife I would *never* have come up with anybody remotely like her. As you say, she's younger, more energetic. She probably runs his life for him and he's glad. But beyond that, what's the attraction? I can't see them discussing art together.'

'She's all front, that one. Literally. Our mother had a saying for it: "Net curtains and no knickers." Anyway, who knows what attracts anybody to anybody else?' He sounded morose.

Kate reached inside her bag for the white envelope Henry Levitte had given her, opened it and took out the stiff white cards. 'We'll have another talk with Levitte on his own.' She waved the cards at him. 'And to please Madame Levitte it will be at this gallery where his Retrospective is being held.'

'I think we might get more out of him without her hanging about.' He looked at Kate. 'Remember my theory about the case, what I think it's about?' He held up the printout. Kate took it, recalling talk of Woodgate Park's unsavoury clientele and the possibility of a motorway-bound Repeater. 'My money's still on a Repeator but how about a local sex type? I asked Julian to search arrests down at the park between 1990 and 1994. Have a look. Nothing for ninety-three, by the way, the year Troy died, and just the one in ninety-four. He searched *last* year as well, got three names and guess what: one of them's the same name as the one back in ninety-four. Read the arrest details then tell me what *you* think this case is about.'

She scanned the information which listed many fewer arrests than she would have anticipated. All three identified for the previous year were for sexual offences, probably the tip of a deviant iceberg, the low number in all likelihood reflecting the difficulty anticipated by officers in gaining a conviction.

'Come on, Doc. Let's hear it. What's the case about?'

She raised her eyes from the printout as Joe walked through the door. '*Sex?*'

He grinned as he walked past her and sat down. 'Glad I decided to drop by.'

'Sex and *time*, Doc. You seen this, Corrigan?'

Joe looked across at the printout and nodded. 'Puts a possible local focus on our case.'

She looked at them. 'And maybe lessens the possibility of an M5-cruising Repeater.'

Bernie shook his head. 'Not so fast, Doc. A Repeater stops in the frame.' He nodded at the printout in her hand. 'That got your interest?'

She nodded, eyeing the details of the three males arrested at the park the previous year for sexual offences: Ernest Phillips, Ronald Dixon and Edward Morrell. Morrell was the one also arrested in 1994.

'Anything else in that info that might float your boat?'

Kate did some swift computations around birth dates. 'Each of them is around forty-five, fifty years old now.' She looked up at her colleagues. 'Morrell has probably been a sexual risk at the park for years. That could also apply to Phillips and Dixon.'

Bernie looked gratified. 'Up to no good in the nineties and *still* up to no good last year. You know my theory: they *don't* change. Morrell proves my point.'

She sighed. 'And *you* know I don't agree with your view. There's a certain proportion of sexual offenders who *do* manage to acquire control if they get help—'

'Yeah, yeah, if you say so. Right now I'm thinking these three might have information for us in exchange for a quiet life.'

She scanned the page again, seeing Birmingham addresses. 'Do you know any of them?'

'Not yet but I will do. I'm paying each of 'em a visit, and soon.'

'You're thinking it's possible that one of these men may have had some involvement in the death of Nathan Troy?'

He gave her a meaningful glance. 'I'm keeping one of them "open minds" you're always on about. Which is why I'm still going with the M5-Repeater theory. I've got Jules onto that.'

'What're you hoping to find?'

'Similar cases to ours in the last two decades. The specifics being . . .' He itemised them on thick fingers. 'Young. Male. Suspicion of abduction by stranger. Close proximity to the M5. We need to twin-track this investigation: local-sex-offender *and* unknown-motorway-Repeater.'

Joe looked up. 'Don't forget Red's third option: we talk to everyone who knew Troy as an individual which could lead us to *why* he was killed.'

Bernie grimaced. 'Which is what we've been doing so far and all we've got is a load of contradiction about Troy from people who reckon they know nothing. We need to move this investigation on or Furman will be looking for excuses to shut it down to save some money.'

* * *

Fifteen minutes later Bernie was alone in UCU, phone to his ear, fingers drumming the table, waiting to speak to a man who was once a familiar figure for many police officers working the city centre. He gazed down at the press cuttings on the table in front of him, a number featuring the same by-line. He'd obtained the current phone number from one of those officers still working at Bradford Street, the old headquarters prior to the creation of Rose Road. He knew that what he had in mind was no longer an approved action.

Since December Rose Road had had its own Press and Public Relations Department with rules and edicts as to what could and could not be divulged or discussed and with whom. Roger the Arse Furman was its prime instigator.

'Afternoon, love. Can I speak to Paul Billington please?'

The female queried his status and how he'd acquired the number. 'Detective Sergeant Watts, Rose Road. I got—' Eyes pressed shut he moved the receiver away from his ear as the handset at the other end slammed against a hard surface. Replacing it he heard the same female voice calling loudly. Seconds later a male voice drifted into his ear. 'That you, Wattsie? How you doing, mate?'

'Fine. You all right?' He got straight to it. 'Paul, I need information. We've got a case from 1993 — student missing from Woolner College, Bournville. Name of Nathan Troy. His remains have been found.'

'I envy you, mate. *The Body In The Library* is about all the crime I get these days. Is this the cold case squad you're now a part of?'

'Yeah, Unsolved Crime Unit.'

Billington's voice grew loud. 'Yes, of course I'll come to Rose Road.' Followed by a quiet, 'The Bell. Fifteen minutes.'

* * *

Bernie was savouring the solitude of the small pub as he sipped amid tapestry-upholstered chairs and pictures of hunting scenes. His kind of place. Traditional. No sports-bar paraphernalia. No winking, jangling fruit machine. As he relished his beer and the tranquillity the bells of the nearby church began an enthusiastic tolling as the door of the small lounge swung open.

Billington came directly to the table and took a seat, eyes lively with curiosity. Bernie shook the extended hand. 'Thanks for coming.'

'I *need* this. Paula thinks retirement means gardening, Waitrose and *Midsomer Murders*. She's gone to her Pilates class so I'm on the loose.'

Bernie nodded. Paul and Paula Billington. Source of many a Force joke down the years, mainly involving variations on the topic of trousers and who wore them in the relationship. He gestured to the other pint on the table. 'Got it in but left you to pay. There's too much in the papers about the Force being open-handed with journos. The Arse would love it if he knew I was seeing you *and* paying for your ale.'

Billington returned from the bar and sat savouring the beer as Bernie cast an eye over him, taking in the sloping shoulders and soft middle, tensing the muscles idling at his own mid-section. 'Looking well, Paul,' he said, and got down to business. 'You covered the Troy disappearance. Remember it?'

He nodded, taking another pull of beer. 'We were all over the area around his college until the investigation started to scale down. What are you after?'

Bernie leaned forward, voice low, big hands emphasising the points he was making. 'This is off the record.' Billington opened his mouth to protest. 'Yeah, yeah, I know you're retired but you're not living on no desert island. Right now we're busy following up two or three different avenues with the case.'

'Meaning you've got no solid leads yet?'

Bernie's face set and he gave him a hard look, prodding the table between them, voice low. 'What I want from *you* is any details you've got of *witness* sightings: people who seen this student, Nathan Troy, coming and going around the time he disappeared. We need dates, we need timings, locations. Our case records are,' he waved a hand, 'a bit limited on detail.'

Billington swallowed beer again. 'I had a quick look through what I've got before I left the house.' He also kept his voice low despite the barmaid being the only other person present. 'Back then the Job was working to the theory that his disappearance was voluntary, on or around the twelfth or thirteenth of November. I'll go through my notes properly later on and let you know what I come up with.'

Bernie nodded. 'There's something else. There was another student at Woolner College in the nineties, name of Joel Smythe. After *he* finished his course he went home to Surrey, got married, had a couple of kids. We'd like to talk to him but we can't because he took a business trip to London a few years back and didn't bother coming home. Apart from a phone call months later none of his family has heard from him since. I want you check out anything you might have for him as well.'

Billington's brows rose along with his hands. 'Come *on*. He was playing away and he decided to go for—'

Bernie gave him another look. '*I* think we know that, *you* think you know it but we don't. The Job has changed since you was about. We don't make assumptions. These days it's about open minds, establishing facts, knittin' up theories.'

Billington grinned. 'I heard you're working with a little redhead, a psychiatrist. Sounds as though she's making her presence felt.'

Not bothering to correct him Bernie rolled on. 'We've been through our records. Now it's your turn to see what you can find from press reports back then.'

Billington rubbed his hands together. 'No problem. Whatever you're after, it's going to save me from Suffocation-By-Afternoon-Telly.'

CHAPTER EIGHTEEN

Kate left her car on an upper level of the old multi-storey car park, eschewed the lifts in favour of the ramps, passing *Pedestrians Forbidden* signs, senses on alert. Walking the short distance to Margaret Street in skin-flaying cold she watched the nineteenth-century red-brick building coming into view, its Venetian Gothic mass looming over the Edmund Street pavement.

Reaching it, she ran up the steps and into the main entrance to introduce herself to the young woman at reception whose black bobbed hair appeared to have been cut with the aid of a spirit level. Having made a phone call announcing Kate's arrival the woman asked her to wait. After fifteen minutes of increasing restlessness, during which Kate thought of several things she might be doing with the time, she saw a man appear at a half-glazed door to one side of the hallway.

'Dr Hanson? Roderick Levitte. Follow me, please.' He disappeared from sight, leaving Kate to cover the expanse of hall at a quick pace then hurry down a narrow obstacle course of low-lit corridor, its walls a resting place for leaning canvases of varying dimensions, through a second door opening onto a wide, empty expanse and on to a cluttered office. Inside it she watched as he went through assorted papers on the desk. He looked up, distracted. 'Art attracts a lot of paperwork, most of which I can't find. Do have a seat. I'm not too clear what you want with me but I'm happy to help if I can, although right now . . .' He sighed. 'You can probably see this is a bad time.'

'I'm aware that you're busy with preparations for your father's Retrospective so I appreciate your willingness to talk to me.' She reached for her bag. 'While we do that I'd like to make some notes.' Her attention was still on the chaos on the desk. Kate looked at it, at the used coffee cups, the small glass tumbler, a couple of green and white slips bearing a single name, and several copies of a catalogue. She tilted her head: *The Henry Levitte Retrospective*. She looked up to see his eyes on her. 'I said on the phone that I work at Police Headquarters, in its Unsolved Crime Unit. We're investigating a local cold murder case and we've already spoken about it to several people, including members of your family.'

'I'm sure they've been much more help than I can be.' She waited, anticipating he would ask her who had been murdered. He didn't. Perhaps his father or stepmother had already told him. She caught more distraction as his gaze drifted around the small office. 'Right now, life as I generally live it is on hold. I'm working eighteen-hour days here although I must say the staff are making absolutely *sterling* efforts to assist me.' He ran a hand through his dark hair. 'As you're probably aware, my father is getting on in years so I'm doing all I can for him. We're a close family and we've all come together to ensure he's not worn down with preparations for this celebration of his work. He's given a lot to art and he deserves all the accolades the Retrospective will bring.' She merely nodded. 'So, Dr Hanson. Who's your murder victim?' He gave her a tired but affable smile.

'Nathan Troy.'

The light in his face went out. 'I've got nothing to say about him.'

Surprised at the sudden change of stance she waited, noting the day-old stubble and the redness in both eyes. *He's just told you he's working long hours*. He stopped the restless activity at the desk and his hands became still. Except for the tremor Kate could still see. 'It sounds to me as though you might have a lot to say about Nathan Troy, Mr Levitte.'

He dropped onto the chair behind the desk, eyes restless. 'I told Henry years ago what I thought of Troy. Did he take any notice? No!' Anger rushed his face as he began a low litany of grievances. 'It's always the same! My stepmother, my sisters tell him something, he listens. But if *I* tell him? Oh, no. He ignores it. Why the bloody hell should *I* care!'

When nothing else came: 'What did you tell him about Troy?'

She watched him struggle for a semblance of calm. 'I'm not raking all *that* up. We're talking nearly two decades ago. That's all finished. I'm . . . everyone's in a different place now.'

Kate gave him a direct look. 'Mr Levitte, if you have information about Nathan Troy, the police need to hear it. It might be relevant to why he died. It could help our investigation.'

'I've got nothing to say except that he wasn't a fit person to be at Woolner. There's nothing else I want to add.'

She frowned, attention snagging on the word 'fit'. 'What do you mean?' He turned away from her without a response. 'I understood he was a very talented student. Dr Wellan his tutor has spoken highly of—'

The anger was back. 'Wellan *would*. He's another *pathetic* — Always making a big deal of how important it is to get on with the students. "Hanging out with the *yoof*",' he sneered, hooking raised fingers in the air. She watched him stand then walk to several rolls of brown paper and bubble wrap in the corner by the door. Gathering several up he spoke over one shoulder. 'Wellan's *always* done as he likes and he still does. My father's "old school". He disapproves of computers for art purposes. It's irrelevant that he's semi-retired. Wellan should still take note of what he has to say. But *no*. He ignores him. Wellan puts himself forward as an innovator. Hah! All that means is that he's first in the queue for *grant* money then wastes it on all manner of flavour-of-the-month technologies and software rubbish! Where's the creativity in *that*?' He gave the door handle an abrupt tug. 'I can't waste any more time on this.'

Kate watched as he left the room, taken aback by his vehemence. Rallying she got up and walked to the open area where he was now standing beside a long trestle table. She watched his efforts to cover a small framed painting with the bubble wrap and paper, the restless hands making a chaotic job of it. 'The impression I have is that Dr Wellan is very committed to his students, is popular and—'

Roderick Levitte's face darkened. 'Oh yes, he's *popular*.' Kate watched saliva fly. He pressed the back of his hand to his mouth. 'He's a phoney, cheap opportunist who dares to sneer at and make fun of a venerable man who's a *million* times the artist he'll ever be.' Red-faced, he stopped, placed his hands flat on the table and let his head drop forward amid silence.

Having evaluated Roderick Levitte's behaviour and his overblown verbalisations to her, a complete stranger, Kate doubted that she would gain balanced information from him in his current upset state. 'Would you prefer to rearrange our talk?'

'What else is there you want to know?' he muttered, head still down.

She pressed on. 'I need to ask you about the kinds of contact you had with Nathan Troy in the week or so prior to his disappearance. We also need to get in touch with your sisters.'

He pulled himself upright. 'I don't recall having any "contact" with him and you won't be able to talk to my sister Cassandra. She's not well.'

Kate nodded, deciding against mentioning the scene she and Bernie had witnessed at the Levitte house, about which he appeared to be unaware. 'When she improves where can we find her?'

He gave her an agitated look. '*Improves*?' His head and shoulders dropped forward again and she strained to hear what he was saying. 'She's at a clinic in Edgbaston: the

Hawthornes.' His head shot up. 'Don't go anywhere near it unless you've cleared it with my father.' He raised a hand, pointing at Kate's face. 'In fact, forget I mentioned it. What else do you want?' he demanded.

She gave him a direct look. 'We'll need to contact your other sister. We can easily phone your father for the information if—'

'Miranda has an art shop. Vine Terrace in Harborne.' He briefly held her gaze for the first time. 'I . . . I'm under considerable pressure here. You're right, you'll have to come back.' He glanced down at the painting. Face contorting he tore the wrapping from it, squeezing it into a ball with both hands, so hard they shook. 'It's been a bad day.'

Surmising that it was probably one of many he'd had for quite a while Kate nodded and prepared to leave. 'When we do meet again, Mr Levitte, I shall ask you to tell me why you think Nathan Troy was "unfit" to attend Woolner College.' She watched his face colour. 'By the way, I haven't told you anything about Nathan Troy's death.' *And you haven't asked.* 'His body was found at Woodgate Country Park.'

The impact of the three words was immediate. His face paled. The bloodshot eyes glared at her as he raised an arm, pointing a quivering finger at her. 'I'll tell you right now about Troy! He was a vile, disgusting, *despicable* —. He revolted and repulsed me. Somebody like that shouldn't be allowed to—' He stopped, gasping for breath. She took a step nearer to him but the glare she received decided her that her best course of action was to leave then phone later to arrange another meeting, when he might be more balanced and receptive.

She lifted her bag onto her shoulder and walked across the wide expanse of emptiness. 'I'll call you Mr—'

'*Wait.*' She stopped and turned to see him drag a hand across his damp forehead. 'As I said — pressure. I'm not usually like this. *Really.* Things are . . . difficult.'

She heard feet approaching along the corridor she'd navigated earlier. Turning, she saw two tan-coated men, each carrying large framed canvases. Roderick Levitte was also watching them. He glowered at both of them. 'No, no, *no*! What did I say not half an hour ago? Carry them *singly*.' As they reached the table he seized the paintings, examining each one. 'And *these* aren't even listed. Take them back!' he stormed. They exchanged glances, hefted their loads and went away.

He looked exhausted. '*That's* the quality of help I'm getting. *Hopeless*. I'm doing all of this alone.'

'I'll see myself out, Mr Levitte, and I'll phone you to reschedule.' Kate walked away from him to follow the crammed, dim corridor back to the entrance hall. Through another half-glazed door on the opposite side of the wide expanse she caught sight of the men who'd brought in the paintings. Ms Spirit-Level was nowhere in evidence as Kate crossed the hall and tapped on the door. One of the men peered through glass then opened it.

She gave him a bright smile. 'I was talking to Mr Roderick Levitte just now when you came in.' His colleague inside glanced at Kate as he placed a canvas in a vertical rack. 'I'm interested in seeing what isn't making the show.' He looked uncertain. 'I'm here on police business,' she added economically.

The man nodded and gestured for her to enter. 'Stan? Get them canvases out again for a sec. Lady here wants to have a look at what His Lordship's turned down.'

Stan brought the pictures over to her, laying them on the wide table in the middle of the room. They were clearly Levittes. But more so, thought Kate. Much larger than *Sun on Land*, currently hanging on her study wall. The undulations she found so attractive in that painting were exaggerated here into a hectic parody. Maybe that's why they'd been rejected?

As she straightened her attention was diverted by two massive canvases in ornate gilt frames leaning against a nearby wall. Both portrait studies, they matched Kate for height. Stan caught her glance. 'That's the Old Man, that is. Henry Levitte. *His* dad. A great bloke. Not like *him*. I bet he told you how hard he's working? Don't you believe any of it. He's a waste of breath. Never been any different. How he come to have a father like that . . .'

Kate's eyes were on the seated figure in one of the portraits, the hair darker, the jawline firm, immaculate white cuff drawn back from the elegant hand resting on the arm of the chair showing none of the pigmentation marks and veins Kate had recently observed. *Must be, what, at least twenty years ago?* She thanked Stan and his colleague, walked to the door and out.

* * *

Regaining her car Kate engaged central locking then leaned against the headrest. If what she'd seen just now of Roderick Levitte was in any way typical of him it was evident that Cassandra wasn't the only member of her family with difficulties. She started the car and directed it to the exit, Roderick Levitte's words inside her head: *Somebody like that shouldn't be allowed to* — What had he been about to say? Shouldn't be allowed to *live*?

As she drove she wondered what it was about Nathan Troy, beloved son, valued student, that had provoked such animosity that he had to die. The animosity Roderick Levitte had for him continued to be felt two decades later. As she negotiated her way through rush-hour traffic she sifted personality types, aware of the implications of what she'd seen and heard at Margaret Street.

She joined traffic streaming out of the city along the Hagley Road with a slight lifting of the spirits. Something else was equally obvious. They now knew the identity of the student whom Nathan Troy had disliked. She'd found 'Rod'.

CHAPTER NINETEEN

Leaving the School of Psychology, Kate was approaching her car as her phone rang. She picked up the call.

'Doc? What you up to?'

'I went to see Roderick Levitte earlier and now I'm leaving work to go home.'

'Think again. Guess who's keeping us company here? I'll give you a couple of clues. His DNA's on the torch that was under the floor with Troy, he's sixteen—'

'I'm on my way.'

* * *

Through the one-way glass, Kate saw the door of the room swing open, Bernie leading the way inside followed by a male teen and a little woman who looked to be in her fifties, possibly younger. Joe entered last, closing the door. Bernie took a seat on one side of the table and motioned for Stuart Butts and his mother to sit opposite. Joe took up position against the nearby wall.

She listened to Bernie introduce himself and Joe to the seated youth then watched as he turned his pen end over end, eyes fixed on the young face across the table. Kate also gazed at

Stuart Butts, in profile. She'd anticipated an antisocial attitude expressed in anarchic hair and clothing. Not this boy. He'd entered carrying an expensive-looking grey ski jacket which was now on the back of his chair and he appeared to be wearing a full school uniform plus trainers. The trainers also looked expensive. They weren't Adidas. She studied the neat, side-parted hair brushed back from the smooth, guileless face then transferred her attention to the whippet-thin woman perched on the chair next to him, clutching a shopping bag on her lap.

Bernie's voice drifted into the room where Kate was sitting. 'Make yourself comfortable, Mrs B. You might be here a while.' The woman eyed Bernie, lips compressed. Clearly reluctant, she lifted the shopping bag from her lap and put it to the floor. 'Good . . . good,' Bernie soothed with a brief nod of his large head. Her son looked relaxed, legs stretched to one side of the table and crossed at the ankles.

In front of Bernie were the details Julian had obtained from the Police National Computer which Kate had read when she arrived. She watched as he looked over them, taking his time as the teenager's feet began to twitch. The Butts family was well known to the police. The father had convictions for violence which included domestic. Stuart Butts was also known: in addition to theft from a local newsagents', he'd attacked a same-age boy when he was thirteen, breaking his nose and damaging an eye-socket. His victim had refused to make a statement about what had led to the violence, then denied Butts was his attacker and the matter was dropped. There had also been a number of call-outs relating to harassment by Stuart Butts of elderly residents in his neighbourhood, involving offers of 'help' accompanied by veiled threats. The young face remained bland but the twitch in the feet had become a relentless jiggle. Kate watched Bernie raise his eyes and give Butts a penetrating glare.

The youth continued to regard him with a look of mild insolence as Bernie made a start. 'You know how these interviews go so let's get on with it. Tell us about Woodgate Country Park.'

'What about it?' he asked, face full of sham innocence.

Leaning on the table, shoulders hunched, Bernie pointed at him. 'You listen to me. This is an informal chat but we haven't got the time to bugger about, right? We know you was at that park a few days back. Tell us about it.'

Stuart Butts returned the intent glare, maintaining his innocent demeanour. 'I don't know what you're on about. My mom says not to go down there so I don't.'

The sudden smirk disappeared at a swift dig in his side. 'You heard what he just said,' hissed the little woman. 'Tell him.'

Stuart Butts turned his face away from her. 'Shut it. I don't know anything.'

Ignoring the mother, his complete attention on the youth, Bernie enunciated his next few words. 'Yes you *do*. So do we. But there's one thing you *don't* know. We've got evidence which puts you at that park.' Kate watched the neat head jerk. 'You might even come up with what it is if you think about when you was down there.' Stuart Butts's face remained unchanged but Kate guessed at hectic thinking, saw the quick undulations of his throat as he swallowed.

'Come on, love,' his mother wheedled. 'Be a good lad. Tell the policemen what they want to know and then we can go home. Your dad will be in for his tea and when he knows about this he'll have plenty to—'

'Leave him be,' snapped Bernie.

Kate leaned towards the microphone on the desk in front of her to deliver advice to the small bug-in-the-ear devices both officers were wearing. 'It might help if you change the dynamics: exclude the mother.'

She saw Bernie's mouth tighten, recognising his reluctance to do as she'd said because of the possibility of Stuart Butts making a spurious complaint about his treatment. 'You was there. We know you was because what we've got proves it.' The youth still made no facial or other response. 'We've got the torch you left.'

'Not me. Haven't got a torch.'

His mother intervened. 'He's telling you the truth! He hasn't. I can vouch for that.'

Kate leaned towards the microphone again. 'You need to get rid of her.' She watched Bernie's face darken, saw Stuart Butts raise candid eyes to the tall, silent officer leaning against the wall, one leg flexed, then back to his interrogator.

Bernie was fast approaching the outer edges of his patience. 'You're no stranger to the police. You know the system.'

'He's a good lad now. He has his medication every—'

'Not interested,' he snapped, eyes still on the youth. 'He needs to give us some answers, starting *now*, otherwise he could find himself having his breakfast here.'

She turned to her son. 'Come on, Stuey, love. Tell him what you know and then we can get home.'

'Your mom's giving you some real good advice there.' The youth's head came up on hearing the deep voice of the detective leaning against the wall. 'Time to give us the information you have.'

Stuart Butts was studying Joe. 'You American?' This got a brief nod. 'You've got your own gun, yeah?' Joe made no response. 'What's it like to shoot somebody?' In the following silence he returned his attention to Bernie, his eyes giving a single, slow blink. 'I don't help the *pigs*.'

Kate saw the mother convulse on her chair, heard her high squeal and Bernie's swift remonstration. 'You watch your mouth, lad! I've had it with you. Now come on!'

'Don't you talk to him like that,' protested Mrs Butts. 'No wonder he don't like you lot.'

Kate leaned to the microphone, tone impatient now. 'Like I said, you'll get more if you send her out.' She watched Stuart Butts's hands form into fists at a third dig to his ribs.

'Pack it in, you moronic cow.' Catching the heavy officer's glare, he pressed his lips into another smirk.

Joe moved from his position near the wall and came to the table. Placing both hands on it he gazed down at Stuart Butts who looked up, met and held his gaze. 'We're investigating an incident at the park and you're implicated. *Listen.*

Like my colleague said, your property was found at a crime scene. Tell us how it came to be there, otherwise we'll consider charging you for lack of cooperation.' A ragged gasp burst from Mrs Butts as she sent her son a fearful look. 'How about it?'

Kate watched Stuart Butts weighing up his options. It was obvious he wanted out. Whatever he said now would be given to them with escape from Rose Road high on his agenda. 'All right. I *think* I went for a walk down there a few days ago. I was only there five minutes, then I left.'

She leaned to the microphone. 'He didn't walk to the park to spend hardly any time there. Ask what he was doing and *where* he was doing it.'

The soft American voice came again. 'Tell us what you got up to there.'

He did with vagueness and probable omissions: on arrival he'd 'messed about' for five minutes. It had begun to rain so he left and went home. At the end of the skeletal, self-serving account he closed his mouth.

'What did you do during this "five minutes" exactly?' asked Joe, voice heavy with disbelief.

'Nothing. Just . . . hung about.'

'Did you see anybody while you was there?' asked Bernie.

His eyes slid to the broad officer and away. 'Like who?'

Bernie gave him a close look. 'Anybody that we can pick up that might remember *you* and verify your story. If you know that park as well as I think you do you'll know it attracts a few regulars.' He stared into the youth's blue eyes and Kate guessed it was like looking into plate glass. 'I'm talking about the Soiled Mac Brigade.' This elicited another shrill squeal from the mother which turned into a cough. The young face lost its smirk. He was staring beyond Bernie, face implacable. 'There was *nobody*.'

Kate studied him through the glass. 'Ask him about money.'

Bernie eyed the ski jacket on the back of Stuey's chair. 'Got a part-time job?'

'You *are* joking,' he sneered. 'Work for minimum? *Do* me a favour.'

'Stop being cheeky to the policeman! When your father hears—'

'*Shut* your mouth.'

Glancing at his colleague Bernie pressed a button to one side of the table. Kate watched as the door opened to reveal two uniformed constables, one male, one female, who had had prior warning of a possible summons. 'Mrs Butts, how'd you like to go with PC Whittaker here? He'll give you a cup of tea and a couple of biscuits.' Bernie eyed the young constable, who gave some energetic nods.

Mrs Butts demurred. 'I think I should stop with my St—'

'Don't you worry, Mrs B. Young feller'll be all right. WPC Sharma will keep your lad and us company for the rest of our chat.'

Stuey flicked a dismissive glance in his mother's direction. 'Sod off.'

The little woman glared at him, picked up her shopping bag and followed Whittaker from the room. As WPC Sharma crossed it and took a seat in the corner Joe came to the table, lifted the chair vacated by the mother, placed it next to Bernie's and sat. Both officers gave Stuart Butts their silent, unwavering attention.

He returned their gazes, ready to tough it out. 'I've told you all I—'

Bernie spoke, his voice deliberate. 'Your mom's gone but PC Sharma's looking out for you. *Now* you can give us the *rest*.' Kate picked up the derogatory glance the youth sent to the young female constable which Bernie, with evident reluctance, was choosing to ignore. 'Get on with it.'

'There isn't any "rest". What I just told you is all that happened. End of.'

Joe took over. 'We know it rained on Monday.'

The blue eyes held Joe's, the voice a whisper. 'I *said* so, didn't I?'

'What time did you arrive home?' demanded Bernie.

Fazed by the sudden change of direction the teenager shrugged. 'Dunno, 'bout three thirty. Who cares?'

Joe gave him an evaluative look, brows raised. 'You arrived home at about the time you'd usually be leaving school? Knowing your mom was there? Not the smartest move.'

'She wasn't there. Nobody was in.'

Not shifting his gaze Bernie tapped a printed sheet on the table in front of him. 'I phoned your mother after you were picked up. According to her you never showed up at home till "well after five".' He leaned forward. 'Three little words of advice, lad. Give. It. Up.'

The youth's eyes slid from one officer to the other. 'I still don't know what you're on about.'

Joe studied him, head on one side. 'You go to the park on your own that day?'

Tight-mouthed, their interviewee gazed at the clock high on the wall as more seconds ticked by. 'Yeah? *So*?'

Kate had picked up the questioning quality of the brief responses and she spoke again. 'Establish *where* he was when it rained.'

Joe regarded the youth. 'What were you doing when it started raining?'

He shrugged. 'Just watching the birds by the—' The young face slammed shut.

'By the . . . ?' prompted Joe as a single word arrived in Kate's head: *lake*.

'Just hanging about in general. Nowhere special.'

Joe gave a careful nod. 'So what did you do when it started raining?'

Butts shifted his attention to the pooled windowsill. 'I left. It was cold. I got fed up. I went. Home.' Kate wrote down the clipped responses. Lying is easier if you don't include detail.

Head on one side Bernie studied the expressionless face. 'You walked over two miles to stop in that place for *five* minutes then *leave*?' he barked, startling the teenager for the first time and eliciting a frown and some throat-clearing from WPC Sharma.

Joe broke the brief silence. 'D'you have any ideas about what we're investigating at Woodgate?'

'Not got a clue.' The feet had resumed the relentless jiggle.

The two officers exchanged sidelong glances as WPC Sharma sent them a meaningful look. Bernie consulted the wall clock. 'That'll do for now.' He pointed a thick finger. 'But *you* listen to me. We'll be in touch again, rely on it. If in the meantime we find you're holding out on us, you'll be sorry, lad.'

The two officers stood and the youth did the same, contempt on his face. Bernie fixed him with a glare. 'You do know that you're on the right road for a young offenders' place? If you don't, then *this* is where you heard it first. You're heading for big trouble.' In the next room Kate nodded mute agreement.

Stuart Butts's brows arranged themselves into a pseudo-anxious frown, mockery lurking behind the pale eyes. 'Oooh, *am* I?' Within another minute he was gone. So was WPC Sharma.

Bernie turned as Kate came into the room. 'What d'you think?'

'That he's well-acquainted with the park and, given his reluctance to co-operate, I think he was there. At the lake house.'

Bernie looked at Joe. 'What do you make of him?'

'Untrustworthy and holding out. He was probably not there alone.'

They left the interview room together and walked the corridor and the stairs to UCU. Bernie dropped papers onto the table with a glance at Joe. 'First thing tomorrow morning we're out there getting what we can on Stuey Butts, starting with his school.'

Kate nodded. 'Find out with whom he usually truants.'

* * *

He was outside in the dull afternoon, head down, moving at a quick pace to put distance between himself, the building and her. Glancing behind him he pulled his phone from his pocket, tapped the number and waited. After three rings the answerphone kicked in, the posh voice offering him tickets. He grinned, waited for it to stop, then spoke, his tone mocking. 'Hell-oooo. Guess who?'

His message was cut short, as he knew it would be, the la-di-dah voice now in his ear. 'I told you *never* to—'

'Listen, you git! Watch how you talk to me if you don't want all kinds of little secrets coming out. I know what you did, *remember*? Guess where I was five minutes ago?' Without waiting he supplied the answer.

'What?'

'Thought you'd be interested.'

'Why were you—? What have you said?'

'Calm down, you tosser. They're looking for a kid I know.'

'So why're you ringing me? What do you want from . . .' The voice trailed off.

He chortled, picturing the sweating face, the trembling hands. 'I'll think of something and then I'll let you know. Count on it.'

CHAPTER TWENTY

The two officers approached the extensive two-storey brick building in mid-morning dullness, Bernie squinting at the loaded sky as they walked through the main doors and into a wide corridor. They were halfway along it when a piercing bell drilled, doors along the corridor flew open and a navy and white mass surged and flowed in both directions.

'Bloody *hell*,' muttered Bernie as youth teemed. He followed in the direction Joe was moving towards an adult male gesticulating above the heads of the liberated mass.

As they reached him he thrust a quick hand towards them. 'Dermot O'Hanlon, head of this academy, so help me. Come to my office.'

They fell into step with him. 'I phoned yesterday to—' said Bernie.

'Lucky you did or you wouldn't have got past the gate.' Bernie's face set as the head halted, throwing open a door. 'Go in, gentlemen.' He followed them inside. They sat without waiting for an invitation and he bustled past, taking a seat behind a large desk on which sat a number of files.

Joe got to the reason for the visit. 'Stuart Butts. What can you tell us about him?'

O'Hanlon stilled. 'What's he done now?' Getting no response he leaned sideways and lifted a thick file from behind the desk, depositing it on top with a thump. 'Experience makes me keep this handy. It's all in here.'

'How about sharing the basics with us?' suggested Bernie.

O'Hanlon leafed pages. 'Stuart Butts is clever, manipulative, with a propensity for violence. But I can sum him up for you in one word: evil.' He gave them a quick glance, as if to make sure that this had hit home, then continued. 'What makes him even more dangerous is that to look at him you'd never know it. He's always in full uniform. No weird hairstyles, tattoos or face-metal. With him it's all on the *inside*. Unless he decides otherwise, that is.' He itemised the problems in Butts's school career to date. It was a bleak list of subtle bullying of pupils and non-compliance with teachers, plus two suspensions, one for keying a staff member's car, the other for tying a younger pupil to the school's perimeter fence, which had earned him the attentions of two educational psychologists, both of whom diagnosed Conduct Disorder, followed by a six-month referral to a special unit dealing with emotional difficulties where he was given a second diagnosis of Attention Deficit Hyperactive Disorder. O'Hanlon regarded them, his face serious. 'Then they sent him back here. He's not allowed direct contact with any of the animals in the science block. He's on Ritalin but my staff have seen no real change.' He glanced at Bernie. 'That's because Butts has about as much attention-deficit problems as you or me. He's cunning, subversive and nasty. He winds everybody up, kids and staff alike.' He looked down at the file then back to them. 'We had a fire here last year. *That* was Butts.'

'Proof?' asked Bernie. O'Hanlon shook his head. 'Who's he hang around with?'

O'Hanlon shrugged. 'He's a loner, basically.'

Bernie gave him a close look. 'We're assuming he's a *regular* truant.'

O'Hanlon nodded. 'You've got that right.'

‘So who does he skip school with?’ asked Joe.

Reaching among the files on his desk O’Hanlon extracted one. ‘Bradley Harper is the only one that comes to mind. That’s an odd pairing. As I said, Butts is smart. Harper isn’t.’ He lifted a few stapled A4 sheets, lips pursed. ‘Definitely not one of our Year Eleven academic successes.’

Bernie got restless. In his day, secondary school kids were in Years One through to Five, Six if they had the brain cells. It was simple then. He delivered a verbal jab. ‘The number of O levels this Harper’s not doing isn’t our priority. What’s he *like*? What’s he interested in? Has he skipped school before with Stuey Butts?’

The head decided against bringing the heavy officer up to date on the current examination system. Delving inside a manila folder he extracted more printed sheets. ‘Take a look.’ They gazed at photocopied register-entries for the last two months of the previous year. He pointed. ‘See? Harper’s a fairly regular truant.’ He extracted another sheet. ‘His student profile doesn’t indicate any interests. None in school. None out of it.’ Dropping the profile on the desk O’Hanlon sat back on his chair, massaging one eye with the heel of his hand then blinking at them across the desk. ‘No academic aspiration, nor the innate ability to pursue any. His family has no interest in nor commitment to his education, although his two siblings come here and they’re doing well. I’ve met the mother once. A large female who offered me a “smacking” if I allowed any of my staff to detain Bradley after close of school. He’s not a bad kid but he’s the human equivalent of wallpaper when he’s here. He does nothing. He’s the eldest child of the family and I suspect the mother has overindulged him. I don’t know what he does with his time. Eating, at a guess. He does that well enough.’ He gave a heavy sigh. ‘All you hear these days is criticisms about what schools do and don’t do. Fact is, we can’t do it all on our own.’ With a shake of his head he replaced the sheets inside the file and dropped it into a nearby tray. ‘Compared to Harper, Butts has real academic potential.’

Joe nodded. 'When was Harper last out of school?'

O'Hanlon looked at him. 'Good question. After you phoned yesterday I checked with his form tutor. His attendance was registered on Monday morning last week.' He pointed to the date. 'But when I checked some more, none of his subject tutors for the remainder of that day could specifically recall seeing him. That's the problem with pupils like him — they sit there under the radar. I phoned his mother to tell her that I believed Bradley was out of school and she was abusive towards me. I know she's got a lot to contend with but I don't take that kind of thing from any parent. I haven't heard from her since and we haven't seen Bradley.'

Exchanging a look with Bernie, Joe stretched his long legs. 'If Stuart Butts and Bradley Harper did skip school that day, where are they likely to have gone?'

O'Hanlon nodded towards the window. 'The options are limited. They wouldn't go to the community centre or hang around the shops or the roads on their estate because they know my staff are likely to be out there looking for truants. I'd say the most likely is the Country Park a couple of miles in that direction, but who really knows with kids like these?'

Bernie had never felt comfortable in schools and the heat inside O'Hanlon's office was starting to give him a headache. 'What might they get up to if they were at the park? Would Harper have gone on his own?'

'I don't think he's got the initiative,' said O'Hanlon to the last question. 'And personally, I would doubt it. A couple of my staff told me of a rumour that he was assaulted there some time last year.'

Bernie gave Joe a sideways glance. 'Tell us what you know about that.'

'Nothing. As I said, it was a rumour that was picked up among the kids in the school which we never managed to verify. And I don't know what he and Butts might get up to as and when they go there.' He looked from one officer to the other. 'We're well aware of the unsavoury types who frequent that place.' O'Hanlon returned Stuart Butts's file to the floor with a thud. 'When you do speak to Butts my advice is not to believe a word he says.' He hesitated, shooting a brief glance across the desk, choosing his words. 'We've noticed that he always has a steady supply of money.'

'Where from?' asked Bernie.

'No idea.' He rolled his shoulders, face already tired. 'In case you're wondering, we warn our pupils about that whole area of parkland. We're well aware of complaints of drug dealing, flashing and the rest of it.'

Bernie stood, holding out a card to him. 'If you think of anything else, give us a bell. We'll see ourselves out.'

O'Hanlon quit his chair, arriving at the door ahead of them. 'Have to escort you off the premises.' He did, as far as the main entrance, where he remained watching them through the glass.

They climbed into the Range Rover, Bernie fuming. 'To listen to him you wouldn't think *we're* the law, his first line of defence against the druggies, flashers and paedos.'

'Guess he's doing his job as well as he can,' said Joe.

Bernie started the engine. 'From what he said it sounds like Butts and this Harper kid left school together that Monday. We need to get hold of Harper. Ask him a few questions. We might get somewhere with *him*.'

* * *

Later that day Kate was assembling dinner as Mugger, whom she'd just let inside, wove around her legs giving high-pitched cries. She looked down at him and smiled. '*Okay*. I'll do it now.' She left what she was doing to fill his bowl with biscuits, stroking his chill coat, an image slipping into her head of Nathan Troy in T-shirt and jeans in November.

Leaving the cat enthusiastically crunching, Kate put her hands under running water, dried them then resumed her preparations, adding fresh vegetables to soya, looking at her watch as the front door opened and banged shut. Hearing the thump of book-bag on wood she glanced up at the clock, her spirits rising. *On time.*

Maisie entered the kitchen, cheeks glowing and approached the range to inspect what was cooking. Kate gave her a quick hug, choosing to ignore the grimace. 'Hi. How did your maths lecture go?'

'Mm . . . Okay.'

Other than those times when Maisie *wanted* to talk, getting any details about school from her was like prising teeth from a hen. Kate suppressed a sigh. 'Is it getting difficult?'

'Difficult?' Maisie echoed, brows drawn together as if considering a strange concept. Which she probably was. 'I'm going upstairs. Homework.'

She was gone and Kate reflected on the subtle change she'd begun to notice in Maisie, an increase in self-sufficiency. She was growing up. Or should that be away?

Walking to the window she stood and looked at her lone self reflected in the darkness beyond; personal responsibilities and professional demands for years to come rushing her head. It had been a long day and she was tired. Details of UCU's new case sidled into her brain and her words misted the glass: 'Please. *Not* another Repeater.'

She heard the phone in the hall ring and quick footsteps on the stairs followed by Maisie's voice. '*Mom!* It's for you. It's Joe.'

She left the kitchen and went into the hall to pick up the phone. 'Hi, Joe.'

'Got a progress update for you, Red.' She listened as he told her about the visit to Stuart Butts's school, the information they now had that another pupil may have been with Butts at the park. A phone call to that boy's mother had established that he hadn't been home since the Monday he'd walked away from the school. 'His mother filed a Missing report on him at her local station early this morning but that's all we know right now.'

Feeling her heart rate climb, Kate stared unseeing at the nearby stairs. 'Why the delay in reporting him missing?'

'We'll be asking that same question. We're pretty certain they went out of school together. Any ideas for jogging her memory for places they might have gone?'

Kate focused her mind. 'Take something tangible for her to look at: a map of the area where the family lives, including Woodgate Park. Highlight the map's key features such as the main roads, the family home, railway lines and so on.'

'Why the railway lines? Something specific on your mind?'

'No. They're all geographical features which influence people's use of familiar territory. There's been some research which suggests that young people tend to stay on the home side of main roads and so forth as they use their neighbourhoods to go about their daily lives. It gives them a relatively wide area in which to roam where they feel comfortable yet at the same time avoid direct surveillance by people who know or might recognise them.'

She knew from the nature of the silence in her ear that he was making notes. 'Will do. Following that we'll visit Butts at his home, ask him why he didn't think to mention this Bradley Harper. And there's something else. The head of the school told us that Harper might have been assaulted at Woodgate Park last year.' She heard Bernie's voice in the background. 'Thanks, Red. Gotta go. Our "evening shift" is about to start.'

Kate lowered the phone, neurones inside her head fired by a flood of speculations and possibilities.

CHAPTER TWENTY-ONE

They strode the weed-filled path and Bernie pounded peeling wood with a heavy fist. Somewhere inside an infant wail started up, followed by a loud female voice: 'Amber? *Amber!* Bring the babby down here. There's somebody at the bloody door!' They exchanged glances. The voice had neared during its brief flow of instruction, ending with the sudden opening of the door. A heavily built woman filled the opening. She didn't need introductions. Her eyes flicked over the immediate area. 'Come on in.' She squeezed to one side of the tiny hallway and they walked inside, Bernie giving the air an experimental sniff: sour; greasy.

Responding to her nod they walked through a door on the right and into a small sitting room to stand amid clutter. She followed them inside, gathering an assortment of clothes, toys and other oddments. 'You've caught me on the hop. All this with my Bradley — I've had a 'mare of a day.' Her chest rose and fell as she lifted her face towards the ceiling. '*Craig?* You got that homework done yet?' There was no reply but a couple of heavy footfalls sounded on the upper floor.

She gestured for them to sit as Bernie did the introductions. 'I'm Detective Sergeant Bernard Watts and this is Lieutenant Joe Corrigan. Rose Road. Mrs Harper.'

'The name's Debbie. I was expecting you. A young policewoman come this afternoon, Asian she was, but ever so nice.' She walked a few paces and dropped the armful of gathered items into the space between sofa and wall then turned slowly back to them, face fearful. 'You *know* something. Don't say . . .'

They shook their heads. 'Easy, now,' advised Bernie.

Shoulders sagging she sat on one of the battered armchairs. 'I'll kill him when he comes back, worrying me like this,' she said, voice tremulous.

A girl of about eight in pyjamas appeared at the door holding a wide-faced infant, its back to her, arms and legs dangling. It caught sight of the two visitors and the corners of its mouth travelled downwards. 'He needs changing, Mom.'

Her mother gave her a distracted glance. 'You know what to do.' As girl and infant disappeared she watched, chewing her lip as Bernie took out his notebook.

'We need some more information about your lad Bradley. First, has he ever gone missing before?'

She looked doubtful. 'There was one time — but he wasn't actually *missing*. I was having the babby and his dad come here for a couple of days to stop with the kids. They don't get on, Bradley and his dad, so he went to my sister's place without telling anybody. She lives over the other side of the estate, towards the community centre.' Bernie nodded. He knew the location. 'My sister didn't know that Bradley hadn't told his dad where he was going.' She looked annoyed. 'Not that he would've done anything anyway. It wasn't until I come back from the hospital that I found my Bradley wasn't here.' She bit her lip. 'He often goes to my sister's place and stops overnight, sometimes longer. It's a casual thing between us. He likes it there because it's quiet. Just her and Jamie, her twelve-year-old. Bradley leaves bits and pieces of his stuff there . . . it's like a home from home for him. That's what I thought he'd done this time. I thought he was there.' Her lips quivered.

'Does he wag school very often?'

She flared. 'So what if he does? They take no interest in him. They reckon he's thick. He *isn't*. He gets bored.' They waited. 'He occasionally goes out of school and I have told him off about that.'

'You have other children at the same school, ma'am?'

She gazed at Joe and fiddled with the bow on her top. 'Yes.'

'They're doing okay?'

She nodded. 'Very well, actually . . . Oh, I *get* you. You're asking about the difference between my kids? My Bradley's my eldest and Ron isn't actually his dad. Bradley was born at a bad time for me. My mom had just died and I know I mollycoddle him, let him do as he . . .' She bit her lip again.

Joe stood, took a single A4 sheet from his overcoat pocket and went to where she was sitting. 'We're interested to hear any ideas you may have as to where Bradley goes when he's not in school, ma'am. See? This is a map of the immediate area around here.'

She bowed her head over it, soon pointing at features. 'That's this road and there's the school . . . *That's* where my sister lives, but, as I said, he's not been there.' She took the map from Joe and studied it. 'There's the community centre but he wouldn't have gone there. He knows they'd phone me or the school if he turned up there in school time. Same with the shops here. The school does wag runs all round there. My Bradley's not stupid.'

Joe reached out and pointed to an extensive area outlined in green. 'How about this place?'

She gave a decisive headshake. 'No. He wouldn't go there.'

From where he was sitting Bernie could see what was being considered: the Country Park. 'How come you're so sure?'

She looked away from them, colour heightening on the plump cheeks as she told them of an incident there the previous year involving an assault on Bradley. They'd reported it to local police but in light of his refusal to give any details about the assault to anyone, beyond saying that he was grabbed by a man, they were unable to proceed further.

They heard the front door open and close. 'That'll be Ron.'

A short, thin man in work clothes, a hat pulled down to his brows, came into the room, along with a blast of cold air. 'What're they doing here?'

'They're from Rose Road. They're looking for Bradley. They want to know about him, where he goes.' The newcomer was still en route to a door leading to the rear of the house.

Bernie struggled to his feet. 'Hang on a minute! We're here to get information about Debbie's lad. You got anything to say about him? Where he might be?'

He spoke over one shoulder. 'No, except that when he finally decides to come back home I'll be wanting to know what he's done with some stuff of mine he's nicked.'

'Including a torch, by any chance?'

Bernie's words brought him to a halt and he half-turned to them. 'Maybe. He's always sneaking about, messing with my stuff.'

'Describe it, will you?' said Bernie with a glance at Joe.

He shrugged. 'Black with a bit o' metal either end. Nothing special. I just don't like him helping himself to my—'

'We've heard that Bradley was assaulted at Woodgate Park last year,' continued Bernie. 'What do you know about that?'

'Nothing.' He took off his coat and the knitted hat, revealing wispy hair. 'Shouldn't have gone down there, should he? He'd been warned. It was me that took him down the cop shop. *Waste* o' time. He wouldn't tell 'em anything.' He nodded across the room. 'He talks more to her. I'm not here full-time. I don't know what all the fuss is about. He's sixteen.' With that he edged through the door and disappeared.

Debbie Harper was chewing her lip, broad face stressed. 'You've got me wondering now. My Bradley used to love that park. I told him not to go but . . . he's always been a loner and then he took up with a lad at school and I thought, "Now he's got a friend it'll be good for him. Better than being on his own all the time." I know what *that's* like. I changed my mind when I found out who it was and I'm wondering if he went to the park with *him*.'

'Who?' asked Bernie.

'That Butts lad, Stuey. He's a bad influence, he is. His dad's been done for domestic.' Tears slid down the plump cheeks. 'Tell me you don't think something bad has happened.'

'We'll make all the inquiries needed,' said Joe, as he and Bernie exchanged a glance. 'In the meantime, do you have a recent photograph of Bradley?'

She got up from the sofa and went to a sideboard supporting a small mountain of household clutter. Opening a drawer she searched it then took out a small item and handed it to Joe. 'This is his school photo from last October.'

Joe looked at it, nodded. 'Can you give a physical description? Height? Weight?' He passed the photo to Bernie.

She swallowed hard. 'He's blond . . . you can see that from the photo. He's not too tall. Five seven, I'd say. Bit on the heavy side. Takes after me, you see . . . big-boned.'

'Any specific reason why you didn't report him missing the day he went? Or the next day?'

'Like I said, I thought he was at my sister's.' She nodded in the direction of the door through which her partner had gone, face hardening. 'And because of *him*. He said there was nothing to worry about, that Bradley's sixteen and it was time to stop fussing over him. I shouldn't have taken any notice. I should have rung my sister to check.' Her face crumpled and more tears flowed.

At the sound of feet on the stairs she rallied, hurriedly drying her eyes as two boys came into the room. She went to them, putting a hand on the shoulder of each. 'This is Craig and this is Jarvis.' The younger of the two held out two sheets of paper to her. She took them, looking at their felt-penned handiwork as the two officers caught the key sentence on the colourful flyers: *Please!!! Help us find our brother.*

She gave them a small smile. 'That's *really* good, lads. You've done a great job there.'

* * *

A few minutes later Bernie was eyeing the downstairs window of another house, picking up a subtle widening of venetian slats as Joe knocked on its PVC front door a third time.

The door opened and Mrs Butts appeared, cigarette in hand. She looked at each of them, face full of animosity, lips drawn inwards. 'Not again! You couldn't have anything better to do. What time do you call this? You *really* upset him the other day.'

Joe took a step forward. 'We need to come in, ma'am. We have a few more questions for your son.'

Ill-tempered, she stepped back and they entered the hall, moving on to a sitting room dominated by smoke, red leather furniture and a wall-mounted television tuned to Sky Sports. Joe tracked her as she followed them into the room then headed for another door. 'Where is he?'

'Give us a chance, I'm fetching him! He's not been well since you had him in Rose Road. His asthma . . .' Her words faded as she disappeared through the door and they waited, Bernie detecting no sound of movement or conversation beyond it. His eyes drifted around the room, seeing money to spare if the furniture and electronic equipment were anything to go by. He doubted it was earned.

They turned at a subtle sound. Stuart Butts was standing in the doorway. No school uniform this time but still smart. Bernie saw jeans pressed with a crease. He looked him in the eye. 'We've got some more questions for you. Come in here and have a seat.' Ignoring the red upholstery Stuey Butts went and sat on a wheeled office chair, his pale blue eyes fixed on them. 'We want to know about your mate Bradley Harper and you can turn *that* thing off.' He gestured with his thumb at the massive television.

'He's not my mate,' he muttered, reaching for the remote on the arm of a nearby chair and aiming it.

'Why didn't you tell us the other day that you and Harper wagged school and went down the park?' Bernie barked.

'Because we didn't.'

He took a few steps towards the youth, index finger pointing, as Mrs Butts came in, wheezy voice intervening. 'Hey! You can't come in here throwing your weight.'

'Yes we can.' Bernie didn't look at her, his eyes still on Stuey. '*Tell* us. Now! Or you'll be back at Rose Road before you can say *arrest*.'

Stuey gave Bernie an evaluative look, trying to guess how much the officers knew. 'Okay, we went down to the park. So what? We never did anything.' Bernie caught Joe's glance and gave an imperceptible nod. Best for Corrigan to carry on. All he felt like doing right now was applying a quick hand to the smooth, young face.

Joe regarded the youngster turning slowly on the chair, insouciance on the face, guardedness in the eyes. 'Tell us all you know, Stuart, and make sure it's the whole deal or you're coming with us. Back to HQ.'

Butts went with an edited version: yes, he and Harper had left their school after registration and walked from there to the Country Park. When it started raining they had left. They'd seen nothing and done nothing.

Joe stood and walked towards him with slow measured steps, hands in the pockets of his overcoat. 'Okay. Now let's have the whole deal. The detail.' He stood over the youth who gave a little more. When it rained they'd taken shelter in a 'shed' by the lake, where they'd 'messed about' then left. 'How'd you manage to slip your flashlight under the floor?'

They watched Stuart Butts's face become rigid, the pale eyes darting from one to the other. 'I didn't. It wasn't mine.'

Within a further five minutes they had a somewhat less edited account. There had been a scuffle between the two which resulted in damage to the floor. They'd pulled up more of it and the torch had rolled inside the hole.

The quiet Boston tones came again. 'What else was in the hole?'

'*Nothing*. There was nothing to see. We didn't even look.'

Bernie hadn't taken his eyes off him during this exchange. He took a few steps towards him and Stuey grew still. 'Course you did.' He watched the young mouth tighten. 'Try this question: where's Bradley Harper?'

'Haven't got a clue.'

Bernie's breathing accelerated as his anger climbed. 'Okay. Try *this* one: what do you know about Bradley Harper being assaulted at the park last year?'

Stuey's face shut down. '*Nothing*. I'm not saying anything else and I know my rights. You can't arrest me.'

* * *

Two minutes later Bernie had made a phone call to Rose Road, to be told that so far there were no further leads on the whereabouts of Bradley Harper. The Range Rover pulled away from the kerb, Bernie fuming as they headed for Headquarters. 'That Butts is a lying toerag but we've *got* him. His DNA places him at that lake house and the torch places Bradley Harper right there with him. They were both there when that floor was up. I think they had a fight. Either Bradley Harper legged it and now he's too frightened to show himself or Butts has done something bad to him. I'm contacting Gander about arresting Butts. Hope you've got no plans for tonight.'

'Nope,' said Joe.

CHAPTER TWENTY-TWO

Loud music thumped the study ceiling and two pairs of feet thudded in unison. Still thinking of what Joe had said to her about Stuart Butts and the Harper boy, Kate had begun an examination of the contents of the box Nathan Troy's mother had given them. She would take it into Rose Road but first she wanted make an inventory of its contents.

She lifted out delicate watercolours, placing them side by side on the desk, all executed on heavy-duty white paper taken from a medium-sized sketchpad, each bearing the ragged square-and-tag edge of the original spiral-binding. She glanced at each one, recognising those she and Joe had seen at the Troy family home. Here was Alastair Buchanan. There, Cassandra. Cassandra Levitte. She lifted another: the fine-featured, fair-haired Joel Smythe. How could these well-crafted, subtle pictures have been created by someone they'd heard disparaged as unreliable, a thief and a likely drug user? She reminded herself that the number of artists, past and present, known for their significant character flaws was legion.

She raised her head as the combination of music and feet intensified. Leaving the study she went upstairs, to the open door of Maisie's bedroom where she leaned against the jamb, arms folded and watched the two girls in white tees, matching red minis, white socks and tennis shoes, well into their enthusiastic routine for a forthcoming show at their school. She tapped her foot to the nineteen eighties hit 'Mickey', watching them dance as one, legs firm and flawless, smooth knees rising in unison. '*Hey!* Up, up, *now* turn,' yelled Maisie as they spun, faces flushed, little skirts flicking to one side then the other. '*Hey Mickey!* Yeah, Chel, three-four *and* . . .' Kate stood, enthralled by the energy, the physical perfection of both girls. Chelsey, well on her way to womanhood, Maisie shorter with the merest hint of mature promise.

She returned to her study to look again at the exquisitely detailed sketches produced by Nathan Troy when he was not that much older than the two girls upstairs. Now he was gone, ruined, and they still had no idea why death had come for him. Resting her chin on one hand she reviewed a discussion she'd had with her colleagues. Murder-by-stranger? By local deviant? Someone he knew?

She gazed, unseeing, towards the study window, thinking of her theory of the jigsaw floor. The smear of blood which had yielded Stuart Butts's DNA placed him at the lake house. Was it he who had so carefully re-assembled that floor? From her observations of him she suspected he had the acumen for such a task but, recalling the restless feet, she doubted he had the patience and concentration. And what would have been his motivation to do it? She wasn't yet able to make a judgement about Bradley Harper's possible role if he had one because she knew little about him. Her thoughts ran on. Was it too fanciful to speculate that at the time the floor was being taken up whoever it was who'd murdered Nathan Troy twenty years before had happened along again? Marauding Repeater? She sat, feeling tension surge through her brain.

The doorbell rang. Kate replaced the box lid and glanced at her watch. Ten p.m. That would be Chelsey's mother. She glanced out of the window, saw Bernie's Range Rover, and walked from the study to the front door to let him in. 'I was on my way home so I thought I'd drop by and give you an update.' He followed Kate into the kitchen. 'We've had another talk with Stuey Butts. He's confirmed that both him and Bradley Harper was at the lake house.'

'Really?'

'It was Harper's torch — or his dad's — so the fact that it was under the floor proves that the floor was up when they was both there.'

'Still no word on the Harper boy's whereabouts?'

He pulled out a chair and sat heavily. 'Nothing. No one's seen him since they was both at the park. It's technically an Upstairs case, but given the link with ours we've agreed to share whatever we find out.'

Kate sat opposite him. 'Why wasn't Bradley reported missing earlier?'

Bernie gave a weary sight. 'Seems there was a misunderstanding as to where he actually was. More an absence of communication if you ask me. His mother's got a lot on her plate but she strikes me as a bit of a doze. We've told Gander we're having Stuey Butts in again. He's okayed it and if he's still uncooperative we'll consider arresting him. Upstairs are starting a search of the area for Harper tomorrow.' Kate nodded, her anxiety growing with possibilities now occurring to her, including that sixteen-year-old Stuart Butts had killed Bradley Harper. 'You got any time tomorrow morning?'

'I'm working from here till lunchtime. Why?'

'Far as I'm concerned the assault on Harper last year and the fact we can't find him now makes an urgent case for visiting them three local sex types.'

'Has anybody said what kind of assault it was?'

'Doc, trust me. It'll be sexual. I'll come at about eight fifteen so we can surprise 'em with early visits. Between now and then I'm going to have a look at maps of the park. Check the locations of any public conveniences on it.'

She gazed at him, brows drawn together. 'You're thinking it's an area for cottaging?'

He shrugged. 'Makes sense. Types who cruise for gay sex need somewhere to meet up, especially in this weather. See you in the morning.'

Deep in thought she closed the door. A meeting place. Was that what the lake house was?

CHAPTER TWENTY-THREE

Kate was in Maisie's bedroom. 'Here's your hockey kit.' She placed folded clothes inside the bag on the bed, her eyes drifting to a large black-and-white poster. *Please, somebody, tell me that lots of twelve-year-old girls have Isambard Kingdom Brunel on their wall.* 'Have you got everything else ready?'

Maisie was texting. 'Yeah. I'm telling Chel I'll be at her place in, what, ten minutes?'

Kate nodded. 'That should do it.'

Maisie dropped her phone into her school bag and walked to the window to lean on the sill. 'Bernie's arrived.' She propped her chin on one hand as Kate left the room. 'You know, if Bernie went on a diet he might be able to get a girlfriend. Somebody oldish.'

'Get your coat on and stop making personal comments.'

* * *

Kate was inside the Range Rover looking again at the details of the three males arrested at the Country Park the previous year. Bernie pointed at the data as he drove. 'Ronald Dixon got eighteen months. He was out in nine. Ernest Phillips and

Edward Morrell both got probation with a condition that they went for sex offender treatment.'

'It doesn't say here what Dixon did which distinguished his offences from those committed by the other two — although I doubt "distinguished" is the right word.'

'Dixon physically threatened his "hands-on" victim and it was his third conviction. The other two, Phillips and Morrell, got complaints against 'em from people using the park that they was hanging about where kids was fishing. They was charged as watchers—'

'Voyeurs.'

'—and when Phillips's place was searched his computer had a load of under-age pornography on it, plus some recordings off the telly: choir boys plus a scrapbook of kids' pictures cut from mail-order catalogues, if you can believe it.'

'All too easily,' she responded.

'Morrell also has a 1993 arrest, remember? Both of *his* arrests involved watching and following adult females as well as lurking around kids, so he's got a wide target range. Like I said, he supports my theory that types stay active for years. If him and the other two are park regulars we need to hear what they know about any park cronies they might have.'

'Who are we going to talk to right now?'

Bernie slowed, indicating a left turn before joining Harborne Lane. 'I wanted to see Dixon first but there was no reply when I phoned him early this morning, nor from Morrell.' He shook his head. 'It's anybody's guess what they're up to.' He joined traffic surging towards the Bristol Road. 'We're heading for Ernie Phillips's place. I decided we'd go on spec. Give him a nice little surprise.'

They drove on in silence, finally making a right turn into a road of semi-detached houses and coming to a stop. Kate turned to him. 'You *really* think it's possible that one of these three might have been involved in Nathan Troy's death in ninety-three — and maybe in the Harper assault if there was one?' *And maybe in his disappearance*?

He switched off the ignition. 'Doc, whenever I see coincidence in a case it makes me want to give it a good going over. A dead youngster, a now-missing kid and "sex types", all at the same place? These three are as good a starting point as any. They was operating down at the park last year when Harper had trouble there.'

She turned to him. 'But there's nothing to indicate a sexual motive for Troy's murder. We don't *know* that he was killed at the lake house or anywhere else nearby.'

He gave her a patient look. 'But if Troy *was* killed there we can't rule out that whoever killed him could also be the type who has a history of hanging around younger kids at the same place.' He nodded at the printouts in her hand. 'You know as well as me that sex types have places, favoured haunts they like to hang about in, but they're also *opportunists*. You've said it often enough yourself in so many words. They take their chances where they get 'em. They might have their preferences in who they get hold of but if that's not available, well — any port in a storm. It's part of their "work day", like you and me going to the office, seeing what's to do. Yes, yes, you know it all already but you've seen their details, their ages and you know my attitude: "*Once* a sex offender, *always* a sex offender." We're here. Come on.'

Leaving the Range Rover she walked the path to where Bernie was already pounding the door. It was opened on the fourth hit by a mild-looking man dressed in what appeared to Kate's eye to be varying shades of beige synthetics, including a golf-style tank top featuring brown diamond shapes on a pale background. *Mr Polyester*. 'Yes?'

Bernie gave him a hard look. 'Ernest Phillips?'

'Yes. Who—' The question was stopped by Bernie's official identification. Phillips's face assumed a long-suffering expression. 'What d'you want?'

'A little chat. Out here or inside?'

Phillips opened the door further and they went in, Kate casting subtle glances as they entered the silent house, walked the neat hall and on to an equally orderly sitting room. They sat where Phillips indicated and she saw high-quality earphones on a sofa-arm, recognisable music drifting from them: Glen Miller. Phillips sat with a nod at Kate. 'Who's this?'

Delving for his notebook Bernie sent a heavy frown across the room. '*This* is Dr Kate Hanson, forensic psychologist, who works with us in the Unsolved Crime Unit at Rose Road. Let's make this snappy, shall we? Tell us about the happy hours you spent in Woodgate Country Park last year.'

'That was a misunderstanding—'

'*Course* it was. I suppose you'd never seen none of that stuff on your computer neither.'

Phillips flushed. 'All that's behind me now. I'm on the programme. I'm addressing my problems.'

'"Problems"? Like, what makes you perv at kids on the television and download pornographic images you get sent by your like-minded mates?'

This brought further colour to Phillips's face. 'You can ask my probation officer.'

'I *will*. Depend on it.'

'She'll tell you. I've got low self-esteem, high anxiety, issues of social isolation because I lost my job after . . .'

Kate steeled herself for Bernie's response, saw him glare at Phillips, thick forefinger raised. 'You're describing much of the human race, there. Everybody's got problems. I'm no Rebecca of Sunnybrook Farm neither but the difference between you and most of us is that we manage to live right.' She watched his irritation climb as Phillips attempted to intervene. 'Be quiet and listen. We've got a picture and a question for you.' He fixed Phillips with a look. 'You ever see this lad?' Kate glanced at the photograph Bernie was holding out. She didn't recognise the round-faced, fair-haired boy but guessed who it was. Bradley Harper.

Phillips looked at it then away. 'No. I'm not allowed down onto the Country Park. One of my probation conditions.'

Kate suppressed an intake of breath as Bernie's brows shot upwards. 'Who said anything about the park?'

'I heard one of the probation officers at my sex offender group mention some kid going missing from that place . . . or being found dead.' He looked disgruntled. 'I lose track of everything, not having a job.'

Bernie stared at him. 'After we've had a word with your probation officer we might get you into Rose Road for another chat. What's her name?'

He gave it and Bernie wrote it down. Five minutes later they were inside the Range Rover.

'That didn't take long,' commented Kate.

'I wanted to check what kind of set-up he's living in so that when I speak to his PO I'll know what I'm on about. No sign of anybody else hanging around in his house. What did *you* make of him?' he asked, dragging his phone from his pocket.

'I don't know what stage he's reached in his treatment programme but he's still denying his offence. It's possible he *is* socially isolated which could cause him to spiral into reoffending. He needs checking out for possible depression for the same reason.'

'I'll tell his PO when I ring. I'm trying Dixon again.' He sat drumming his fingers on the steering wheel then ended the call. 'Still out gallivanting, doing God-only-knows-what. I'll give Morrell a bell.' After six rings he cut the call, looking belligerent. 'No answer from him, neither.' He eased the vehicle into the traffic flow. 'They need chasing up, soon as.' He looked at Kate. 'Get anything else from Phillips?'

She lifted her shoulders. 'The personal difficulties he referred to are typical for certain types of sex offender. Do *you* think he heard about Bradley Harper at his treatment group?'

'Your guess is as good as mine. Possible he might have picked up something about Troy being found.' He looked vexed. 'One of the things that gets my goat about investigation isn't the talking. It's the tracking down so you *can* talk.'

Kate had her notebook open on her lap. 'We haven't managed to encourage much "talking" from our leads so far but I saw Roderick Levitte on Monday. He talked. A lot.'

'I saw your notes on the screen. Give me the gist.'

'It wasn't only what he said, it was the way he said it.' She delivered a truncated account of her meeting with Levitte.

Slowing for more traffic, Bernie huffed. 'He sounds just this side of barmy to me. Perhaps it's one of them family traits you hear about, seeing we now know that that Cassandra is his sister. By the way, I phoned the other sister, Miranda, again. Left another message. No response. That's twice now. *If I* was the judgemental type I'd say she's avoiding us.'

Kate's eyes slid to an address and phone number in the notebook. She looked at her watch. It was only ten thirty. She wasn't due at the university until one thirty. 'Can you drop me on Harborne High Street? Roderick told me where she works. I'll try the direct approach.'

* * *

When Kate had almost reached Vine Terrace she called ahead to identify herself and announce her imminent arrival. She got only an answering machine. She increased her pace, curious now to meet Henry Levitte's other daughter. The narrow road opened into an attractive, spacious area of evergreens in hardwood tubs and a mix of specialist shops facing onto the central courtyard, among them a photographic studio, a designer baby-wear shop and a patisserie, aromas of newly baked bread and fresh-ground coffee drifting from it on the chill air.

Kate crossed the courtyard and walked in the direction of the unlit grey and white double-fronted premises of Artworks to read the sign on the door: *Closed*. 'Rats,' she muttered. As she neared she read another: *Hours of Trading. Monday to Saturday: 9.30 a.m.–4.00 p.m. Wednesday: 9.30 a.m.–12.00 noon.* Kate checked her watch. It was only eleven o'clock.

Shading her eyes she looked beyond window glass and works on display to the shadowy interior. Dropping her hand she glanced round at the other small enterprises then turned back, raising her hand again. That's when she saw it.

Movement. Deep within the shadows of the little gallery. She knocked on the door. No response. No one there. She'd been mistaken.

Chilled and frustrated she turned away, following the tempting aromas of fresh-baked bread. She entered the patisserie where a heavy-set man in a white apron was leaning on the counter reading a newspaper. He straightened, smiling. 'Morning! What can I get you? I've got some French sticks that haven't long come out.'

She indicated the white-painted chairs and tables. 'You do coffee to drink in?'

He nodded. 'Americano, latte — we've got Blue Mountain if you're happy to pay the price.'

All work and no . . . why not? 'Blue Mountain would be good.' She crossed to a table that afforded an unrestricted view of Artworks.

The man bustled to and fro behind the counter and soon she heard the metallic burr of a coffee grinder, following which he appeared with a tray bearing a small cafetière, a pale blue cup and saucer and matching jug. He placed them before her on the table. 'Sugar's there. Would you like something to go with that?'

Kate declined, nodding across the courtyard. 'Artworks opens on a Wednesday morning but there's no one there.'

Tucking the tray under one arm he leaned sideways to look through the window. '*Should* be. Miss Levitte's one you can set your watch by. Yes, the lights are on. She's there.' Kate turned quickly to the window. The lights were indeed on. Eyes on the small gallery she drank the Blue Mountain, which was good, then looked at the bill. It needed to be.

Leaving money on the table and giving a nod to the man she left the patisserie and recrossed the courtyard to the gallery. The sign on the door still proclaimed it closed despite the glow of interior spotlights. Once again she knocked on the glass of the door. Silence. She tried again, louder this time. Still nothing. Irritated, she got out her phone, located the number and listened to her call ringing inside. After six rings the answerphone took over. Ending the call, she checked her watch, debating what to do as she gave another quick glance inside. Now her earlier observation was confirmed by quick movement deep within.

She raised her hand to the door then stopped. It would keep. And it hadn't been a wasted journey. *Now I know you're avoiding us, Miranda Levitte. And I'm really interested to know why.*

CHAPTER TWENTY-FOUR

Kate opened the door of her room that afternoon, one arm around several files. A brisk walk to her desk and she leaned forward, letting them slide, her attention caught by a yellow slip bearing a message from Julian: *Developments at Woodgate*. She recalled her phone ringing during her drive to the university. She picked up the message and went to the connecting door where Crystal was engaged in some speedy word processing. 'Did Julian say anything else?'

The cropped blond head indicated a negative. 'Only that everyone was going down there.'

'I'd better go. I've got nothing timetabled until the three-thirty lecture but if any student does call in asking for me can you take a name and say I'll get back to them?'

'Sure,' said Crystal with a smile. She gazed up at Kate, large-eyed. 'I've told my mom about you and your job. She loves watching reruns of *Cracker*. I bet they're all waiting at Woodgate for you to tell them what's what.'

Kate grinned. 'If that's the case—' She checked the message time: 1.20 p.m., ten minutes ago. '—I'd better get going and sort them out. I'll be back in time for the lecture.'

* * *

Calling into Rose Road first she found a disgruntled Julian. He answered her one question. 'They left as soon as the news came in and as *usual* they wouldn't allow me to go with them. I've not seen or heard from them since.'

'Could you do something for me? The assault against Bradley Harper. Make a comprehensive search: every single available database for *any* description of his alleged perpetrator?'

He nodded. 'I'll have a — *Hey*, can't I come with you?'

* * *

Kate parked behind Bernie's vehicle, walked down the slope and in the direction of the lake, muted voices there becoming increasingly distinct. Her two colleagues were standing on the flat land below the lake house as white-suited SOCOs examined the muddy strip bordering the nearby lake. As she drew nearer to them Kate was startled by a glossy, featureless shape rearing from black water. One of Rose Road's forensic dive team. She looked again. Two of them. She continued on to where her colleagues were standing. Wordless, she looked up from one to the other, needles of frozen rain now hitting her face.

Joe nodded to her. 'Marathon runner in training reported seeing a body in the water early this morning. It took a while to locate. They're still checking for anything else.'

'I never thought all that running about did nobody any good,' muttered Bernie, pulling up his coat collar as he turned to her. 'You've missed the action. Connie was here till ten minutes ago. She provisionally identified him from the photo his mother give us.' There was no need to ask. Bradley Harper. They gazed in silence at the lake, dark and still below motionless trees and slate sky as the specialist work continued around them. 'Rotten place for a kid to die. Or anybody else, for that matter.' He flexed his shoulders. 'Any road up, Connie's got him now. She'll do what she can for him. And us.'

'Did she say anything about the cause of death?' asked Kate.

He shook his head. 'You know better than that.'

They followed Joe as he moved in the direction of their parked cars. 'I'm due at the practice range in fifteen minutes.'

'I'll drop you, Corrigan, and then I'm going to see Stuey Butts again.'

Kate looked up at him. 'Now that we've placed him down here with Bradley Harper are you going to arrest him?'

She listened as Bernie outlined the need for caution due to Stuart Butts's age and the possibility of legal complications if they were seen to act too quickly and without good evidence. 'I'm hoping we'll hear something from Connie soon and then we'll get him into Rose Road.'

'Did she give any indication as to when she might report back?' asked Kate.

'Tomorrow morning,' responded Joe. 'Where you off to, Red?'

'Back to the university.' She went to her car, thinking of the visitor she was expecting that evening. 'You two free later? Dinner at my house, courtesy of Wongs?'

Joe clicked his fingers. 'Darn it. Washing my hair.' She glared up at his mock serious face. 'Just so you know I'm not easy.'

As she unlocked her car he folded his arms on its roof and leaned against it. 'I've been thinking. Two young guys out of school. Spending time here. They find Troy under the floor. They get scared. *One* of them hightails it.' He raised dark brows. 'Why not both? There must have been an incentive to keep Harper here, alone, after he saw Troy's remains.' He stepped away from her car. 'And human nature being what it is, I'm guessing it had to be a sufficiently attractive or valuable incentive to stop Stuey Butts running too far.'

* * *

Bernie examined his watch for the third time in fifteen minutes. He wanted to be out of here with information but it would be a one-way street. He wasn't about to divulge anything about the discovery of Bradley Harper. The gas fire hummed on its highest setting and smoke curled its way towards him from Mrs Butts's second cigarette since he'd arrived. Squirming to avoid a spring of the red leather sofa on which he was sitting, he did another quick survey of the room, the wall-mounted plasma-screen television above a combination DVD-CD player flanked by speakers way out of his own price range, wires snaking the dusty laminate. His mouth curled. He could make some guesses about where this household's money was coming from. How many times over the years had he been in houses like this? He sighed, wondering how many years more. He knew it wasn't the Job that was getting him thinking like this. It was to do with having an arse like Furman for a boss. But if he didn't have the Job what would he have? Thoughts of Billington the reporter crept into his head. No. He wasn't about to go down the shopping-expedition-afternoon-telly road, and unlike Billington he no longer had a wife. He still wanted, needed, to be out there. Still wanted the policing. He liked his UCU colleagues. More to the point, he liked Connie Chong.

A regular metallic squeak dragged his attention back to the room. Dressed like the archetypal schoolboy he wasn't, Stuey Butts was rotating on the wheeled, swivel chair, a chasm of negativity. Bernie dropped his gaze to his feet. Today it was highly polished black lace-ups with thick soles. The mother was hunched in a chair, a mate to the red sofa, sending furtive glances to her son and Bernie.

As the youth rotated, exuding insolent contempt, Bernie looked around for a diversion, his attention claimed by an object to his immediate left, something he hadn't noticed on the previous visit: a roomy glass tank filled with vegetation above a layer of pebbles. Quick movement within it snagged his attention further. It wasn't unusual for people he routinely visited as part of his job to keep 'exotics' as pets: he'd seen them all. Alligators. Tarantulas. Iguanas. His eyes narrowed on something small and fur-covered pulsing in one corner of the—

'Get moving, Donna!' The shout from the hallway was punctuated by the slam of the front door. Bernie glanced at Mrs Butts who had refused to let her son answer any questions until her husband arrived home. She was on her feet, face and shoulders rigid. Stuey stilled as the door thrust open and a medium-height man came through it, stomach swelling the greying T-shirt, hanging over the scruffy jogging bottoms. No coat, despite the cold. He stopped when he saw Bernie. 'What's the *bastard* done now?' he demanded, immediately recognising him as 'Job'.

Stuey tracked his mother as she darted forward, upending the ashtray. 'Nothing, Wes. I told you about it, remember? Mr Watts is looking for that Bradley Harper. I've got you something on a plate in the . . .' The ingratiating tone faded as she scurried from the room.

Picking up subtle rustlings from within the tank Bernie gave Wes Butts another cool once-over. 'Your Stuey was one of the last people to spend time with Bradley Harper the day he . . . left home.' He gave a fleeting thought to the possible implications for Stuey of his next words. Needs must. 'Thing is, we're not sure he's telling us everything he knows.'

With a cold glance at Bernie, Stuey flicked his eyes towards his father who was quickly covering laminate, veering sideways as he stood over him, hands fisted. 'No, Dad, hang on! I was just going to—'

'Tell him! Tell him what he wants to know, you bastard, so he can sod off out of here and I can eat my bloody tea in peace!' Breathing heavily he glared downwards then looked in Bernie's direction, unfurling one fist to point at his son. 'You know the trouble with these today, don't you? I do, and I'll tell you what it is for nothing. They've got no experience of doing as they're *told*. When I was a cadet it was what I had to learn: *standards*. Following orders. Discipline.'

Bernie's eyes slid again over the T-shirt, the beer belly. 'From what I hear, your Stuey's not responding too well to any of that at his school.'

The lips curled. 'You think I'm coming down on my lad just because a few stuck-up teachers say he's done this, that and the other?'

Bernie reviewed Butts's earlier words. 'In the Services, were you?' he asked, again eyeing the scruffy T-shirt, the dirty trainers then transferring his gaze to Stuey's polished shoes. In this house it would be a case of 'do as I say'.

'Yeah. For a bit.'

Bernie looked from the elder Butts to the son, still leaning away. Give the kid a year or two and there'd be major changes here. Then the Buttses would know what real trouble was. That's if they cared. He spoke directly to Stuey. 'Tell me again about the day you and Harper were in the lake house. What did you find?'

'I already told you everything. Weren't you listening, or what?' Stuey ducked his head to avoid the palm of his father's hand.

Bernie shot forward, his eyes on the elder Butts. '*Hey!* You looking for an assault charge? You're on the right road to getting one!' He turned back to Stuey. 'When you looked in that hole, what did you see? The truth, this time.'

'You obviously know what was in there. That *thing*. Why do you need me to tell you?'

Wes Butts looked from his son to Bernie. 'What's he on about?'

'Leave it,' Bernie snapped, not looking at him, his full attention on the son. 'Tell us about it.'

He went straight to denial that he'd taken anything. His father glared at him, his face a mix of greed and menace.

Bernie fixed Stuey with a look. He agreed with what Joe had said, that there had to have been an incentive for Harper to stay. Something which may also have brought Stuey Butts back. 'I still want to know what you saw under that floor.' The brief description when it came fitted what they'd all seen in the post-mortem suite. Brown, leathered, rictus mouth in a mute scream. Bernie's eyes drilled Stuey's. 'Now tell me what *else* was down there.'

'There wasn't—'

As Wes Butts pushed himself upright, face congested, Bernie's tone sharpened. '*You*. Keep out of this.' Then to Stuey. 'Come on. What else?'

'Nothing!'

Bernie was holding on to his temper. 'You legged it and then you went *back* to get whatever it was.'

'No!'

Bernie fumed. 'Yes! Either *you* had it or your mate had it and now he's . . . gone.'

Wes Butts stared at Bernie. 'What's he had?'

Stuey Butts's eyes flicked from his father to the big officer. 'It wasn't *me*. I didn't take it. I *didn't*.'

'So it was your *mate* Harper that took whatever it was! Come on! What was it?'

'I'm telling you I don't know! When I saw that other thing, the one with the mouth, I got out.'

'So why go back?'

'I didn't. You haven't got any proof because I *didn't*.'

Bernie got to his feet, staring down at Stuey. He knew he wouldn't be getting anything else from him here. They'd have him into headquarters again. Not wanting to provide Butts Senior with any excuse for physical reprisal once he'd left, he nodded. 'That'll do for now.'

He turned to Wes Butts slouching on the chair. 'Physical assault of kids, including your own, is an offence. You do it and I'll know about it. You haven't seen the last of me. That's a promise.' Now he wanted to be gone, away from the oppressive atmosphere.

Heading for the door he turned, directing a question to Stuey. 'What size shoe do you take?'

'What?'

'Shoe size!'

'Eight and a half but . . .'

He glanced at the father. 'How about you?'

Heavy brows descended. 'Who wants to know?' At the sight of Bernie's face he backed down. 'Okay, keep your hair on. A nine.'

Hearing a sudden rush-and-skitter Bernie looked back across the room to the glass tank. The small furry creature he'd seen pulsing in the corner was gone.

CHAPTER TWENTY-FIVE

That evening, during a merciful lull in conversation, Kate deposited plates inside the oven then walked from the range, recalling Maisie's recent body angst as she gave the statuesque woman perched on one of the high stools a brief glance. Celia had been warming to a theme. One she often warmed to with Kate, given a chance. Not wanting to encourage further comment Kate moved around the large table, distributing placemats then walked to a nearby drawer for cutlery, feeling Celia's eyes on her.

'You're looking well, despite the lamentable lack of action — and I like *that*.' She nodded at the blue linen knit Kate had on. 'Was it your Christmas jumper? Anyway, what was I saying? Ah, yes. You need to keep your ear to the ground — which isn't that much of a distance.' She grinned at Kate. 'Find out what he's up to. Make a few discreet inquiries. Tap into the gossip at Rose Road. I bet some of the females there are keen on him so you need to make a move.'

After a difficult late afternoon Kate was in no mood for it. 'I'll do no such thing. It's none of my concern what Joe Corrigan does with his time and it's none of my business who he's doing it *with*!' She took a quick breath. 'For all I know he might be seeing somebody. And so what if he *is*? What will that tell you? *I've* been out with him a couple of times for drinks.' She shook her head, irritated that she'd been drawn back into the discussion.

Celia wasn't having any of it. 'Who's interested in "out"? You and Joe Corrigan staying *in* is what we're hoping for.'

'*I'm* not hoping for anything,' snapped Kate.

'Liar, liar, pants on fire,' grinned Celia.

The front door opened and a deep voice yodelled from the hall. 'Hi, honey, I'm home!'

Kate gave her delighted friend an annoyed look. 'It's a *joke*.'

Joe came into the kitchen carrying takeaway bags. 'There's more being conveyed by Ber-*nard*, my glamorous assistant.' He placed his burden on the granite worktop. 'And now I morph into barkeep. What're you girls drinking?'

Maisie strolled into the kitchen. 'Aunt *Cee*! I didn't know you'd arrived.'

'You would've done if you'd come down when I called you and not waited until you smelled food,' said Kate on her way to the plastic bags.

'Hello, sweetie. Love the little winter shorts. My choice if I were a hundred years younger.' She towered over Maisie and hugged her.

'Mom? Can we go over to Aunt Cee's, *please*?'

'When I've got some spare time,' she responded, trying to identify Chinese dishes as Bernie came in with more.

Within five minutes all had been conveyed to the table and they were taking their seats. 'Where's my spare ribs and sauce?' demanded Maisie.

'In front of you.' Kate pointed, feeling harassed. She glanced at Joe as he approached the table. He gave her a wink as he set down lager for Bernie and a glass of juice near Maisie.

'Thanks, Joe — *Mom*, this is wrong. It's got squiddy things in it. *Look*.'

Kate clicked her fingers. 'Give it here. If I hadn't had to wait three-quarters of an hour for you outside the Think

Tank, being constantly moved on, I could've phoned Wongs with our order an hour ago.'

'I'm still not eating squids.'

Joe returned with two gins and tonics, one of which he handed to Kate. 'There you go, Red. Get yourself around that.' He lowered theatrical brows and his voice. '*Extra* strong.'

Celia took a small sip of hers, closing her eyes. 'Mmm. This is the life.' She glanced around the table. 'How's the case going? Any arrests imminent?'

'Mom doesn't like two questions in a row, Aunt Cee. She says she can't cope with it.'

'Cold cases can take a while to reinvestigate,' said Bernie.

After a couple of minutes of near silence, Maisie jumped up from the table. 'I'll eat the rest in a minute. I have to get my stuff together.' Kate absently watched her go then stole a sidelong glance at Joe as he ate and drank, following the subtle movements of his mouth. Looking up she saw Celia grinning at her. She responded with a narrowing of eyes.

Bernie looked across at Joe and Kate. 'I had an interesting visit this afternoon involving a useless git of a father and a kid who I think's dabbling in gay sex.'

Celia's brows rose. 'I'm seriously wishing I hadn't mentioned work. Where's Maisie off to?'

'Kevin's, overnight. We've re-established weekend contacts and its going well so I've agreed to this midweek stay. He'll have to get her to school in the morning. I think he's turning a corner and starting to see where his—'

'Ha! And I'm Dolly Parton,' scoffed Celia, rolling her eyes.

* * *

Kevin's arrival thirty minutes later was signalled by a beep and Maisie rushed for the hall. Kate went more slowly, watching as he came inside in his dark pinstriped suit looking smooth and also defensive. He nodded to Kate, with a fleeting look to Celia in the kitchen doorway. 'Come on, Mouse. Stella's waiting in the car.' As Maisie picked up her backpack and raced outside he glanced past Celia into the kitchen, speaking to Kate in a low voice. 'Entertaining? Cops and an old, inebriate friend.'

'Which is no longer any of your business,' she responded in a similar manner.

'It is while my daughter's living here.'

Kate felt anger surge. 'There's no "while" about it.'

He sighed. 'Stop being such a redhead.'

'How about you stop being annoying?'

Celia arrived at Kate's side, nursing her one drink of the evening, giving him a steady look. 'Heard this one, Kevin? Man walks into a bar and sees a stunning blonde. He goes up to her. "Hi," he says. "I'll fuck anyone, any time, anywhere. What d'you say?" The woman replies, "Oh, hi, you're a barrister too!"'

He gave a grin but Kate saw the essence of the joke had found its mark. 'Heard it already. You should lay off that stuff.' He turned and headed out of the door.

They returned to the kitchen to find Bernie and Joe in conversation. Joe looked up. 'Rachel Troy rang late this afternoon, Red. Our visit started her thinking. She's remembered Nathan telling her that Joel Smythe was upset about something. Or somebody.'

'Did she say what? Or who?'

'She never knew.' Kate's sigh ended on a small hiccup. Hearing it he leaned on his forearms, eyes on hers, his tone 'official'. 'Excuse me, ma'am, but I believe there are sufficient grounds here for me to take you into my custody and breathalyse you.' Celia eyed Kate and grinned.

Bernie looked across the table at Joe. 'What I said earlier about Stuey Butts. You was right in what you said this morning down at the lake, about incentives and him going back. I asked him if he took anything. Know what he said? "It wasn't me." It was Harper who had whatever it was and I still think there's a sex angle.'

'How about we lighten the tone, Ber-*nard*?'

'Right — how'd you get on at the estate agent's?'

Kate's head came up. 'Estate agent?'

With a glance at him Joe responded to her question. 'The lease on my apartment is due for renewal in a few months. That means I've got some decisions to make. About the future.'

Kate propped her chin on one fist. His secondment. Less than a year left and then — he'd be gone. Back to Boston. She felt the effects of the gin evaporate as Celia looked on, exasperated.

CHAPTER TWENTY-SIX

The extraction system in the post-mortem suite was at full throttle next morning, three of its stainless steel tables already occupied. The hydraulic scissor-lift hummed in the cold store and Igor emerged, pushing a covered trolley, greeting them with a 'Welcome to the Inner Sanctum'. Aligning the trolley with the post-mortem table beneath strong examination lights he depressed the footbrake, he and another worker lifted the body onto the table, removed the green cover sheets and left with a squeak of latex boots and wheels.

They gathered in coveralls and gloves, waiting for Connie to enlighten them. 'Bradley Harper. Aged sixteen,' she said, eyeing them through the clear perspex face shield. Kate and her two colleagues followed her gaze to the porcelain-white body, its skin wrinkled and puffy, the surface textured with what looked to be goose pimples. Kate stared down at them. *He'll never feel cold again.* She transferred her attention to the head, where there were a number of abrasions.

Connie moved to the other side of the table. 'Body seen early yesterday by a runner. Officers who first attended took a statement from him: he watched the body surface. Gases would have caused it to rise, by the way. Runner says he saw no one else around the area of the lake. That's the sum of what he provided.' She pointed. 'See these?' She indicated the head abrasions.

'Beaten up prior to going into the water?' queried Joe.

She did a quick head-shake. 'My opinion is that he was killed then placed or more likely thrown into the water and sustained those when he came into contact with submerged debris.'

Bernie looked at her. 'Like what?'

'Old tree branches, domestic rubbish. The dive team did a full search. Found an ASDA shopping trolley and a fridge and they weren't even trying.'

'But he *could've* been beaten up beforehand?' persisted Bernie. Kate guessed he was thinking of Stuey Butts.

'Sorry. In my opinion, the injuries to his head are post-mortem. Right now my guess, for what that's worth, is that after throwing or placing him in the lake and seeing him float, his killer went in after him to push the body under submerged tree-roots.' She pointed at the head. 'There's evidence of waterlogged bark in those cuts. But enough speculative information. I've got a cause of death.' Three heads jerked upwards simultaneously. 'See this? Here, let me make it easier for you.' With gentle hands she manipulated the pale head, extending the puffy, white flesh of the neck, causing its folds to spread. 'That is a ligature mark. My examination confirmed a lack of water in the stomach, lack of foam in the airways and absence of middle-ear haemorrhage. He *didn't* drown.' They waited. 'In my opinion, despite there being no ligature present, Bradley Harper died from strangulation prior to immersion in water.' She did a quick head to toe survey of the body. 'Poor lamb.'

'How was the body dressed when it was recovered . . . or was it like this?' asked Kate.

'Ah, me. How often do I need to encourage medical students to ask the what-where-when-how questions. UCU? *Never*. He was fully dressed. His clothes are over here.' Connie beckoned and they followed to a nearby table on which sat a grainy, blue plastic sack. Opening it she removed the now dry contents, laying them out: black shoes, school uniform-style trousers, white nylon shirt, navy V-neck sweater, boxer-style underwear and a blue and brown parka. 'I've done an extensive examination of all of it. Sometimes we get lucky even with immersed clothing but not this time. No fibres, no hairs that aren't his.'

'No necktie?' queried Joe.

'No and if you're thinking ligature, don't. Whatever was used was of a different nature entirely.'

Bernie gazed at her. 'Like what?'

She turned to him with a faint smile. 'Gratified as I invariably am by your *keen* interest, that's a "can't say" at the moment.' She looked at the three intent faces. 'How about you ask me what else I have?'

'What else do you have, Connie?'

She sent him a smile across the table. 'Thank you, Joseph.' Three heads converged as she reached inside the blue plastic sack and withdrew a small object nestled within its clear plastic evidence bag. She placed it gently on the examination table. 'Take a look.'

Bernie broke the brief silence. 'Where'd you find it?'

'It went into the water with him,' said Connie.

'He was wearing it?' he asked.

She shook her head. 'No. It was in a concealed pocket in this.' She laid a gloved hand on the parka.

Joe was now taking a close look at the small item. 'Based on what we know of the young people involved in the investigation I seriously doubt this belonged to any of them, including Nathan Troy.'

Kate straightened from her own examination of it to look up at him. 'Why not?'

'Because its monetary value would probably rule out ownership by any young guy of their economic backgrounds.'

Bernie was still eyeing the small object. 'We'll check with the parents. I hear what you're saying, Corrigan, but it doesn't look that special to me — leather strap, plain face.'

'It's an IWC: International Watch Company Schaffhausen. See?' Joe pointed to tiny words on the face.

Bernie peered down at them. 'Never heard of it. Now, if you'd said Rolex I'd be with you.'

Joe glanced around at his colleagues. 'I saw one of these at an auction house back home. This looks to be vintage IWC.'

This got him a grin from Connie and a folding of arms from Bernie. 'Full marks, Joseph. It's a 1936 IWC Special Pilot's watch. Igor's had the catalogues out. Whoever bought it, *whenever* it was purchased, would have paid a *lot*. No cues as to ownership in terms of a helpful engraving, by the way, and don't even entertain the idea of DNA.'

Kate had continued to study the watch. She understood Bernie's viewpoint. It was plain and looked . . . ordinary. 'So this is what Stuart Butts and Bradley Harper saw under the floor when they uncovered Troy's remains. See? The buckle is broken.'

Bernie half turned to Joe. 'Like you said, an incentive. This is why young Harper stopped at the lake that day and I'd lay odds that it was the same thing that brought Stuey Butts back again. I'm thinking Stuey Butts saw Harper with it, Harper wouldn't give it up, there was a struggle. Butts couldn't find it. He lost his temper, strangled Harper then threw him into the lake.'

Kate looked pensive. 'I know Stuart Butts has a record for violence and I can envisage him getting angry and pushing Harper into the water, but strangling him? I can't see it.' Bernie's words had caused some of Kate's earlier ideas to surface inside her head, where they drifted like leaves on eddies. *Impulsivity was a likely characteristic of Stuart Butts . . . But not patience. He wouldn't have bothered to replace the floor . . . Had no motive to do it, surely?* . . . But somebody had. And somebody killed Bradley Harper. One and the same? *Or did Harper replace the floor? But why would he? Maybe to conceal the source of his find? A bid to prevent police investigation of Troy's remains*? She gazed down at the cold young body. Questions, questions. She sighed, looking up at her colleagues. 'Do his parents know yet?'

'His mother.' Connie nodded. 'We'd provisionally identified him from his photograph late yesterday and two officers went out to see her first thing this morning, brought her back here. She's formally identified him.'

Kate looked at the remains again. 'Does she know the cause of death?'

Connie shook her head. 'It hadn't been established when she came in. She needs to know.'

'I could go and see her after I leave here. Tell her,' offered Kate.

Joe looked at her. 'How about some company when you do? She already knows me.'

She nodded, leaning her head back for a couple of seconds to rid her shoulders of the tension which had settled there. 'I think Bradley Harper was killed by someone who had a strong motivation for Nathan Troy to remain concealed under that lake house. Because that person put him there twenty or so years before. We know that neither Bradley Harper nor Stuart Butts could have done that.' She glanced down at the table. '*Two* young, dead males. *One* killer.'

'Yeah?' said Bernie. 'So how do you explain that Troy's killer just happened to be hanging about at the lake when Butts and Harper showed up?'

Eyes still focused on the table she shrugged. 'I didn't say I have an answer for everything.'

He gave a wheezy laugh. 'No, it was me that said that about you.'

She looked across at him. 'You suggested that this case is sexually motivated and I'm following your line of thinking. Maybe the lake house is a favoured "haunt", like you've said. If so, how about whoever murdered Nathan Troy was also watching Bradley Harper?'

Bernie frowned at her. 'You might have something there. Could be the same bloke who assaulted him there last year. You're right on my wavelength, Doc.'

* * *

They returned to UCU and Joe went to the refreshment centre as Kate walked to the glass screen to circle the two victims' names. 'Let's hypothesise for now that Troy's murder, Harper's assault and his subsequent murder are all linked. What I want to know is how did Troy come to be buried with this watch? It's unlikely it was his. Too expensive.'

'How about a struggle between Troy and his killer and the watch come off that way?' suggested Bernie.

She shrugged. 'What might that tell us about whoever killed him? That he's young and well-off? Not impossible. What about Buchanan? I suspect his family is quite well-to-do. He spoke in disparaging terms about a Rotary watch his parents bought him back in his student days. If, as he said, that was stolen — maybe he claimed on insurance, got the IWC to replace it?' She groaned and covered her face with her hands.

Bernie eyed her. 'What's up with you now?'

'Now I've said it, it doesn't sound all that plausible. The IWC would have been many times the value of the watch that was stolen. And anyway I'm not even convinced of what Buchanan said about that. Every time I follow an idea in this case it poses more questions or goes nowhere.' She took a deep breath. 'Okay. Let's think a bit more about your idea of a struggle between Troy and his killer: how about there *wasn't* one?' She watched his face darken.

'Kate's right,' said Joe, appearing with coffee. 'Remember what Connie said?'

She nodded. 'Connie suggested that Troy was compliant.'

Reluctant to let go of the possibility of a struggle Bernie proceeded to outline a situation in which Troy's initial contact with his killer was amicable then turned to disagreement. 'I'm not saying they slugged it out — just some low-level arm-grabbing which caused the watch to come off, after which Troy is dead and he's shoved under the floor — and the watch falls in there with him. His killer has to act quick. He can't hang about looking for it. He has to get out of that lake house, out of the park. Heat of the moment. Stress.' He glanced at her. 'I'd have expected *you* to think of that. You ask me, Troy met his killer for iffy reasons.'

She shook her head. 'I'm going off your theory. It makes no sense to me that one of your sex types or "lowlifes" was wearing a vintage watch worth thousands of pounds when he made some kind of overture towards or contact with Nathan Troy? Anyway, there's nothing to suggest that Troy was anything other than heterosexual?'

He looked irritated. 'How about I remind *you* to keep an open mind where young Troy's concerned? Whatever his mother told you about him *we* don't know it's reliable, *plus* sex types ain't all riff-raff. A local *magistrate* was arrested down there a couple of years back.'

Looking less than convinced Kate picked up her notebook and flicked pages. 'Tell me of one "type" *you've* known in the last, what, quarter-century, whom you can categorically identify as remotely likely to own a watch like the one we've seen?'

Giving her a look he headed for the refreshment centre to spoon additional sugar into his coffee as Julian appeared with a printout. He reached out a large hand. 'Give us them details, Devenish.'

Joe had been listening to the exchange about the watch. 'Back in the thirties the original owner had to have been financially good 'n' heavy.'

'True,' agreed Kate.

'And it could've been sold, bought and thieved umpteen times in all the years since,' muttered Bernie, his attention on the printout.

Julian was at the screen, studying the details of the watch. 'Well-off people don't sell things. They hang on to them. Then they get more.' She glanced up at him, guessing he was speaking from experience of his own father: wealthy, one hundred per cent committed to money-making. Absent.

Kate flipped more pages of notes, lifted the phone and listened as her call rang out. 'There's probably one or two *unlikely* owners we can rule out.'

'Hello?'

'Mr Troy?'

'Yes?'

'This is Kate Hanson. We met recently.'

'Yes. Any news?'

She bit her lip, speaking quickly to forestall any further questions. 'I'm really sorry to have to ring you like this, but I have a question. Has anyone in your family or Rachel's ever owned a watch made by a firm called IWC? A watch that was known to either of your families as very special. Very expensive.' She listened, thanked him, replaced the receiver. 'No.'

Julian turned from the screen. 'Special Pilot's watch. How about the original owner was an actual *pilot* in the thirties. Like a flying ace! I watched this programme on television—'

Joe shook his head. 'Wouldn't bet the farm on it.'

Bernie gave an absent huff, his eyes still on the printout. '"Pilot's watch" is just a name.' His face broke into a slow grin as he looked up at each of them. 'Well, well, well. The search of disappeared youths aged fifteen to twenty-one years with an M5 connection. Well *done*, Sherlock.' He flapped the printout in the air. 'There's *five*. They're the right age range. *All* discovered in shallow graves in woodland areas ranging from Birmingham to Devon.'

Joe broke the silence. 'I can see the future: it's got a lot of miles in it.'

Kate now had the printout. She read the cause of each of the listed deaths: strangulation. She examined the locations of disappearance and subsequent discovery of each of the bodies. Each disappearance had occurred at points somewhere between Birmingham and Devon within marked proximity to the motorway, the same for the remains. Kate frowned. *There's something about these cases. Something . . . familiar*. She looked again at the detail, searching her memory and the multitude of cases she knew of, had lectured on, a few she had been consulted about.

She paced, frowning at the printout, running her fingers through her hair. 'The first in this series was in the early nineties . . . and the last known victim was in *2006*. Nothing since then. The killer of these five young males could have relocated. He could be dead.'

Bernie was nodding at her. 'There's something about these cases you don't know.'

She looked up at him. 'Tell me.'

He grinned at her. 'They're all *solveds*.'

She looked at the details in her hand then back to Bernie. 'Philip Noonan!'

'Got it in one.'

Kate's eyes widened. 'Now I remember. He was caught a few years ago.'

'In 2006. Which is why there was no others in the series. Way back when he was "operating", he had his own building firm and he wasn't short of a few quid neither. He had work contracts all along the M5. On his travels from one contract to another his MO was to strike up conversations with youngsters, offer them jobs, after which nobody saw 'em again till they turned up dead and buried. I'll arrange for us to go and see him. Maybe he'll have something to tell us about Woodgate Country Park.'

She shook her head. 'But he was caught, what, five, six years ago? He couldn't have killed Bradley Harper.'

Joe came to stand next to her. 'But he *could* be in the frame for Troy.'

Kate looked at Bernie, watching the grin stretch across his big face. 'If we find out he's ever had one of these pricey watches we can count Troy as a solved, leaving Harper as a current case with either a sex-type or young Butts in the frame for it.' He raised a fist. '*Result*.'

'Where's Noonan serving his sentence?' she asked.

'Secure Hospital, Berkshire. Ever been there, Doc?'

'Yes.'

* * *

Kate and Joe were sitting in the untidy lounge having informed Debbie Harper of the cause of her son's death. She was sitting across from them weeping but struggling to get control. The door drifted open and a small girl of seven or eight was standing there, mute, her eyes huge in her small face. Unaware of her presence Debbie spoke. 'He never liked water . . . cold water. He . . .'

Kate quickly stood, went to the door and led the girl by her hand back into the tiny hall where she got down on her heels. 'My name's Kate. What's yours?'

'Amber.'

'Let's go back in here, shall we?' Kate straightened, took her hand again and tapped quietly on the half-open door of the room on the other side of the hall. Inside she found two young boys watching television, a baby sleeping nearby in a buggy. Identifying the elder of the boys she entrusted Amber to him. 'It's a good idea if you all stay here until we've finished talking to your mom, okay? We won't be much longer.'

Joe was speaking as Kate returned to the room. 'We're really sorry, Debbie.' He fetched his notebook and a pen from his pocket. 'If there's anyone you'd like us to contact, ask to come and be here with you, we can do that.'

Debbie Harper shook her head. 'You're all right. My sister's on her way. She's going to stop over with us tonight. She's waiting for a girlfriend to come and look after her lad.' She bit her lip. 'I agreed with her it might be better if he didn't come as well.' Her voice wobbled and her eyes swam again.

'Is there anyone you can think of who might give you some practical help?' he asked.

'I used to have a social worker but not now.'

Joe nodded. 'How about I ring the duty team at the local office? That okay with you?' She agreed and he stood, taking his phone from his pocket and leaving the room.

Looking at the woman, Kate knew how terrible her last few days had been; first, the realisation that her son was missing, then to be told he'd been found dead, and now she knew the cause of his death. Kate felt helpless, recalling that in their previous case it had been Bernie who had organised help for a vulnerable elderly woman. *It's what police officers do. You do what you do.* Was it possible that Debbie Harper had information but wasn't aware of it? she wondered, gazing across the room at her, uncertain whether she should ask. 'Mrs Harper, do you feel able to talk to me?' Getting a nod she pressed on. 'I'm wondering if Bradley said anything to you which made you think he was worried or nervous about something. Or someone?' Silence. 'Did he ever mention anyone following him or . . . ?'

Debbie Harper shook her head, staring at the carpet. 'No. The only trouble he ever had was with that chap at the park last year but I told Mr Corrigan and the other policeman, the big one, about that. Not that there was much to tell.'

Kate nodded. 'Apart from that incident Bradley never said or maybe hinted to you about some problem or worry?'

'No. Nothing. My Bradley was a happy lad. He loved his family, he loved his home. The only thing he didn't like was school.'

Kate gave her a steady look. 'Was there anyone there who he had problems with, as far as you know?'

She shook her head. 'No. He was an easy-going lad. He even got on with that Stuart Butts.' Kate tensed, anticipating that Debbie Harper was about to query Stuart Butts having had some involvement in her son's death but none came. Kate thanked her. She'd had to try.

She was relieved when the door opened and Joe came inside. 'Debbie? They're sending somebody out. She's on her way. Her name's Elaine.'

'I know her.' Her eyes brimmed. 'Thanks ever so much.'

Five minutes later Kate and Joe walked from the house together. 'Learn anything?' asked Joe. She shook her head, feeling inadequate.

* * *

Kate arrived home to find Phyllis making initial preparations to leave. 'I'm sorry I'm late. I should have let you know.'

Phyllis adjusted her hat. 'Stop fretting. It's only ten minutes and I'm in no rush, am I?'

The nearby phone clamoured and Kate picked it up. It was Bernie. 'Doc? I've been on to the Special Hospital in Berkshire and told 'em we need an urgent visit. They said it's either tomorrow or in three weeks' time because Noonan's down for some kind of surgery between now and then so I agreed tomorrow. Friday's a quiet day for you at the university, right?' Then he told her the time of their agreed arrival at the hospital. 'We need to start out early.'

Kate put down the phone and looked at her housekeeper. 'Tell me if you can't, but is it possible for you to stay overnight, Phyllis?' She thought back to the first time Phyllis had come to her house more than ten years before, when Kate was struggling to manage her university job, her court-related work and a small inquisitive toddler who needed little sleep, all of it against a backdrop of dazed shock that Kevin had left a month before. Since then, Phyllis had proved to be one of Kate's most loyal sources of support.

'I've only got myself to suit. Course I can.'

* * *

Kate had gone with Maisie to take Phyllis home to collect what she needed and she was now settling into the spare room she normally occupied when she stayed over. Alone in the kitchen Kate felt more relaxed than usual because Phyllis was there. Maisie bounded down the stairs and into the room. 'Guess what? Me and Hannah Blum have been picked to give a maths demo to some old professors.' Kate went slowly to her, wrapped her arms around her and gave her a fierce hug. 'Mom, it's not *that* big a deal.'

CHAPTER TWENTY-SEVEN

'This morning was the first time in years I heard the birds coughing their lungs up.' Bernie peered through bright winter sun as the Range Rover passed a roadside sign. They were entering Berkshire. He glanced at Kate in the rear-view mirror, her head down as she examined the notes she'd prepared the previous evening. 'I phoned the Director of Secure Services and she give me some instructions. Here you are, Doc. I wrote 'em down.' Joe took them from him and held them out to her.

'Can you read them to me, Joe? I probably know them anyway.'

Bernie grinned as he eyed her in the mirror. 'Must be great to know everything, Doc.'

Joe was studying Bernie's notes. 'Let's see . . . there's some stuff about taking documents and photographs inside.'

Bernie intervened. 'I've got clearance for one photo. You'll have to ask about your notebook as we arrive,' he said to Kate.

Joe continued. 'And there's advice to visitors to remove *all* clothing and leave it in their vehicles.' He turned to look at Kate, eyes skimming the charcoal grey trouser suit topped by a black overcoat. 'Mm . . .'

'Stop it.'

'Then we go see the consultant forensic psychiatrist — possibly a pal of yours, Red?'

'Name?'

He glanced down at the sheet. 'Dr Ellen Forbes.'

Kate nodded. 'She was here when I came to—' She rolled her eyes at Bernie's head-shake. 'I did *one* month here following a conference I attended *years* ago, and—'

'They decided to keep you in for a bit. That figures. What's she like?'

Kate cast her mind back. 'She's good at her job. Friendly and very pleasant, is what I remember.'

They were silent as the road started to climb, the sombre high walls now visible. Within a few minutes they had reached the barrier of their first security check, the Victorian red-brick buildings very close now. Bernie showed their identification and details of the arrangements for their visit. They waited whilst a phone call was made to the main building then, watched by two uniformed security guards each with an Alsatian on a lead, they were told to drive on to a designated parking place.

Reaching it, they got out of the Range Rover, leaving their coats inside as a male member of staff appeared to accompany them to security where they were searched and their phones, watches and Kate's handbag were surrendered. She was allowed to retain her notebook and told that she would be provided with a pen. After a few minutes wait Dr Ellen Forbes arrived. Of similar age to Kate, in black trousers and pale blue twin-set, blond-brown hair secured behind her head, she gave each of them a warm greeting, particularly Kate. Accompanied by a male guard she led them along pale yellow corridors, through several doors, each of which the guard unlocked and relocked after them, and on to her departmental office, talking as they walked. 'I was looking forward to seeing you again, Kate. We're still using one of your ideas as part of our current behaviour modification scheme.'

'That's the Doc for you. Full of ideas,' muttered Bernie, becoming less enamoured of the place the further they ventured.

With a smile for him Ellen led them into her office, indicated seats then went to sit on the other side of the desk, its neat surface devoid of paperclips and other items which might be fashioned by an inmate into a tool for self-harm or violence to others. She reached inside a drawer, took out a Biro and handed it to Kate, regarding her visitors in a solemn manner, voice low and matter-of-fact. 'Philip Noonan. He has one of the UK's life terms. He'll never leave here. What else do you need to know about him?'

Kate's notebook was on her lap but she didn't need to check what she'd written. She knew what she wanted to ask. 'The murders he committed. What was his methodology exactly?'

Ellen gazed at her. 'Manual strangulation.'

One difference between Noonan's murders and our case, thought Kate. 'Each of them?' Ellen nodded.

'How's he responding to the regime here, ma'am?'

'We don't talk in terms of "regimes", Lieutenant.'

Joe dipped his head. 'My apologies.'

Ellen continued. 'It depends on what you mean by "responding". We're habituated to slow or minimal progress but we continue to work for it wherever possible. We're responsible to the patients for providing them with the skills they need to control their violent and sexual impulses.' She gave them a calm gaze. 'We also have an equal responsibility to everyone on the outside to do the best we can, given the prospect of eventual release.'

Bernie frowned. 'You said just now that Noonan will never leave here?'

Ellen nodded. 'There are a proportion of patients with psychopathic personalities who will remain unsuitable for release. Philip is one of those but it would be unethical to withhold treatment from him.'

'Has he taken responsibility for all five murders?' asked Kate.

She shook her head. 'Four of them. He's consistently denied murdering the youngest victim.'

That got Bernie's attention. 'Why's that?'

'He was fifteen,' responded Ellen. 'His other victims were aged nineteen to twenty-two.'

There was a short silence, broken by Kate. 'Ellen, has there ever been any theory or suspicion . . . *anything* at all which has led you or other professionals who work with Mr Noonan to suspect that he may have had *more* than five victims?'

She nodded. 'We're fairly sure of it.'

Kate's thoughts were now on their imminent meeting with the five-times murderer. Probably more. 'How confident are you that he'll listen to our questions? That he'll give honest responses when we ask him about our case?'

Ellen looked at each of them in turn. 'I'm confident that he'll listen. As to how honest he'll be about the victim in your case, we'll have to see, but I think it's likely he will be, given your victim's age.'

Joe gave her a direct look. 'So age is the single reason he's denied responsibility for that one victim you mentioned?'

She nodded. 'Highly disturbed as Philip Noonan is, he's not lacking in awareness. He knows that people tend to find younger victims, those below the age of sixteen, particularly upsetting.' She paused. 'He doesn't like to be judged. But, if he doesn't feel the need to defend himself the odds are reasonable that he'll give you a truthful response. Can I take a look at the photograph you've brought?' Kate passed her the head and shoulders picture of Nathan Troy and Ellen studied its detail. 'What was his overall appearance like?'

Joe responded with a glance at his colleagues. 'Tall, about five-ten, with a slim build.' Kate and Bernie nodded confirmation.

Ellen looked doubtful. 'Well . . . I've seen photographs of Philip's victims. They conform to a type: stocky, well-developed. This young man doesn't fit but that's for Philip to say.' She passed the photograph back as the phone on the desk gave a single, short ring.

Glancing at her watch, a small frown appeared on her smooth brow. 'Philip is on his way. We'll hear him and his escorts coming before we see them. I need to warn you about his appearance before he arrives. I suggest you conceal any shock you experience when he does. He'll need time to consider the photograph. His sight isn't good. He's scheduled for surgery very soon which we're hoping will give him some improvement.'

Bernie frowned as he and everyone else in the room picked up the approaching sounds of jangling keys and doors opening and closing. 'What's wrong with him? From the information we've got he's no more than late forties.'

Ellen's hands rose, palms uppermost. 'In every establishment there's a social pecking order. Here it's no different. He's a big man but mild-natured. He comes way down.'

There was a peremptory knock on the half-glazed door. It opened and Ellen stood. 'Come in, Philip.' She nodded to the two burly escorting staff who had entered, their status indicated by the multiple keys secured by chains to the inside of their trouser pockets and the plastic badges on their white shirts. Kate knew that the badges were attached solely by velcro. They led the middle-aged man they were flanking into the room. He was dressed in a black jumper, black joggers and slip-on casual shoes. The escorts accompanied him to a vacant chair, waited for him to sit then turned and left the office, taking up waiting positions beyond but close to the door, eyes on the interior of the office.

Kate and her colleagues each gave the arrival the non-invasive glances Ellen had advised. Noonan was well over six feet tall and heavily built, much of his weight accumulated around his middle. His face was a ruin. One eye was milky and narrowed, the other pulled downwards at its outer corner by a scar which coursed down one cheek to his mouth. When he smiled, as he was doing now, the cheek formed concertina pleats, the eye all but disappearing.

It had been agreed with her colleagues that Kate would do the talking. She kept it simple and brief. 'Good morning,

Mr Noonan. We're very grateful to you for agreeing to talk to us.'

There was a brief silence. His voice when it came was light, almost feminine. 'No problem.'

'My colleagues and I are investigating the death of a young man whose remains have been found in an area of parkland in Birmingham.'

The goodish eye was on her face. 'How old?'

'He was nineteen.'

'Where's the park exactly?'

Kate's heart rate climbed. This was going better than she'd anticipated. He hadn't denied being 'active' in the area. 'It's on the southwest side of the city. Woodgate Country Park. It's very close to the M5.' He nodded, saying nothing. 'The area is attractive. It's big and it has special areas for cycling and jogging.' She paused. 'And a lake.' She paused again. 'Is it a place you think you might know?'

His one functioning eye was on her face. '. . . Maybe.'

'Do you think it's possible that you've visited it?'

Tension rose in the room as everyone waited, only Kate giving him direct glances. He appeared unfazed by her question. 'Maybe,' he repeated.

Knowing that she had to get Noonan talking, Kate framed what she hoped was a non-accusatory question. 'Do you think it's at *all* possible, if you were there, that you might have been involved in an incident with a young male who—'

'Hard to say,' came the light voice. *Did he get what I just asked him*?

'Mr Noonan, what I'm asking you is—'

The mild voice cut in. 'I know. I understand. Problem is, when I was . . . able to offer my boys my special services, it was such a long time ago. I'd have to have some prompts to say if he was one of mine. I'd have to know about the actual place where he was and what he was like before I could say if he was one of my Dear Departeds. You have to give me that kind of detail.' The tension in the room was now palpable and Kate's head was in overdrive. *Dear* . . . ?

She gave a quick glance around the room. Bernie's gaze was on the floor. Joe was leaning on the arm of his chair, a hand across his mouth, his attention also on the floor. Whilst she didn't want to risk any negative responses from Noonan Kate knew they needed to get quality information from him, including a direct yes or no as to whether he was responsible for killing Nathan Troy, if that were possible. Kate had also had her own agenda when she came here. She had wanted that information without providing Noonan with any details about Nathan Troy or his death which he might later use for masturbatory purposes. Accepting now that it was an unrealistic aim, she continued. 'He was nineteen. A student. He died in November, 1993. His remains were found at a lake house in an area of the park. He was wearing a Nirvana T-shirt and jeans and—'

Noonan's face pleated. She guessed he was smiling again. 'What's a lake house?'

She kept her eyes on him. 'The place I'm talking about is a small wooden structure, like a summer house.'

His face creased further and now she noticed an odd, chant-like quality in his light voice. 'I don't understand. You need to be more explicit. If he was in there all those years why wasn't he found a long time ago?'

Kate kept her voice businesslike. 'His remains were concealed. Under the floor of the—'

The goodish eye stared and the pleats disappeared. 'That's . . . awful. That's horrific. I wouldn't do that.'

Kate's attention went briefly to the psychiatrist who was listening, her face impassive, then back to Noonan. 'You're denying any involvement in a . . . an incident in such a place?' He nodded. 'How can you be so sure, Mr Noonan?'

The cheek pleated again. 'I *honour* my boys. I give them respectful burials.' His voice dropped to a whisper and he nodded several times. 'I did the *right* thing by each of them.' He looked at everyone in turn. 'Nothing over the top. I put them in clean sheets, brushed their hair. Then there was a short prayer, a hymn to fit the occasion and interment.'

Noonan began a low, undulating hum. It took Kate a few bars to recognise 'Nearer My God to Thee'. She knew from peripheral vision that Bernie was a thousand miles beyond his comfort zone. Joe looked calm but she knew better. The humming stopped.

'Thank you, Mr Noonan.'

'The name's Philip. What's yours again?'

'Kate.' *I have to be thorough. We can't come back again.* 'I hear what you've said, Philip, but would you be willing to look at a photograph we've brought with us?' He nodded, one eye shuttling between her and Joe as the photograph was produced.

Ellen took it and showed it to Noonan, retaining hold of it. 'Can you see it or do you need more light?'

'More, please.' She switched on the large Anglepoise fixed to the desk, her thumb and index finger still on the photograph. Noonan's head bowed over it, one finger hovering. What felt like several minutes passed but in reality was only twenty seconds. Kate had counted them. He straightened and sat back on his chair, his attention lingering on Nathan Troy's face. 'This is the one you've come here about?' She nodded. 'I don't think so.'

She gave him a quick, searching look. 'Does that mean he *could* be?'

'My boys are built for physical work. Broad. Muscular. He isn't. *Wasn't.* That's what I'm getting from his face . . . and his . . . upper body.' Kate felt restlessness to one side of the room as Bernie folded his arms. 'But like I said, if he was one of my boys I would never have abandoned him under the floor of some outbuilding. They *have* to lie within God's good earth.' Kate frowned. *Was lying on sand equivalent to 'good earth'?*

Given the bizarre nature of what he was saying Kate felt able to introduce a change of direction without any preamble. 'Have you ever owned an expensive watch, Philip?'

'Yes, I have,' he said, not missing a beat. 'A nice *special* one.'

Tension thickened again. 'Can you tell us about it?'

'I bought it years ago and I had the idea that one day I might . . . keep one of my boys with me. Treat him like my son, you know? And after years and years and years,' he breathed out the repeated word, 'give the watch to him.' He paused, then, 'Trouble was, I couldn't work out how to keep him.'

Kate broke the silence, recalling a comment of Julian's about inheritance. 'What happened to the watch?'

'Nothing happened.' His eye swivelled to the psychiatrist.

Ellen nodded to him then looked to Kate and her colleagues. 'It was too expensive for us to hold here.' She opened a drawer and took out a simple manila folder, no metal clips, and turned pages until she came to what she was looking for. 'This is the inventory of Philip's belongings when he first arrived.' She passed it across the desk, pointing at one item. Head on one side, Kate looked at the list of innocuous items including: *Gold Patek*. 'Philip had to give it to his mother for safekeeping. Do you want to add anything to what you've told our visitors?'

He nodded, the milky eye and the goodish eye both turned towards Kate. 'I want you to understand. You have to understand. There are some terrible people in here.' He pointed to his own face. 'Look what they did. I'm not like them. What I did, I did with care. Out of love. Each of my boys had a *proper* burial. Tucked up snug-as-a . . . covered, cared for, like a mother or a father would do.' The one functioning eye went back to Ellen. 'Can I go back now? I want some coffee and an iced bun.'

At a nod he stood and his waiting escorts were immediately inside the room, ready to walk him to the door. He stopped and turned back to the room as he reached it. 'Will you be coming again? I'm always ready to help the police.' On an afterthought the cheek creased once more. 'Any of you got sons?'

The two staff members escorted him away, faces implacable.

* * *

They reached the car park, Bernie venting the fury he'd had to contain for the last hour or so. 'I'm *telling* you — people like him, it's like "Blackpool" through rock! No matter what anybody does, they *never* change.'

'What he told us needs careful analysis—' began Kate.

'Right now what I need is to get off my chest what I think of him, the murdering bastard.' He wrenched open the driver's door and Kate felt the onset of a headache.

CHAPTER TWENTY-EIGHT

In the diminishing light inside UCU Kate was at the glass screen, eyeing her two colleagues sitting at the table. They looked as drained as she felt. 'I'm reluctant to rule out Noonan as having killed Nathan Troy on what we've got. He wasn't sufficiently categorical that he didn't do it. I've looked at what he said. He may have his own reasons for denying killing Troy, as he has for denying the murder Ellen told us about. We need a search of the park.' She looked at each of them.

Bernie returned her gaze. 'You're saying we should scour bloody acres at that bloody park for evidence of that bastard's handiwork?' He leaned against the table, head supported on one fist. 'Searches like that cost a mint . . . but, there again, he has got a liking for expensive watches.'

Joe was pointing at the screen. 'What's the significance of "Present-Past Tense"?'

Kate looked up at the words. 'That's partly what makes me wonder whether Noonan did kill Troy. When I showed him the photograph his response was that he "isn't" built for physical work. He self-corrected to "wasn't" but when he spoke of his acknowledged victims it was in a similar way — as though they're still living.'

'And what does ringing every bit of meaning from them few words tell you this time?'

She approached the table and gave Bernie a direct look. 'His use of the present tense for his victims relates to his fantasising about them on a regular basis: what they looked like, what he did to them. It's his way of "keeping" his victims with him. It passes the time for him. I'm saying that Troy might well be another victim because he spoke of him in a similar way. Is that enough rung-out explanation for you?'

Bernie looked thoughtful. 'I did think he sounded straight when he said he didn't like how Troy was left — plus he manually strangled *his* victims.'

She nodded as she returned to the screen. 'But we've talked about this in the past, yes? Repeaters often change their patterns. Searching the park is probably the only way we have of establishing whether Noonan was "active" there. If a search identifies remains which show signature behaviours reminiscent of those he described to us, we might legitimately consider that he killed Nathan but changed some of those behaviours, perhaps for practical reasons.'

'And you've heard from somewhere that this Force has money to burn,' he rasped, getting up from the table. 'Yeah, yeah, okay.' He stood and looked at her. 'How about a drink o' tea? I'll make it.'

Joe was reaching for the phone. 'I'll ring Adam. Ask him about an infrared search. It might reduce manpower.' He dialled an internal number. 'Adam? Joe. We need some help, a search of the park at Woodgate to see if there are any clandestine burials. Would ground penetrating radar help?' he asked, switching the phone to speaker.

Adam's voice drifted into UCU. 'It depends because it involves sending electromagnetic waves into the ground and timing the bounce-back. Ideally there needs to be good contrast between the search item and the soil around it so there are variables to be considered: soil type, how long the body has been buried, whether it's naked or clothed. Our limited experience so far is that clothed or wrapped gives better results.'

Nodding, Kate approached the phone, Noonan's description of his burials inside her head. 'Hi Adam. We're thinking in terms of six-plus years buried and almost certainly wrapped. As to the soil type at the park' — she looked at her colleagues — 'we can't say, but do you think there's the likelihood of success if there is anything to find?'

'Winter's the best time to survey but six years could be pushing it, plus the park's a big place. Got a likely area for the search, bearing in mind that tree roots can be a problem?'

She thought about it. 'The open area of land that lies back from the lake, but it's only a guess.'

'Okay, leave it with me. We'll spend some time doing a visual search as we mark up the area. I'll have to get authorisation for it, though.'

Kate's face fell. 'Who?'

'The Arse, unfortunately, but how about we proceed in hope? I'll get back to you in a couple of days or so.'

Bernie carried the tray to the table, passing steaming mugs to her and Joe and taking one for himself. His bulldog-with-a-gripe face was gone. 'Relax, Doc. Wait to see what happens.' He gulped his drink. 'Our mother always had the kettle on. Always had a pot o' tea on the go. She said it watered down trouble. Mind you, you could cut our mother's tea into squares.'

Following a brief silence Kate put down her mug and looked at each of them. She was about to test out Bernie's mother's theory of the efficacy of tea. 'As there's nothing else we can do right now in relation to Noonan, how about we consider another possibility?' She walked to the glass screen. 'You've seen the notes I wrote up about my visit to Roderick Levitte?' Getting two nods she outlined the possibility of Roderick having had some direct involvement in Troy's murder or knowing something about it.

Joe sat back, hands clasped behind his head. As she finished he said, 'I'm wondering how likely he is as the killer. He sounds too volatile. My impression of Troy's murder is that there's kind of a coolness to it.'

'I've already said that this Roderick sounds mental to me,' huffed Bernie.

Kate looked across the table to Joe. 'I'm convinced he's the "Rod" Rachel Troy mentioned. He may present as odd but that's not a reason to exclude him as a possible POI. His presentation, his discourse, is indicative of an emotionally unstable personality. He thinks in black and white terms about people and situations, judges everything by way of extremes: good–bad, wonderful–hopeless, with him–against him and he has the capacity to change those stances several times in a short space of time. He's suspicious and distrusting and there's probably a degree of paranoia.' She left the screen and came to the table. 'We can't discount him. His attitude to Nathan Troy was pure vitriol. He described him using the words "vile" and "disgusting". He said that Troy revolted and repulsed him and wasn't fit to be at Woolner, possibly suggesting that he wasn't fit to "live".'

Bernie put down his mug. 'That bit did get my attention, even if it is another bloody opinion about Troy that don't match anybody else's.' He looked at Kate, frowning. 'Hang on a minute. Them words he used. Do you think they're a hint that Troy had some sex problems?'

Kate's attention went from the glass screen to her colleagues. 'You're saying what I'm thinking, Bernie, but how about switching the focus from Nathan? Firstly, consider this: most of us are aware of our own internal functioning — our thoughts, motivations and interests, yes? What happens if we experience those as *so* morally *repugnant* they make us feel *really* uncomfortable and anxious? What do we do?'

Joe's eyes were on hers. 'Recalling my Psych-101 class we lay them on somebody else?'

Kate nodded. '*Exactly*. That goes straight to my second point: I think Roderick Levitte's words about Nathan Troy are an example of his projection.' Seeing Bernie's face crease into a frown she continued. 'It's a psychological defence mechanism. He feels so uncomfortable with what he views as his own repellent ideas and desires that he has to attribute them to someone else. In Roderick Levitte's case I think that someone was Nathan . . . although I'm no Freudian.'

'Perish the thought,' Bernie muttered.

'It's a handy way of distancing himself from all the angst caused by what he considers to be deviant thoughts in his head.'

He looked across at her. 'Which gets us exactly where?'

'It *tells* us about Roderick the person, as does his personality type. He's no stranger to impulsivity and recklessness. I saw confirmation of it when I met him: betting slips on his desk, a drinking glass, and his personal appearance backs up what I'm saying. He's tired, overweight, unkempt and unable to execute simple tasks. I suspect he uses alcohol regularly as a self-soother. In short, he's a mess and probably depressed.'

Bernie frowned at her. 'You're saying he told you Troy had some dodgy ideas, disgusting ideas, but they was really *his*? You're saying Roderick Levitte could be a nonce?'

She put down the marker. 'I'm saying he's another POI. Rachel Troy told us there was friction between him and Nathan. I have a picture in my head of a time twenty or so years ago when Roderick Levitte was around Woolner, maybe basking in reflected glory generated by his father the professor and eminent artist, and in all likelihood being obnoxious to any student who made him feel inadequate. Such as Troy. We can't rule out that back then he was having extreme difficulties coping with his own thoughts and emotions and was envious of Nathan Troy. A powerful combination.'

She came and sat on the table. 'By the way, he let slip where his sister Cassandra is right now: a private mental health facility called the Hawthornes in Edgbaston. We need to see her. Soon, if we can.'

Bernie rummaged his pockets. 'You mentioning Troy when he was still around Woolner has reminded me, I had a call from Billington the journo about last reported sightings of him.' He brought out a scrap of paper. 'Listen to this. There was one on the tenth of November 1993 — that's your pal Wellan's tutorial with Troy. He told the original investigation about it. Billington says there was another sighting by Alastair

Buchanan. Seems he made a statement at the time that he saw Troy on the thirteenth, heading off campus towards Linden Road carrying a backpack. That's the last sighting Billington was able to turn up.'

As Bernie walked to the screen to add his information Kate and Joe exchanged glances. 'Buchanan didn't mention that to us,' she said.

'I rung him and asked him about that,' said Bernie. 'According to him he "forgot", plus you two never asked.'

Joe frowned. 'Pain in the ass.'

'He was sure it was Troy?' asked Kate.

'Said he was.'

'He's playing *games* with us,' she murmured.

'Don't think he liked us, Red.'

'He didn't like *me*. He *stays* as a POI.'

Having added some words to the glass Bernie returned to the table. 'Billington told me that none of the journos on the story back then were able to track down this Joel Smythe and neither was the police. Looks like he made himself scarce around the time Troy disappeared.'

Kate sat back, musing. '*If* Buchanan's sighting was reliable, where might Troy have been going on the thirteenth?' She looked up at Joe. 'Remember what Bill Troy said about Nathan and he planning a trip together around that time?' She looked at her watch. Five p.m. She needed to get home. Searching the screen for specific detail then winnowing notebook pages she stopped. 'Got it. Bill Troy told us that he and Nathan were taking a trip to London together which was planned for' — she flipped to the next page — 'oh, the eleventh of November. Bill said he bought the tickets but the trip didn't happen because Nathan never arrived at the station.' Kate sat back. 'So where does that get us . . . ?' She stood. 'I don't give a damn what Buchanan said he saw back then. I don't trust him. If we disregard what he said and there was no other sighting after the tenth, Nathan could *already* have been dead by the thirteenth.'

Joe nodded. 'Like you said, Buchanan remains Numero Uno POI.'

CHAPTER TWENTY-NINE

Revived by a hot shower and now dressed in a loose knee-length woollen dress over thick tights, Kate was inside her study that evening, resuming her inventory of Nathan Troy's belongings. Frustrated by lack of space she returned the items to the box and carried it to the kitchen. Placing it on the table she examined each item as she lifted it out, adding a brief description to the list she was making. As Mugger wound himself around her legs, she removed the last item and counted what she had. Seventeen sketches and watercolours plus: a cylindrical metallic object, a rolled-up item of paper and a plastic wallet. As she was re-counting, Maisie appeared, executing a practised pirouette as she approached the table. 'Would you give Mugger some biscuits please, then make us some tea?' asked Kate.

'Of course.'

Glancing at Maisie she saw her swoop on the little cat, scoop him up and twirl him around the kitchen before setting him down and reaching for the cat biscuits. Kate narrowed her eyes, guided by a sixth sense. *What's she up to*?

Maisie came to stand next to her. 'What's all this? Hey, these are really good. Ooh, I like that.'

'Leave them where they are, please. I'm writing them down on this list.'

‘And this is nice. Who did it?’ She was holding up one of the small watercolours.

‘They all belonged to a young person who . . . went away a long time ago. I’m looking through them to get an idea of the kind of person he was.’

‘He was *artistic*, Mom.’

‘Thanks for that. He was an art student.’

‘What’s this?’ Kate gave a sideways glance at the metal object under Maisie’s hand, her small fingers laid over it as she rolled it across the table top. ‘What’s it for?’

Kate held out a hand. ‘I don’t know. Can I have it, please?’ Maisie surrendered it and she replaced it in the box feeling her daughter’s warmth against her skin. She reached for the rolled-up paper item and smoothed it on the table. It was a poster bearing the Woolner College name and a motto: *Let’s Take Art to the Community!*

‘He’s a good drawer, Mom. Or *was*.’

She gave an inward sigh. ‘How about that tea?’

Maisie gave an enthusiastic nod. ‘Hot chocolate for me, thanks. Do you ever think that maybe these people who are dead *know* you’re looking for them and they’re like, *willing* you and Bernie and Joe on — *Find me! Find me!*’

‘Never,’ said Kate, tone repressive.

‘You lack imagination, Mom. Daddy says the same.’

‘Does he,’ responded Kate, keeping an even tone.

‘Can you speak to Daddy when he comes tomorrow morning about him taking me swimming later? He says he’s “too busy to fit it in”.’

Kate replaced the lid on the box and went to switch on the kettle. ‘If that’s what your father says then—’

‘What about the things *you* say when he doesn’t do what you want?’

She sighed, feeling guilty yet determined not to give in to Maisie’s manipulations. ‘How about tomorrow you try *imagining* you’re swimming?’

‘You’re *so* sarcastic. That’s something else Daddy—’

'So I've heard. It's late. Time you were getting ready for bed.'

* * *

After yet another re-count of the contents of the box Kate made her way upstairs, seeing a seam of light under Maisie's door. She frowned, looking at her watch. Ten forty-five. *Why do I always have to be after her? Because she's full of life and there's no one else to ensure she does what she's supposed to.*

She tapped on the door and waited. Getting no response she opened it. 'It's time you—' In pyjamas, Maisie whirled from the computer, face flushed. Kate walked further into the room. 'What are you doing?' she demanded, ideas crowding her head, none of them attractive.

'Homework, see?' She pointed to textbooks and written notes on the desk beside the computer. 'And you're supposed to knock.'

'I did. You were obviously too engrossed.' She looked at the computer screen masked by a screen-saver as Maisie watched her, eyes rounded. 'What's on there?'

'Nothing — Mom!'

Kate had moved the mouse and the screen changed. Maisie was on Google. She straightened. 'Tell me about your sudden interest in Woodgate Country Park.'

Maisie pointed at the screen. 'It's been on the news. About that boy that's been found drowned there.' She waved the handwritten notes at Kate. 'It's a scoop. Look. I'm writing it up for the school's bulletin.' Kate reached out and exited the search engine. 'Hey!'

'Now you listen to me. We've already discussed that place. It's not safe and you're to stay right away from it.'

Maisie glared up at her, angry and mutinous. 'That's *typical* of you, Mom. Can't you see? I'm keeping myself and other pupils informed of what's going on! That boy was young and he died in a dangerous place. Don't you want us to be aware of local risk?'

'Very plausible.' Kate pointed to the bed. 'In.' She watched as Maisie muttered her way to her bed and climbed in. 'And I'll consider whether you're sufficiently trustworthy to keep your computer up here.'

'Oh, for—'

'Maisie.'

Kate returned to the kitchen, placing the items on the table back into the box and carrying it to her study. She put the box down gently on the desk. *That's the last time Maisie sees anything remotely connected with what I do at Rose Road.* She flipped the lid and took a last look inside, one snagging her attention: the small plastic wallet. She opened it. It was stiff with age and empty. Tiredness encroaching, she dropped it back into the box, hearing a chiding voice, its tone reminiscent of her mother: *That wasn't very thorough, was it?*

With a sigh she retrieved it and switched on the desk lamp. Leaning towards the light she gently prised the unyielding interior pockets apart. It wasn't empty. There was one thin item inside one of the pockets. She drew it out, holding it under the lamp, her pulse picking up tempo. Not a single item. Two. She placed them gently on the desk, side by side, and examined them then raised her eyes to the window and looked out on darkness, a single thought in her head.

You didn't go to London or anywhere else did you, Nathan?

She reached for the phone on her desk and left two brief phone messages.

CHAPTER THIRTY

Kate strode into UCU early next morning. 'Thanks for coming in on a Saturday but . . . I've got something.'

Joe gave her an appraising glance. 'You'll get no argument from me.'

'You two are *really* going to like this.' She dumped her coat and bag on the table and pulled out her notebook. From between the pages she carefully withdrew the two small items and held them up between thumb and forefinger.

Bernie gazed up at them. 'Train tickets. So far I'm not getting a lot of "like".'

She waved a hand at him. 'Come *on*. Take a closer look.' Putting on glasses he and Joe came to stand either side of her. 'Not just any old train tickets. *These* are a cheap day return from Birmingham New Street to London Euston.' She looked up at them, eyes bright.

Joe whistled. '*Hot* dog! The date . . .'

'Is the eleventh November 1993,' she finished.

'Where'd you find 'em, Red?'

'The box we got from Troy's parents? Inside a wallet. *See?* They were never used. No punched hole. No pen squiggle. Bill Troy told us that Nathan never came to the station to meet him that day. Nathan had his London tickets but he never used them.' She pulled the desk phone, tapping numbers from the screen. When she got a response she pressed the loudspeaker button. 'Mr Troy?'

'Dr Hanson? Any progress?'

Kate saw head-shakes and kept it brief. 'We're continuing with our investigation and I'm sorry to bother you again but I need you to confirm something about the train tickets for the trip to London you told us about. You said you bought them?'

Bill Troy's words flowed into UCU. 'That's right. We'd arranged to meet up at New Street Station early in the morning but Nathan never arrived.'

'Did you contact him to find out why?' Silence. 'Mr Troy?'

'No. I didn't. I was annoyed with him after I'd laid out the money. I . . . thought he couldn't be bothered to turn up.'

Her eyes on the tickets, thoughts jostling, she chose her words. 'You were planning to give him his ticket when he arrived that day?'

'No. I sent them to him so he could get his seat on the train. In case I was delayed.'

She nodded. 'Thank you, Mr Troy, and I'm sorry again for having to ring you.' She reached out and disconnected the call. 'Nathan already had his train ticket on the eleventh of November. Any ideas as to *why* he didn't meet his father?'

Bernie massaged his jowls. 'He could've just decided not to go. *Or* his killer might already have got hold of him which would make what Buchanan said—'

Kate nodded, feeling adrenalin surge. 'I think Nathan may have been dead or in mortal danger by the eleventh, which prevented him meeting his father, thus making it *impossible* for Buchanan to have seen him on the thirteenth?'

'Possibly,' cautioned Joe.

Bernie broke the following silence. 'We'll have him in.' He reached for the phone, dialling a number from the screen, and waited. 'Mr Buchanan?'

Kate recognised the self-assured tone drifting from the speaker phone. 'This is Alastair Buchanan. Who is this?'

'Detective Sergeant Bernard Watts, Police Headquarters, Rose Road, Birmingham. Remember I called you after you'd had a visit from two of my colleagues? About our investigation into Nathan Troy's death?'

The voice became terse. '*Yes*, and I'm in the process of preparing a letter of complaint about one of them.' Kate rolled her eyes.

'Tell you what, Mr Buchanan. How about you come into Headquarters for a chat and bring your letter with you. How're you fixed?'

CHAPTER THIRTY-ONE

Following an early Monday start at the university, Kate walked into UCU to find Bernie and Joe standing by the glass screen. Bernie gave her a nod. 'I was just saying that when we see Buchanan we'll get out of him exactly what he knows about Troy's disappearance, but for now we carry on working our other theories.' He pointed to the names of the three local sex offenders he'd written up there. 'We've seen Phillips and in another five minutes I'm off to see *him*.' He jabbed Morrell's name. 'Okay, his history of adult female victims doesn't fit our case but I still want to check him out because so far he's avoided my phone calls and messages.'

The door swung open and Furman appeared in a finely tailored charcoal grey suit, moving with his customary self-regarding swagger. 'Watts. I want you to get over to that art student's family — what's-his-name—'

'Nathan Troy,' Kate snapped.

'Get a list of their son's associates at the time he—'

'We've already visited Mr and Mrs Troy,' said Kate.

'And I want them visited again.' His eyes were on the screen. 'Get more names, Watts, no matter how tenuous the parents think they are.' He looked across the table. 'And I want an hour of your time, Lieutenant. I've got a Home Office delegation upstairs, plus some local business people with deep pockets. I'm leading a discussion forum: "Armed Policing in the Twenty-First Century". Five minutes?' Joe gave an imperceptible nod.

On his way out Furman turned. 'I'll be calling a meeting next week to evaluate progress on the Troy case. Seems to me it's floundering. Try and come up with something useful, Watts.' He pulled the door closed with a firm hand.

Bernie stood, patting his pockets. 'When I get to be in charge around here I'll have a nice brick wall built and he'll be the first — where's my bloody keys?'

Kate pointed to the window sill then looked at Joe. 'He wants to show you off.'

'Armed Response: The Star in Furman's Firmament.' He shook his head. 'What a sap.'

She watched as he and Bernie disappeared through the door. *I'll go back to the university. Grade some more assignments.* She gazed at the screen, thinking of Bernie's thwarted plan to visit Morrell, seeing the name of the third sex offender, Ronald Dixon, and his local address. Probation officer details were also there. Kate recognised the name. Dixon needed to be spoken to. Either he might have been responsible for the assault of Bradley Harper the previous year or he may know something about it. He was also old enough to have been pursuing a deviant agenda in the early nineteen nineties at the time Nathan Troy was killed. But first, there was something else she needed to check. She lifted the phone and dialled, writing Dixon's address into her notebook as she waited. Her call was picked up after three rings.

'Wellan.'

'It's Kate Hanson. Have you got a minute?'

'For you, yes.'

'We've got some new information about Troy. He was going somewhere on the eleventh of November. Did he mention anything to you?'

'Eleventh of November? No, it doesn't ring any bells.'

'You don't recall anyone else saying that Troy was planning a trip with his father?'

'Can't say I do. My impression of Troy's father was that he had no time for what he was doing at Woolner and he and Troy didn't get on. I don't recall hearing anything from the students. Henry wouldn't have mentioned it as he took no interest in the students' lives.'

Thanking him, Kate replaced the phone, lifted it, dialled again and waited. 'West Midlands Probation Service. How can I help?' She identified herself, asked for the officer by name.

A businesslike voice arrived in Kate's ear. 'Salma Huq.'

She grinned into the phone. 'Hello, Salma.'

The brief silence was ended by a squeal of recognition. 'Kate! What the—? How *are* you?'

Kate pictured the bright young woman who'd been part of her Criminology course at the university three, four years ago. 'Fine, thanks, and you?' She listened then, 'I'm calling from the Unsolved Crime Unit, Police Headquarters, Rose Road. I need some information about a client of yours. Ronald Dixon. He was arrested early last year for a sexual assault on a fifteen-year-old boy at Woodgate Country Park.' There was a small silence. 'Salma?'

'Along with your other talents you're also psychic?'

Kate's eyebrows rose. 'Why's that?'

'He's currently out on licence after serving nine of his fifteen-month sentence but as we speak I'm completing the forms to have him breached.'

Wondering what Dixon had done to earn his imminent return to prison she listened to the reasons now arriving inside her ear: he was known to be associating with some dubious people in recent weeks and it was suspected that he was grooming a local single mother of two young boys who had described him to a friend as 'Mr Wonderful'. Salma was on a roll. 'He's been increasingly non-compliant recently: avoided two appointments with me and missed his sex offender treatment programme group meeting this morning. *More* than enough to send him back.'

'Can you give me a brief profile of him?'

Salma did, indicating that Dixon was rated as high-risk for reoffending due to his offence history which included hands-on and non-contact offences against adult females and under-age children of both genders. His treatment programme reports showed that his attitude towards children in particular remained highly distorted. 'Basically he regards them as fair game. What else? Oh yes. Propensity for violence. He's had two adult female partners over the years, as far as we know. One lasted a few months, the second three years. He beat *her* up and she called it quits. Described him as a "split-personality". Our records don't show his having any children of his own, mercifully, although you can never be certain.'

Kate nodded, recognising the raft of significant indicators which had contributed to Dixon's high-risk status. She also recognised his difficulty in appropriately asserting himself with adult females, intuiting that he probably veered between grateful doormat and implacable tyrant.

Salma had more to tell her: during the course of his treatment Dixon had reluctantly confirmed using violence-themed pornography featuring teenagers of both genders. 'Plus another client in his group dobbed him in for visiting a massage place in Lozells, staffed by under-age females. Get the picture?'

'All too clearly. I've got an address. Fourteen Jannings Road. Does he live alone?'

'Yes. We've had surveillance on him for the last ten days. No indication that he's got anybody with him.'

Kate thought of her plan for a visit to Dixon. 'I also wanted to know if he's considered a risk for violence to professionals?'

'Mmm . . . Belligerence yes. Nothing to support direct physical violence. Why?'

'I'm going to see him.'

'After tomorrow you won't have the chance.'

Kate replaced the phone. It was now or never. She seized her bag and coat, pausing only to remove the photographs of Bradley Harper and Nathan Troy from the screen.

CHAPTER THIRTY-TWO

Stepping out of her car into suburban early-afternoon quiet, Kate scrutinised the sombre Edwardian semi. It looked abandoned, almost derelict. She'd checked the address. This was it. Collecting her bag from the boot she approached the house, eyes on the large dust-filmed ground-floor bay window. *Are you here, Mr Dixon?* As she walked the overgrown shale drive she looked beyond dusty glass to light seeping into the room from windows at its other end and falling onto an ornate, high-backed wicker chair. There was a figure lolling there. *He's home.*

Approaching the shadowy vestibule she pressed the bell just inside and listened to the faint ring reverberate inside, her eyes still on the dim scene through the large downstairs window.

Her head whirled at the whine of little-used hinges. Unnerved, she watched the door drift slowly inwards. She'd seen no movement within the room beyond the window. *He couldn't have moved from the chair, from that room to the front door without my seeing. There must be someone else here.*

The frisson of anxiety across her scalp and shoulders increased at the appearance of a grey, whiskered face now visible in the gap between door and jamb, its voice hoarse.

'You're not from the Social about my claim so you can piss off. Wha'ever you're flogging, I don't wan' it.' The gap was already narrowing.

She put out a quick hand to the door. 'Mr Dixon?' He made no response. 'You and I need to talk.'

'You reckon?' The door continued on its way. She held up identification. He caught the West Midlands Police logo and the door halted. He looked towards but not directly at her. 'I've got nothing to say to you people.'

'I'm sure you don't but I have some questions for you.'

'And I've got no answers so sod *off*.' The door was on the move again.

'Here or Rose Road, Mr Dixon,' said Kate, voice firm. 'You choose. You've got five seconds before I phone for assistance.'

The face glowered through the narrow opening. 'All right, all right. No need to get shitty.' He opened the door, jerking his head. She walked inside the dim hall, picking up the strong smell of sweat. He shut the door, leaving Kate where she was, and headed for another at the far end of the long hall. Alert for sounds elsewhere in the house, glancing at the closed door on her immediate left, she followed him, seeing newish trainers below baggy grey trousers. Adidas trainers. He shoved open the door onto a chill kitchen where he sat, arms folded, face defiant.

She chose a chair between him and the door, going straight to the purpose of her visit. 'Mr Dixon, you assaulted a young male at Woodgate Country Park last January.'

Quick rage appeared on his face. 'I did *nine* months hard, just because some *stupid* kid . . .' She let him rant, barely listening to him fume about the unreliability of his victim. She'd heard similar diatribes many times. He stopped, breathless, out of steam, looking at her through narrowed eyes. 'You're short for a copper. What's your game?'

'I told you. I'm from Rose Road. I want you to look at a couple of photographs.'

The sallow face suffused again. 'Why am I always the one that gets picked on?' he demanded. 'There's a good few others you could—' He stopped as she placed the first photograph on the table in front of him. She tapped it. 'This teenager was assaulted last year by an adult male at Woodgate Country Park. All I want from you is that you tell me if you've ever seen him.' She reinforced the words with another tap.

Face weary but guarded, he gave it a cursory glance. 'Never seen him in my life.'

'Take a proper look, Mr Dixon,' she ordered. 'You might change your mind.'

He gave a heavy sigh and did as she'd said. 'Like I said, no. I've never laid eyes on him.' His face creased, exposing crooked front teeth. 'Or anything else, for that matter.' He caught Kate's change of facial expression. 'Don't you look at me like that. This is my house and I can say what I like in it.' He shook his head. 'You lot can never take a joke.'

'Have you seen him?' repeated Kate.

'No. I haven't and it wouldn't matter if I had. My preference is kids that are on the slim side, blond—'

'He *is* blond,' snapped Kate. *Was.*

'And a heavyweight, by the look of him. I go for a light build.'

She used his response to extend her questioning. 'You also go for sex offender treatment. How's that progressing?' She'd anticipated a lie and got it.

'Going well.' Avoiding her eyes he produced a pack of cigarettes from his trouser pocket. He cast about then looked at her. 'Got a light?'

Kate wasn't about to be distracted. 'What about your associates, Mr Dixon? Might any of them have approached this young man?' She watched as he got up to lean over the greasy gas hob, cigarette between his lips.

He straightened, blew smoke, and returned to his seat. 'I *don't* "associate". That's what I've learned from the programme. I don't hang about with nobody. I don't see nobody. I've got enough aggro in my life and—'

She stopped a likely flow of further self-pitying phrases. 'What about friends? A partner?' she asked, still mindful of the figure she'd seen through the window.

He hunched his shoulders, dragging on the cigarette, avoiding her eye. 'Got none.'

'You were violent to your last partner,' she said, matter-of-fact.

The whiskery, yellow skin reddened, rage flaring his face again. 'Only because of what she *done* to me!'

Kate waited. When nothing more was forthcoming: 'What did she do?'

He was silent for some seconds, the rage dissipating as quickly as it had arrived. 'She cut my toast into quarters. *Nobody* treats me like some little kid. Who the *fuck* did she think she was?' She waited again, knowing his limitless inadequacy, guessing childhood years so negative that *any* behaviour towards him in adulthood which reminded him of his own early vulnerability was likely to trigger spiralling fury and physical violence. She gave Bradley Harper's photograph another tap.

He glanced at it again then shook his head. 'I can't think of anybody I know who might've had a go at him but . . . but now I think about it there was this bloke I saw down there a couple of times, chatting to one or two big lads. I just happened to be around — this is months before I got arrested.'

'Tell me about him.'

He shrugged, raising a hand to uncombed hair, the pungent smell of body odour rolling towards Kate. 'Nothing to tell.' He gave her an up and down glance. 'Posh type. That's probably why I noticed him. Bit out of place.'

'Why "posh"?'

'His clothes. His voice. I heard him on his phone the one time.'

'What was he saying?'

'Dunno. Too far away.'

'Describe him further,' Kate ordered.

Dixon looked nettled. 'You lot ever say "*please*"?' He gave a heavy sigh. 'The couple of times I saw him he was wearing a dark jacket, shirt and tie — even though it was warm out.' He squinted upwards. 'Shortish. Around five-seven. Fat face, like, round. Close cut hair . . . receding a bit here.' He pointed to his temples, triggering a sudden picture of Alastair Buchanan in Kate's head. *How tall was Buchanan*?

'Colour of hair? Age?'

'Dark, maybe turning grey. I'd put him somewhere towards mid-thirties to mid-forties.'

'Give me your best guess.'

'Fortyish, best I can do. I don't go round noticing how people look.' He paused. 'Another thing. He was wearing glasses.' His index fingers and thumbs formed circles. 'You know: Harry Potter style.'

She reached for the photograph. Buchanan hadn't worn glasses when they visited. Which was no confirmation that he didn't wear them. She still wanted to know more about Dixon. She asked her next question without any expectation of an honest reply. 'How long have you been committing sexual offences at the Country Park, Mr Dixon?'

His eyes slid. 'That was the *only* one.'

Kate's eyebrows climbed. 'And you got arrested for it?' she asked, marvelling that he wouldn't have realised that prior to coming here she'd have obtained details of his extensive record.

Face hostile, he flared again, not missing a beat. 'Yeah? It happens!'

'Seems to me that makes you the unluckiest person I know, Mr Dixon.'

His face twisted into a sneer. 'That's because you don't know me.'

She got out the other photograph and laid it before him. 'What about this young man?' Nathan Troy smiled up from the table.

Dixon blew smoke, giving the photograph a dismissive look. 'You're *joking*. Way outside my range: he's too big, too old and too dark. I've told you my preference: young and blond with a light—'

'You said.' Replacing both photographs inside her bag she stood, walked from the table then turned. 'What size shoe do you take?'

He gave her a sideways glance but no quibble. 'Eight.' The glance changed to a leery grin. 'That mean I can ask you what size—'

'Who's in this house with you?' Kate demanded.

He stared up at her. 'What you on about now?'

'Don't mess with me,' she advised, repeating the question.

He looked bewildered. '*Nobody*. I'm here on my own. I can't have nobody . . .'

'I *saw* someone. Through the front window when I arrived. Who is it?' she demanded again, confident now in her ability to keep the upper hand, no matter what.

'It isn't anybody, I'm telling you. You come in here issuing your orders and you don't know *nothing* about me.'

She took slow steps back to him, her face set. 'If you think I'm a fool you're making a *big* mistake. I know all about you, Mr Dixon. I know your offence history, your extreme-high-risk status, and I know why you do the things you do because I *know* what's inside your *head*. I *know* your personality in all its inadequacy. I *know* that you can't or won't control your sexual behaviour — I suspect it's "won't" because you like that aspect of your life *just* the way it is. *Don't* tell me what I know!' She took a breath. 'I know *you*. Never doubt it.'

In the silence of the cold kitchen she glared at him. The bluster had left him and he was sagging on his chair. She thought again of his likely early years and gave a mental shrug. Like everyone else he'd had choices. So far he'd made all the wrong ones. 'I'm waiting.'

Dixon stared at her, face sulky. He stood, shambled past her to the door, and out. 'All right. Seeing as you *know* everything.'

She followed, recalling Bernie expressing a similar opinion. More than once. She followed him along the shadowed frowsty hallway then waited as he halted at the closed door of the front sitting room, his hand on the handle, looking down at her.

'Sure you want to see?' His breath hit her face.

'*Open* it.'

He gave the door a push and she walked inside. Here it was. The wicker chair she'd seen through the window and its occupant in a school-uniform travesty, sagging at a drunken angle, hair awry, face fixed on the floor, red mouth agape.

Kate turned away and walked back to where Dixon was standing, knowing that all she'd seen and heard supported Salma's plan to have him breached. A glance at his face as he stood in the doorway showed that he was enjoying the scene. She recognised his poor self-awareness, one of the reasons he was oblivious to the fact that his freedom would be curtailed within hours.

She glanced up at the wide bay window as she left the room and continued to the front door. 'Your "girlfriend" needs more air, Mr Dixon, and you need curtains.'

* * *

On her way home Kate reviewed the information she'd gained on Dixon. Everything she knew about him, including his link to Woodgate Park, made him a prime candidate for having murdered Nathan Troy. She shook her head. She intuited that, even twenty years ago, Dixon hadn't had the self-assurance and the personal presentation required to have initiated a social exchange with Nathan Troy, nor the ability to control him. *All roads in this case lead to the damned park*. She changed lanes, earning an irate beep from a car too close behind.

* * *

He was waiting for his call to be picked up. He got a response after six rings.

'What?'

He kicked out at a nearby sapling. 'Where *are* you? You said to be here and you'd bring me some—'

'On my way.'

'Hurry *up*. You know how much I hate it here and — Hang on a minute.' He turned, lowering the phone. There was somebody calling him. By *name*. He frowned, staring upwards, listening.

'Stuart? *Stuart!* I need to talk to you.'

He lifted the phone, stress climbing. 'Listen there's somebody here.'

'I'm nearly there. Stay.'

'I don't like this. I don't know who the fuck she is but she's calling *me*. She knows who I am!'

'What does she look like?'

Agitated and now on the move he shrugged. 'I dunno. Just a woman.'

There was silence inside his ear, then: 'Small, slim? Long, red hair?'

'Yeah, I suppose, but—'

'Get out. *Now*. Come to the road.' The call was cut.

* * *

Knowing of Bernie's determination to get the teenager into Rose Road again, Kate placed her hands either side of her mouth. '*Wait!*' He was gone and she knew it was pointless to go after him in the now diminishing light. She thought of what she'd heard him say when he was last inside Headquarters. She thought of the expensive jacket, the trainers. If her reasoning was on the right lines and taking his young age into account he could be vulnerable to—

Some distance away to her left she heard the muted *thunk* of a car door and listened. An engine roared into life then faded away to a smooth purr.

CHAPTER THIRTY-THREE

The following afternoon Kate was adding Dixon's details to the screen. She turned as Julian approached holding a photograph. She took it and studied the detail of the Adidas ZX trainers. She shook her head. They were nothing like the ones she'd seen on Dixon's feet.

She put the photograph on the table and went to the computer to look at other photographs Julian had accessed: the males convicted of sexual offences at the Country Park since 1990. She scrolled downwards once, recognising Phillips and Dixon, thinking again how few arrests there had been. She'd anticipated far more to warrant the park's reputation as a place of deviant sexual activity. *How many other men might have been arrested there but not charged for lack of evidence? Or not even arrested*? 'This is all there was?' she asked.

He gave her a sidelong look. 'If there are other records I've got no clearance.'

She understood what he was saying to her: that he wouldn't access prohibited databases for her as he had done in their previous case. She nodded. 'I wasn't suggesting that you break any rules.' In any case, what was on the screen confirmed Bernie's previous search. She read the name under the other photograph: 'Morrell'. None bore a similarity to the man Dixon had described. She sighed. *How trustworthy was Dixon anyway? About as much as a sack of ferrets.*

She was returning to the glass screen to add the description Dixon had given of the man he'd seen at the park when the phone rang. 'UCU. Kate Hanson.'

John Wellan's voice drifted into her ear. 'Kate, I've found my contemporaneous notes of the last tutorial I had with Nathan Troy if you still want them?' The door swung open and Bernie and Joe walked in. She pointed to the information she'd added to the screen as she listened to what Wellan was saying. 'There's not much detail although they helped me recall the actual conversation I had with him. If you've got a minute . . . ? Let's see . . .' She heard paper rustle. 'I asked Troy what he thought he might contribute to the exhibition we were mounting in the new year — 1994. He said, and I'm reading this directly from the basic notes I made at the time: "I might not be here." Now I've looked at it again it sounds as though he was planning to . . . go. What do you think?'

Kate raked her fingers through her hair, frustrated at her inability to fit what he was saying about Troy with the description his parents had provided. 'Leaving when he loved his course and was doing well?'

'I probably thought the same at the time.'

'Did you question him about it?'

'I actually added a question mark at that point in our discussion so I think I probably asked him what he was intending. The next words of his I wrote down were: "Got plans but rather not say right now."'

'What did you think he meant? Did you have any ideas?'

'None. I can tell you that my attitude would have been that I had to accept it, that he was old enough to make his own decisions, and anyway it seems pretty clear that he didn't want to tell me what the plans were. You probably know from your own experience that students can surprise us with the decisions they make.' She nodded agreement into the receiver. 'Want to see the actual notes?'

‘Please.’ She looked at her watch. ‘I have to drop in at the university in half an hour. I could come to Woolner on my way—’

‘I’m occupied with faculty meetings. Just came out for a smoke and to ring you. I could drop them at Rose Road about seven this evening?’ Hearing nothing he continued. ‘Or, if you live locally I could bring them to your place, whatever’s best for you.’

Kate fingered the tiny line above her nose. She wanted to look at the notes as soon as possible. Meagre as Wellan’s description suggested, she wanted to be the judge of their usefulness. ‘If you don’t mind bringing them to me?’

‘Not a problem. I’ll call in on my way to Brindley. I’m taking some stuff to the White Box Gallery for the old tart’s Retrospective. Always the dogsbody. Give me your address.’ She did. After a pause he said, ‘See you later.’

Kate put down the phone, relating the gist of the conversation to the others, then, ‘Do we know anything about Stuart Butts’s whereabouts following my sighting of him at the park yesterday?’ They shook their heads and she realised that she was concerned about him. ‘I know he comes across as unpleasant but — he’s young and that makes him vulnerable. Just as Nathan proved to be.’

Bernie’s eyes rolled. ‘If you say so, Doc, although I don’t see any similarity myself. Describe what you seen again.’

‘He was alone, some distance away, on his phone. He was wearing the same ski jacket. When he saw me he looked really rattled and then he ran. A few seconds later I heard a car start up — I think he was picked up by somebody.’

‘You didn’t see the car?’ asked Joe.

She shook her head. ‘But it sounded expensive.’ What else did she need to tell them? She pointed to the screen. ‘See what I got from Ronnie Dixon.’

Joe gave her a steady look. ‘You went to see Dixon *and* to the park alone?’

Kate bridled. ‘I can take care of myself, *thank* you,’ she snapped.

'Yeah, right,' sniffed Bernie. 'Like you did last year when Harry Creed got hold of you.'

She approached the screen and tapped what she'd written. 'Dixon gave me *this* description of a man he saw hanging around the park at the time Bradley Harper was assaulted.' She pointed to specific words then looked at her colleagues. 'I've seen the photographs of the sex offenders arrested at the park. Morrell doesn't look much like this but he might have something to offer.'

'I visited yesterday and he doesn't,' said Bernie, shaking his head.

Kate gave him a surprised glance. 'I thought you went to see the Troys like Furman—'

'Sod Furman. They don't need us at their house for nothing.'

She nodded. 'Tell us about Morrell.'

Bernie pointed at the screen. 'He's on the short side but he's not "posh" and he don't wear jackets and ties. Jeans is more his style. There's nothing about him that's likely to snap your suspenders. He's got no form for under-age fiddling.'

Kate replaced the marker on the small lip at the bottom of the screen as Joe stood, picking up his phone and jacket. She knew better than to ask: Armed Response Team.

She looked at Bernie. 'What are *you* doing now?'

'Going Upstairs to see if they've picked up any info on Stuey Butts following your sighting.'

She nodded, brows together, musing. 'He knows the concerns about the park. Why isn't he distancing himself from it? Why's he still going there?'

Whittaker leaned into the room as Joe exited with a hand wave. 'DS Watts? There's a man in reception asking for you. He says he knows there's current police interest in Woodgate Park, that he's got "experiential knowledge of the vicinity", and—'

'You can't find me.'

Kate shot him a disapproving look then nodded to Whittaker: '*I'll* see him. He might have something useful to contribute.' Seizing her notebook she followed him from the room, ignoring Bernie's voice calling after her.

On arrival in reception Whittaker veered behind the high counter to stand next to a female civilian co-worker dressed in the regulation white shirt and epaulettes. She directed Kate with a subtle head-nod in the direction of one of those waiting and rolled her eyes. Of the three males, one was a sulky teen, another was nursing a black eye and the third was wearing a hat skewered with a feather atop lank grey hair. Even without the nod from the civilian worker it was obvious to Kate which of these she'd come out to see. She walked over to him. 'Mr . . . ?'

He leapt to his feet, executing a bow. 'Kirk. James Kirk,' he broadcast in grandiose manner. Eyes drifted to him across the reception area.

'If you'll follow me, Mr Kirk?' said Kate, recognising the name but not sure how or why. She indicated the small room off reception and waited for him to enter.

He remained where he was, his audience small but attentive. 'I've heard of police activity at Woodgate Park and I know the area extremely well.'

'Good. If you'd like to come this way?'

'I used to frequent that area to the point where I became something of an expert. But not any more. *Oh*, no.'

Kate was now well aware that she had a problem on her hands and was formulating a few words she'd have for Bernie when she saw him. 'You know, I *think* it might be a good idea if you write out a statement—'

'Not since the last time I was abducted.'

She looked at him, knowing there was nothing to be gained in trying to locate sense in what he was saying. She eyed Whittaker and his co-worker. 'Okay, Mr . . . Kirk. If you come over here the officer will give you what you need to make a brief statement—'

He was off again. 'I'll *never* forget it. It's all in your records. I'll wait while you fetch 'em and take a look. I came here to report it last year. Fifth of March, at 2030 hours. Rather than you wasting time locating my file, I'll tell you:

I was *probed* and subjected to a number of other degrading, scientific procedures . . .'

Heavy footsteps were coming down the corridor from the direction of UCU. Kirk turned and pointed. '*He'll* tell you all about it. He's got a *dossier*. Ask Chief Inspector Watts what he knows, but,' he tapped the side of his fleshy nose, 'once you know, *you'll* be at risk as well.'

Bernie and his voice arrived in reception. 'What you after, Nige?'

He pointed at Kate. 'Tell this woman what happened to me at that park in Woodgate.'

Bernie was searching his pockets. 'Come on. If I can find my keys, I'll drop you home. You go and wait by my car while I talk to my colleague here.' Nige, aka James Kirk, quit the building at a smart clip.

She glared at Bernie. '*Thanks*.'

'I tried to tell you. You're too keen for your own good sometimes, like him.' He nodded towards Whittaker.

'A pointless question but we're sure he's got nothing worth contributing?'

'We *are*. That's Nigel-No-Mates, mad as a bloody herring, speaks fluent Klingon, been abducted by aliens ten times to my knowledge *and* he's a right pain in the bum to get rid of once he's in here. You could have been stuck here for hours with him.'

Kate rolled her eyes. 'Unlikely. It's obvious he's got problems and—'

'Now he's freezing his whats-its off out there. You finished?'

'Yes. I'm going back to the university where I can rely on getting sense out of people,' she snapped, turning on her heel.

* * *

Early that evening Kate was inside her study, immersed in grading student assignments when she heard the rumble of engine followed by the doorbell's ring. She looked at her watch then out of the window, unable to see who was at the door but getting an unrestricted view of the glossy blue-green vintage car. Walking into the hall she heard feet thumping the landing.

'*That'll* be Lauren.'

'Not unless she's driving a nineteen fifty-something Jaguar,' murmured Kate, continuing across the hall.

'Wha'?'

Kate heard no more beyond an upper-floor door slam. She opened the front door. 'Hi. Come in.' She led the way into the kitchen. 'Coffee? Tea?'

Wellan followed her, carrying a folder. 'Can't stop, thanks. Here's the notes from Troy's last tutorial I told you about. I've also brought what I found of previous tutorials. I don't think there's much in there. I'd like them back when you've finished with them.' He laid the folder on the table. 'After rereading a few I'm ashamed to admit I haven't given him much thought over the years.' The doorbell sounded again and he looked in the direction of the hall. 'I'm on my way . . .'

'That'll be for my daughter.' They heard footsteps on the stairs, the opening of the front door, and a cacophony of little squeals before the footsteps pounded upwards.

'The young mathematician I've heard about? Must be great to have a bright child.'

She glanced at him. Clearly he wasn't totally resistant to the gossip mill. She recalled comments she'd heard about him: his professed liking for the single life and a succession of girlfriends over the years. 'It has its moments.'

His hand patted the folder. 'Must be off. Henry wants the stuff in my car at the White Box Gallery by seven fifteen.'

She looked at her watch. 'You'll never make it. The Hagley Road's a nightmare at this time.'

He grinned at her as they walked into the hall. 'Did I ever intend to? He can wait. The latest from today's faculty meeting is that he's planning to spend more time in college, even take a few classes. I think he's losing his grip but Johnson's going to let him because he's too damned spineless to say no.' At the door he paused. 'Ignore that. You probably know what they say about me: "A moody sod with a chip as big as the West Midlands".'

'Could you spare another minute?' He nodded and followed her into her study. Flipping open the black, glossy box she took out the rolled poster. Unfurling it she held it up. 'Know anything about this?'

She saw his eyes widen. 'Good *grief*. "Let's Take Art into the . . ." Where'd you get it? That's almost prehistoric!' He grinned, shaking his head. 'My idea for getting art into kids' clubs and community centres. I ran it for about twelve months, *years* back.'

She looked at it then back to him. 'Why's it got Roderick Levitte as the contact name?'

He shook his head again. 'Because the Old Man wanted Roderick to have a project. He told me to hand it over. Roderick took it on, ran it for two months and it died.'

She chose her next words. 'When Henry Levitte retired they gave the chair to Matthew Johnson.'

He nodded. 'That's right.' He studied her. 'And *you* think I might have been nursing a grudge over that ever since?' He gave an easy laugh. 'I knew I'd never get it. My face doesn't fit but the truth is I didn't want it. I enjoy the teaching. I don't want to sit in some office at Woolner, messing about with development plans and worrying over finance.'

Kate nodded, understanding his viewpoint. She wanted to ask him something else but was unsure of how he might respond, given that they didn't know each other that well. 'Is it difficult working at the college and feeling as you do — sorry, I know it's nothing to do with me but from what you say you seem . . .'

He grinned at her. 'Out with it. I won't be offended.'

She shrugged her shoulders. 'You seem distanced from everyone there.'

'Which is exactly how I like it. I teach my students, I do what has to be done and the rest of the time I live my life. Speaking of which, I have to go.' He turned and stopped. 'Good God! Is that a Levitte over there?'

She followed the direction of his gaze and nodded. 'My ex-husband bought it, oh, ten years ago.' He took a few steps towards it and she followed him, waiting as he gave the painting consideration. 'I'm guessing you have an opinion on it?'

He looked at her. 'Oh, yes. Don't I, just! It might be my turn to wonder if I'm about to offend *you*.' She grinned up at him as he turned back to the painting, giving it a cursory glance. 'All I'll say is that Henry always had very well-hidden shallows.'

They left the study and walked into the hall, Kate opening the front door.

'How's your investigation going?' he asked as he stepped outside.

She shrugged. 'We're following up all the leads, as the police tend to say. The picture we're getting of Nathan isn't helping. Very contradictory.'

Wellan nodded. 'Yes, well, that's often what we get with students of that age, isn't it? One minute happy with what they're doing and the next wanting something else — like Troy and his plans, yes?' He gave her a wry smile and a wave and walked away.

Back in her study, hearing the classic car's engine sputter throatily into life and fade, Kate sat at her desk, gazing at student assignments. She'd grade two more and then look through Nathan's notes. She raised her head, listening. The upper floor was silent. *Stop being so suspicious*. The doorbell rang again.

With a sigh she threw down her pen and went to the door. It was Bernie. She led him into the study. 'You just missed John Wellan. He dropped these off — Troy's tutorial notes. If I get time this evening I'll go through them before I bring them in to UCU. I'm curious to know if they're of any use.' She looked at him. 'What's brought *you* here?'

He'd eyed the notes and wandered from the desk, now gazing at posters and other decorations on the wall. 'I was passing. You in UCU tomorrow?'

'I was planning some assignment-marking. Why?'

'Buchanan's agreed to come in first thing for a chat. Said he wanted it "out of the way" before he goes to an "important" meeting he's got in town. And after that you and me have got a gig. At the White Box, Brindleyplace. Your emer-i-tus prof is available to see us.' He'd reached the far corner of the room and was pointing to the small painting there. 'This it? This what Levitte was on about when we went to see him?'

Kate walked over to him. 'Yes. *Sun on Land*. Kevin bought it as a wedding anniversary present.'

'Mmm . . . Not my kind o' thing,' he murmured, moving away.

Kate's eyes moved slowly over the painting, stung at having received two criticisms of it during the last hour. 'Well, *I* love it. It's . . . reassuring. See how the land curves, like a bowl held by two cupped hands? It looks—'

Bernie glanced in her direction. '"Reassuring". Yeah, you said. Why's it stuck over there?'

She frowned. 'What do you mean?'

'Why's it over there in the corner where you can't see it?'

'I *do* see it. You're supposed to keep paintings away from direct sunlight.'

He sniffed. 'Right. I'm on me way. See you tomorrow. Buchanan's arriving at nine.'

After he'd gone Kate returned to the study and the corner to stand in front of *Sun on Land*, eyes drifting over the rounded contours, the multiple curving striations and the broiling, orange disc of sun centred in the azure sky. *Why is it here*?

Unable to come up with a satisfactory answer she shook her head impatiently and returned to her desk.

CHAPTER THIRTY-FOUR

At nine the next morning Whittaker showed Buchanan into the informal interview room where Bernie and Kate were waiting. On seeing her Buchanan halted. Bernie stood and waved him to a chair. 'Thanks for coming in, Mr Buchanan. Have a seat. Hope it hasn't put you out.'

'I told you on the phone. It's convenient for my meeting later — *and* this.' He reached inside the heavy camel overcoat and drew out an envelope. 'I want to give it to the most senior officer here.'

'That'll be *me*. Detective Sergeant Watts.' He held out a hand. After some hesitation Buchanan passed it to him. 'Okay, Mr Buchanan. Let's get down to why we've asked you to drop in. On the thirteenth of November, 1993—' The door swung open. 'Ah, you know Lieutenant Corrigan?'

Buchanan looked up and nodded as Joe took a seat. 'What's all this about? I told you all I know the other day. I can't help you with this.'

'You might do if you cast your mind back to something you told the police back in 1993.'

He stared from Bernie to Joe then back. 'You're not serious?'

‘Oh, I *am*.’ He glanced at the few words on the single-sheet statement in front of him. *You* said, “I was leaving Woolner at ten a.m. on the thirteenth of November and I saw Nathan Troy walking away towards Linden Road.”’

‘I vaguely remember saying something like that. What of it?’

‘You stand by that statement?’

Buchanan looked at each of them and Kate saw his gaze waver. ‘If that’s what I said . . . Yes . . . I *do*. I was doing my best to help the police . . .’ He lapsed into silence, looking edgy, then, ‘The view I had at the time might have been—’

Bernie’s eyes were back on the statement. ‘You confirmed to officers that “visibility was good” and you positively identified the individual you saw as Nathan Troy.’

The atmosphere inside the room was expectant. Buchanan’s face darkened. ‘I’m very uncomfortable with this. If *this* is an example of what happens when people assist the police . . . It was *years* ago.’ Kate watched him, noting the arms clamped across the chest, the tension in the face. She’d agreed not to actively participate in view of his complaint about her but she’d wanted to be here. To observe him. Note his reactions. ‘I was only nineteen when I made that statement. Why am I getting the third degree?’

‘That’s not a situation that applies, sir,’ said Joe, tone cool. ‘We need assistance and you’ve agreed to give it.’

Buchanan gave him a bad-tempered glare and stood. ‘I’m leaving.’

Kate saw uneasiness in Buchanan’s face as Joe also stood, looking down at him. ‘What’s your response if I tell you that on the thirteenth of November 1993, when you claimed to have seen Nathan Troy, we have reason to believe he was already in harm’s way, possibly dead?’

She watched Buchanan absorb the quiet words, his face paling. He tugged at his coat collar, squaring his shoulders. ‘So I was wrong twenty-odd years ago. So what? I don’t know anything else,’ he snapped. He walked to the door then turned and pointed. 'What is relevant is *that* letter. I expect a response from a senior officer.'

Bernie followed him, placing a restraining hand on the door. 'One more thing before you go. Tell us about Cassandra Levitte.'

'What? Now look here . . .' he blustered.

'Did you and her ever have a relationship?' Buchanan's face was furious but he remained silent. 'Nothing to say, Mr Buchanan? No matter. We'll be asking her dad about her when we see him later on today.' Buchanan glared at him then turned and disappeared through the door.

Bernie walked back to the table. 'Nervous, ain't he?' He picked up the envelope brought by Buchanan, waving it towards Kate. 'He's a slippery bastard doing what slippery bastards *do* when they feel threatened: saying nothing or going on the attack.'

'What would most people say in his situation, in response to questions on what they told police years ago?' Joe mused. '"Sorry. I must have got it wrong"?'

'Or variations on — *Bernie!* What are you *doing*?' She watched, aghast, as he opened the envelope. 'You can't *do* that. It's an official complaint.'

'Stop frettin'. He hasn't addressed it to a named officer.' His eyes skimmed words and he grinned up at her. 'Blimey! He don't like *you*, does he?'

He dropped the letter onto the table and she and Joe looked at it. '"Cavalier and aggressive"!' She was incensed.

'Take no notice, Doc. If he knew you better he'd realise the reality's a lot worse.'

* * *

'Hey, Red!'

Kate turned from locking her car to see Joe approaching. 'What are *you* doing here?' She smiled, pleased to see him.

'Thought I'd come for the ride. Meet the artist. View the art.'

They fell into step. 'Where's Bernie? We agreed to meet at the White Box Gallery.'

'I dropped him off there and came in here to park.'

'Has anybody managed to make contact with Stuart Butts?'

He shook his head. 'According to Upstairs, his folks are sticking to their original story that he's staying with people they know. Upstairs are planning to send a couple of officers out to scan the area where he lives.'

She nodded, feeling apprehension climb. 'The last thing we need is for him to be at risk of becoming another victim.'

They walked out of the Brindley car park. Ahead of them the White Box's stark interior, visible through the plate glass walls, was a beacon amid the muted offices and restaurants in the dreary afternoon. She looked up at him. 'Another toney place?' she asked.

'Undeniably. But not much art visible from here.'

Kate had a sudden thought. 'Did Bernie tell you I've got John Wellan's notes from Troy's tutorials?'

'Yep. Anything of interest?'

'They confirm what he already told us but also that Troy mentioned having plans in the New Year which might take him away from the college. Leaving aside the question of the reliability of Buchanan's sighting, for all we know Troy *might* have been intending to leave Woolner.' She frowned. 'But he didn't get far, did he?'

They had reached the glass doors where two men in work coats were standing to one side to allow them in. Acknowledging them she realised she'd seen them before. At Margaret Street when she'd met Roderick Levitte. 'Hi, Stan!'

He turned, surprised. 'It's *you* again.' He looked from Kate to Joe. 'Is this the police you're helping?'

She nodded. 'Is anyone else here, do you know?'

Stan lowered his voice. 'Not the idiot you saw the other day but his old man is.' He pointed to the gallery's interior. 'Up those stairs.'

'Thanks.' She had a thought. 'Is there anyone else?'

'There's a tall, heavy-looking bloke in the small display room along there having a look at some of the stuff that's already hung.' With a wave he and his colleague walked away and Joe showed identification to the uniformed security guard who'd appeared during the exchange.

They entered the gallery and crossed the huge ground-floor wasteland. 'I've already suggested to Bernie that I talk to Henry Levitte first,' said Kate. 'As we're slightly acquainted he may volunteer more detail.'

'Makes sense. I'll go see what Bernie's doing. He seems to be getting into art.' He moved in the direction of the room Stan had indicated and Kate headed for the stairs.

Reaching the first-floor space her attention was diverted by the massive vaulted glass ceiling, a narrow walkway snaking some way below it, protected by a metal balustrade. She moved forward, staring upwards into cool, grey light.

'Good afternoon, Kate.'

She spun, startled by the soft voice from somewhere below her left shoulder. Henry Levitte was seated on a canvas chair, almost hidden behind an enormous canvas. As he stood she saw that he was wearing what looked to be an old-fashioned artists' smock, below which she saw pinstripe trousers and elegant patent leather shoes. 'I do apologise if I startled you, my dear.' He was at her side, a hand on her forearm, gazing down into her face, his own good-humoured, the wide mouth stretched.

She returned the smile. 'No need. I was so taken with the light, I didn't notice anything else.'

The hand dropped and he regained his seat, taking up his brushes. 'Incredibly striking in here, isn't it? Even on a dull day like this one. I like to work here whenever I can.'

'Do you mind if I take a look?' She went to stand behind him, to study the androgynous nude, the side-on face sketchy yet compelling. He appeared to be painting from memory. 'You don't need your model to finish this?'

He gave a quiet laugh. 'No, my dear. Not at this late stage.' He glanced up at her then beyond. 'As the gallery is closed to the public I'm assuming that you're not alone and that *that* is a colleague of yours?'

She turned to see that Joe had come up the stairs and was examining the few pictures hanging some distance away. She turned back, nodding. 'That's Lieutenant Corrigan. Shall I introduce—'

He gave a brief shake of his head. 'I'd really rather you didn't. Ah — he appears to have other things to do.' Raised voices were drifting up from the ground floor, and they watched as Joe went to the stairs and disappeared from view.

Alerted by the tired quality in Henry Levitte's voice Kate glanced down at his face. Now she saw the shadows beneath the deep-set eyes, an absence of life in the eyes themselves. He looked exhausted. She thought of the imminent Retrospective. It must be a considerable emotional and physical demand for someone of his years. 'Are you feeling all right? Can I get you anything?'

'I am extremely *tired*. In fact, I do feel a *tiny* bit unwell. I'll sit over there for a few minutes, if you don't mind.' Not knowing whether she should offer him assistance, Kate watched as he rose somewhat unsteadily from his chair and walked with uneven gait towards an extensive red sofa some feet away. Kate was now aware of the emptiness of the upper floor. *If he's ill I need to alert someone.*

'Kate, please — sit.' Waving a hand towards the sofa, the smock hanging from his bowed shoulders, he moved slowly to a small refrigerator nearby and removed two small cans. 'This is all there is up here, I'm afraid.' She looked at the cans. Alcohol was probably the last thing he needed right now.

She peered inside the fridge. 'How about the water? On the bottom shelf there.' Replacing the cans he removed one bottle, handing it to her. She gazed up at him. He looked dreadful. 'Professor Levitte, if you don't feel able to talk to me today we'll postpone it. In fact, I think I should . . .' She began to rise.

He put a finger to his lips as he came towards her. With a ponderous turn he lowered himself onto the sofa. Before she could move he was down, so close she could feel his heat.

She sat forward. 'I'm going to go downstairs. I'll ask someone to come up and—'

'No, no. *Please*. Start your inquiries.' The weak voice wavered. 'Be a good girl — help me take my mind off the frailties of age.'

Still concerned, Kate gave him another close look. During her visit with Bernie to the Levitte home she'd formed the impression that he was a proud, rather vain man. John Wellan's words came into her head. *Old tart*. It might agitate him if she insisted on getting help. Repositioning herself she got ready to start the process. 'As long as you're sure?' This got a weak hand wave. 'When we came to see you the other . . .'

The large head fell back and his body sagged. 'You want to talk about my daughter Cassandra.' Kate heard a deep, wracking sigh. 'She was hyper when you saw her and now she's plummeted. She's *very* unwell. We're taking each day as it comes. She's like her mother, my first wife. She was Canadian, you know. She never truly settled here.' He lapsed into a heavy silence, too close for her to see his face.

Kate softened her voice. 'Professor Levitte, we'll need to talk to Cassandra at some stage because she was a friend of Nathan Troy's.'

He lifted his head. 'Is your life a *fulfilling* one, my dear?' She looked at him, confused. 'I know you're divorced but you're a bold, daring girl, I think. Do you live your life to fit your dreams for your daughter?' She made no response, confused by the conversational turn. 'My children are very special to me, especially Cassandra. I had to care for them, you know. Their mother was totally incapable of doing it. Cassandra was the most needy. She sought me out. She was my special girl. I regarded her as a companion rather than a daughter. Seeing how she is now is heartbreaking for me.' Distracted by his words, Kate was now worried that he might be about to cry. 'She was a delight to me. That is, until she entered adolescence. Your daughter must be nearing that stage? Prepare yourself for mood swings, anger, resentment, wilfulness. Our relationship, mine and Cassandra's, changed. She became . . . unmanageable. It was never the same afterwards.' He gave a deep sigh.

Kate searched for reassuring words. 'Surely all of those things you mentioned, the moods, wilfulness, they're a natural part of dev—'

'Oh, what does that mean, Kate, "natural"?' She was nonplussed by the sudden, unexpected verve in his words. 'I'm unashamedly old-school. I've always known what Cassandra needed and it's been my commitment to provide it but her anger has come between us so I can no longer do that.' Her eyes strained sideways as she tried to judge how he was, aware that he was still upset. Should she leave him now and get — 'Kate, my dear, we don't know each other well but I feel able to speak with you about painful experiences such as these.' He appeared to lose his agitation and again she was conscious of his heat. 'I feel so terribly tired again.' Feeling the weight of him she made the decision she should have made minutes ago. *He needs medical attention. Go downstairs and tell Bernie and Joe to alert paramedics.* With subtle leg movements to avoid disturbing him she moved sideways and forward to the sofa's edge. She'd seen how frail he was when they'd visited him at his home. She shouldn't have listened to his protests. She should have alerted someone as soon as—

Sudden, powerful hands came from behind to clamp her breasts, then slid downwards, exerting a tight grip on her waist. Rendered motionless by shock Kate felt one of the hands slide downwards to her thigh where it grasped and squeezed. Hard. She shot forward, limbs flailing, hair flying, face hot and furious. '*Don't . . . How . . . Stop!*'

The steady tap-tap of approaching heels and a strident, northern voice cut through Kate's distressed words. 'Whatever are *you* two doing?' Theda Levitte was now standing a couple of yards behind the sofa, eyes gleaming.

Hot and disorientated Kate stared at the heavy face, aware of her two colleagues also approaching. She tried to pull words together. 'I thought . . . he was . . . unwell.'

Theda Levitte's eyes were on her face, the vivid mouth pursed. 'Actually, *you're* the one who's looking rather odd.'

In a succession of easy movements Henry Levitte rose from the sofa, removed his smock, adjusted the formal suit then smoothed his hair with both hands. 'Theda, darling! How lovely.' Ramrod-straight, he looked at his watch then back to his wife. 'And how timely! Let's get some lunch. Which would you prefer? Cielo? Edmunds? Or perhaps the Shogun? *You* choose. Ah, here are the detective sergeant and the lieutenant.' He thrust out his hand to Joe as Kate looked mutely on, a character in a strange play whose part she hadn't yet learned.

She heard Joe, his voice coming to her from a distance. '. . . Kate?'

Theda Levitte's amused voice drifted to her. 'She and Henry were having a nice little chat, apparently.'

Kate put a shaking hand to her forehead. 'He was talking about his . . . children.'

Theda Levitte's eyes glittered. 'We *must* be going, Henry.'

All Kate knew was that she had to get away. From the gallery. From *him*. He was coming towards her, arms outstretched. 'How about we reschedule our little talk, Kate? Are you all right? You look a little . . .' She backed away, watching as he turned and looked down at his wife, mouth stretched, tongue moistening his lips.

She turned and rushed for the stairs.

'*Kate*. Kate! *Stop*.'

She'd reached the doors, cold air hitting her face, when Joe's last word halted her. She stood, grasping one of the door handles for support, watching as he walked towards her, holding her coat and bag, face full of concern. 'We were dealing with a couple of drunks trying to get inside. What happened up there? What the hell was it?' She didn't respond. She felt . . . stupid. He took her arm. 'I'm taking you home. Bernie can drive your car.' She looked dully at his outstretched hand then located her keys and handed them to him.

Later, inside the Volvo, aware of quick glances coming from Joe, Kate replayed events in her head, recalling Henry

Levitte's weight, his heat, his hands and their proprietary grip on her chest and waist, the press of him on her thigh. She thought back to the visit to Hyde Road with Bernie, to behaviours scarcely noticed, misunderstood at the time: his physical closeness; his touch. Today, she'd been lulled and manipulated once more. Anger surged. How could she have been so *slow*? Henry Levitte, renowned artist, wasn't ill and he certainly wasn't tired.

* * *

Hours later Kate was in a corner of her sofa in near darkness, knees drawn up to her chest, trying to bring sense to what had happened earlier. She was still angry. Not only about what he'd done. About her own lack of awareness. Here she was in her mid-thirties with what she'd always considered to be a reliable antenna for sexual threat as developed as that of any woman. *More*, given the nature of her training and work. Yet it had arrived like a train, leaving her shocked, incapable of action and furious. She thought about the face of the androgynous model in his painting. She knew whose face it was. She recalled his words when he talked of Cassandra. They'd brought to mind a number of sexual offenders she'd evaluated over the years. She rested her head against her knees. All of his sentiments phrased in innocent words, but taken as a whole their underlying meaning was clear. She recalled the smooth segue from the ease he'd described in talking to her to his making sexual contact.

Kate rested her head against the back of the sofa. It had been hours ago yet she was still shocked at what he'd done, at his severe lack of sexual boundaries, the *risk* he'd taken, given her work and her role with the police.

She straightened. Where exactly *was* the risk for him? He was a renowned artist in line for a significant honour. There was no witness to the afternoon's events apart from herself. Justice often failed in cases of sexual crime. If she made an allegation against him he would merely deny it. She pressed her lips together, feeling her head start to ache. He hadn't put himself at *any* risk. Because he regarded himself as fireproof because of who and what he was. In all the years he'd taken sexual advantage he'd never, *ever* considered himself at risk of denunciation. So he'd continued. She glanced at her watch: eleven thirty p.m. She got off the sofa and went to her study for a notepad.

CHAPTER THIRTY-FIVE

The sound of the Chamberlain clock striking nine drifted across the campus and into Kate's room where Bernie and Joe were listening to her, their faces grim. She took a deep breath. 'I walked into that situation, into his sexual attack, because I *thought* I knew him. I now realise how misplaced my confidence was. I'd bought the whole persona of a well-known, venerable and charming elderly man, whereas in reality Henry Levitte is a well-practised sexual manipulator. He has to be because he managed to con *me*. Any professional awareness I thought I had counted for nothing. He still managed to draw me in. What he did yesterday shows his supreme arrogance. He believes he can do as he likes. We've already said that this case is about sex. Henry Levitte is involved in it somehow.'

They regarded her in silence then, 'If you say it, that's enough for me,' said Joe. Bernie nodded.

She continued. 'Last night I reviewed his behaviour when we visited his home: his touching, his close proximity. I didn't pick up on it at the time but with hindsight I know that Henry Levitte is a *frotteur*. He has a sexual drive to touch and press against females. But what happened yesterday was much more than that. The painting he was working on — I believe Cassandra was the subject, not only because the face looked familiar but because of the way he spoke about her, his choice of words, his perceptions of her as a child. Henry Levitte has zero sexual boundaries. I believe he sexually abused Cassandra during her childhood.'

Bernie's eyes searched her face. 'I noticed he was a bit . . . touchy-feely around you at the house but I put that down to you and him knowing each other.' He shook his head. 'What I'm struggling with here, if what you say is right, is why he risked carrying on like that around us, *you*, bold as brass, sitting there painting *that* picture, saying the things he did and *then* doing what he done to you.' He shook his head again. 'I don't get it.'

Kate understood what he was saying. Hadn't she had to work out for herself what they were dealing with? 'Henry Levitte is a highly devious sexual manipulator who got away with abusing his own daughter and, in all likelihood, other unrelated females over the years. He has the confidence to continue because he believes he's immune from censure. I doubt he sees the police as a threat. Consequently, his actions are brazen, he revels in giving intimations of what he does, what he *is*. Because of his years of getting away with it. John Wellan's attitude to him probably sums up what a lot of people think: that Levitte's a harmless old eccentric.' She pushed her hair back from her face. 'It's all a game to him.'

Bernie gazed at her. 'No offence, Doc, but what you're saying — yes he done what he done to you but there's no proof he's done anything to anybody else. Okay, Wellan don't like him but a few others we've talked to seem to think he's okay.'

'I'm saying there's already an indication of a pattern of behaviour. We daren't hang around, not acting on what we know until we're sure.'

'Levitte's not afraid that Cassandra might blow the whistle on him?' asked Joe.

Wearily, Kate forced herself to sit upright. 'No. If she managed to make an allegation against him who would listen to her, give anything she says credence? That's what he relies on.' Kate glanced across the table at Bernie. 'You've seen her. What do *you* think?'

He shook his head. 'From a Force point of view, Cassandra as a victim-witness is a non-starter. And how do we follow up all this about Henry Levitte when we've got Troy's reinvestigation?'

'They're connected,' she said.

She heard the exasperated sigh, saw his eye-roll. 'Where's the facts for that, Doc? The evidence?'

Joe was studying her. 'How do you want to move this forward?'

She glanced up at him. 'Henry Levitte is a duplicitous, cunning, sexual threat. Doing nothing isn't an option. I want him moved to prime POI in this investigation. I want him at Rose Road for a formal interview and I want Gander to okay it.'

Bernie was shaking his head. 'You'll need to come up with some good reasons to support that.' He hesitated. 'How do you feel about telling Gander and Furman what Levitte done — to you?'

Her heart squeezed. 'I'd have to think about that.' She gazed out of the window. 'I always thought I understood how difficult it is for people who've had experiences like Cassandra's to speak about it. Now *I really* understand. Trouble is, if no one speaks there's no justice for anybody, is there?'

Kate stood and went to the window to look at the stark winter campus. 'Going back to what you said, Bernie, about facts, evidence — Cassandra talked to Nathan Troy, didn't she? Remember what Rachel Troy told us about him? That he was a "moral" person who would take a stand against anything he considered wrong? He was a friend of Cassandra's.' She turned to her colleagues. 'On those occasions when they talked, what if Cassandra divulged her family history and experiences to Nathan? What if it was *that* knowledge which got him killed? I'm concerned about Stuart Butts's whereabouts but right now I'm even more worried about Cassandra. We have to see Gander. *Today*.'

* * *

They walked inside the chief superintendent's overheated office, watched by the ever-present Furman. Within half an hour Kate had delivered her theory and her rising concerns about the whereabouts of Stuart Butts and the safety of Cassandra Levitte, without any direct reference to her own experience at the White Box Gallery. She would disclose it only if she had to. In the following silence, she gave the chief superintendent a steady look then, 'Henry Levitte has to come here. To Headquarters.'

Peripheral vision showed Kate that Furman was barely holding on to exasperation. Now he erupted. '*He* doesn't *have* to do anything.' In her unsettled state the words pounded Kate's head. 'Knitting up some mad theory about Professor Levitte as a sex maniac because *you* say it fits what you *think* you know about this case and this dead student's character isn't *proof*.' For once he was looking directly at her. 'Without any proof, what makes *you* think you can demand a formal interview?'

Kate had felt emotionally flat during the last few hours. Now she felt anger rising but kept her voice low, controlled. 'I've already *told* you. I believe he had some involvement in the murder of Nathan Troy. He has the financial background to have owned the watch buried with Troy's remains—'

'You don't know that! Anybody could have left it.'

She closed her eyes then looked at him again. 'What I *suspect* is that he's a familial sexual abuser, that he preys on females, that he was involved in the murder of Nathan Troy which could mean that he's somehow linked to the murder of Bradley Harper who, with Stuart Butts, found Troy's remains.' She turned to Gander. 'We don't know where Stuart Butts is. He needs to be found—'

Furman intervened, turning to Gander. 'There's already been a couple of patrols on his estate. We're not sanctioning any more financial outlay on *that*. He's streetwise—'

'*Vulnerable*.' snapped Kate. 'And you're forgetting Cassandra Levitte—'

'There's nothing to "forget"! She's a mental health case. She's got professionals already involved with her. She's not this Force's concern.'

Kate turned to Gander. 'I believe Stuart Butts and Cassandra Levitte would be safer if her father was arrested. Surely, there's sufficient grounds in what I've said to at least interview Levitte so we can get proof—'

'*Get*?' Furman barked, whirling to Gander, his finger jabbing in her direction. 'Hear that? She's asking for a formal interview so she can use it as a vehicle to *make* a case against him. That's a one-way ticket to an official complaint!' He turned back to her, face pale and furious. 'Are you out of your *mind*? Do you realise how well-placed, how well-connected he is? That whole family's known in this city. He's on boards and—'

'How's that relevant to what I've told you about him?' she demanded, hot-faced.

His lips all but disappeared. He was seething. 'You *civilians* are all alike. You don't get it, do you? Well, think on *this*.' He pounded the rosewood with a fist as Gander rose from his chair. 'He's got money, he's celebrated, he's on the next Birthday Honours List. *That's* what we're dealing with. No — *you* listen.' Kate saw Bernie's mouth open, saw Joe rise from his seat and gave them a furious head-shake. 'Any action this Force takes is on the basis of *facts*.'

Kate was now on her feet. 'When it should be on the basis of *understanding* what we're dealing with—'

'That's *enough*!' At Gander's voice the room lapsed into silence. He glared at each of them, his eyes settling to Kate. 'If you're as sure about Henry Levitte as you appear to be, the next step has got to be very carefully orchestrated. I'm not sanctioning any demand to have Henry Levitte brought in here. If he comes at all it'll be on a *voluntary* basis. Apart from anything else he's getting on in years.' She opened her mouth and he raised his hand. 'I know you've got little patience with procedure. *We* don't have that luxury.' He glanced towards Furman. 'This Force has to pursue all its cases with an awareness of potential consequences. We need solid grounds to act. If the grounds aren't robust there needs to be careful consideration as to how to move forward.' Gander sat back on his chair, determined and uncompromising, his eyes on

Kate's face. 'You and your colleagues go away and come back when you know how this theory of yours can be actioned.'

'I *know* how.'

Furman's face was incandescent. He turned it on the chief. 'Sir, you have to put a *stop*—'

Gander sat forward, the back of his jacket rising above his massive shoulders, his eyes on her, clasped hands beating an inaudible rhythm on the desktop. '*How*?'

'We contact Levitte today. We request a brief meeting with him. We suggest it takes place at Woolner College — *No*, wait. There's a better place: the White Box Gallery. The reception for his Retrospective. During *that* meeting we inform him that he's now a prime person of interest in the murder of Nathan Troy and raise the issue of his coming *voluntarily* to Rose Road.'

Furman stared at her. 'He'll say *no*—'

'No he won't. I think he'll agree to seeing us at the Retrospective,' said Kate, her eyes still on Gander. 'Because it will be where his art is. He'll consider it his terra firma where he's in control. Henry Levitte likes to be in control and his wife has already requested that any future talks with him be elsewhere than their home.' Both Bernie and Joe nodded confirmation.

'What about the formal interview itself? Here!' stormed Furman. 'If he doesn't come in with legal representation, which would be a bloody *miracle*, he's bound to ask what proof, what evidence you've got for making him a prime person of interest, and the answer's *none*.'

'I've already told you. He's a sexual danger.'

'According to you! All anybody else knows is that he's seventy bloody years old! At *least*!'

Kate closed her eyes. 'I think that when we question him here we'll get supporting evidence.'

Furman looked as though he was about to have a stroke. 'You *think*?'

Gander looked troubled. 'Inspector Furman has a point. If Professor Levitte does agree to come in and you can't produce any evidence, things could get very difficult for us, and also for you, Kate.' She understood what was being said. As the civilian driving force behind the plan, if she was unable to justify UCU's action then she could be in Levitte's legal sights if he so chose, out on her own with possible implications for her professional reputation and financial security. Something clutched inside her chest. She breathed. She wouldn't back down. She couldn't. The silence in the room seemed eternal.

She looked at the chief inspector. 'So, is it a yes?'

* * *

After a detour to run cold water on her hands, Kate walked inside UCU as Julian was speaking. 'She *didn't*! Kick-ass or *what*!' His head spun towards her. 'I'm only saying what Joe just said about the meeting.'

'I've been thinking.'

'When do you never?' asked Joe looking at her, arms folded, head on one side.

'The Levittes implied that Nathan Troy was a drug user. Connie found only lithium in his remains and she didn't report any indications of poor self-care.' She went to the screen, searching the mass of information there. 'Alongside their disparagement of Troy they also presented as hardly aware of him. What if that was merely a bid to distance themselves? What if they *had* had direct contact with him? After all, Troy and Cassandra were friends. What if he was a visitor to the Levitte house? And if so, why not say so?'

Kate returned to the table and lifted the phone. 'No one else has confirmed Troy having a serious drug problem. His mother told us specifically that he was against them. Buchanan told us that Troy took ecstasy although we don't trust anything he says. If Troy was taking drugs why didn't Henry Levitte, in his professorial role, do something about it? That's what I'll be asking him when he comes for interview. Among several other things.'

'Hello, Kate. How's it going?'

She switched the phone to loudspeaker and John Wellan's voice became audible. 'John, were you ever aware of Nathan Troy using drugs?'

The laid-back voice drifted over the room. 'No, but it is possible. You probably know that a lot of the kids smoke—'

'I'm not asking about weed.' She looked at her colleagues. 'It's been suggested that Troy was a cocaine user.'

'What?'

'You never heard that?'

'Never. Who said that?' Kate didn't respond. 'I don't know what to say. What *can* I say? Look, I'm on my way to Brindleyplace. Roderick's making total mayhem of the displays down there so I need to—'

'That's okay. That's all I wanted to ask.'

Kate put down the phone. 'Theda and Henry Levitte distanced themselves from Troy because they didn't want it known that he'd been a regular visitor to their house.' She walked to the window and looked out, unseeing. 'Nathan and Cassandra were friends. She confided in him. She told him what her father had done to her. But how . . . why does Bradley Harper fit in to all of this? And Stuart Butts?' *Where are you, Stuart? And is Cassandra safe where she is*?

Searching the glass screen for a number, she went to the phone again, dialled, gave her name and asked to speak to whoever was in charge.

A pleasant voice drifted down the line. 'Leila Jones speaking. How can I help you, Dr Hanson?'

Kate gave a brief outline of her role in UCU and its current investigation. 'I'm very concerned about the safety of one of your patients, Cassandra Levitte—'

The voice which interrupted was now cool. 'Miss Levitte is with us as our *guest*.'

'We need to see her.'

'That's not possible at the moment. She's much too emotionally fragile but I can assure you that she's perfectly safe here at the Hawthornes.'

CHAPTER THIRTY-SIX

Connie came into UCU later that afternoon, carrying what looked to be a large photo album. Bernie eyed the small, neat pathologist in charcoal trousers and gleaming white shirt as she walked towards Kate, looked at them as they stood together, both small and neat. He knew from experience that both were direct in what they had to say, but that was where the similarity ended. Connie was most often calmness and peace whereas Kate could be impatient and in your face, with a right mouth on her at times. He stood and with a quick tensing of abdominal muscles went over to them. 'Got something for us, Connie?'

'Nothing dramatic but delivered with care and interest for your case.' She placed the square, spiral-bound volume on the table. 'This is my ligature book, my own collection. Essential bedtime reading.' Bernie ran an index finger around the inside of his shirt collar as Joe and Julian also gathered. She lifted the sturdy black cover to reveal the first array of six samples, each in a clear plastic pocket, each neatly labelled and annotated.

'This is about Bradley Harper?' asked Kate.

'The very same.' She turned several of the rigid pages. 'I looked through each sample last night. This morning I checked three possibles against his remains.' She stopped and pointed. 'This is the one.' They peered at strong-looking white cord. 'Of the seventy or so samples I have here, *that's* the nearest in terms of thickness and surface pattern. See? The faint herringbone appearance of the weave?' She looked at each of them. 'In my opinion this is *very* similar to what was used to strangle Nathan Troy.'

Kate touched the plastic, gazing at the cord within. 'What's its legitimate use?'

Connie shrugged. 'It's very sturdy, so any number of applications, including domestic, particularly those involving a pulley-type operation, for example sash windows or even something as basic as hanging heavy items on walls. Unfortunately for UCU, it's commonplace.'

Glancing at Joe, thinking of some sash windows they'd seen fairly recently in Worcester, Kate watched as Connie picked up the album and prepared to depart, sending a question to Bernie. 'Where shall we meet?'

Bernie rubbed his jowls. 'Reception in ten minutes? I'll drive us.' She nodded with a grin as she opened the door, through which came the sound of heavy feet on the stairs.

Kate frowned. 'What's happening?'

'Officers on their way to the park to do a quick search for Stuart Butts and it's going to get even busier there: Forensics are ready to start using ground penetrating radar tomorrow morning,' responded Joe.

She absorbed what he'd said then placed both hands over her face, leaving them there for a few seconds. *The search of the park suggests that Gander is taking seriously what I said.* Dropping her hands she looked at Bernie with a tired smile. 'What *else* is going on?'

He gave her a vexed glance. 'Nothing's "going on". I was in at eight this morning and I could do with a break. Connie suggested we have a quick look at some of the paintings at that Barber Institute place at the university.'

Joe stretched his long arms. 'I think we could use some downtime, Red. What d'you say to a glass of wine at Malmaison before you head home?'

She shook her head. 'Sorry.'

'Then how about a brief diversion? Just a few minutes?' He stood and reached for car keys and his cashmere overcoat. She hesitated then gathered her belongings and followed him out of UCU, picking up a speculative glance from Bernie.

They started across the car park in freezing mist. 'Where are we going?'

Joe gazed down at her. 'I'd like your opinion on something.'

Kate veered to her own car. 'I'll follow you then go on home.'

Within minutes the Volvo was signalling and pulling into the kerb and she did the same. They were parked outside a terrace of three-storey Edwardian houses in Regent Road running parallel to the High Street. She left her car and went to where he was now standing, looking up at the houses. After some more seconds she glanced at him, brow furrowed, arms folded around herself. 'It's *freezing* out here. What am I looking at?'

'What do you think of it?'

'Of what? I'm too tired and cold for guessing games. Tell me.'

'The one with the blue door. It's mine.' The two small words hit her square in the solar plexus. She couldn't think of anything to say. 'I bought it last week. What do you think?' he asked again, looking down into her face.

Kate recalled a reference to an estate agent when they'd all eaten dinner together at her house. She looked at the Oxford Blue door, at wisteria stick-dry and leafless but which would probably be glorious in future months. She also saw crumbling external plasterwork around the bottom of the ground-floor bay, and windows of two upper floors in similar condition. 'It's lovely, Joe. Or it will be. It needs . . . work. Was it expensive?' *Is it your business?* She bit her lip. It was an idiotic question anyway. Prices were high around here, even in a recession.

'Reduced due to condition. It's a Fixer-Upper.'

She gave him a cautious glance. 'So . . . you bought it to make some money.'

'I bought it to make a home.'

The last word hung on the air between them. 'You already have a home.'

'That's a rental.'

She realised he was referring to his Edgbaston apartment. 'No, I mean your home in Boston.'

'I sold that the end of last summer.' She was disconcerted. Something else she hadn't known. *Still not your business, Hanson.*

She turned away and he opened her car door for her. She looked up at him. 'What about your secondment? It's down to less than a year now. *This* one.'

She got into the car and he dipped his head, giving her a direct look. 'Who knows what might be going down by then?'

CHAPTER THIRTY-SEVEN

Distracted, checking her watch, Kate moved through her silent house. Maisie wasn't home and should be by now. She drifted into her study, head full of the day's events, her attention snagged by Henry Levitte's painting on the wall. She turned away from it, unable to integrate its beauty with what she knew about him. The hall phone rang and she hurried to it. It was Whittaker on reception duty at Rose Road. Could Kate collect Maisie who'd been picked up by officers at Woodgate Park?

Within ten minutes she was walking through the door at Headquarters. Maisie was talking in animated fashion to a grinning Whittaker and his colleague as they leaned on the counter in reception, looking down at her. 'So, *then*, Adam who does the forensics arrived—' Animation evaporated as she saw the newcomer. 'Oh.'

'What have you been up to?' hissed Kate when she reached her.

Whittaker looked from Maisie to Kate. 'It's okay, Doctor Hanson. Gus Stirling was with the officers at the park. He recognised your daughter and organised a car to drop her here as soon as—'

She cut him off. 'It isn't okay. She had no business there.' She turned to Maisie. 'And on the way home you can try and think of an explanation as to why you left school and went there when I'd expressly said you weren't to go. Make it one I *might* find believable.' Kate turned on her heel and Maisie followed, low-browed, with a wave to the two smiling officers.

Half an hour later they were in the kitchen as Kate threw chopped vegetables at a wok. Maisie had delivered her explanation: the girls at her school all knew of Kate's role with the police and what was happening down at the Country Park so Maisie had gone there with 'one of the weird twins'. 'We were looking for information for another article I'm thinking of writing. I don't see why you're so upset about it. It's like a public place and we were interested. We only went to look around. For all you know we might have picked up a clue.'

Kate glared at her. 'That park is *not* safe.'

'Actually, *Mother*, there were police already there when we arrived.' Remembering her current position, Maisie went for a change of approach. 'Guess what? I met your friend Adam, the forensics man. He was testing out some equipment, like a little trolley on wheels, moving it along the ground and he had this cool laptop connected to it and I had a look at how—'

'Be quiet! When I found out where you'd been I was *very* worried. Don't you understand?'

'Okay, no need to yell,' muttered Maisie.

Kate raked her hair from her face. 'Look, Maisie. It's not my aim to scare you but there are some *really* risky people around. You know that from what happened last year to Chelsey,' she said, referring to the abduction of Maisie's friend by a murderous Harry Creed during UCU's previous case.

'Yeah, and it looks like I'll never live *that* down. I never went with Chel that time and today I stayed when the police saw us. Weird Twin legged it.'

Although still exasperated, Kate understood what Maisie was saying. She was generally sensible but bad things happened, even to the sensible . . . 'All I'm saying is when I tell you not to do something just . . . please, don't do it.'

‘Sorry,’ said Maisie, looking briefly contrite. ‘But the thing is, Mom, what Adam told me was *really* interesting. I’ve decided! I’m going to be a forensic anthropologist.’

Kate was searching freezer drawers. ‘Give me *strength*,’ she muttered into frigid air.

CHAPTER THIRTY-EIGHT

After spending much of the morning catching up with her work at the university, Kate was preparing to leave. The connecting door opened and Crystal appeared holding out an email. 'Glad I caught you. This has just come from the vice chancellor. He wants to see you at three thirty.'

She took it and pushed it into her bag. 'Thanks. I'm going to Rose Road now but I'll be back later.'

Twenty minutes later Kate walked into UCU to find her colleagues in muted discussion. Seeing her they stopped speaking. She looked from one to the other. 'What?'

Bernie rubbed his jowls, a sure sign of discomfort. 'Goosey's just called in looking for you. Said to tell you to go to his office, soon as you arrive.'

Throwing her coat over a chair she took her notebook from her bag. 'He didn't say why? Well, I can guess. Furman's been dripping his gutless views into his ear and he's going to say "No" to the plan for the Retrospective.'

She went through the door, passing Julian on his way in. Bernie called after her. 'I'll ring to say you're on your way. *Don't* kick his door down. Just hear him out before you start on him.'

* * *

She knocked then walked into Chief Superintendent Gander's office. He was at his desk, tapping rosewood with clasped hands, talking to Furman. Gander waved her to a chair and she sat then glanced at Furman. 'As you took the call you'd better tell Kate what the CPS said.' She frowned, trying to work out how the Crown Prosecution Service might be involved with their current case.

Looking exhilarated Furman told her. 'The CPS has informed me this morning that Creed's trial preparations are well in hand.' Kate grew still as the scar on her thigh gave a small twinge. 'They're going to let us know when the case is down for Plea and Directions and after *that* they'll give us a trial date.' His eyes skimmed hers. 'They're confident Creed will go for a Not Guilty plea. *You'll* be called as a prosecution witness.'

UCU's previous case slammed into Kate's head. Harry Creed had been one of their own, a colleague here. Or so they thought. Not only had he abducted Maisie's friend Chelsey, he'd also murdered several young women whom he'd demeaned and violated before and after they died. Creed was a manipulative, duplicitous psychopath, but despite the evidence UCU accumulated against him Kate had lost none of her fear that he might, somehow, walk free. She kept her voice cool, despite rising tension. 'I know how the criminal justice system works and I'm more than ready to assist it where Creed is concerned.'

Furman was looking directly at her, his face elated. 'How about something you *don't* know? He's planning to represent himself.' Her heart flip-flopped. 'Which means *he'll* be cross-examining you at his trial.'

Face strained, she walked back into UCU. Joe had arrived and she told her colleagues what she'd learned. In the ensuing silence Bernie walked from the table, returning after a couple of minutes with a mug of tea which he placed next to her, plus a white sandwich bag. 'Lunch. Eat.' She looked inside the bag. It contained a hefty, cheese-filled bread roll. Or 'cob' as Bernie would have it. 'I'm cutting down,' he muttered.

Julian's eyes went from one to the other of his senior colleagues. 'So — you don't think — it's not like Harry Creed could get off . . . ?'

'Don't talk daft, lad,' chided Bernie, his eyes on Kate as she ate.

'Don't worry about it,' said Kate. 'He's playing his usual games.' She finished her tea then glanced at her watch. 'Oh, for—'

She leapt from her seat, grabbed her bag, searching it for the vice chancellor's email. They watched as she rushed for the door.

CHAPTER THIRTY-NINE

By three thirty-eight p.m. Kate was sitting in the ante-room to the vice chancellor's office. Surely he hadn't heard about Maisie being picked up by the police at the park? Her forehead creased. If he had it was possible he wanted to talk to Kate about it. She bit her lip. He might even be planning to exclude Maisie from maths lectures . . .

The panelled door swung inwards and the vice chancellor appeared, beckoning her with an urgent hand. She followed into the high-ceilinged room and took the chair indicated. 'I'll get straight to the point, if you don't mind.' The formal words put her heart in a vice. *It is about Maisie.* 'Aiden Bennett is leaving in September for a year in South Africa.' Kate stared at him with a belated nod at the reference to the department's professor of Criminological Psychology. 'And in addition, Professor Frankel has at *long* last come to a decision about his retirement.' Kate gazed across the desk, wondering what he was leading up to. 'I can see that you're as surprised as the rest of the faculty at *that* news, given the time it's taken him. For this department it means that two professorial posts will be available in the next academic year.' He looked up at her, his face serious. 'By the way, I'd rather we kept this meeting between ourselves. You know what it's like here for rumour and gossip. I don't want any accusations of favouritism.' He gave her another close look. 'In my opinion you are by far the best candidate for either position. I think you'd do an excellent job. Unfortunately, Kate, I have to say . . .' Surprised at what he'd said so far, she tensed again. Surely it couldn't matter to the vice chancellor that Maisie was taken to Rose Road the other day? '. . . although I support your current work with the police, I wouldn't be able to support your application for a professorship if you intended to continue working with the Unsolved Crime Unit. That would be too much demand for anyone, including you.'

The vice chancellor's words fragmented Kate's jumbled cognitions. She was aware of his sharp eyes still on her as he waited for her response. She pulled together scrambled wits. 'I'm naturally very pleased to . . . know this. I shall bear in mind what you say about the Unsolved Crime Unit.' She closed her mouth, stifling an embryonic argument against the vice chancellor's stance already forming inside her head.

* * *

Five minutes later she was crossing the freezing campus, head teeming with possibilities. If she *were* given a professorship it would mean increased financial security for Maisie and her. The additional demands, the weight of responsibility would be considerable, but she would have more time. But less student contact. And no more UCU. She wouldn't be working with Joe and Bernie. She walked on, eyes on the ground. Joe. He'd just bought a house here but that probably had little relevance for her. He was a single man, free to do as he wished, change his plans when his secondment finished at the end of the year.

Hands thrust deep in the pockets of her overcoat she walked on through mist, thinking that the situation at home would radically change in the next five or six years. Maisie would be making choices about her own life and her future. Maybe it was time she put some planning into her own career? Kate got into her car, recalling the vice chancellor's request that she keep the information to herself, a reference to the rampant gossip mill which ground away at the university and inside all other academic establishments. *But not Woolner College, seemingly.*

* * *

Kate was in her kitchen, feeling apprehensive and edgy from the day's events. She'd tried blocking the thoughts surging into her head as a result of what Furman had told her about Creed's plans for his forthcoming trial but when she did, thoughts of her own professional future insinuated themselves. She banged the kettle onto its base. *Damn Furman! Damn it all!*

Crossing the kitchen she threw open one of the garden doors and went outside in bleak chill to walk the long paths illuminated by light from the house until she was breathless, following which she came inside with a decisive pull on the door. She would consider what the vice chancellor had said when she wasn't so overstretched. *And the next time I think about Creed's trial will be within two weeks of its start and I'll be totally prepared for it. Until then: enough.*

She went into the hall, lifting her face to the upper floor. '*Maisie*?'

* * *

They'd gone to an early screening of a comedy and now they were on their way home, Maisie laughing as they neared the house. 'And did *you* notice the bit where he — Mom?'

Kate had already seen it. A police car's blue lights strobing the house and drive. She spoke, keeping her voice even, anxiety tightening inside her chest. 'Did you set the alarm like I told you?'

'I think so.'

They came onto the drive and Kate turned off the ignition, watching the blue-white oscillating lights flaring the front of the house. Her mind was racing from room to room, words rushing her head: pearl necklace; her mother's ring. Damage? Had she paid the premium?

She opened her door with a glance at Maisie. 'Stay here.' Seeing two unfamiliar uniformed officers emerging from their vehicle and putting on their hats, she got out of the car and waited for them to come to her. 'This is my house. I'm Kate Hanson. What's happened?'

'Bradford Street received a report of a burglary in progress. We responded,' said the taller of the two.

She gazed at her house. *Somebody has been inside*. It looked alien. She gave the officers her attention. 'And you are?'

They both showed identification and the one who'd spoken continued. 'DC Trent and PC Nicholls. We've just arrived. If you'll stay here we'll go inside and—'

'I'm coming with you.' She started forward.

He turned back to her with a stern look. 'Madam, the front door is open so it's best you stay out here until we ascertain the nature of the situation inside.' With a second stern glance he walked with his colleague towards the house and she watched them disappear inside. Folding her arms around herself in the bitter evening, she paced the drive.

Maisie was standing on her side of the car. '*Mom!* What's going on? What's happened?'

'I'm not sure. We need to stay here until they tell us.' After waiting for what felt like an eternity DC Trent reappeared and walked towards them, face inscrutable. 'The house is empty.'

Kate was on the move. 'I want to check if anything's been—'

'Just a minute.' His tone halted her, his facial expression unfathomable. 'This your daughter?' She nodded, wondering why it was relevant. 'I need a brief word with you. Alone.'

She turned to Maisie. 'Get back in the car and stay there, please.' She turned and walked with DC Trent towards the house and stepped inside. '*Oh!*' The hall was littered with books and items of clothing. Stepping around them she followed him into the kitchen, noting that the coffee maker was gone. And the radio. She looked at DC Trent and his colleague. 'What about the rest of the house?'

'If you'll come over here, please?' Unsettled by his formal tone she approached where he was standing beside one of several open drawers. He pointed. 'Take a look in here.'

She did. Inside the drawer, sitting on what was part of a set of placemats, the others tossed on the floor, were several round white tablets, each stamped with a stylised cat's face. She stared at them, hearing voices coming from the direction of the front door, one of them familiar. Joe walked into the kitchen, calm and soft-spoken as he addressed the two officers. 'Joe Corrigan, Rose Road here.'

Trent's facial expression indicated that he knew who Joe was. 'Lieutenant.' He nodded.

PC Nicholls was now coming through the door, Maisie close behind. 'Checked the houses either side,' he said to Trent. 'Nothing to report.'

Joe glanced at the various items on the floor, looked at Kate's shocked face and finally at DC Trent. 'What's going on here?'

'We responded to a call-out of a burglary in progress.' He lowered his voice. 'We've found evidence of drugs and I'm considering charging—'

'Sure, you are. Let's discuss that.' Low words were exchanged as Kate watched him subtly move the two officers across the kitchen, corralling them on the other side, where more low words flowed. Kate saw Trent peer around Joe to look at her, after which both officers headed for the front door.

Kate went to Maisie and slipped an arm around her. 'Mom. What's going on?'

I don't know. 'It's okay, Maisie. It's all sorted now.'

* * *

Kate came into the kitchen with a quick glance at her watch. 'Superficial chaos restored within twenty minutes.'

'Strangest break-in I ever saw,' muttered Bernie, who'd arrived at the house following a call from Joe. They turned as one of the forensic workers from Rose Road's team, summoned by Joe, came into the kitchen. 'Find anything?' he asked.

The forensic worker gestured over his shoulder. 'Somebody disabled the alarm then forced open the laundry window. I've managed to lift a palm print off the window frame. I'll need elimination prints from everybody who lives here.' He proceeded to do it, using a hand-held device.

'Where's your *ink*?' demanded Maisie.

'We use these mobile scanners now.' He grinned at her. 'If you've got "form" I'll know it within fifteen seconds.'

She watched as he scanned her hand. 'Wow!'

Within a few minutes he and his colleague were gone, leaving Kate frowning at a two-item list of what had been taken.

Joe beckoned to Kate and she went to him. 'I'm guessing you know what these are?' he said, indicating the tablets still inside the drawer, keeping his voice low.

She nodded. 'The picture on them indicates Mephedrone. "MCat".'

'Yup.' He regarded her, his face serious. 'I can come up with *one* idea as to why somebody might pull a charade like this.'

Bernie had been listening nearby. 'Somebody's having a go at your reputation, Doc. I've got my own theory as to who might have done this. That laundry window's not very big.'

Kate's brows rose. 'You're thinking this was Stuart *Butts?* But he doesn't know anything about me.' She looked at Joe. 'Lucky you came by, otherwise I could have been arrested.'

He grinned. 'All part of the service, ma'am, and now we'll secure the laundry window.'

* * *

Kate completed another circuit of the kitchen and shook her head. Still just two items gone from the whole house. A very strange break-in, as Bernie had said. The hall phone rang. Looking at her watch she frowned and went to answer it, anticipating more trouble. She got it.

It was Stella, Kevin's on-off girlfriend of the last eighteen months. 'Kate? Listen, a bit of a . . . situation has come up.' Kate listened as the other phone was covered then, 'I'm calling from the QE hospital.' Something grabbed inside Kate's ribcage. 'It's Kevin. He was brought in . . .' The voice drifted off again and Kate knew exactly what had happened: a heart attack. He ate all the wrong things and in the last twelve months he'd put on weight. She closed her eyes. *What do I say to Maisie*?

Stella was back. 'We've been in A and E for the last three hours. He's ruptured a calf muscle playing squash and—'

Kate's overheated thought processes reinforced by the day's tensions skidded to a halt on a thick residue of resentment and annoyance. '*I* don't need to know about this.'

'He'll be unable to get around for the next few days.'

'Very inconvenient for both of you,' said Kate.

'Kevin and I aren't together since we got back from Paris.'

Kevin's familiar, forthright voice replaced Stella's. 'Kate, I'm in a spot and I need somewhere to stay for the next week or so.'

Her eyes stretched at his words. 'You're *not* coming *here*.'

His voice turned fractious. 'Why not? Phyllis can fix me snacks and drinks in the day. There's a downstairs bathroom. I'll sleep on the sofa in your study. Stella's just left so come and get me.'

'Ring for a *taxi*.' Kate looked at the dead receiver in her hand then slammed it down as Maisie leapt down the last few stairs. 'What's happened *now*?'

CHAPTER FORTY

Kate marched into her room at the university on Monday morning, frazzled and twenty minutes late for her tutor group. The students had been allowed inside under Crystal's supervision where they were talking amongst themselves. Reaching her desk, Kate took a breath, picked up the file of prepared notes she'd left there, and disseminated them among the group with a brief apology for lateness. Crystal gave her a look and motioned *Drink*? She nodded, subsiding behind her desk as the students read what she'd given them. A mug of tea arrived within a minute or so, accompanied by two paracetamol tablets.

Bloody Kevin. Kate cursed him silently as she took the painkillers. She cursed herself, too, for allowing him to rile her. He invariably laid on the charm when he needed something from her, and Maisie was thrilled to have her father staying, but from now on until he returned to his own place he'd expect to be waited on, given his poor mobility. She'd had to bite her tongue last night when he'd suggested that Maisie stay up past her bedtime.

The paracetamol and tea did their job and within another hour, tutor group despatched, Kate was sitting at her desk, eyes drifting dully over a new batch of assignments requiring her attention, mind flitting to thoughts of the potential professorship and all that went with it.

The phone rang. She snatched up the receiver. 'Yes?'

It was Joe. 'Hey, Smarty-Pants. I rang at nine and you were a Not-There. Now you sound like you're in one *unholy* snit. Not worrying about Friday night?'

'No, but I've been thinking about it and what you and Bernie said. Whoever reported what was happening at my house *chose* Bradford Street rather than Rose Road because he, they, know I work at Rose Road and wanted to make sure that the officers who responded didn't know me, that they would find those drugs and arrest me. I think Bernie's right. Somebody wants me discredited.'

'Right on the money, Red.'

She leaned back on her chair. 'Wonder what Furman was up to on Friday night?' She sighed. 'Ignore that. It was a bad joke. I'm edgy and—'

'Also late because?'

'Kevin's come home.' It took a few seconds plus the silence in her ear for her to realise what she'd said. 'No!' She stopped, admonishing herself to calm down. Joe wasn't interested in her domestic problems. 'He's got a leg injury. It's a temporary arrangement. He's been at the house barely two days and I'm already fed up with him.'

'Well, it's kind of nice when folks support each other in times of crisis.'

She grinned at him, despite her mood. 'Drop the Norman Rockwell-style philosophy. It doesn't travel. What are you after?'

There was a quiet laugh. 'I need you.'

'Don't *you* start.' She massaged one temple.

'We've had a call from the Hawthornes. Cassandra Levitte is now well enough for a visit.'

Kate sat up. 'Really? At last! And at a really good time. She might give us some information which could assist us when we interview her father.'

'How about I be second string, given the gender and mental health aspects.'

'When?'

'Three thirty this afternoon.'

* * *

Kate and Joe were inside the Hawthornes, a large, one-time family home circa 1900, now divided into small, self-contained accommodation for those with serious mental health needs and the personal resources to pay for it. They listened to Leila Jones the manager, her black hair in intricately woven corn-rows disappearing into a bright fabric headpiece, as she explained the Hawthornes' role in relation to Cassandra Levitte. 'A number of our residents need constant specialist care. Cassandra isn't in that category. She comes to us when she's in crisis and requires short-term support, protection and guidance on self-care.' She glanced at Kate. 'This is a place where she feels safe.'

Kate nodded. 'What happens if there's no room for Cassandra when she needs it?'

The manager smiled at her. 'Cassandra's family is *very* caring and financially generous.' This prompted a quick glance between Kate and Joe. 'Her father pays to ring-fence a room for her in what was the original stable block.' Kate made a quick note as Joe studied the flamboyant woman across the desk.

'Does she often use that resource, ma'am?'

Leila Jones gazed down at brief notes in readiness on the desk. 'Since Cassandra first came here in January, 1994, she's stayed with us on twelve occasions, mostly on an emergency basis.' She gave Kate an evaluative look. 'Are you aware of the nature of Cassandra's difficulties?'

'I haven't seen any formal diagnosis.'

'The Hawthornes has regular input from a psychiatrist who has diagnosed mood disorder. We help her manage her "high" episodes and her depression by ensuring that she takes her medication regularly. She's most often depressed. The highs when they occur are more problematic for Cassandra's daily life: at those times she's unable to recognise her need to continue with her medication. Nor is she able to monitor her own personal safety.'

Kate recalled the scene she and Bernie had witnessed at Hyde Road very recently. 'Has Cassandra absconded from the Hawthornes recently?'

Leila Jones gave her a direct look. 'This isn't a secure establishment, Dr Hanson. We monitor our guests closely during their stays and their families alert us when problems occur within the community.'

Which means that Cassandra was living at home when we saw her the other day? Kate felt concern stirring again as she made quick notes. 'Her condition is kept stable with medication?'

Leila Jones gave a nod. 'Mainly lithium.'

She and Joe exchanged another quick glance. 'Is it still okay for us to meet with Miss Levitte today, ma'am?' he asked.

She gave him a wide smile. 'She'd be disappointed if you didn't. She's gone to a lot of trouble for you. I'll take you to her.'

They followed her through a door at the rear of the house and into a walled garden. To one side of it was a single-storey brick building. As she led them into a small terracotta-tiled hall, she spoke, her voice low. 'Please bear in mind that she tires very easily.'

A nearby door opened and Kate recognised the woman standing there: the girl in Nathan Troy's sketch. The woman at the window of the Levittes' sitting room. Cassandra Levitte, her face paper-white with deep purple smudges under the eyes, her fair hair drawn back from her face. Kate noted a little mascara and lip gloss. When she spoke Kate heard a voice that was almost childlike and entirely devoid of emphasis. 'Would you like to come in for tea and cake?'

As Leila Jones left they entered the small, neat flat where a table was laid with china, cakes and biscuits. When they were seated around it and Cassandra had brought the makings for tea, Kate smiled at her, voice low. 'Is it okay if we use first names?' The question produced a shy nod. She chose her next words. 'Joe and I work together. He's a policeman.' She was silent for a few seconds to allow Cassandra to absorb what she'd said. 'We need to ask you some questions and I'd like to write down what you tell us because it could be important. Is that okay?'

'Yes. I'm glad you've come this week. I was really ill last week.' There was no indication of awareness that Kate had been a witness to the incident at her family home. 'Before that I couldn't sleep. Too much to do . . . I didn't sleep for a whole week.' She frowned. 'I spent lots of money. Daddy was really angry.'

Kate followed the conversational line. 'What did you spend the money on?'

'I don't know . . . It . . . went. Disappeared. I think my boyfriend spent some.'

Kate's interest spiralled but she kept her inquiry low-key. 'Your boyfriend.'

'He was really nice . . . I don't know his name.'

Buchanan's oblique reference to Cassandra's historical promiscuity came into Kate's head as she considered how to turn the conversation to the purpose of their visit. Cassandra did it for her. 'Leila said I should talk to you. About my friend Nathan.' They watched a frown form on the pale brow. 'I'm being good now, taking my medication . . . it's hard for me to remember things. Nathan went away and that was a long, long time ago.'

'Can you tell us about him?' asked Kate. No response. 'He was your friend.'

A mix of emotions crossed Cassandra's face, so quickly that Kate was unable to reliably identify them. 'A good friend. Sometimes I went to his house . . . I didn't like it there. The other boys . . .'

When nothing further was forthcoming Kate gave Joe a quick look and went with a direct question. 'Can you tell us about Nathan visiting you at *your* house?'

She watched the large grey eyes become unfocused. 'The only time I do remember was when I was sick. Daddy was angry and things crashed and rolled and then I was sent to bed and everybody went away.'

Kate's pen flew. She looked up at Cassandra's vague face. 'What about the very *last* time Nathan came to your house? Can you remember that?'

The pale face saddened and she shook her head. 'No . . . That was it. I liked him. He was my true friend.'

Kate nodded as she wrote. 'We've been told that he liked you too.'

'He talked to me . . . We talked to each other.' Her face underwent a sudden, startling change. She looked fearful, her body rigid. 'No, no . . . I didn't talk. He talked. I didn't . . . I didn't.'

Slowing her own movements Kate leaned forward, her eyes on the woman's distressed face. 'Cassandra, it isn't a bad thing to talk. It can be a *good* thing to do.' She still looked distressed so Kate changed direction. 'Were you taking medication when you and Nathan were friends?' She got a nod. 'Do you know what it was?'

She nodded. 'It was lithium. I still take it. Sometimes the doctor gives me another drug but I don't remember what it's called.'

Kate chose her words. 'Was there ever a time when Nathan used your medication, Cassandra? Maybe by mistake?'

She gave a head shake. 'No. Nathan didn't take things. He thought it was bad and anyway he was strong and happy . . . and then . . . then he went on the floor and . . . there was crashing and rolling around and . . . I need to lie down.' She looked at Joe from beneath heavy lids. 'If I was still really ill I would ask you to lie down with me. But I'm not ill like that now so . . .' The voice trailed off to a whisper. 'I won't say it.'

Kate and Joe stood. They could come back another day. Cassandra walked with them to the door. As they neared it Kate noticed an object hanging there: a large, dark blue disc of glass, about ten centimetres in diameter, suspended from a hook by a blue plaited cord. In the middle of the dark blue was a circle of white, another of turquoise and within that, at its dead centre, a stark black spot. Kate went closer. 'That's very striking.'

'*No!* Don't touch it. You mustn't take it!'

Kate turned to Cassandra. 'I won't. I promise.' Cassandra's breathing was now ragged and the minimal colour had drained from her face as if a stopper had been pulled. It was now sallow, tinged with grey, the violet shadows under the eyes stark on the waxy skin. Kate breathed the powerful smell of stress. 'It's very important to you, isn't it?'

Cassandra looked from Kate to the disc and back. 'It's my life,' she whispered, clasping her hands to her mouth.

Kate gave the ornament another swift look. 'Where did you get it?'

Again, the mix of emotions passed over her face. 'It has a name. A strange name . . . I don't remember,' she whispered, eyes enormous, the pupils dilated as she raised a hand to it but stopped short of contact. 'It . . . protects . . . I've got another here.' She turned back the lapel of her shirt and they saw a tiny, quivering bead of similar colours suspended from a gold safety pin. 'And another . . . In my bedroom.'

Kate looked to the disc hanging on the door. The 'eye' in the centre stared back, baleful. 'So, it's a kind of charm?'

'No. It's an am-u-let.' She pronounced it as a child might when taught a new word. 'I take it down at night and hold it. It's restful. Safe.'

Kate was confused. 'You know the Hawthornes well, Cassandra. You've stayed here many times. Miss Jones and all the other people here look after you. You know and trust them?' This got a nod and she pointed to the glass. 'Why do you need this?'

'You don't understand. You can't. The Eye guards me. Without it I'll . . . *die*.' She lapsed into silence then, 'I'm sorry.'

'Please, don't apologise,' said Kate. 'Where did you get it?' she asked a second time.

'I don't know where . . . It came from the East. It's a secret.'

Her suspicions of Henry Levitte's abuse of his daughter rose inside Kate's head again. She looked at the troubled woman, feeling more anxiety surge. 'It isn't good to keep secrets, Cassandra, especially if it's about something that's troubling—'

'No.' Following the quiet single word she opened the door, Joe and a reluctant Kate stepped outside, and the door closed.

* * *

They returned to Leila Jones's office and Kate described the glass ornament. 'I thought you should know because it appears to be a source of both comfort and upset for Cassandra. I'm not sure if it has any significance for your care of her?'

Leila Jones nodded as she made a quick note. 'On previous stays she's brought it here and tended to fixate on it. We don't routinely search our residents on arrival so I didn't know she still had it. But thank you for alerting me. I'll ring our psychiatrist and ask for his advice on how to manage her needs over the next few hours.' She stood and came to them, holding out her hand. 'Thank you for coming. I know it was important to Cassandra.'

Kate turned to her. 'How long do you think she'll stay here?'

Leila Jones studied her, seeing her anxiety. 'As I said before this isn't a secure establishment. We can't prevent guests discharging themselves or leaving, but whilst she's with us she's safe.'

She led them out of the main door and watched them get into the Volvo. Returning to her office and her desk she lifted the phone.

CHAPTER FORTY-ONE

'Lithium!' Bernie rubbed his hands together.

Kate nodded. 'We thought you'd like that.'

He sent her an evaluative look. 'I know this theory you've got about Henry Levitte but can you be a hundred per cent certain that *she* didn't do Troy in? In one of her "states"?'

'Cassandra?' She shook her head. 'From what we've seen and been told I can't envisage her ever having had the organisational ability, the strength to open up the lake house floor, place a body under it, then conceal it.'

Head down, he was silent for some seconds. 'What about if she had some help?'

'From whom?'

He lifted his shoulders. 'I don't know. I'm raising it, right? Like a possibility.' He paused. 'Did she say anything relevant that we might use when we interview her dad?'

Kate sighed, flicking notebook pages. 'Not directly. As I said, she mentioned not liking the student house. She referred to not liking "the boys" there. She glanced across at Joe. 'What did you make of her?'

'She is one very scared woman and I think it's lucky she's where she is.'

She nodded. 'I agree. She's terrified of something. Or somebody.'

Bernie's eyes were on the glass screen. 'When we get Henry Levitte in here for interview he has to tell us all about Troy's connection with his family. We also want to know where Buchanan and Johnson fit in, if they do, and this Joel Smythe that nobody could find back then and nobody else has been able to find for the last half-dozen years.' His eyes moved over the screen's contents. 'And *then* there's that Roderick. Bloody odd, he is. They all are in that family, if you ask me. Just thinking about 'em leaves me knackered before we've even seen their old man again.'

Pushing his chair back to recline, Joe stretched both arms and laced his fingers behind his head, eyes on Kate. 'You reckon Troy visited the Levittes' place because of his friendship with Cassandra and that she told him about what her father did to her.' He was silent, then: 'I think you're on the money there.'

'Proving it is something else.' Kate contemplated the notes she'd made earlier. 'The house on Hyde Road could hold a lot of secrets but we can't do anything until we talk to Levitte *here*.' Feeling frustrated, she rested her chin on one hand. 'I want to know who or what has made Cassandra so terrified. Either she obtained that ornament, the "Eye", herself or somebody gave it to her. Either way, she's been manipulated into a dependence on it. Who would do that and why? I think it's *him*, her father. He's not at all the foolish figure John Wellan describes.' She gazed ahead, chin propped on hand. 'And there's a question I *keep* coming back to: what happened to Nathan's Troy's coat?'

Bernie frowned. 'I'm not so sure that's relevant. Go down Broad Street any Friday or Saturday night, Doc. They're all out there: kids with hardly anything on in the winter. Devenish is the same. It's like a young macho thing. Having met this Cassandra again are you *more* confident in your suspicions of old man Levitte than you was when you seen Gander?'

Kate thought about it. 'The same. Cassandra has confirmed that Nathan Troy visited the Levitte house. From what she said, one of his visits became contentious. It's a pity Cassandra doesn't remember the last occasion he was there.'

Bernie dropped his hands on the table and pushed himself to standing. 'That's the trouble with her, Doc. Her reliability. You need to face it. Like Stuey Butts, she'd make a lousy prosecution witness.' He looked down at Kate. Think what a dogs' dinner your ex-husband would make of either of them or any of his barrister cronies if it come to that.' Kate watched as he left the table, heading for the refreshment centre. He was right, of course. Bernie was speaking again. 'I've been thinking about her name. "Cassandra". That's one you don't hear very often.'

Kate stood and began to gather her belongings. 'According to Greek mythology Cassandra was a powerless female whom no one listened to.'

CHAPTER FORTY-TWO

The following day Kate and Joe walked across Rose Road's car park and stopped next to her car. 'You're sure you don't want to come along?' he asked. They'd discussed the need to visit Miranda Levitte and he had agreed he would do it.

She shook her head. 'Miranda Levitte has managed to avoid calls, messages from Bernie and a visit by me. She might be more forthcoming with you.' She grinned up at him. 'Consider yourself UCU's secret weapon. Gender plus the American accent might be on your side. I'm interested to know what she's like, given what we know of her family.' She paused, then, 'Behind the facade the family is a mess. For years it's had a satyr at its head, a biological mother whose mental health difficulties prevented her from actively engaging with her children and protecting them and a second wife whose capacity to emotionally engage and protect *any* children, let alone someone else's, I seriously question. Roderick and Cassandra have significant mental health difficulties which have prevented their moving on from the family and creating stable lives, enduring relationships and children of their own.'

She unlocked her car, watching him walk away with a wave of his hand. 'We've not heard that Miranda's life is any different. Come back with the goods, Corrigan.'

* * *

Kate walked into the room adjoining hers. No Crystal. Notebook in one hand she sat at the computer and scanned pages of notes. It was yet another long shot but she needed to understand what Cassandra had told them. If that were possible. Getting onto Google, she tapped in 'the Eye'. It produced little of use. Refining the search to 'Evil Eye' was more informative. The word 'amulet' caught her attention and she clicked on it, staring at the photographs which appeared on the screen, so similar to what she and Joe had seen on the back of Cassandra's door. She gazed at another, showing the same design on the tailfin of an aircraft. She read the text: *Amulet believed to protect against the evil eye . . . crystal blue eye has always . . . common in Turkey . . . Egypt.*

Kate went through every note she'd made since their investigation began. She flicked pages, running a finger across lines of strokes, searching all that was there for cues, something, *anything*, she might have missed. Matthew Johnson was in Istanbul in the early nineties and John Wellan had been in Greece. Which wasn't unusual for academics. She flicked more pages, facts and utterances coming off the pages and out of her memory, their meaning not fully appreciated when she first heard them and not connected since. Turkey. Egypt. Eastern Mediterranean. She stared ahead. Cassandra had said the amulet came from 'the East'.

* * *

In response to Joe's ring at the door of Artworks a tall blonde woman appeared from the rear of the small gallery, approached the door, opened it and motioned him inside. Her voice when it came was well-modulated. She looked him directly in the eye and smiled, displaying even, white teeth. 'I assume you're the lieutenant who phoned? Come on in.' He did, noting the languid, confident movement as she walked ahead of him into a comfortable room at the rear of the premises where she indicated a seat on a chesterfield. 'Coffee? Tea? Or something a little stronger?'

'Thank you, ma'am. Nothing for me. We appreciate your agreeing to this visit.'

She gave him another direct look. 'No problem at all.'

He waited until she took a seat at one end of the sofa, crossing her legs. He took the nearby chair. 'You know about the discovery of Nathan Troy's body, Miss Levitte?'

'Yes, of course, and it's Miranda. Unfortunately, I don't see how I can assist you with that.'

'I have a couple of questions. Shall we see how it goes?'

She half smiled, eyes on his face. 'Mm . . . Let's do that.'

'Did you ever meet him, Nathan Troy?'

Miranda Levitte recrossed her legs then smoothed her hair behind her ears, her actions casual, self-possessed. 'Ye-es but only once, I would say.'

'Where was that?'

Clear blue eyes considered the ceiling then lowered to Joe's. 'At my father's house.'

He gave a slow nod. 'Can you recall when that was, ma'am?'

The half smile appeared again. 'Oh . . . heavens — it's *so* long ago, isn't it?' She gazed upwards again, the fingers of one hand lightly stroking the front of her neck. 'I'd have to say . . . the beginning of Nathan Troy's first year at Woolner.'

Notebook in hand he looked up. 'And what would have been the reason for his visit?'

Miranda Levitte's elegant eyebrows moved upwards. 'The reason? Goodness, I have no idea. I wasn't living at home then.'

'What was your impression of him on that occasion?'

She looked beyond Joe then refocused. 'Over-impressed with the house, overawed by my father. I don't recall hearing him say a word in the hour or so that I was there. People like that, they're keen to align themselves with the family.' She gave Joe a direct look. 'Because of my father's reputation in the art world, you understand. I suspect Nathan Troy was an ambitious type. "On the make", as one might put it.'

Joe gave her an appraising glance as he wrote. 'Your sister wasn't the reason for Troy visiting the house?'

Cool blue eyes regarded him. '*Cassandra*? Have you met my sister, Lieutenant Corrigan?' He gave the briefest of nods. 'Then you'll know that she proves the point I'm making. I'd say it was very unlikely that she motivated his visit.'

He sent her a steady gaze. 'Your sister has her problems for sure but she seems to be a kind, gentle person. Maybe Nathan Troy saw that?'

Elbow on the arm of the chesterfield, index finger across her upper lip, she gave him a steady gaze. 'I seriously doubt that. Cassandra finds daily life very difficult. Always has done. She's had no life, no work, no partner in the . . . accepted sense of the word. My father does all he can but she's a drain on him both emotionally and financially. I don't know whether you're aware that he's anticipating a knighthood in the not-too-distant future?' Joe nodded. 'Cassandra's behaviour has the potential to embarrass him and that really isn't fair on him.' She sighed and recrossed her long, smooth legs. 'There's something you should know about my father. He cared for our mother until she died. He looked after and cared for all of us and he's *still* looking after Cassandra. After all those years of work and caring he doesn't deserve to have this business with Nathan Troy raked over again, particularly if it reaches the media. It's just not — *fair*.'

'I guess Troy's parents don't think it fair what happened to him.' She stared at him as he went to another line of questioning. 'Maybe he was at the house because he was friendly with your brother?'

He watched the blue eyes widen and the full lips part in a mocking smile. '*Roderick*? You clearly haven't met him. My brother doesn't get on with most people. He likes his own company. "Likes" might be a little too emphatic.'

Joe nodded as he wrote then looked up at her. 'Anything else to add about Troy, other than he was a kid on the make?'

She laughed, vermilion lips drawn back from white teeth. 'I *do* like Americans. The directness. No, I haven't. Except that he was young, immature, and I suspect rather boring.'

'He *was* young back then. You also, ma'am? Maybe your judgement of him at that time was influenced by your being used to older males? More mature suitors?'

She smiled into his eyes. '*Suitors*. How delightful. Yes. Some. None that stayed the course.'

He regarded her, deciding to test Kate's view: 'I'm surprised that neither you nor your brother and sister married or had children.'

The cool gaze was on him. 'That surprise of yours is somewhat misplaced where *I'm* concerned, Lieutenant.'

* * *

Kate's phone rang as she was making her way through a throng of Woolner students.

'Hi, Joe. How did it go?'

'Red, there's something you need to know. I've met this tall, cool, blonde and you're history.'

She laughed. 'What did you find out?'

His tone become serious. 'She doesn't seem to think much of her sister and brother. She comes over as very confident, very self-assured. Regards both of them with distant curiosity is about the size of it. Know what? She confirmed Troy visited the family home.'

'I *knew* he was a regular there,' breathed Kate.

'She didn't go that far, Red. What she said was she saw him once only.'

Walking among milling students Kate put her hand over her free ear. 'Did she say anything about Troy? What she thought of him?'

'Yep. Her take was that he was impressed with her father and trying to further his own ambitions.'

Kate stopped. 'She said Troy was *ambitious*?'

'She did.' There was a small silence on the line then. 'She spoke of her father in a warm way. Have to say it, Red — I didn't get the idea that *she'd* had any problem with him.'

She walked on. 'Maybe Cassandra was the only child he victimised. He made his choices depending on his children's personalities — from what you said about her manner Miranda sounds cool, confident. Nothing like Cassandra.'

'Mmm. Cool with definite hot spots here and there.' Kate raised her brows. 'But what you said about their adult lives, there's one thing you've not anticipated.'

'What's that?'

'She has a son.'

Kate stopped again. 'How old? Where is he? Who's his father?'

'He's nineteen. He's at Cambridge and she's not a kiss 'n' tell gal.'

* * *

Kate ran up the steps and inside Woolner. Within a couple of minutes she was at the wide-open door of the studio, watching John Wellan sweeping the floor, his lined face more morose than usual. She watched as the broom pushed sparkling debris. 'What happened?'

'Rupe! Stay. Good dog.' He carried on, giving Kate a brief glance. 'Better keep your distance. Out of harm's way.'

Kate went to stand near the row of face masks and protective clothing, giving the studio a quick survey. The source of the glass on the floor was now evident: one small vacant square amid several glazed panes to one side of the door to the studio. The side next to the lock. She hadn't noticed it when she came in. Now her thoughts were on her own recent experience. 'Know who did it?'

'Not a clue.' He crouched, swept glass into a dustpan then carried it and the broom to the far side of the studio, releasing the contents into a large black bin.

She started towards the door with a small wave. 'I'll come back another—'

He gestured her to stay, pointed to a chair. 'Sit,' he said, going past her to the kettle.

She took another look around the studio, eyebrows climbing when she noticed gaps on the wall. 'They stole your *pictures*?'

'What?' He looked up to where she was indicating. 'No. That was me, tidying. Getting rid of the stuff that's accumulated over the years. All of it worthless rubbish. After your visit I decided it was time.'

Kate went and sat down. She took the hot mug from him. 'Thanks. Since I saw you I've met Cassandra Levitte.'

'Oh, yeah?' He searched the pockets of the coat thrown over his chair. 'Did you find out what you wanted to know? *Ah!*' He seized the roll-up tin.

'We talked to her but she's clearly unwell at the moment.' She sipped as he lit his cigarette, her eyes drifting over the work surface. Everything had been rearranged. A lot of it was gone. 'I see you've still got the painting by the door.' He looked up at her. She pointed. 'The Madonna type with the baby.'

He shrugged. 'Good job I have. That's a set piece by one of my third-year students. She'll be wanting it in July when she finishes.'

Kate looked surprised. 'A student painted it? She's very accomplished.' Another sip then, 'Did whoever it was actually take anything?' she asked again, deciding not to mention her own break-in.

He exhaled smoke, looking tired. 'You probably don't know this but I'm keen on quality, on workmanship. I like classics.'

She nodded with a grin. 'I've seen the car.'

He dragged more smoke into his chest. 'A few years ago I bought a classic pen, a claret and gold Montegrappa "Dragon". Lovely thing. *That's* disappeared. Haven't had a chance to find out if anything else has gone.' He glanced at her. 'You're not here to listen to me wallowing — Quiet, Rupe.' He transferred his attention back to her. 'Something on your mind?'

Kate nodded. 'Yes. I don't know if you're aware that Cassandra Levitte is in a nursing home at the moment?'

He looked at her. 'Can't say that's a surprise.'

She chose her words, not wanting to divulge too much about Cassandra's current problems. 'On a recent visit to her I saw something, a kind of protective ornament she has. Blue glass with concentric circles — like an eye. She appeared very attached to it.'

John Wellan nodded then looked at Kate. 'And you're telling me because . . . ?'

'Because I think it's a Mediterranean type of decoration and I thought you might have an idea where it might have come from.'

'I can only guess it would have come from somewhere like Turkey, but as to how she acquired it, God only knows.'

She sighed, resting her cheek on her hand. 'You've known the family for a long time. I thought some comment or other might have drifted your way.'

The downward lines of his face deepened. 'I've worked with Henry for years. Since I started here in ninety-two. I know *him* pretty well but not the rest of them. I make sure I'm pleasant when I meet any of them but I've never been part of *that* social circle. Too much bloody hobnobbing with Birmingham's great-and-good for my liking. Got no time for it.'

'What do you think of them as parents — I mean Henry Levitte and his second wife?'

He shrugged. 'I've got no children so I'm in no position to judge although on the face of it Roderick and Cassandra wouldn't earn them any prizes.' He looked in the direction of the windows. 'Parents, families.' He shook his head. 'My parents' vision extended as far as the end of our street. I had nothing in common with them, my brother or my sister. I was glad to get away from it all and out of Doncaster.'

Kate felt defeated but pressed on. 'You told me about Roderick and his problems and you knew Cassandra when she was a student here in the nineties.'

He shook his head. 'You couldn't "know" Cassandra. Nobody could. She was hardly here and when she was she was all over the place. Medication, I suppose.'

'What about their lives in recent years?'

He gave Kate a direct look. 'If I knew anything I'd have told you already.'

She looked pensive. 'I thought you might have picked up something from Academe's old rumour mill.'

He gave a decisive head-shake. 'I don't get involved in *any* of that back-biting rubbish. If you want details of their personal lives I'm the wrong person. As far as the academic hierarchy here is concerned I'm persona non grata. I don't make it on either Levitte's or Johnson's Christmas card list, trust me.' He grinned, drew on the cigarette again, swallowed smoke and gave her a speculative look. 'Maybe if I'd kept my mouth shut, followed Henry's ideas of "good art teaching" I might've made prof and a lot more money. Too late now. Never going to happen.'

'Do you think you're over-stating your bad-boy image?'

He grinned at her again. 'I hope you're right. I need a couple more years here.'

She stared into her drink as a thought occurred to her. 'I seem to know more about the people here than you do.'

He shrugged then raised his hands, looking around the studio. 'See all this? Painting, sculpting. This is what brings me in here every day. This and the students.'

She took a final sip and put down the mug, ready to leave. 'We met Cassandra and now I'm beginning to understand her, starting to get an insight into her likely childhood years.'

He gave her a brief glance. '"We"?'

'Lieutenant Corrigan and I both went to see her.' She stood, looking pensive. 'It's odd, you know, but despite the years I've been doing my job I never fail to be surprised, shocked even, by the long shadow people's history, their early years, can cast on their lives.' She picked up her bag. 'And I'm guessing you can't tell me anything about Miranda?'

He began constructing another roll-up. 'Apart from an impression of iciness and a tendency to survey the world from a great height, literally and figuratively, no. But that might be how she is towards me. The only one I've had any real contact with is Roderick.' He shook his head. 'I've told you what a pain in the behind I think he is. Everything he does for this Retrospective I have to redo.' Kate gazed down at him, seeing the tiredness in his face. 'He's probably responsible for me leaving my bloody pen here so somebody could nick it.' He looked up at her with a brief smile. 'That's enough of my griping.' He stood and they walked to the door.

'We're attending the Retrospective reception. I'm assuming you'll be there?'

He nodded. 'More's the pity. Are you planning to observe the Levitte tribe meeting and greeting?'

'We're planning to speak to Henry Levitte early in the evening then agree a date very soon afterwards for him to come into Rose Road.'

He struck a match. In its flare she saw the tremor of his hand as he applied it to the thin cigarette. He breathed out smoke. 'A sound idea. The only way you'll get anything out of that old tart is on *your* terms. I'll see you at the Retrospective.'

* * *

Kate's phone rang as she approached her car. 'Hi, Bernie.'

'Got something for you, Doc. The handprint at your place from the break-in the other night. Guess who?' She stopped. 'Stuey Butts.'

Despite having heard Bernie's suspicions already, she was surprised by the news. 'But he doesn't know me, my connection to the case. And even if he did, how would he know where I live?' Another thought occurred. 'You don't think this has any relevance for our plans tomorrow evening at the reception?'

'Don't see how.'

She ran a hand through her hair, trying to organise the ideas and concerns vying inside her head. 'He hasn't been found yet, Stuart?'

'Nobody knows where he is. Mother Butts is downstairs bawling her eyes out.'

'How come?'

'She's finally admitted they haven't had a clue as to his whereabouts for a few days.'

Kate was walking again. 'Why didn't she say before now?'

'I'm guessing years of avoiding the police and the bruise she's wearing on one side of her head might have something to do with that. Officers from Upstairs are still looking for him. I don't think we'll get any answers until we locate him.'

CHAPTER FORTY-THREE

Twenty minutes later Kate walked into her house to find Kevin leaning against a work surface making tea. 'Want some?' he offered. She nodded and waited until the tea was poured then carried both cups to the table. 'How was work?' he asked.

She sipped. 'Busy. Haven't stopped.' She looked at him. 'How's the leg?'

Kevin lifted it, grimacing, and she could see below the robe that it was still swollen. 'The end of my squash days.' He sighed. 'Thirty-eight and a squash has-been.' He leaned back against the chair to look at her. 'Ever wonder where it all went?'

She glanced at him. 'Where what went?'

'You know. Time. Us.'

Kate took another sip. 'I think you'll find it was you who "went",' she said. Anticipating the usual rush of self-justification she was surprised to hear another sigh.

'I know.' There was a few seconds' silence. 'It wasn't all bad before that, though. Was it?'

She put down her cup. 'Not all of it,' she said carefully, willing to go along with him in the interests of ex-marital harmony.

He looked at her, regret in his brown eyes. 'I'll never forgive myself for what I did to you, you know.'

'I'll never forgive you either,' she quipped to lighten the atmosphere, adding a grin to take the edge off her words.

'I have thought at times I was a fool.' She saw sadness in his face and was about to speak when he hit the table with his palm, causing her to jump. 'But there it is. *Nulli usui ploravit super effuso lac*, eh?' He grinned, leaving Kate to slowly parse the Latin as he struggled to his feet. He'd reached the study by the time she got it. 'No use crying over spilt . . .' She got up from the table, face grim, thoughts on her ex-husband and her father. She'd trusted them. They'd both left.

Carrying cups from the table to the Dishdrawer she stared at the wall. And then there was Joe: tall, attractive, amusing. She liked him and guessed he liked her given the jokey way he interacted with her. She deposited cups and saucers into the plastic racks. *It doesn't matter. At thirty-five I'm now in charge of my life. Never, ever again will I risk inviting the kind of chaos Kevin brought into it. It took too long to get order back*. She could do without that kind of commitment.

She followed him to the study. 'When are you going home?' she asked, then frowned, now aware of the quiet of the house. 'What's Maisie doing?'

He shrugged. 'Gone to some friend or other.'

She stared at him. 'When? You told me she was doing homework. Which friend? What time did—'

'I forgot she'd gone. She said something about Chelsey. *I've* had a tough day as well, you know. Stop fussing over her. She's twelve. The way you're carrying on she'll still be living here when she's forty.' The doorbell rang. 'See? Pathological worry, ill-founded.'

It was Joe. He came inside and the two men exchanged curt nods through the study door.

Joe looked at her. 'Thought I'd drop by. Bad time?'

Hearing muttering from the study she shook her head. 'No but I have to ring Candice.'

They both heard a beep from beyond the house, a rush of feet on the other side of the front door. It opened. 'Hi, Mom. Hi, Joe, saw your car.'

'I didn't know where you were,' said Kate, keeping her tone light.

'I told Daddy I was going to Chel's.'

Kate looked at Joe standing by the open door. He nodded. 'See you tomorrow, Red.' She watched him go.

CHAPTER FORTY-FOUR

Kate was sitting at the table in UCU teasing out the most likely investigative thread they now had: Henry Levitte. Bernie's voice broke into her efforts. 'Before I forget, what time are we getting to your place tonight to pick you up? I said I'd let Corrigan know.'

She glanced down at her watch. 'Six thirty. You'll also be picking up Julian. He's getting changed at my house. Where's Joe?'

'Accreditation Board Review for his firearms training. About this meeting with Levitte tonight: you and me need to agree what we say to him and, more important, what we *don't* say because my guess is he'll be talking to a lawyer by nine tomorrow morning, sooner if he has a friend who's one.'

'You know the procedure best so how about you tell me your views and I'll consider them alongside Henry Levitte's psychology and what we need to achieve?'

His hand rubbed shadowed jowls. 'Right, and as soon as we've got it together Goosey has to see it.' He reached for the phone. Two minutes later he hung up. 'He's calling in. In half an hour.'

Something in her notes of the recent visit she and Joe had made to Cassandra snagged Kate's attention. She traced a line of shorthand strokes with her finger and stopped for a few seconds then looked up at Bernie. 'Have you ever thought how difficult it can be to get true meaning from what people say if their voices lack emphasis?'

He frowned at her, patting his pockets for a pen. 'Now you mention it, can't say I have.'

She stared at her notes. Cassandra had been on strong medication when they met with her. Again she tracked specific strokes. When she'd asked Cassandra about the occasions on which Nathan came to her home, Cassandra had described a time when she was ill and her father was angry. She looked at the actual words Cassandra had said: 'No . . . that was it.' Looking up at Bernie she spoke. 'Listen to these two sentences. First one: "No . . . that was it." And the second: "No . . . *that* was it." What do you think?'

He gave her a brows-down look. 'You know my attitude to all this words-under-the-microscope stuff.'

She mustered patience. 'This was Cassandra speaking about a visit Troy made to her home. I asked her if she could remember the last time he visited. I thought she was saying "No, that's the only one I remember." She wasn't. She was saying that the one she'd described *was* the last time! See?'

He came to Kate's side to look down at the notes, seeing only hieroglyphics. 'You're saying she was telling you that the time she was on about *was*—'

'Troy's last visit. Exactly. Now listen to what she said about it: *she* got ill, her father was angry, things crashed and rolled.' She stared up at him. 'I think there could have been a row between Troy and Henry Levitte. Levitte was much younger then. There may even have been a physical fight.'

He slowly nodded. 'I'm with you, Doc. You're thinking that Nathan Troy never died down at the lake but at Hyde Road? We need to watch what we say to Levitte when we see him tonight.'

* * *

Minutes later they heard the approaching heavy footfalls of Chief Superintendent Gander. He came through the door shooting distracted glances at each of them. 'Let's get to it and I want to see a plan that's got "Careful" written all over it.'

Bernie described a meeting that would be low-key. They would inform Henry Levitte that he was now viewed as a prime person of interest in the murder of Nathan Troy. They would explain to him that he was not necessarily a suspect but they believed he might possess knowledge of what had happened to Troy.

'We'll word our request for an interview here in such a way that he knows it's going to happen,' said Kate. 'We'll wait to see if he mentions bringing legal representation.' Gander studied the floor as she continued. 'We're going to contact him in the next half-hour to agree the best time to talk to him this evening.' Furman had strolled inside on the last few words and was now standing near the door. 'We won't give him any details. It will be a case of "We have some 'insights' about Nathan Troy's murder and we want to discuss them with him here, tomorrow".'

Bernie handed the single A4 sheet to the chief inspector as Furman's eyes slid to Kate and then to Gander who was nodding agreement. 'You're still confident about the quality of the information you've got?' he asked, looking from Bernie to Kate. They nodded. 'Lieutenant Corrigan is of the same mind?' More nods.

Furman broke into the conversation. 'Just to restate my position. I don't agree with or support this.'

She gave him a direct look. 'Having identified Henry Levitte as a Prime we need to hear as soon as possible what he has to—'

Furman glared at her. 'I'm still querying the lack of evidence.'

She pointed at the screens. 'The psychological indicators are all there.'

He shook his head. 'Nearly two years you've been here and you still don't get it.'

Gander gave him an irritable look. 'Leave it. Kate's a part of UCU because of her psychological expertise. If she says these indicators are reliable, we go with it.' Wisps of uncertainty unfurled themselves inside Kate's head as she watched him button his straining jacket. 'You've not heard any more about what's happening at the park?' he asked. She and Bernie shook their heads and he turned and strode from the room, Furman in his wake.

CHAPTER FORTY-FIVE

At six fifteen Kate was in her bedroom before the full-length mirror, fighting mounting anxiety as she turned from one side to the other, scrutinising her reflection. She hadn't worn the knee-length midnight blue dress for two years, and then only once. As on that occasion it was undeniably body-hugging from shoulder to knee. She turned again, squirming to gaze critically over the other shoulder. The same.

Unease was now replaced by a crisis of confidence. She walked carefully to the dressing table, picked up a hand mirror and returned to the full-length version to check the back view, registering a ring from the hall phone. *It's like a second skin. Why didn't you try it on before?*

She glanced at her watch. Too late? Maybe not. She could do a quick change into the black lace with the back slit. Taking a few steps away she turned and watched herself approach the mirror in the vertiginous suede heels. *What the hell's going on?* With no assistance from her the shoes, never previously teamed with the dress, were adding an undeniable sexual aspect to her movements.

A voice floated into the bedroom from beyond the door. 'Mom? *Mom!* Bernie and Joe are on their way — they'll be here in a couple of minutes.'

Frazzled, she shifted her attention to the heavy curtain of hair resting on each shoulder. Pushing it back she thought of the planned event for the coming evening: Henry Levitte had agreed on the phone to meet them between seven forty-five and eight o'clock, after which there would be a formal presentation at nine attended by a number of city dignitaries when he would deliver a brief speech of thanks. *Our involvement should be long finished by then.*

She took a deep breath. Time she went downstairs.

* * *

Julian loped into the sitting room, slowing as he realised he was there ahead of Kate and that Kevin, its only occupant, was staring at him over his newspaper. Discomforted but lacking the social aplomb to make a smooth exit, he sat on the edge of a chair, feeling and looking cornered. Kevin eyed him. 'So, where exactly are you all off to? Somewhere formal?' He surveyed the circa 1980s dinner jacket with wide lapels and too-long sleeves. 'Fancy dress thing, is it?'

'It's the private viewing of the Levitte Retrospective at the—' Picking up the subtle sound of car doors Julian made a springbok leap towards the sitting room door and the hall beyond.

'Yes, you deal with callers,' encouraged Kevin, his leg propped on a low stool. 'Ah, too late,' he added as Julian returned amid the sound of the front door being opened.

Maisie bounded into the sitting room and onto the sofa as Kevin put out a warning hand. 'Watch the leg!'

'Bernie and Joe are here and they're looking *really* special.' She looked across the room. 'Hi, Julian. You look nice too.' Kevin watched as the sitting room door swung open again to reveal the new arrivals. He didn't greet them. Maisie took the social initiative. 'Mom said ages ago that she'd be one minute. I'd sit down if I were you.'

Joe crossed the room to look out on the darkened rear garden as Bernie lowered himself onto a chair, nodding at

Julian. 'That dinner jacket works a treat, Devenish. I might start wearing it again.' Julian glanced at Bernie's solid girth. 'Y'know, as we drove here I had a thought. If I hold onto the job a bit longer I might consider a place round this part of Harborne.'

Kevin gave his newspaper a quick shake and fold. 'There goes the neighbourhood,' he murmured, so quiet that only Joe heard it.

They all heard the next sound: footsteps on the stairs, followed by the rhythm of heels across the hall. They turned as one to the sitting room door as it drifted open. 'I'm ready.'

Maisie was the first to find a voice. '*Wow*, Mom! You've got these "wiles" Chel's mom's been telling us about.' Kate's colleagues watched as she turned back to the hall then they and Maisie followed her.

Kate's voice drifted back to the sitting room. 'I won't be late. Don't forget, Maisie, bed at—'

'I *know*.' As the sound of the car engine faded she yelled after them, 'Have a great date!' Closing the door she returned to the sitting room and her father's irritable face. 'Wha'?'

CHAPTER FORTY-SIX

The White Box Gallery was full of heat and brittle social noise, its ground floor now transformed with extravagant arrangements of flowers, floor-standing displays of Henry Levitte's work and populated by a sophisticated, evening-dressed crowd. They stood together, searching for familiar faces. Henry Levitte's for one. He wasn't in evidence, but one or two others were. John Wellan was standing some distance away on one side of the room. Kate noted that he was wearing full evening dress. Nothing anarchic such as the cartoon character T-shirt she'd observed under his dinner jacket on one occasion. She watched him nod absently at Theda Levitte who was talking avidly at him in above-the-knee shiny black satin, hair stiffly coiffed. As Matthew Johnson appeared to one side of them Wellan glanced up looking morose, saw Kate and raised his champagne glass. Following his gaze Theda Levitte turned, sending her a tight-mouthed glare before turning back to speak to Johnson.

Somewhat nearer, Kate noticed Roderick Levitte talking to a tall, slender blonde in a red taffeta sheath, her hair in an elegant French pleat. Maybe he'd got himself a date? she thought, noticing that despite the dinner jacket, he didn't appear to have shaved. He looked as exhausted as when she'd met him at Margaret Street. She watched his companion talking in animated fashion to him and two other males, one she didn't recognise, the other Alastair Buchanan. *What's he doing here?* If he'd noticed Kate he gave no indication. The tall blonde was now laughing, bright lips drawn back from white teeth, diamonds sparking at her ears. She turned her head, making sudden eye contact with Kate. The wide mouth freeze-framed for two seconds as the eyes swept over her head and beyond.

Leaving Bernie and Joe to survey the crowd Kate moved to where a small knot of guests was gathered around a man in a pale blue satin dinner jacket who was expounding on the merits of a canvas on a nearby wall. 'And this is, of course, a *prime* example of what I'm saying. In *this*, one can see *every* artistic decision made by Henry Levitte during its execution. One can appreciate the true *appeal* of his work on an *immediate* level but also . . .'

She turned away, heart rate increased by the mention of the word 'prime'. Bernie appeared at her side, handing her a glass, frowning at the satin-clad critic. 'Here you go. One gin and tonic. Corrigan's gone to do a quick recce. Who's the arty git?'

Kate swallowed a mouthful of her drink then transferred the glass to the hand holding her evening clutch to examine the commemorative programme she'd been handed on arrival. 'Have you seen him yet? Henry Levitte?'

'No but I heard somebody say he's here. When I phoned him he said he'd send a message when he was ready to talk to us but one of the waiters has just told me they're already expecting things to run a bit late. The sooner we get to see him the better. I'd like to wrap this up by half nine.' He nodded his head towards where Julian was standing, a glass of champagne in each hand. 'I'm going to have a quick word with *him*.'

Kate distracted herself from thoughts of the imminent meeting with Henry Levitte by searching the invitees again. John Wellan and Theda Levitte were no longer in evidence. Neither were Matthew Johnson nor Roderick Levitte although the elegant blonde was still there, talking to appreciative males. Kate searched the throng once more, finding no trace of Buchanan.

* * *

By eight thirty p.m. it was looking increasingly unlikely that they would get to meet with Henry Levitte prior to the formal presentation and his speech. Kate had started on her second gin and tonic and was now aware of the heat. There was nowhere to sit. She squirmed leaden toes. Feeling a slight ache behind her eyes from the combined effects of heat, noise, perfume and the scent of multiple lilies, she was beginning to doubt that she'd make it to whenever Henry Levitte was due to speak if she had to remain vertical for much longer.

Scanning the ground floor for the Ladies, she caught sight of Joe, his head close to that of the tall blonde. He looked up at her and winked. As she watched he said something to the woman who inclined her head towards his and gave him a wide smile. He detached himself and walked towards Kate and not for the first time she thought how striking he was. The tall blonde evidently thought so too.

'How's it going, Red?'

'Fine. I didn't realise you have a particular liking for women with faces on a level with your own,' she snapped. *This is what comes of one-and-a-bit gins and tonics: not only getting green-eyed but letting him know it, you idiot.*

He raised dark brows at her. 'I like women.' Seeing the expression on Kate's face he grinned. 'Strictly in the interests of our investigation, I was unselfishly giving Miss Miranda Levitte my undivided attention.'

Kate looked back to where Miranda was still standing. 'That's *her*?' She looked up at him again. 'Mm . . . I could *see* you were. Any idea of Henry Levitte's whereabouts?' She looked at her watch. 'It's already gone eight thirty.'

Joe scanned the room over most of the heads around them. 'Don't see him.'

She held out her glass. 'Can you take this please, Joe? I'm going to find the Ladies and try to encourage the blood supply back into my feet. I noticed one upstairs when we were here the other day.'

She turned and made her way towards the stairs, coming face to face with Miranda Levitte who looked down at her, eyes evaluative. 'So, *you're* the psychologist who's planning to speak to my father this evening.' She turned away. 'Please keep it brief. He's rather tired.'

'We'll bear that in mind,' answered Kate in a crisp tone, aware of a bulky presence now on her other side. She felt a firm hand on her upper arm and heard Theda Levitte's voice above the hubbub. '*Mrs* Hanson.'

'*Mrs* Levitte,' responded Kate, now thoroughly fed up with the noise and heat.

'I'm *very* surprised that you and those two policemen arranged to come here *this* evening. Henry told me you want to speak to him. What's all this about? I *want* to know.'

'I'm sorry, I can't discuss it with you. We need to speak with your husband first.'

'Well!'

Joe arrived on Kate's other side. Theda Levitte gave him a sweepover glance and was gone. They watched her gesture impatiently at a waiter, baring her overbite at a nearby official photographer. 'Who's the shrink-wrapped heavyweight?' he asked.

'That's Mrs Henry Levitte the Second,' said Kate, heading for the stairs. 'I won't be long.'

* * *

On pulsing feet Kate walked amid the tumult to the thick red rope looped across the staircase. Shrill laughter and high-pitched voices followed her as she unclipped it and stepped onto the first stair, secured it behind her and continued upwards, now very aware of the combined effects of gin, noise and heat.

The upper floor was cool and quiet. Vestigial light seeping upwards from the ground floor scarcely penetrated the darkness here. Unable to locate a light switch Kate moved away from the stairs towards the nearby wall. Disorientated, wondering if maybe it was too soon to be up here after what had happened the last time, she skimmed the wall's smooth surface with one hand, bumping into some narrow shelving on which she dimly discerned a white table napkin and an abandoned metal tray.

Continuing in what she reasoned was the direction she needed she reached a dim corridor off the main floor, a glowing sign above the door at its end: *Ladies*. With a rush of relief she walked the corridor and pushed open the door. It was empty. Kate walked inside and sank onto one of the high-backed gilt chairs facing a mirror surrounded by light bulbs. She closed her eyes and remained there for a couple of minutes, revelling in the quiet and the opportunity to sit down. She straightened and opened her eyes to assess her reflection. She looked okay, if a little flushed. But the *feet*! She wriggled her toes again, feeling them start to pulse, cursing the shoes but deciding not to risk removing them. Better to sit here for a minute or two and hope for some improvement.

Opening the small clutch, she took out lip gloss and applied it, giving her watch a quick glance. The presentation was now imminent. Where had Henry Levitte got to? She glanced at the programme she'd been holding since she arrived, a portrait of him reproduced on its front. She looked inside, read the summary of his long and distinguished career and his considerable contribution to art and various charitable bodies. The presentation of his award was to be made by the city's Lord Mayor. She folded the programme, pushed it inside the clutch, got to her feet with a quick wince, walked to the door of the Ladies and out.

The upper floor was now in almost total darkness. *Probably the effect of the brightness inside the loo*. Aware of vast empty space and having somehow misplaced the wall she took measured, cautious steps, wondering what had happened to the meagre illumination from downstairs. There was now only the merest hint of it and the whole place had quietened. *They're starting the presentation! The lights have been dimmed. He's down there. Now we'll have to wait around until he's free.*

Kate edged forward then stopped, conscious of a steady, rhythmic creaking sound coming from nearby. Unable to identify its direction she listened, took a few more steps, stopped again this time to sniff the air. There was a smell. Not flowers. Not perfume. Her nose drew in odour molecules, the neurones beyond it sending signals to her brain. Pungent and meaty, it filled her head and she was once again a seventeen-year-old hospital volunteer distributing books and magazines to elderly patients.

Confused and disturbed she took a few more tentative steps into a wall of sodden, malodorous wool which brushed against her face, her lips. Panicked, disorientated, gasping at the wetness, Kate dragged air into her mouth as the wool yielded. Wrenching her face away, arms raised involuntarily, the satin clutch fell from her hand as one glossy sole slid forward on the smooth, wet floor. Head jerking backwards, flailing against wool and gravity, Kate crashed downwards to solid wood. She lay, unable to move, her head turning to light now penetrating upwards from the lower floor, hearing raised voices. She floated, her eyes closed.

When she next opened them she saw the vast vaulted ceiling miles above her. Much, much nearer was Henry Levitte, his lopsided face gazing down at her, his moist lips slackened, eyes yellow-white and pupil-less, neck engorged. He swayed, frail and elegant as she tracked him: To the left. To the right. To the . . .

Kate's brain called time and she fainted.

CHAPTER FORTY-SEVEN

She gulped air. Tried to stand. Failed. Urgent footsteps were approaching. Light from the stairs seared her eyes. She drifted in shock, hearing a woman's harsh shouting. How was she supposed to think, with all of this? Time slid, treacherous and unreliable, stealing whole minutes.

Kate was now wrapped in a red waffle blanket, inside a small, meagrely furnished room. She felt sick. Bernie's large warm hand patted her shoulder. 'You're all right, Doc. Relax.' She heard Joe's voice nearby, saw Julian's white face, his eyes wide. Nausea was now coming in waves. Lifting one hand from the blanket she placed her fingers against her mouth, perspiration on her forehead and upper lip, saliva surging into her mouth. *No. Please. Not that. Anything but . . .* She swallowed hard, looked up to see Bernie's concerned face, saw Joe's hands move as he fashioned a newspaper into a cone shape. Kate squeezed her eyes shut as the nausea came again and her diaphragm rippled. *Think other things . . . Think other things.*

She did. She thought of her demands to Chief Inspector Gander that UCU see Henry Levitte this evening. Their prime POI in the death of Nathan Troy. Levitte would have known why they were coming here, guessed their suspicions of him.

Kate frowned. *Her* suspicions. He knew what was going to happen and he'd killed himself. Her heart rate climbed as she recalled the sight of him hanging above her. *What have I done*?

'Kate?' With a swish of protective clothing Connie Chong was beside her, voice urgent. 'Look at me.' Kate opened her eyes and stared. 'Tell me where you are,' instructed Connie. Kate's eyes lost focus again, drifting haphazardly to the desk and on to two large, framed paintings leaning against a nearby wall. '*Kate*?'

She dragged her attention back. 'Do' know . . . White Box.'

'Good girl.' There was the double click of a case being opened followed by Connie's voice again. 'She's in shock.'

'He . . .' Kate closed her mouth on another surge. Swallowed.

Connie was holding up two small tablets. 'Listen to me, Kate. Put these under your top lip, one each side. They'll stop the nausea.' She did as instructed, hands shaking, jaws clamped.

Connie transferred her attention to the others in the room. 'What happened exactly?'

Joe was still holding the newspaper cone, eyes on Kate. Bernie responded. 'We were down here on the ground floor waiting for a message from Levitte to say he'd see us. We didn't get one. The Doc went upstairs and found him. Walked *into* him.' Kate squeezed her eyes closed and her lips together. 'The family knows something's happened but they haven't been told anything yet. Joe stopped Levitte's wife going up there.'

Listening as she examined Kate's pupils, Connie gave a brief nod. 'I've seen her drinking brandy. Somebody pointed her out to me.'

Bernie looked from Kate to Connie. 'You examined him yet?'

She nodded. 'Forensics did the snaps, got him down and I've done a *very* quick prelim. Igor's keeping him company along with two PCs. There are more officers from Rose

Road on this floor, crowd-managing, stopping anyone leaving.' She turned back to Kate and gave her a searching look, noting the return of some colour. Closing her case she stood, her attention now on the other members of UCU. 'Want to take a look at him? No, not you Kate,' she said, seeing the red blanket being pushed away.

Kate let it fall and stood, still shaky. 'I'm . . . okay but not Julian.'

'That's not *fair*.'

'Settle down and be quiet,' snapped Bernie. 'Wait here.'

Her two senior colleagues in the lead, Kate left the small room and walked with Connie along the short corridor. 'Leaving aside the awful experience you've had, *love* the outfit,' whispered Connie, on a mission of distraction as they emerged into the spacious ground-floor area and continued to the stairs, watched by the now silent and captive crowd. 'I think *all* UCU personnel should "dress" more often. Don't you agree that Bernard looks *particularly* pretty?' she murmured, eliciting a shaky smile from Kate.

Reaching the now well-lit upper floor they walked on to where the body of Henry Levitte lay on a still-open body bag. Connie made a staying motion. 'Not too close and keep to that side, away from this area. It's still damp.'

They looked to where his body was lying. Kate's eyes drifted over it, starting at the patent leather shoes then upwards to the darkened trouser front and on to the upper body, the face. The eyes were half closed, a red rash now evident on the slack skin beneath each of them. One cheek, one side of the neck and both ears were also flushed. Connie pulled on gloves, following the direction of Kate's attention. 'Petechial rash associated with asphyxia.'

Kate watched Connie's movements. 'He knew we were going to accuse him of involvement in Troy's death and . . . he did this,' she whispered, beginning to shake. Joe removed his jacket and placed it around her shoulders.

Connie gave her head a firm shake. '*No*, Kate. I very much doubt the cause of his death was hanging.' She was on her knees pointing a latexed finger at Henry Levitte's neck. Kate shut her eyes as her colleagues studied the well-delineated, dark red furrow snaking its way around it. 'If he'd died from hanging I'd have anticipated seeing livid bruising caused by coagulation of blood beneath the skin where the instrument of hanging exerted pressure on the surrounding tissue. There isn't any.' She gazed upwards, to the balustrade and the long cord dangling there, then back to the body. 'And the mark you can see on his neck would have included a suspension point, where that cord pulled upwards. I've checked. The furrow you can see is continuous. There is no suspension point. He was killed before he was suspended.'

Kate's eyes flew open, bright spots of colour forming on her cheeks. 'So, what caused his death?'

'Unless he tells me something very different later, in my opinion he was strangled. From behind.' Kate watched as she eased away the wing collar. 'See how unmarked the neck is, apart from the groove? No indication of fingertip bruising, no nail marks.' She looked up at them. 'Strangulation by ligature. Looks like his killer wanted to hide the cause of death. Hoping for it to be deemed a suicide, maybe?' She sat back on her heels looking up at them. 'As usual at this stage, what I'm saying is tentative.'

'Any idea as to time of death?' asked Joe.

Connie lifted eloquent shoulders. 'Two hours prior to Kate finding him, maybe more, maybe less.' She pulled off her gloves. 'If what I've said about cause *is* correct we have three fatalities: Nathan Troy, Bradley Harper, Henry Levitte. All strangled in a similar way.' Kate stared at the body then looked at each of her colleagues as Connie's voice filled the silence. 'There's a pattern, UCU, and Henry Levitte's death is part of it.'

CHAPTER FORTY-EIGHT

'DS Watts!' A breathless Whittaker was looking upwards from the bottom of the stairs. 'Can you come down? The family's getting restless, particularly the older woman.'

'Where are they?'

'We're keeping them in separate offices down a corridor off the main floor and *she's* going bonkers. *Listen.*' They did, picking up harsh sounds muted by distance. 'Gus is asking if you'll have a word with each of them, then we'll get written statements and let them go.'

Leaving Connie they followed Whittaker's swift departure down the stairs. On the ground floor Julian joined them, his face pale and sweating. 'We'll take the wife first,' said Bernie.

The dumpy figure turned her head to the door and erupted as they came inside. 'About bloody time! What's *happened*? What's going on? They wouldn't let me up.'

'Okay, Mrs Levitte. We need to have a quiet word.'

'*Stick* your "quiet word"!' She swung round on her chair, plump legs parted, pointing at Bernie's face. 'Tell me! What's happened to Henry? Is he ill? I want to see him. He *needs* me!' Kate stared at her. Events of the evening had stripped away the social voice and her chest and throat were covered in a fiery red mottling. 'Just you wait till our solicitor hears about this.' Heads turned as a young constable came into the room and they watched him set a mug down on the desk next to her. 'You can get rid of that! I'm not drinking that crap!' She shoved it away, causing the contents to spill.

Bernie walked to her, placing both hands on the desk, his eyes on the irate face. 'You need to calm down Mrs Levitte because—'

'Don't *you* tell me—'

'—I've got some bad news for you and you need to be quiet and hear it.' She stared. 'I'm sorry. It's your husband . . . He's dead.' Everyone in the room steeled themselves for a verbal onslaught that didn't come. 'You understand what I'm saying, Mrs—'

'Yes. yes. I *get* it.' Kate heard irritation in the voice, saw hectic thinking behind the coarse face.

Bernie straightened. 'I'm not sure you do. I've just told you what's happened to your husband but you don't seem to be upset.'

Theda Levitte lifted her face to his. 'I understand what you've said. I *know* what you thought about him and you were *wrong*!' Kate closed her eyes. 'But he's dead now and my priority is my stepchildren. Where are they?'

Bernie took the chair on the other side of the desk. 'The way this works, *we* talk to them first—'

'You keep *away*! I want to talk to them. *Now*. I want them fetched. I want to talk to Miranda.' Her face suffused. 'That brother of hers—' She stopped, eyes hooded. 'I want to see Roderick.'

Bernie was fast approaching the end of his patience. 'And like *I* said, you need to calm down.' She drew her arms around her squat body, red mottling stark against the white flesh. He nodded. 'That's better. We'll make it as quick as we can.'

They left her and walked to the door, Bernie lowering his voice as he gestured at a young constable there. '*You*. Find Whittaker.' He jerked a thumb. 'Get him to take her statement. Keep her here as long as you can.'

They continued down the corridor to the next office. Roderick Levitte stood as they came inside, body wavering, hands on the back of the chair to steady himself. His eyes lingered on Kate. 'I heard my stepmother's voice—'

'Sit down please, Mr Levitte,' Bernie interrupted. 'We want a word.' Levitte sat, rumpled and glassy. 'First, I've got some bad news for you. It's about your father. I'm sorry to have to tell you but . . . he's dead.' Levitte lowered his head, hands going to the short hair, his upper body beginning a steady rocking motion. Bernie watched him, uncomfortable, his voice gruff. 'Sorry but we need to—' The words were stopped by a low feral sound from deep within the rocking man which intensified then forced its way out of his mouth, high and rolling.

They looked at each other. With a second glance at Bernie Kate went to where Roderick was sitting. 'Mr Levitte? There's a doctor upstairs. Would you like—' They watched as the hands left the plump face, saw the wide mouth, the exposed teeth, eyes narrowed and streaming. Roderick Levitte was laughing.

Within a couple of minutes he'd gained a semblance of control. Looked up at them he gave a series of rapid blinks, fingering the moist skin directly beneath his eyes. '*Damn* these contacts. I'm okay. I'm . . .' The sound came again, another high, rolling laugh, subsiding after a few seconds. 'The King is dead, eh?' More laughter bubbled. 'And *I'm* still here.'

Bernie strode to the door and spoke in a low voice to the young constable lurking there. 'When Whittaker's finished with the stepmother get him in here to take this one's statement.' He turned to his colleagues. 'Let's get on with it.' They left Roderick Levitte slumped on his chair, still grinning.

'Why leave him? Why don't *you* take his statement?' Kate asked as she watched Joe walk ahead of them along the corridor.

'*Because* I want to be away from that madness and there's a couple of other people still to see.' They'd reached the last door and Bernie threw it open. The room was empty. He turned and beckoned to the constable. 'Where is he?'

The young constable looked unnerved. 'Where's who, sir?'

Kate watched Bernie's colour mount. 'There should be another witness. His name's Buchanan. Nobody's been allowed to leave so where *is* he!' he railed.

'He must have left earlier, sir, before all of this kicked off.'

Bernie was on the move, back along the corridor, Kate beside him. 'What do you think?' she asked.

'Plenty, but it'll keep.'

She looked at him, frowning. 'Buchanan may not be the only one who left early. Where's Matthew Johnson?'

'God knows. He's not here, that's for sure. Wait till I get back to Rose Road! I'll have *plenty* to say about how to secure a bloody scene.'

They'd reached the bar area which was now empty of attendees, except for John Wellan sitting alone some distance away and Miranda Levitte seated at a table, pen in hand, staring down at a piece of paper. Joe was at the temporary bar, beckoning one of the idling waiters. 'One single, straight bourbon and a jug of iced water.'

Kate watched him take the alcohol to Miranda Levitte then return to fill glasses with water. He came to her holding one. 'Here you go, Red. You'll probably keep this down now.'

She shuddered. 'I see John Wellan's still here.'

'He's given his statement and he's offered to take Miranda home.'

'How is your cool blonde?' she asked as she sipped.

'Looking like she's finishing her statement so let's go find out.' They approached her. 'Miss Levitte? Not sure if you know my colleague Kate Hanson. Could we speak with you, please?' She looked at Kate, nodded, then away. Joe picked up the very brief statement and read through it.

Miranda Levitte put down her drink, voice indistinct. 'My father is dead and I can't . . . respond.' Kate saw confusion on her face. 'I never really . . . understood my family. How it worked. My brother and I — we were never favoured, like Cassandra. I always wondered what was wrong with us. With *me*.' Tears fell onto the red taffeta, splotching it black. Kate's head was full of ideas and questions as she watched the elegant head bow, the blond hair now escaping from its pleat. 'I was never the favourite but I was treated well. Roderick was the one who got all the criticism and Cassandra got . . .' She lifted her face, eyes wide, pupils dilated. 'Isn't the human mind amazing? We know what we know but we tell ourselves we *don't* know.' She pushed back her hair. 'I always wondered what our real mother knew. She loved Cassandra but . . . Mother was so unhappy living here. She was dependent on . . . him.'

Kate took a deep breath. She knew she'd been right about Henry Levitte. At the sound of approaching footsteps they all turned. It was Roderick. 'I've given my statement. Can I talk to my sister, please?' He sat next to her, taking her hand. She didn't resist. 'I've got a lot of problems but it's time I faced—'

Sharp heels clicked across the floor. Theda Levitte approached her two grown stepchildren and, before anyone could stop her, delivered a resounding blow to Roderick's head with her open hand. Joe and Bernie arrived at her side, each seizing an arm. She struggled against them. 'I heard you laugh, you *bastard*, now shut *up*.' Kate saw Wellan's shocked face and Miranda squeeze her eyes and mouth closed as Roderick put a hand to his head. Theda Levitte looked at her stepchildren. 'They've got their statements. We're leaving. Now.' Kate watched them go, John Wellan getting up and following, his face weary.

A few minutes later she and her colleagues approached the gallery's doors where a lone male in a pale blue satin dinner jacket was standing. Bernie stopped. 'Who are *you?*' he demanded. Kate recognised him as the man who'd appraised Henry Levitte's work earlier in the evening.

'My name's Sylvester Seale.'

'Gerraway. What're you doing hanging about here?'

'I was told to wait.'

Bernie gave him a look. '*Who* told you?'

'One of the police officers. I told him I saw something and—'

Bernie's interest climbed. 'What did you see?'

Seale pointed at the stairs to the upper floor. 'I saw a waiter going up those stairs.' He turned to Kate. 'I also saw *you*. I noticed your hair and the—'

Bernie narrowed his eyes at Seale. 'Get on with it,' he barked.

Seale lifted satin shoulders. 'The waiter went up first. It was about . . . mmm, I'd say around seven thirty although I can't be absolutely *precise* about—'

Bernie gave him an irritable glare. 'How'd you know he was a waiter?'

The man gave brief consideration to the question. 'He was wearing a black dinner jacket . . .' Bernie gave an exasperated eye-roll, '*and* he was carrying a drinks' tray. My *impression* was that he was between forty and fifty years old — although, now I think about it, the way he moved. Good body tone. He *could* have been younger.'

Kate nodded. 'I saw a tray up there.'

Catching sight of Whittaker and another constable walking down the stairs Bernie gestured at them. 'One of you get a statement from *him*.' The constable nodded and hooked a finger at Seale. Bernie turned his attention to Whittaker. 'I want you to nip back up them stairs. There's a drinks' tray—'

'It's on a shelf. It has a white napkin on it,' said Kate.

They watched Whittaker's quick progress up the stairs. Bernie shouted after him. 'When you find it give it straight to Forensics to bag it!' They watched him cover the stairs at a fast pace. 'Good job one of 'em knows what he's doing and jumps to it,' Bernie muttered.

* * *

They were outside the gallery. Joe had gone to fetch the car. Julian was sitting on the kerb, Kate beside him. She felt better in the cold night air. She glanced at Bernie. 'What's next?'

'After we've read their statements we'll decide if we need to interview them. We'll get hold of Buchanan tomorrow. Ask him why he left in such a hurry. And that Johnson.' He looked tired as he gazed down at Kate wearing Joe's jacket. 'What d'you think about the Levittes? All bloody weird, if you ask me. Mother Levitte didn't give a damn about her husband and that git of a son *laughed*. As for the daughter, what was *she* on about?'

Kate stared at the brick-laid road. 'Miranda was making a lot of sense. What she said has confirmed for me that Henry Levitte *was* a sexual abuser. He singled out Cassandra.' She looked up at Bernie. 'It happens. Levitte knew his children well, recognised Cassandra's extreme need for attention. Miranda was probably much more confident as a child and therefore potentially too risky to be victimised. Roderick's role in relation to Henry Levitte was to be criticised and denigrated.'

'I still think the way they all carried on is weird.'

Kate nodded. 'I can see what you mean but in my forensic work I've learned that people can say and do odd things in the aftermath of traumatic situations.' She looked up at him. 'Do you know what Jackie Kennedy is quoted as saying shortly after President Kennedy was shot? She said, "They have killed my husband. I have his brains in my hand."' A faint groan came from Julian. She looked at him. 'How are you feeling?' He shook his head.

Hands in his pockets, Bernie looked unimpressed, despite what she'd told him. 'I've had to give bad news to a few people in my time, Doc, but I never saw anybody react like them three. How about one or all of them seen the old man off because we was getting close?'

Kate shook her head. 'I might be wrong but from what I heard tonight none of them knew in a real sense what was happening to Cassandra in that family.'

Bernie gave a sigh. 'In my book, Doc, you *know* something or you *don't*.'

She turned to him. 'You heard Miranda. She was telling us that she couldn't allow herself to know what her father was doing to her sister.'

'And Mother Levitte? What about her? Don't tell me she didn't know anything.'

Kate shrugged. 'By the time she joined the family a lot of what happened to Cassandra and Roderick had already occurred but if she did hear or guess she *chose* to ignore it. Theda Levitte has two interests: money and status. If she wanted those she couldn't allow herself to know. So she kept herself distanced.' *Distanced.*

'Right, so nobody's responsible for nothing.' Bernie transferred his attention to Julian. 'Hey! You still with us?' Julian raised his head, his face still pale. 'Seven glasses of champagne is six too many and I warned you. I'm glad it's the Doc's you're stopping at, not mine.'

Kate gazed along the road at the long line of cars leaving the multi-storey. 'I'll go and see Furman tomorrow. Imagine how he'll react about what's happened.'

He glanced down at her. 'It don't matter, does it? Our prime has turned victim. It's all part of our case.'

Kate pulled Joe's jacket close. 'Henry Levitte *was* a sexual risk, but did he murder anyone?'

Listening to her words Bernie's gaze was on the middle distance. 'Forget about it for now.' He gave her a sideways glance. 'By the way, you looked a treat tonight.'

She looked up at him, surprised. 'Thank you. At least *somebody* noticed.'

'Trust me, I weren't the only one.'

'He didn't say anything.'

He grinned at her as Joe's car came into view. 'Maybe he was knocked for six, Doc.' The car came to a halt in front of them and Kate slid inside it, exhausted.

CHAPTER FORTY-NINE

At eight o'clock the next morning Kate was calling upstairs for the third time. '*Maisie*? Down here, *now*, please.' Julian had appeared at the top of the stairs halfway through the loud words. Turning with care he disappeared. A hand to her head Kate retreated to the kitchen.

Kevin was at the table looking tired and irritable. 'That *bloody* student of yours was up and down the stairs fifty times during the night. Sounded like a herd of wildebeest. I'm supposed to be here for rest and recuperation.'

Standing at the table, dressed for a workday, her head thumping, Kate handed buttered toast to Maisie as she trolled past. 'Cereal afterwards. Plenty of milk.' She saw clear cornflower blue eyes roll then transferred her attention to the table's sole occupant. 'If this establishment isn't meeting your needs, please feel free to leave.' *You know how. You've done it before.*

'*Mom*. Don't be so horrible to Daddy. He's not well.' Hearing her mother's muttered response she gestured with toast. 'I heard that. You said, "My arse". When I said it that time, you went—'

Kate put a hand to her forehead. 'Be quiet, Maisie, for goodness' sake. You're not out of the woods yet, let me tell you.'

Kevin looked from one to the other. 'What's she done?' Kate ignored his question. She had no intention of telling him about Maisie being picked up by her police colleagues at Woodgate Park. Neither did he know about the break-in. Kate wanted it to stay that way.

The doorbell rang and Maisie darted towards the hall, picking up her book bag en route. 'That'll be Chel.'

'Maisie?'

'Wha'?'

'Home by four fifteen, latest. Don't miss the bus.'

Pulling at knee socks, giving the jaw-gaping head-quiver Kate disliked, Maisie opened the front door and disappeared through it to where Chelsey and her mother were waiting.

Kevin watched her as she returned to the kitchen. 'Maisie's getting out of hand if what I'm observing is the norm here: you ranting and she backchatting.'

'Kevin? Shut up.'

'You know your problem?' he said. 'You're doing too much, unnecessarily. You've got the university. Why don't you focus on that? Why this determination to involve yourself with this . . . this crime unit?'

She turned to him. 'It's a unit for unsolved crimes.' She studied him. 'It doesn't bother you at all, does it, that offenders don't pay for what they've done, that victims don't get justice?'

He let his head drop back. 'Not this again. *No*, it doesn't, because I'm part of the system and I understand it. You know where you're going wrong?' She closed her eyes. 'You're an academic trying to play detective. It's not working. Stick to what you know.'

'I know that the system is unfair and denies people the—'

'Most get justice!' he snapped. 'Can't that be enough for you—?' He was alone in the kitchen, the door hurtling towards its frame.

* * *

Two hours later, her morning lecture finished, she was inside her room at the university, chin on fist, staring at nothing. Her gaze dropped to a telephone message from Bernie timed at eight forty-five that morning: *Nothing of obvious interest in Statements. Buchanan, Johnson contacted. Ditto. Ronnie Dixon in custody at Birmingham Prison and Ken visiting this a.m.* She read the last few words again and frowned. Ken was the EvoFIT specialist based Upstairs. Bernie had arranged for him to visit Dixon to ask him about the man with Harry Potter glasses he said he saw at the park the previous year. No matter how good the facial composition software was, it would be a considerable feat of memory for Dixon to accurately recreate the features of someone he'd briefly seen many months before. And if he managed it what were the odds of the man he'd seen being identified and arrested? Particularly if he had no prior record. She came out of her reverie as the communicating door opened. 'Hi, Crystal.'

Kate watched as the cup was placed on its coaster on the desk. '*Drink*,' said Crystal, looking down at her, prepared to wait it out whilst she did so. She picked up the cup, sipped tea and leaned back against her chair. 'How're you feeling?'

She looked up at her young admin assistant. 'Last night—'

'Detective Sergeant Watts phoned this morning to tell me what happened.'

Kate sighed. Crystal wouldn't have had the whole story as Kate saw it. 'I made a judgement about someone. Now I've realised that I got it partly right but also very wrong.'

'We've all done that,' said Crystal. 'You know what? If I'm even partly right I just forget about it. Can I get you anything else?'

'No thanks.'

Alone, she sat, hands clasped at her mouth, then reached for the student assignments on her desk. *When was there ever a point in sawing sawdust?*

* * *

Six assignments later she pushed them to one side, thinking of what Connie had said: that the hanging of Henry Levitte was a subterfuge to conceal the fact that he was strangled. Kate sat back in her chair. *Who could have had that kind of motivation? Concealment of Troy. Concealment of hanging . . . I want to see Buchanan's and Johnson's statements from last night, no matter how brief.*

She stared out at the leafless campus. Henry Levitte had wielded power of a kind within his family. Power. What else does power afford people? She thought of Buchanan's lucky career trajectory and Johnson's meteoric rise within Woolner's faculty. With power came the ability to dispense largesse. She frowned. Everything she'd known about Levitte indicated him to be a sexual abuser. It didn't make him a murderer.

She thought of Cassandra. Was she still at risk now that her father was dead? And what about Stuart Butts? She looked down at names: Cassandra and Roderick. Nathan and Bradley. All victims. She added Joel Smythe's name, convinced it belonged on the dismal list. She picked up the phone and dialled John Wellan's number. He answered almost immediately. 'Do you know of anybody on the faculty at Woolner who might have kept in contact with Joel Smythe after he finished there?'

'Highly unlikely, I'd say, and how does he fit . . . Never mind, I'd rather not know. Even if I thought it worth asking the staff about Smythe, I can't. There's hardly anyone here. Lectures are cancelled as a mark of respect.'

She closed her eyes. 'I wasn't thinking. Forget it, okay?'

She put down the phone and stood. She had to get out of her room. In any case, there was something she had to do at Rose Road. Bag in hand she walked to the door, pulling on her coat, calling as she went. 'Crystal? I'll be back later.'

* * *

She walked down the corridor towards Furman's office to give her account of the previous evening's events. As she neared it she slowed. Voices were coming from the half-open door. She identified one as Gander's. 'Roger, you've said all this before—'

Furman's voice drifted towards her. 'That was before this latest debacle. I was against it from the start but she was adamant — and she got it *wrong*. It isn't the first time. She doesn't get police work. She's a loose cannon, she's impulsive and she won't be told anything.'

'She's highly qualified.'

'So what if she is? That doesn't change what I just said. This "interface" between policing and psychology isn't working. Watts finds it difficult, *plus* I don't trust that student of hers being allowed on the computer system.'

'Both the vice chancellor of the university *and* Kate are supervising young Devenish,' came Gander's weary voice.

She heard a mocking snort. 'She's as bad! For her rules are there to be disregarded. And *now* we're having to wait to find out the outcome of last night for this Force. The Levittes will have their lawyers—'

Kate spoke and looked towards the door. 'I'm concerned about the safety of Cassandra Levitte and I want some surveillance of the Hawthornes to ensure that she doesn't leave without our knowing.'

She watched Furman drop back on his chair, a hand over his eyes as Gander came towards her. 'We can't do that, Kate.'

* * *

Kate was walking across the car park, Gander's sympathetic face and his words in her head. There could be no surveillance of Cassandra because of a lack of manpower and no evidence to suggest it was needed: Miss Levitte was being cared for by mental-health professionals. She threw her bag into the boot and got into her car. Henry Levitte was dead but still casting his long shadow. They now knew a lot about him in life. Was there anything more to know? Shaking her head she started the engine, recalled the day she and Bernie had gone to see him at Hyde Road. She thought over the conversation they'd had and Levitte's reference to a location. A church.

CHAPTER FIFTY

Parking her car on the space in front of the Bell, Kate pulled up her collar and pushed her hands deep into her coat pockets. Her head was fuzzy and she still felt unwell from the events of the previous evening. As she walked amid winter bleakness her mood dipped. What would she achieve by coming here? It was the longest of long shots. She crossed Old Church Road and walked beneath the lich-gate set into the stone wall and overhung with dark evergreen, eyes on the mellow stone tower ahead.

Following the rough pathway through the churchyard she slowed to examine leaning gravestones on either side: sources of familial history. She halted beside a large stone structure. A family tomb. Taking a few steps nearer to read the words carved into it she struggled to see what lay beneath the grey-black surface pitted with whatever ailment old stones fall prey to. All she could make out were isolated letters.

Returning to the path Kate walked on. The stone she'd come to find was probably as old and as difficult to decipher. It might not even exist. She was wasting time whilst UCU's case foundered — they faced legal threat if what she'd heard Furman say earlier was reliable — and her university work piled up. Maybe she should go home and rest for an hour?

Then she remembered. Kevin was there. She didn't have the energy for him at the moment.

A rhythmic sound nearby pushed her senses to high alert. She stopped, scanning the churchyard for its source. A tall, spare man in padded coat and heavy scarf, a traditional besom broom in his hands, was sweeping the last dead leaves from around some of the headstones. Yet another long shot but she was here so she might as well ask.

'Excuse me? . . . Hello?' He halted his efforts, looked up, then in her direction. 'Do you work here? I mean, regularly. Do you know the church well?'

He leaned the broom against a headstone, face flushed from exertion and cold as he approached her, unwinding the scarf, giving her a friendly grin. 'I'm a volunteer. Have been for years. What is it you want to know?'

Kate was unprepared for such a direct inquiry. She improvised. 'A friend of mine, well, she's not a friend exactly, but she told me that she and her husband . . . belonged to this church years ago and . . . I was wondering if . . . the family had much direct connection with it. We've rather lost touch with each other.' *You're lying on church premises.* She didn't care. Poorly constructed as her improvisation was it had clarified the thinking behind her decision to come here.

He nodded, holding out his arm towards the church. 'I'm entrusted with a key. You'll know your friend's name so why don't we go inside? The church has maintained records of births, marriages and deaths among its parishioners for many years.' She walked with him towards the old building, listening as he talked. 'They're the church's own records, you understand, but we often get people coming to look at them when they're trying to construct family trees. A very popular pastime now. You're welcome to do the same. See if you can find any information relating to your friend.'

On reaching the rear of the church he led Kate between dark yews to an almost concealed door. She watched as he applied a large key to it. 'It's sad we have to do this but . . .' He gave a shrug and led the way into a small, chilly room lined with modern bookcases. Turning to Kate he asked: 'Young friend or old friend?'

She looked at him, startled. 'Oh, well, there are two, actually — in their fifties and seventies . . . One of each,' she ended lamely.

Nodding, he went to the shelves, running his fingers down shiny brown spines. Watching him she saw that they were in alphabetical order and grouped under the three headings he'd mentioned. As she waited he selected three hefty, leather-bound volumes and carried them to a table on one side of the room. 'Sorry it's so cold in here. I can't even offer you anything to drink, Miss . . . Mrs . . . ?'

'Hanson. Kate Hanson. Please don't apologise. I've interrupted you when you're busy.'

'No problem. I hope you don't mind my asking but do you feel all right?'

Kate knew what he meant. She'd seen her own reflection before she'd left her car: face pale and shadowed, hair in disarray. 'I'm fine. Thank you.'

'Then stay as long as you need.' He indicated the volumes he'd selected. 'If these don't have the information you require, feel free to search the shelves. I'll be outside. Let me know when you're ready to leave.' He gave her a thoughtful glance followed by a smile, went to the door and out, closing it after him.

Kate shook her head as she reached for the first volume. *After that cover story and looking the way you do no wonder he thinks you're odd. Or worse.* Checking dates and words stamped into leather she selected one of the volumes and settled to her task.

After fifteen minutes she'd gone to the second volume and found the first reference of interest to her: Henry Levitte's marriage to his first wife Flora Tremblay had taken place here. She absorbed the detail: he was born in Hertfordshire, she in Montreal. His second marriage had also occurred here to Theda Barr, spinster and nurse from Sheffield. Reaching for the third volume she turned pages, eyes scanning elegant, penned words: Henry Winston Levitte. Born 1902. This had to be Henry Levitte's father. She read on. He'd worked as a design engineer with De Havilland. Her eyes widened at the name. The aircraft building company? Kate's breathing quickened, recalling what Julian had said about an expensive watch found with a dead boy: that it could have belonged to a pilot. She looked again at the information: Levitte Senior died in 1985. She knew it wasn't 'real' evidence, wasn't incontrovertible proof, but it made sense. Henry Levitte would have inherited his father's watch on his death. The question now was did Henry Levitte still have it at the time Nathan Troy died? If not, then in whose possession was it when Troy was interred under the lake house floor?

Kate closed the volumes, thinking of an engineer who had a son who became a painter. As she carried the books back to where they belonged her thoughts spun on, to another son: Nathan Troy and his beautifully subtle pictures. His pictures. *Portrait.* The word arrived inside Kate's head with such suddenness that she almost felt the jigsaw pieces turn, slide and arrange themselves into a unified whole with a sudden, satisfying *click!* She *had* to get home. *Now*. She had to *see*. Hurrying from the church she walked in the direction of the sweeping sound. He turned as she approached. 'I've come to let you know I've finished. Thank you. I have to go . . .'

He watched her quick progress away, calling after her: 'You found . . . who or what you were searching for?'

She turned, still moving. 'I did.'

CHAPTER FIFTY-ONE

Kate was inside her car, its engine humming, phone to her ear. 'Julian, I need an urgent database search. *Really* urgent.' She gave him the details, ended the call and pulled away. Within minutes she was thrusting open the front door. *Surely* if she'd seen it she would have realised last night.

A petulant voice drifted into the hall. 'Kate? That you, Kate?' Ignoring it she pounded the stairs.

Flying to her bedroom and on to her wardrobe, her hands churned scarves, belts and handbags, looking for a particular item. She stopped. It was here. She picked it up, the cool satin against her fingers. Opening it with unsteady hands she removed the programme, smoothing it with her fingers, turning it over. Here he was. Henry Levitte in portrait, the detail itself very small. She took it to the window. It looked similar but she had to be sure, had to examine the original. She ran down the stairs and out of the house, Kevin's irritable voice drifting after her.

* * *

Approaching the White Box Gallery's glass doors she saw a large white van parked nearby, words on its side indicating it to be the property of the Institute of Art and Design (Margaret Street), alongside the red and blue V of the Birmingham City Council logo: 'Two Fingers Raised,' according to Bernie. The van was under the close supervision of a security guard.

She walked to the gallery's open doors and was stopped by another uniformed figure. 'Excuse me, madam.' He glared down at her from under the peak of his cap, blue serge arm barring her progress. Agitated, she searched inside her bag for identification. She *had* to get inside. *Had* to see it. The security guard took his time perusing her Rose Road identification, under-impressed. 'Is there a *named* person you have business with?' Kate's gaze swept the ground floor, seeing that most of what had been here the previous evening was dismantled, the art works gone. She bit her lip. *Why* hadn't she been quicker last night to realise? *Too busy holding onto two gins and tonics and whatever dignity you had left.* She glanced at the van. 'Stan from Margaret Street. Is he here?' Looking even less impressed, the guard raised his arm. 'Up there.'

Heart quickening, Kate went to the stairs and began to climb. By the time she reached the upper floor it was hammering with re-experienced stress. 'Stan? *Stan!*'

Hearing a muffled response she spun, seeing him some distance away, an A4 sheet clutched in one hand. He smiled as she walked towards him. 'It's you again. I'm nearly done here. Just checking the list of exhib — Are you okay?'

She gave a quick nod. 'Fine. I want to look at something—'

'You're as white as a sheet. Come over here. Sit down on this sofa—'

'*No!* Listen, when I was here last night I was in a small room. Somewhere down there. It was windowless with hardly any furniture.'

'I think I know which one you—'

'I *must* look inside it.'

'I'll take you down — sure you don't need anything?'

'Let's *go*.' She started down the stairs. By the time she reached the vast almost empty expanse of ground floor he'd caught up with her and was directing her along a corridor. He stopped at a pale wood door and threw it open. 'This is it.'

She walked inside, memories of the previous evening flooding her head. Here was the table, the chair, even the newspaper . . . She looked around the small room, then at him. 'Where are they? Where've they gone?'

He eyed her, dubious. 'Where's what?'

She jabbed a finger at one corner. 'There were two paintings there last night, leaning against that wall. One was a portrait. I *must* look at it again.'

He held up his hands. 'Okay, okay. No need to get excited. It's outside.'

He followed her out of the office, across the ground floor and out, still with a wary look on his face. Unlocking the van doors he threw them wide, gesturing at its contents. 'I think I know the one you're on about. If you'll give me a—'

Kate was already inside, bent low, examining paintings slotted inside a metal and wood structure. He followed her. 'It's over here.' Within the confines of the vehicle and its considerable load he edged towards two large canvases in heavy frames. Breath quickening with exertion he manoeuvred the largest so that it now faced Kate who crouched on her heels before it. 'This the one?'

She stared at it, the dark hair, the strong nose, the fleshy mouth. 'This is it.' Leaning closer she focused her attention on the area between the hand and the lower arm. She would know it anywhere. She reached for her phone.

Thanking Stan she left the White Box Gallery and hurried to her car. As she left the city centre she contemplated her next step. Nathan Troy had died for a specific reason. Not because some deviant stranger had had an urge to destroy him. Henry Levitte *may* have killed him. If not him then someone else Levitte knew. She needed facts relating to Cassandra's teenage years. She knew of only one place which might have them: the Hawthornes.

CHAPTER FIFTY-TWO

Leila Jones opened the door. 'Dr Hanson, come in. I'm afraid you've had a wasted journey. Cassandra isn't here.'

Kate stared at her as she stepped inside. 'Where is she?'

Miss Jones held out a hand towards her office. 'Her mood stabilised and she left yesterday to stay at her sister's house so she can be cared for over the next few days.'

Concern surged through Kate's head. Was Miranda aware that her sister needed protecting? Miranda herself might be a risk and . . . who'd been caring for Cassandra the previous evening? She pushed her hair from her face. Right now there was something she had to do. 'It's you I came to see.'

Looking surprised Miss Jones led the way into her office and gestured Kate to a seat, then walked behind her desk on which was sitting a thick file, a pen balanced on top of it. 'I'm adding details of Cassandra's latest stay to her patient records so I'm very—'

Her eyes on the medical records Kate asked, 'You've heard about her father?'

Miss Jones's head nodded beneath another multi-coloured turban, face sombre. 'Yes. We're hoping it doesn't precipitate another crisis but if she's well-supported and her medication intake is monitored, I think there's room for optimism.'

'I need your help.'

The manager shot her another surprised look. 'I'm not sure how I can help but if I can I will.'

'You like Cassandra, don't you?' The other woman nodded. 'During my visit here with Lieutenant Corrigan Cassandra wasn't explicit but what she told us — and other information we've acquired about her — gives me reason to believe that the Levitte family has some very . . . *problematic* dynamics.' The manager sent her a direct look and Kate knew that she'd understood her allusion to Cassandra's abuse. 'We started our investigation with the death of a young man in 1993. Two other people have died and as you know I'm worried about Cassandra's own safety. Increasingly so.' Her eyes dropped to the thick file. 'I have to see Cassandra's medical records.'

Leila Jones folded her hands on top of the file in front of her and fixed her with a look. 'I can't help you. You must be aware that they're confidential. They were released to the Hawthornes, to my keeping, for the express purpose of managing Cassandra Levitte's treatment here—'

There was a peremptory knock on the door and a young woman in a pale lilac overall came into the office. 'Sorry, Miss Jones, but can you come *now*?'

The manager's face tightened and she rose. 'You'll have to excuse me, Dr Hanson. We have a situation here with one of our residents.' She gestured towards the door. 'I'll show you out.'

Kate was ushered out of the office and stood in the echoing hall, hearing a loud crash from somewhere along the corridor. The young woman in lilac was fast disappearing in the direction of the noise, Leila Jones following her, pointing to the front door. 'See yourself out please.'

Kate walked across the hall and opened the door, stood for some seconds then released it. As it closed she turned back and looked along the corridor. No one in sight. She returned to the office, went inside, closed the door and leaned against it. Not for the first time a voice was shouting inside her head about rules, professionalism, ethics.

Pushing herself from the door, listening for sounds beyond the room, she hurried to the desk and reached for the file. There was no time to search it. Leila Jones might be back very soon. Giving the file a quick glance she saw a couple of pink Post-its protruding from it. Ears straining, she flipped pages to the first pink marker: Details of Cassandra's medication. Lithium. They already knew about that.

Kate flipped more pages to the second marker. She was way back in Cassandra's medical history, her eyes scouring multiple handwritten comments. She was stopped by three letters: *EDD*. All they'd been told about Cassandra as a young woman had led Kate to suspect it. Here it was. 'Expected Date of Delivery'. Years ago, when she was nineteen, Cassandra Levitte had been pregnant. Hearing faint sounds from somewhere beyond the office she read on, looking for more. She found it, further down, next to the words *Putative Father*, two initials which made her catch her breath. *MJ*.

Closing the file she went quickly to the door, listened then opened it, peering out. She could hear voices, one of them recognisable: Leila Jones. Kate left the office, ran soundlessly across the hall, opened the front door and slipped through it.

CHAPTER FIFTY-THREE

Kate sped into Rose Road's car park, slowing as a couple of uniformed officers turned to look as she approached. She parked, hearing her phone ringing inside the boot. Locating it she picked up the call: 'Hell — Oh, hello, John.'

'Kate.' Wellan's voice sounded troubled. 'Would you mind telling me what's going on? I've had Miranda Levitte on the phone just now.'

'Did she mention Cassandra at all? Did she say she was with her?'

'What? No, she didn't. She said her stepmother's expecting to be arrested and she asked if I'd speak to you.'

She slung her bag onto one shoulder, locked her car and hurried to the main doors of the building, telling him that she'd just arrived in Rose Road but it was likely that Theda Levitte had been requested to come for interview. 'Miranda and Roderick might get similar requests.'

'Oh, I see.' He sounded mollified. 'I don't want to get involved in this mess but I feel I'm being dragged into it. According to Miranda, Theda has been going on about some "youth" she's heard about who was at the lake recently. She's got it into her head *he* murdered Henry. I told her that no matter how well turned out he was a young kid couldn't have got into the White Box.'

Kate was through the doors and into reception. 'Sorry, I have to go.'

Call ended she looked to Whittaker. 'Everyone in?' she asked, breathless, still on the move.

'Only Julian. Lieutenant Corrigan's at a meeting with the Terrorism Team.' Whittaker's increasingly loud voice followed her as she continued the corridor. 'And DS Watts is also upstairs.'

She thrust open the door of UCU and Julian looked up. 'I'm trying to do the search you asked for about Theda Levitte but the system's on a go-slow. I've offered to work on it to speed it up but Goosey said no.'

'Forget the search for now.' She dumped her bag on the table and shrugged off her coat, looking up as Joe came through the door. 'I've got a lot to tell you. Where's Ber — Never mind,' she said as he followed Joe into the room.

'Looking aggravated, Doc. What's up?'

'Cassandra has left the Hawthornes and I'm really concerned about her. But first, I've got *loads* of information you need to know about. First, something pictorial.' She picked up her phone and tapped *Camera Roll*, located what she wanted and examined the full-screen version: not bad. 'Here. Take a look.' She handed it across the table. Three heads came together to examine the picture of a disembodied arm, its focus on the area of the wrist.

'It's the watch!'

'Give it here, Devenish. Can't see nothing with you waving it about.' He took the phone and examined the photograph through rarely worn glasses, glancing at Joe. 'What d'you think?'

Joe took the phone, looked then nodded. 'The IWC. Where'd you see this, Red?'

She spoke quickly, looking from one to the other of her colleagues. 'First time I saw this portrait was at Margaret Street when I met Roderick but it meant nothing. Then I saw it again last night, *twice*, first on the commemorative programme and then in that small room . . . when I had other things on my mind. This morning I checked the programme but the detail was too small. I've been to the White Box to see the original.' She took a quick breath and went to look at the picture on the phone in Joe's hand. 'The pilot's watch. A detail from a formal portrait of Henry Levitte dated around . . .' She frowned. 'Well, I don't exactly know but it has to have been years ago judging by his appearance and obviously *before* 1993.' She crossed to the glass screen. 'Remember when we went to the Hyde Road house and Henry Levitte mentioned a family connection to St Peter's church, Harborne?' She began to write, simultaneously relating the historical information she'd found about Henry Levitte's family, including his father's connection with de Havilland.

Fists clenched, Julian jerked both arms downwards. '*Yes!* His father worked on *planes*. He handed on his *pilot's* watch to his son.'

Kate turned from the glass. 'Either the watch places Henry Levitte at Troy's murder scene, or someone else left it — someone who stole it or was given or lent it.'

'If it was a family member how about son-and-heir Roderick?' suggested Joe.

Kate pushed her hair from her face. 'Possible, but I've been thinking about Henry Levitte. His role as a father was about power. Powerful people are able to victimise. They're also able to reward. Where are Buchanan's and Johnson's statements?'

Bernie walked to the table then back, holding out two emails. 'Here.' Kate took them. They were no more than three lines each, Buchanan's stating that he saw nothing untoward at the Retrospective and that he left before eight thirty as he had a long drive home. Johnson's was similarly brief, indicating that he felt unwell and was home by nine. Both denied knowing about Henry Levitte's death until they were informed that morning and statements demanded of them. 'Told you there wasn't much in 'em.' Kate looked at

Johnson's email, distracted. She needed to tell them what else she'd learned.

'You're not the only one with info, Doc.' Bernie waved a large square envelope in her direction. 'This arrived from Upstairs five minutes ago. Want a look?' He took out the single A4 glossy sheet bearing an image in varying hues from gun-metal to pale grey and laid it on the table. 'Result of the EvoFIT. Ronnie Dixon's confirmed it's a very good likeness.' He was watching her. 'See anybody you think we might know?'

Kate stared at the image on the table, recalling his behaviour the previous evening at the gallery after the discovery of the body when he'd cried tears of laughter. She also recalled his reference to 'contacts'. Contact lenses. Her thoughts spun back to a collection of family photographs that Henry Levitte had called the Rogues' Gallery, one of a young boy. She'd thought him studious. He'd been wearing spectacles. 'Are you getting him in?'

Joe came to the table for a second look at the surprisingly accurate EvoFIT likeness of Roderick Levitte. 'He's downstairs. Came in an hour ago. Tanked. Totally schwasted. The medic's given him the once-over, we've charged him with drink-driving for now. He's sleeping it off as our guest.'

Kate rubbed her temples as she walked back to the screen and picked up the marker. 'There's something else. Something really important about Cassandra.' She wrote the initials she'd gleaned from the records at the Hawthornes plus a few additional words and turned to her three colleagues.

Studying the information, hands propped either side of his girth, Bernie read the words again then looked at her. 'How'd you find that out?'

She gave him a look. 'Leave it. What matters is we've *got* it. We need to see Matthew Johnson.'

CHAPTER FIFTY-FOUR

They were at the door of Professor Matthew Johnson's second-floor apartment, part of an elegant Georgian building overlooking St Paul's Square in the midst of Birmingham's Jewellery Quarter, Bernie talking from one side of his mouth, voice low. 'He's in this case up to his neck, given what we now know about him and Cassandra Levitte *and* I'll be asking him why he wasn't straight with us when we saw him before.'

Having been let in by a silent Johnson who was expecting them, they walked into the sitting room. As he hadn't invited them to sit Kate stood beside an upholstered ottoman, gazing around at walls painted in neighbour-colours of the spectrum, from cream to gold, peach to red. *Wonder what his wife is like? Probably an artist too.*

Professor Matthew Johnson hadn't yet spoken. He was waiting. Bernie got down to it. 'We have evidence that at the time you was a student at Woolner you had a relationship with Cassandra Levitte which resulted in her getting pregnant.' Johnson's face suffused with colour which then faded to nothing. Still he said nothing. They waited. Bernie gave him a hard look. 'You got any comment to make about what I just said, Professor?'

Johnson looked at him then at Joe and Kate before responding to the broadside. 'Was it necessary for *three* of you to come here? Are you planning to charge me with something?'

'No, sir,' replied Joe. 'But we do need a response from you to what my colleague has said. Do you have *any* comment to make about your being identified in 1993 as the father of Cassandra Levitte's unborn child?'

Kate watched jaw muscles working beneath the smooth planes of his face, saw his eyes dart from one to another of them. He was upset. And he was thinking. She got impatient. 'Mr Johnson, when we came to see you previously I asked you about the nature of your relationship and that of your housemates with Cassandra Levitte.'

'Yes, and *I* recall that what you suggested was outrageous.'

'And *you* never told us about fathering a child with her.'

He glared at Bernie. 'Because it's preposterous. I told you. Henry Levitte entrusted me with Cassandra's care because of her vulnerability.'

'We need to know about Cassandra Levitte's pregnancy,' said Kate. 'We need you to tell us about it. We're now investigating three murders.'

His head snapped up. 'I thought Henry committed suicide.'

She looked him in the eye. 'You missed the action last night by leaving so quickly. The pathologist examined him. She's decided otherwise.' He looked away towards the window. 'Why weren't you open with us before? Why didn't you tell us about your relationship with Cassandra Levitte?' she demanded.

'Because there wasn't one.' He took a few steps from them, running a hand over his hair, then turned. 'No matter where or how you got this information I'm telling you that it's not true. I was never involved with her. It's a lie.' They watched as he continued, voice low. 'I'm assuming this "information" can be kept confidential?'

Bernie glared at him. 'Worried about what the wife might say? About something you never told her?'

Johnson's eyes narrowed. 'Who said I had a relationship with Cassandra Levitte?'

'Would Cassandra Levitte herself lie about it?' asked Kate.

He looked at her, uncomprehending. '*What?*'

Joe intervened. 'Professor Johnson, are you categorically denying having had a sexual relationship with Cassandra Levitte and being the father of a child she conceived in 1993?'

'Of course I am.' He stared at Kate. 'Cassandra said *that?*' He put his hands to his face then let them drop. 'The only explanation I have for her telling you this is that she's not well. If you've met her you'll know that she has considerable problems. I haven't seen her for years but it was evident even then. She's given you false information. I don't *know* why. I don't *care* why. I'm a private person. I keep my work and personal life separate.'

Bernie regarded him, his face disapproving. 'Well that's your bad luck because we'll be asking your colleagues, your friends and your family what they know.'

'Stay away from my family or I'll take legal advice.' He glared at each of them, then: 'When did Cassandra tell you this?'

'We can't divulge that information, sir.' Hearing Joe's words Kate bit her lip.

Johnson was angry. 'What *can* you tell me so that I can refute it? I need to know the details she gave, when she says this happened.'

Kate looked across to Bernie and got a nod. 'Miss Levitte was two months pregnant in mid-October, 1993,' she said.

He stopped pacing and stared at her. A few seconds elapsed. 'That proves it. It rules me out. I wasn't even in the country in July, August or the first half of September, 1993.' As they watched he turned and walked to the small writing desk under the window. Opening one of the drawers, he removed an item with a dark blue cover and handed it to Joe. Glancing at Kate then Bernie he took the small item and opened it as they moved closer to examine it.

Bernie turned to Johnson. 'All this shows is that you was out of the country during that time frame. Cassandra Levitte could've nipped over to see *you*.'

They turned as the front door of the apartment opened and a pleasant voice drifted from the hallway. 'Hi, sweetie. I've got the smoked salmon and the — Oh. I didn't know we had company this evening?'

The latecomer entered the sitting room amid a profound silence. 'Can I get anyone a drink?' he asked.

* * *

They were inside the Range Rover in the parking area of the apartment building and Bernie was railing: 'Why didn't he say outright that he's . . . and *that* don't rule him out, neither. He could be a Tommy-Two-Ways. What's he wearing a wedding ring for!' Kate rhythmically tapped her head against the seat in front of her. 'And *another* thing! He put his hands on that old passport pretty damn quick if you ask me. It'd take most of us bloody *hours* to find something like that.'

'Strikes me as an orderly guy,' murmured Joe.

Bernie wasn't finished. 'It *don't* rule him out as Cassandra's kid's father. Like I said *she* could've gone over to see *him*. All them years ago he could've been "confused" about his . . . what's-it . . .'

'Sexuality,' murmured Kate, on autopilot, gazing out at illuminated Georgian architecture and thronged restaurants.

'Exactly! I say he should be a POI alongside Buchanan and Roderick *bloody* Levitte.'

Joe turned to look at Kate. 'We'll check but it does look like he was in Istanbul for that period in ninety-three.'

Kate nodded, making quick notes. They would check. Right now she was clarifying her thoughts on the question which had come into her head the instant the final scene in Johnson's apartment had played itself out. She looked up at her two colleagues. 'Cassandra has her pregnancy confirmed by her GP. He asks her the identity of the father. *Question:* Why would Cassandra Levitte name Johnson as the father of her unborn child? *Answer:* Because it would be assumed if anyone ever found out about the pregnancy that her identification of Johnson wouldn't cause him problems. Because it wouldn't be believed. Because she knew back in the early nineties that Johnson was gay. She named *him* to shield someone else.' Kate cast her eyes over pages of notes, recalling John Wellan's laughter when she made tentative enquiries about Johnson as Troy's 'competitor'. So Wellan knew that Matthew Johnson was gay. Others would know. 'Who was Cassandra protecting?' She stared out into darkness. '*Was* it her own father?'

'Have you thought, Doc, that it could've been Nathan Troy?' was Bernie's response.

Joe turned to look at her, seeing her frown. 'You don't think much of the idea that Troy might have been killed because he'd made Cassandra pregnant?'

Kate was staring through the windscreen at the apartment building. 'You mean familial retribution? A dynastic act of revenge?' She thought of the two Levitte males: Henry; Roderick. As the Range Rover moved forward she gazed out at stark trees supporting strings of tiny white decorative lights. 'We don't know that the family was ever aware of her pregnancy. If they weren't then there couldn't have been a retributive act.' She put a hand to her forehead. 'And why, in the liberal sexual climate of the last twenty or so years, would it be thought necessary?'

Bernie eyed her in the rear-view mirror. 'Seems to me the pregnancy was kept secret because whoever the father was, he was on a sticky wicket. *You* say her own father but it could have been somebody else who took advantage of her because of her problems or he was married. When we get back to Rose—'

'*No*. I want to know more about the pregnancy. I want to know if Cassandra had her baby and if she did, what happened to it? *Miranda had a baby around that time*. Take the next left.'

Kate watched Bernie's large head shake. 'I've guessed where you got your info from. Do you *like* trouble?' She shrugged. If her search of Cassandra Levitte's medical records did come to light she'd live with the consequences.

CHAPTER FIFTY-FIVE

They were at the Hawthornes, inside the manager's office, Bernie nearing the end of what he had to say to Leila Jones. 'Our case is moving fast.' He avoided looking at Kate. 'We suspect that Cassandra Levitte was pregnant twenty or so years ago and we need a look inside her records to find out what happened to that pregnancy.'

'I can't let you do that,' said the manager, tight-lipped.

Bernie's eyebrows lowered. 'Listen, we can get an order.'

'Then please do. It's the only way you'll see them.' She gave Kate a cool glance then back. 'I suspect your colleague has already looked inside, which was *highly* unprofessional of her.'

Kate felt frustration rising. 'We have to know what—'

'I take the confidentiality of records very seriously. I refuse to be directly involved in disclosure of information. Get your order.'

A possibility occurred to Kate. She pointed to the file on the desk. 'You've read all of the records. We need very specific information from it. How about we ask you one, two, specific questions at most and—'

The manager sent Kate a level look. 'Dr Hanson, I appreciate that you're a very resourceful and also a very determined person. So am I. The answer is *no*.'

Kate heard Joe's low voice in her ear. 'Let's go. We can start the process for obtaining a court order as soon as we're back at Rose Road.'

She turned away from Leila Jones and followed him and Bernie across the room. At the door she turned. 'I understand your concern for the protection of people in your care. I'm wondering if you appreciate our concerns? Two young people and Cassandra Levitte's father have been murdered. Until their killer is caught there's a continuing risk to others. I don't know whether you've heard from Cassandra or had contact with her since she left here but I'm worried about her. I think she could well be at risk.' She saw the steady gaze waver. 'How about an indication from you to just one key question?' Leila Jones made no response. Kate went with her question. 'Is there any reference in those records to a termination?' They saw the imperceptible nod.

Within five minutes they were inside the Land Rover, Kate staring moodily ahead. Bernie turned to her. 'There you go, Doc. I think that takes care of any theory you *might* have been knitting up about Cassandra's kid being brought up by her sister Miranda.'

She shrugged. 'Coming here's reminded me of my visit with Joe to see Cassandra, her abject fear. Her pregnancy didn't bring about any act of retribution. *She* wasn't shielding anyone. Someone was controlling *her*.' She thought of the glass Eye. 'And has been for years.'

CHAPTER FIFTY-SIX

Early Monday morning in bright winter sun Kate ran up the steps, into the wide, deserted hallway and on towards the stairs. The investigation could only benefit from historical information and she was here to get it from the one person she thought might provide it. Even if he was way outside the academic gossip loop. She tapped the door and looked inside. Wellan was alone except for Rupe. He waved her inside. 'Welcome to the mausoleum. Lectures are still cancelled so I'm spending some of the time catching up with student grading. Six months of it, so help me. Have a seat.'

'I won't hold you up for long. Commiserations about Henry, by the way, although I know you weren't friends.'

He gave her a speculative look. 'You found him. Was it awful?'

She nodded. 'Yes. It was. I need some background on the college if you have time.'

'Fire away.'

'When were you appointed here?'

He grinned. 'Back in the last Ice Age — more precisely in September, 1991. I went back to Athens to complete my contract there so it would have been around . . . October, November when I finally started here.'

'And Henry Levitte was Head of Fine Arts then?'

'Yes. He was on my interview panel.' He leaned forward. 'Do you know, I found out years later he was against my appointment?' He sat back. 'But don't knit *that* up into a solution for your investigation: "Dr Gesso in the Gallery with the Palette Knife" or whatever it was that did for him.' He took out his tobacco tin. 'Everybody knows I disliked the old tart but the nineteen nineties are a lifetime ago and over the years I'd perfected the art of totally ignoring him unless it was unavoidable.'

Kate massaged the tiny line above her nose. 'I hear what you're saying but you probably knew him as well as anyone outside of his family, given that you were colleagues for so many years. Would you say he was a man who liked to wield power over others?'

Fingers moving expertly, his eyes on the roll-up: 'Henry Levitte was a vain, self-centred old man with an ego the size of a small planet and no, I didn't like him. He controlled that family. As far as I could see he wasn't that interested in his daughters. *One* child would carry the Levitte name to future glory: his son. You've met Roderick. He couldn't carry water in a bucket and the old tart never lost an opportunity to tell him so.'

Kate watched as he blew smoke. 'You don't actually like any of them, do you?'

He shook his head. 'No, and *now* I've got Henry's sulphurous old bat of a wife on to me about Roderick drinking and running off somewhere.'

Kate chose her words. 'I can see that he was powerful within his family but how about outside — here, for example?'

He sent her a mild glance. 'You wouldn't be referring to our Esteemed Leader, by any chance? Asking what lifted Johnson up the greasy faculty pole so quickly?' He grinned at her. 'If that makes me sound bitter, I'm not. Wouldn't want to be in any club which would have me, et cetera.'

Kate gave an absent nod, looking at a question she'd written. It had to be asked and Wellan might recall something relevant. 'Did you ever notice anything particular about Levitte's personal presentation over the years? His clothes, things like that?'

He shot her a sideways glance. 'Apart from the fact that the old tart favoured cream linen suits and a panama in the summer? He's the only walking cliché I ever knew. That the kind of thing you're thinking of?'

She shrugged. 'Something more personal, a ring, maybe . . . or a watch.'

He blew out a steady smoke stream. 'I don't recall anything specific such as a watch or a ring.'

The brief knock on the door was followed by a young female face appearing round it. He stood. 'Wait outside, please. I'll be one minute.' He turned back to Kate. 'Look, I'm sorry. It's lectures which are cancelled, not tutorials.'

Outside the college a frown settled on Kate's face. She walked on, thinking of human nature and covetousness. The Montegrappa taken in the break-in. The classic car. Each a testament to John Wellan's discerning eye for elegance of design. Yet he hadn't noticed the IWC. Her thoughts drifted on. Because by the early nineties it was no longer in Henry Levitte's possession? Maybe he'd already lent it or given it to someone? More patronage?

Her thoughts were interrupted by the sound of her phone. She slipped it out of her pocket and answered it.

'Doc?' It was Bernie. 'You remember we asked Adam to do that radar search of the park to check for any indications of Noonan's past activity?'

'Yes?'

'So far they've picked up signs of human remains and everybody's going down to—'

Kate was running. 'I'll see you there. Where exactly?'

'Within fifty or so yards of the lake.'

CHAPTER FIFTY-SEVEN

Kate drove onto the high ground and squeezed her car into a space there. Bernie's words were borne out by the high degree of activity she could hear and see below. Feeling that she was now fixed in some awful routine, she stepped out of her car and walked down the steep incline. No Hunters today. Cold mud oozed around her shoes. Catching sight of the tall figure in the navy overcoat, hand raised, she raised hers in response. She was also counting the number of forensic workers present: fifteen. UCU's investigation was now a major concern at Rose Road, rating a big financial outlay. Furman would be furious.

She walked towards Joe. He gazed down at her. 'Starting to feel like "Groundhog Day" to me. How about you?' She nodded, acknowledging Bernie on hefty haunches as he watched Connie's delicate movements with a trowel-like tool, gently dislodging the raw earth exposed earlier by a couple of shallow scrapes from the nearby yellow digger.

Kate looked down at what was claiming their attention and asked a sudden, illogical question, an indication of creeping tiredness. 'You're not going to tell me this is Stuart Butts?'

Connie sat back on her heels, white forensic suit soiled, her hair spiky. 'Not a chance.' She pointed with the metal tool. 'To be in this condition he'd have needed to be missing for the last five or six years.' She resumed her work as Kate surveyed the pattern of darkened lines in the rich earth, all that was visible so far, her thoughts now on a more logical identity. Connie stopped again to look up at her then on to Bernie and Joe as forensic workers moved in and began setting up large lights in readiness for when the natural source gave out. 'I won't have anything to tell you until this,' she gestured towards the slight undulations, 'is entirely uncovered, lifted out, taken inside the PM suite and given at least a preliminary examination.' She returned to her work. 'Which won't be until *late* tomorrow. And that's if we're lucky and my locum is prepared to do some overtime.'

Kate eyes drifted over the indistinct remains as a small breeze arrived and passed over them, causing small dried leaves and tiny spikes of vegetation to lift. A scarcely discernible wafting near to where Connie was working caught her attention. Connie also caught the movement and raised her eyes to Kate's. Kate took another, closer look.

The light breeze blew again, lifting wisps of fine hair. *Evidence of Noonan's murderous activities? Or someone who's part of our investigation?*

* * *

Back in UCU Kate asked her colleagues if they had heard anything about Cassandra or her whereabouts. She got headshakes. Cassandra hadn't been located at Miranda's home, and Theda Levitte had screamed 'No' down the phone to Joe and hung up when he'd asked her a similar question. A subsequent visit had caused more rage but producing nothing helpful. Cassandra hadn't returned to the Hawthornes. Kate went to the window, scanning the road beyond in a futile effort to convince herself she was doing something. *Where are you, Cassandra?* She turned away. 'We have to *do* something. She's unwell, she needs regular medication and she's in danger.'

Joe looked up at her. 'Six officers are out there right now, revisiting the Hawthornes, Hyde Road, even Woolner.'

'And if she's at none of those?'

That got her a direct look from Bernie. 'This is basic police business. Give us credit for doing what we know how to do.' She returned to the table and sat across from him, struggling to quell unease.

He was still eyeing her. 'I've been thinking about what you said yesterday about Cassandra's pregnancy — that it might have been her own father. Okay, he done what he done to her, but I can't see her putting up with it by the time she's a teenager, a *college* student.'

Impatience added to Kate's tension. 'We've *had* this conversation before. Habituation to years of intrafamilial sexual assault can make it extremely difficult for victims like Cassandra to break that cycle.'

He looked at her, doubtful. 'If you say so.'

'I do.' She flicked notebook pages. 'Mid-October 1993 it was confirmed that she was nine weeks pregnant. If the dates are reliable she's likely to have conceived some time in August of 1993. It could have been her father . . . or any other male caught up in this investigation.' She pushed the notebook away.

Julian turned to her. 'That's only a few weeks before Nathan Troy disappeared.'

Bernie leaned on his forearms, big shoulders hunched. 'I've been thinking along them lines as well. Her relationship with young Troy weren't *none* of this platonic rubbish. How about he was set to be a daddy at nineteen? In August ninety-three his great future in art is well and truly behind him because he'll soon have a kid to support. He was planning to hop it.'

Kate turned on him. 'What did his mother say about him? That he was a *moral* person.'

'Yeah, well. She would, wouldn't she?'

Julian eyed his colleagues. 'Maybe Buchanan was the father?'

'Did you hear what I just said?' demanded Bernie. 'Troy's the likeliest—'

The door swung open and Whittaker appeared. 'He's ready now, DS Watts, Lieutenant.'

Kate watched Bernie pawing papers. He looked up and saw her watching as he located the EvoFIT. He waved it towards her. 'Roderick Levitte don't know about this yet. You coming?'

'What about Cassandra?'

He got to his feet holding a clutch of A4 sheets. 'We can't do no more than we're doing. Roderick Levitte needs interviewing about the assault of Bradley Harper last year and we're thinking he might confess to his father's murder. If we don't get on with this and he walks because we can't hold him no longer he might be a threat to his sister for reasons we don't yet know. *Now* are you coming?'

She followed them out of UCU. 'What actual grounds do you have for keeping him? Just the drink-drive?'

'For now,' said Joe.

Bernie nodded as they took the stairs. 'He was going on about wanting to make a "confession" when he arrived. We'll have a talk with him, show him the Evo and then move onto the subject of what happened to his dad. If he says anything even a bit iffy we'll hold him. We don't want him on the loose, talking, tainting any other information we might get from his bloody family. No wandering psycho murdered Henry Levitte and we can knock that theory on the head for Troy and Harper. Let's see what Roderick's got to say.'

* * *

Kate was running a critical gaze over Roderick Levitte through one-way glass as Bernie intoned the usual preamble at the start of the interview, the PACE machine's lights attesting to the fact that it was recording. Levitte had waived his right to legal representation. So far there hadn't been much to record. He looked dreadful.

Joe and Bernie were facing Levitte across the table. Bernie glared, giving Levitte another verbal nudge. 'When I arrested you for the drink-drive offence you said you wanted to tell us something. You used the word "confess". Now's your chance. Let's hear it.' Levitte didn't raised his eyes from the table.

Kate watched as Joe got an imperceptible nod from Bernie. 'Sir? Is there anything *else* you want to say or tell us?' Still no response.

Bernie glared at Levitte. 'Come on!'

Scarcely breathing she waited for him to speak. Or move. Now he did both. He straightened, looked from Bernie to Joe. 'I was drunk. I didn't know what I was saying.'

Her colleagues looked at each other. Bernie sat forward on his chair. 'Drunk but still very specific in what you said. "Confession" is one of them words everybody understands — particularly when it's said inside a place like *this*. To police officers.'

Levitte raised a shaky hand to his face. 'I have to get out of here. Go home. I'm the head of the family now. They need me.' Kate tensed. *Is he wanting to get out of here to get to Cassandra?* The two officers regarded him in silence. Colour washed his face and his expression changed to one of anger. 'Look, I'm under considerable strain. The whole family is. You know that. Okay, I was in a state when I arrived here. Is that surprising?' He was rapidly losing composure as he had when she saw him at Margaret Street. He banged the table with an open hand, voice rising. 'You can't keep me here. I've done *nothing*. All I did was have too much to drink. Everybody does sometimes. *You* do. I didn't know what I was doing or saying. I've sure as hell got nothing else to say to you.' He sat, chest heaving, face turned from them.

She caught the look which flashed between her colleagues, watched as Bernie reached inside the envelope, withdrew the single item and placed it before him. 'For the tape, DS Watts is showing Mr Roderick Levitte an EvoFIT likeness. Do you have any comment to make about this?'

Levitte looked at it, his face turning from pale to ashen. His stared at them then back to the likeness, lights inside the room picking up the perspiration which had sprung onto his forehead. The shaking hands darted forward as the EvoFIT was moved beyond his reach. Sweat was now pouring from his face, his mouth slack.

Returning the likeness to the table Bernie tapped it. 'We have a witness who's identified *this* individual as being at Woodgate Country Park last year when an assault was committed against a fifteen-year-old male. It matches physical details taken from the victim at the time.' Reaching into the envelope again he brought out a photograph. 'DS Watts is now showing Mr Roderick Levitte a photograph of Bradley Harper. This what you want to tell us about?'

Levitte looked as though he might vomit. 'No!'

'You ever see this youngster before, sir?' asked Joe quietly. Levitte's eyes flicked from one officer to the other, his mouth tightening.

'Come on. We've got somebody who says he saw this man, who looks a lot like you, approach this lad. A lad who's recently been found dead at Woodgate Country Park.' He pointed a forefinger. 'But you know all about that, don't you? *You* killed him. You killed Bradley Harper.'

Kate stared at Roderick Levitte's face. It was chalk. His chest rose and fell and he raised a hand to the wetness on his forehead. 'This is all wrong. That's not what I . . . I was confused. I'd wished my father dead so many times and I felt guilty . . . That's what I meant by "confess", and I was drunk.' He looked down at the EvoFIT then at Bradley Harper's face. 'Okay. Yes. I saw him down there a couple of times, ages ago. I only wanted to talk. I didn't *do* anything to him. I *never* did anything to him, I *swear* I didn't!'

Kate watched the muscles in Bernie's shoulders tense and his face redden, making Levitte's pallor all the more stark. 'Roderick Levitte, I'm arresting you on suspicion of the assault of Bradley Harper at Woodgate Country Park—'

'This is a nightmare!' he screamed over Bernie's words.

'I'm also arresting you on suspicion of involvement in the murders of Nathan Troy and Bradley—'

'*No! No!* Let me out of here.'

It took three thickset officers to remove him from the interview room and transfer him to the custody suite in the basement.

CHAPTER FIFTY-EIGHT

They returned to UCU. Kate sat at the table, head supported by both hands, eyes searching the glass screen. 'I can't believe it. I can't believe he killed Bradley Harper. Or anyone else.'

Bernie turned to her. 'What about the Evo? What about the state he's in? What about what he's said? We've only just started with him. We're keeping him. As soon as he's calmed down we'll have another go with him.'

Joe watched her as she stood. 'He did use the word "confess" and you know that he's a volatile kind of person.'

Kate stood. 'It's possible that when he said he wanted to confess that he was referring to his guilt around his father or having assaulted Bradley Harper. That I can believe.'

'Where're you going?' he asked.

'I've got a study group in half an hour. Can you let me or Crystal know as soon as there's any news about Cassandra?'

* * *

Kate had hardly entered her room when Crystal appeared. She was stopped by the look on the young woman's face. 'What's happened? What's wrong?'

A pink message slip in her hand, Crystal stared at her. 'I'm glad you're here. I've had a phone call.' Tension rising,

Kate took it. 'She rang but she said she didn't want to speak to you, but wanted to leave you a message.' Crystal read what she herself had written. '"Please tell Kate I'm now in hell, where I should be." She sounded *really* upset, and then she started singing this strange song, something about "ears", and it sounded awful.'

Kate took the slip, knowing only one person whom the details fitted. Cassandra Levitte. The quick surge of unthinking relief vanished as she reread the few words again. 'She didn't give a contact number?'

'No. I dialled 1471 — it's on the back.'

Kate turned the slip over, recognising the phone number of the Hyde Road house Bernie had written on the screen in UCU. *Cassandra.*

She sped to her desk, lifted a thick file and returned with it to Crystal. 'When my study group arrives give each of them one of these and apologise for my absence, please.' She was opening the door then stopped. Bernie and Joe were busy interviewing Roderick Levitte. 'Call Rose Road and leave a message for UCU that Cassandra has phoned and that I'm going to get her.'

'Kate?' She turned at the apprehension in the young voice. 'Don't be angry. You told me you don't like your mobile number to be given out, but . . . I did. I gave it to *her*. I thought she might . . . need to speak to you.'

'You did the right thing.' Crystal watched as the door swung shut.

CHAPTER FIFTY-NINE

Kate pulled into the side of the road and switched off the ignition. She was about to place herself in yet another bad situation. Cassandra hadn't wanted to speak to her when she phoned. Hadn't asked that she come here. She had no professional role in relation to her. Theda Levitte would certainly have an opinion about Kate coming to her house uninvited. She didn't care. She'd had to come. She had to know that Cassandra was safe.

Leaving her car she walked the short distance along the road until she came to the dim, overhung driveway. Walking along it she peered through heavy tree cover at the house. A dark blue Mercedes was sitting outside. Theda Levitte was in.

Sudden, explosive sobs coming from somewhere in the direction of the house startled Kate. Inching forward she peered through branches towards the sound. She *was* here. Cassandra Levitte, hands clasped to her chest, hair wild, face as bereft and disturbed as the day she and Bernie were inside this house. Something had to be done.

With measured steps to avoid startling her, Kate stepped from the trees, making herself visible, face calm. The sobbing had abated and another sound drifted to Kate. She realised Cassandra was singing to something in the crook of her arm, a keening sound at odds with the few words Kate could hear: '*Do your ears hang low . . . can you tie them . . . in a bow*?' Pitching her voice so that it was not much stronger than a whisper, Kate spoke. 'Cassandra? It's Kate. I've come to help.'

The anguished sobs continued. Kate thought she'd never seen a living face so tormented, so devoid of colour. The bare, chilled arms dropped and whatever Cassandra was holding fell to the ground. Kate watched her turn and run along a path at the side of the house and away.

'Cassandra! Please don't go! *Wait!*' Reaching the spot where she'd stood Kate halted, then bent to pick up the brown plush rabbit, pliable from years of handling. She reached into her pocket for her phone. She had to ring the Hawthornes to tell them that Cassandra had relapsed, that they should send someone. The woman who answered the phone informed her that the Hawthornes was unable to intervene. Mrs Levitte had assumed responsibility for Cassandra's care and their intervention had to be requested by a family member.

Ending the call, frustrated, Kate approached the house, scanning the surrounding trees. As she neared it she halted. The front door was open, not wide, but not fully closed. Cassandra must have left it unsecured. Kate glanced at the tree cover again. She couldn't leave the house like this. She needed to alert Theda Levitte or whoever else might be inside.

Reaching the door she pushed it wide and stepped into silence, a trespasser amid a riot of painted leaves. 'Hello? . . . *Hello*? . . . Anyone here?' she called, absorbing the quality of air and sound within the house. It felt empty.

Pushing the door closed Kate crossed the hall and stood on the bottom stair gazing upwards, uncertain. 'Hello?' she called again. 'Is anyone home?' Leaving the little rabbit on one of the stairs she continued upwards to the landing from which several doors led off, only one standing half-open. It was the only door with a lock, a key protruding from it. Curious, she walked inside.

The room was huge, fitted with claret-coloured long-pile carpet but otherwise unfurnished, all its curtains drawn.

Bemused, her illicit status forgotten, Kate stood in its centre, looking upwards. It had originally been three rooms. The central section of the ceiling was mirrored. Absorbing that peculiarity she became aware of an odd, muffled quality around her and went to the windows to lift one of the thick curtains. The window behind it was double — triple? — glazed.

Turning away back into the room Kate's eyes drifted over it. *Why so big? Why so . . . anonymous? What function do you serve?* She walked the claret pile to the shorter wall and stood before it. Set into it were two massive doors. Reaching out she laid her hands flat against them, staring down at their handles. Dragging air into her chest she grasped them and pulled.

The doors swung towards her on well-used hinges. She gazed inside at deep shelves, all empty. *Why such a large cupboard and nothing in it?* Kate closed the doors and was halfway across the room's wide expanse when a piercing shaft of winter sun hit one of her eyes then disappeared. Facing the opposite wall she moved a few centimetres to one side then back, again to the side then back, the shaft hitting her face then missing. Hitting. Missing. She crossed the room, eyes on a specific point on one side of the door, and put one eye to it. The light was coming from a high window on the landing. She ran a finger over the hole. It had a defined edge. Not a hole. An aperture. It told her the room's function because she knew the aperture's dual purpose: voyeuristic for anyone looking inwards from the landing, and precautionary for someone inside looking out.

Kate followed the stairs down to the hall then turned to gaze up at the landing. Who routinely walked these stairs to that room? She'd met one of them already. It was his house. She leaned against the wall at the bottom of the stairs, eyes still on the room's open door. Behind her the wall moved.

Heart lurching inside her chest Kate leapt and whirled. There was nothing to see. Nothing except multi-green leaves and peeking, waxy blooms. Lifting a hand to the wall she gave it an exploratory push. The lush, tropical mass yielded then stopped. Mind in overdrive she traced a finger downwards to the small handle of an outward opening door, not quite closed when she'd leaned against it. She'd never have known of its existence if whoever had been there last had secured it.

Kate pulled the door towards her.

CHAPTER SIXTY

It was a storeroom, small and cold, meagre light filtering through a narrow, stained-glass window at its far end. Descending the three shallow steps beyond the door Kate stood amid storage boxes, listening as she breathed stale air. Nothing but thick silence. She lifted a lid from one of the boxes. Empty. She lifted another. Full of old shoes, all sizes and styles, from large leather Oxford lace-ups to child-size ones of patent leather with a strap. Ahead of her at the end of the room was a clothes rail crammed with garments, light falling on one full, off-white sleeve. She walked towards it and lifted the thin, rough material. Cheesecloth. Next to it hung a man's heavy black jacket. Why keep old, dated clothes in a concealed room?

She turned to another box, its lid askew. Its contents left her motionless, a profusion of leather, masks of all types and styles, some with zips, others featuring ornate studwork. Protruding among them were switches with handles fashioned from wood with 'tails' of leather. She dropped the lid and lifted another. Inside were countless plastic envelopes. She stared at the round white tablets inside, many stamped with the stylised cat's face she'd seen in her own house. She was standing amid the contents of the upstairs cupboard. Placed here where it was safe. Secret. Until needed.

She turned back to the crammed clothes rail seeing low, dusty shelves beyond it, filled with old toys. Cassandra had been inside this room and probably the one upstairs. Moving forward Kate felt a smoothness underfoot. Looking down she saw a shoebox on its side, its lid some distance away, contents strewn. On her knees she reached out to the scattered photographs to stare in soaring horror at pale, youthful slimness among mature male bodies—

Tap — tap — tap — tap.

Kate's head jerked in the direction of the door, eyes wide. Someone was here. Inside the house. Eyes on the almost-closed door, ears straining, she pictured pudgy feet in high heels crossing the hall. She listened. Nothing now. Not a sound. The door moved a few, slow centimetres away from its frame.

'Do you want me to bring this lot in, lady?'

Kate leapt at the loud male voice coming from the hall, followed almost immediately by another just beyond the storeroom door, irritable and familiar. 'Put them down there and be *careful*! There's glass in that one. How much?'

'Eleven quid.'

She listened as more taps moved away. Heavier footsteps receded, followed by the bang of the front door and the muted sound of a diesel engine. Kate was scarcely breathing. She was in a fix and she knew it. She knew enough of the woman beyond the door to predict her response to trespass into her home. She had to wait it out. When she left she had to take some of what she'd seen with her as proof.

Eyes still on the door she went to her knees, running her hands over the floor, lifting a handful of the photographs to push them inside her pocket.

'Come out, come out, wherever you are . . .' Kate froze at the sing-song voice, the photographs slipping from her grasp. *She knows I'm in here. How could she? She's seen the rabbit! She's guessed something's happened. She's coming inside.* 'Roderick? Ohhh, Ro-der-*ick*? Have they let you go?' The voice became harsh, drifting inside the hallway just beyond the door. 'Come on, you sad bastard. I want to know what the police said to you. What you've told them.'

Kate was rigid, ears straining as the voice faded and the heel-taps ceased. *What's she doing? Is she going upstairs? If so, she'd soon be back. Or was it a ruse?* Kate stood light-headed with tension, forcing herself to wait. After another two minutes it was intolerable. She couldn't remain in here. Not only would Theda Levitte have seen the rabbit, she would have seen that the big upstairs room was open. She'd been to this door already and Kate could imagine the speculation on the heavy face as she'd reached for the handle. She'd be back.

Kate knew she had to do something. She was halfway across the small room on her way to the door with no plan when the tapping heels sounded again. She stopped, not breathing, listening as they neared, then passed. Another slam of the front door followed by the muted thrum of a powerful engine fading away. She frowned. The Mercedes. Theda Levitte was leaving. After a minute of tense waiting Kate emerged into the hall. It was empty. All was as quiet as before. She had to go back, get as much evidence as she could carry, particularly an item she'd seen which she now realised was key. She ran back across the room to the clothes rail. Reaching out her hand she touched the shoulder of the black jacket. Heavy, serviceable, inexpensive, its style would have had no appeal for anyone living in this house. She ran a hand over it. Nathan Troy had been in mortal danger in this house. And today Cassandra had seen his coat and everything else inside this room.

Kate tensed as quick muffled footsteps crossed the hall and stopped. Turning towards the door she watched it open. The coat slipped from her hand to the floor.

CHAPTER SIXTY-ONE

She watched the movement of the door, transfixed, heart hammering. 'Kate? Kate!'

Running across the room she hurled herself through it. 'Julian!'

Julian's fisted hands were at his chest, ready. As she hurtled through the door he lowered them and staggered back to lean against the nearby banisters. '*Jees-us,* Kate! I'm too young for a heart attack!'

She clasped her hands, gasping words. 'I'm *sorry*. I didn't mean to scare you but I've never been so pleased to see anybody. How did you know I was here?'

She watched as he pulled in air, exhaled then straightened. 'I picked up your message, came over and saw your car down the road. Then I saw the taxi arrive. When the driver carried the shopping inside I followed him and hid in the sitting room over there. 'Come *on*, Kate. She may not have gone far.' He watched her turn away. 'What're you doing?'

'I've found a lot of things, evidence in—'

He grasped her wrist. '*No*, Kate. If she comes back and finds us here, we're toast. We've got no right to be here so anything we take won't count as evidence.'

'It's worth a try!'

He was on the move, pulling her with him. 'No, it isn't! Come *on*.'

They came out of the front door at a run, crossing open space to the heavy cover of trees as the Mercedes nosed its way back up the drive in fading light.

* * *

They were inside the car, Kate resting her head back. 'I've *never* felt so relieved to see anyone.'

'After I got your message I took a call from Bernie's journalist mate. He's put together more or less the same information as we have about the Levitte family. Then I biked over.'

She took out her phone and called Rose Road to alert them to the mass of evidence she'd seen inside the Hyde Road House. As Julian climbed out she started the engine. 'Where're you going now?' She asked.

'Rose Road.'

'See you there and . . . thank you.'

He gave a quick mock-salute.

* * *

For the second time Kate read the information on the glass relating to Theda Levitte née Barr, then continued pacing the floor of UCU. Joe and several other officers were now on standby a mile or so from the Hyde Road house, waiting whilst Bernie obtained a search warrant. As soon as he had it they would descend on the property.

Julian was watching her. 'Good job we left when we did.' Kate gave a brief nod, thinking of all she'd seen there, wondering how far Theda Levitte was involved in any of it but most of all concerned for Cassandra whose whereabouts were still unknown.

The desk phone clamoured. Kate lifted it. 'UCU. Kate—'

'Hi, Red.'

'Joe! Where are you?' She could hear sirens. 'What's happening?'

'Theda Levitte's incinerated a load of stuff in the garden. Most of it's ash, the rest charred and unrecognisable.' Still clutching the phone, Kate let her head drop forward onto her forearm. 'Kate?'

Her voice was muffled. 'I can't bear this . . .' *And Cassandra is still out there, alone somewhere.*

* * *

Later that evening Kevin was making careful progress across the hall as the phone rang. On its sixth ring he reached it and picked it up. 'Yes?' Following a brief pause his mouth compressed as he watched Kate walking towards him. 'Who's this calling?' She took the receiver from him.

'You know who this is,' Joe responded.

Kate spoke into the phone. 'It's me, Joe.'

'What's his problem?' asked the deep voice in her ear.

She glared at Kevin's back as he made his slow way to the study. 'It would take too long.'

He got straight to his reason for calling. 'Been thinking. We have nothing which places Troy in that house. We need to get our focus back to where he went, what he did in the days prior to his disappearance. Seems to me we've got just one reliable sighting before he disappeared: John Wellan's tutorial. I've fixed to go see him tomorrow morning at Woolner.'

She did a quick review of her next day's commitments. 'What time?'

'Ten thirty.'

Kate frowned at the small pink feet which had appeared on the stairs, toenails painted neon-glare orange. She looked up into Maisie's face, moving the receiver to one side. 'It's for me. Time you were in bed.' Pouting, Maisie swivelled and disappeared as Kate repositioned the phone. 'I've got a lecture from nine thirty until ten thirty, although you haven't actually asked me.'

'I was getting to it. How soon can you make it?'

'Ten forty-five?'

'Sounds good to me. See you then.'

'Wait, Joe!' She eyed the half-open study door. 'What's your specific purpose in seeing him?'

'We need to know exactly what was witnessed of Troy in the short time frame before he went. I'm discounting what Buchanan said. Can't trust him. But we've got John Wellan and I want it direct from him exactly what he saw. Do you think it's possible he'll come up with some new detail if you do some of that smooth, memory stuff I've seen you do?'

'It's possible, if you mean cognitive interviewing to enhance recall of—'

She heard a deep sigh. 'Red, you're the only woman I know who can talk like that and make a red-blooded guy . . .' She laughed. It felt like it was for the first time in days. 'How're you feeling?'

'I'm fine. I'll be there in the morning. Any news of Cassandra?'

'Sorry.'

She sighed, aware of yet another fleeting impression from her experience at Hyde Road. One of a number she'd had which she was unable to recall, testament to the extreme fear she'd experienced there. Something she'd seen at that house, something she'd heard . . . 'See you tomorrow.'

'Sleep well, Red.'

Upstairs she found Maisie sitting cross-legged on her bed, surrounded by books and papers. 'It's a little late to be still working. What's all this?'

Maisie pointed to some printed sheets. 'It's my civil rights project on Martin Luther King. Have you heard of him?'

'Vaguely,' said Kate, giving her a sideways look as she moved books aside to sit.

'So you'll know he was this *brilliant* orator who went on a lot about justice and freedom.'

Kate nodded, her eyes drifted along printed lines on one of the sheets. She picked it up, recognising it. It was King's

'Mountain-top' speech. She read on: . . . *ain't gonna let nobody turn me around* . . . *Let justice roll down like waters* . . . She replaced the sheet with the others. 'You need to be getting ready for bed.' She looked at her watch. 'Oh, look. It's well into my child-free time.'

'Yeah, right — and I'm not a child.' Maisie jumped off her bed and headed for the bathroom. 'You do realise, Mom, you've always got something to say? Daddy calls you "Last-wordy".'

Kate watched her go. *Like mother, like daughter.*

CHAPTER SIXTY-TWO

By ten forty-six the following morning Kate was at John Wellan's door. Inside she found him and Joe seated in companionable silence, Wellan smoking, Joe nursing a hot drink, his long legs crossed at the ankle and stretched before him, Rupert supine beneath his chair. Wellan looked round at her. 'Come on in. We were having a chat while we waited. Here.' He stood and pulled a chair forward. 'Drink?' She nodded, giving Joe an enquiring look.

'I've mentioned the technique and John's willing,' he said.

'Only on the understanding that there are no thumbscrews involved.'

She smiled. 'You're in luck. Never on a Tuesday.' She glanced round the low-lit room. 'This setting is ideal because it's where your tutorial with Nathan Troy took place. I'll be using some basic memory-jogging techniques to encourage maximum recall by you. Some of what I ask may seem trivial but if you can stay with it it'll help the process. Shall we get started?'

'You're the boss.'

She looked at him. 'Is that where you were sitting during the tutorial? In that chair?' Wellan nodded. 'Okay. It might help your focus if you close your eyes . . . Listen to what I say.

Ignore everything else.' In the silence she began, voice low, pen poised. 'You were waiting here that afternoon for Nathan to arrive for his tutorial. Describe the studio.'

His eyes closed, Wellan's face relaxed a little. 'Warm. Like it is now. Looked like it might snow . . . and . . . I had a couple of the lights off so it was . . . calm in here and . . . there was another chair back then. One of those Swedish things with a curved frame.' She watched as his index finger moved, sketching the shape. 'Right where you're sitting.' Rupe yawned widely under Joe's chair and he reached down to stroke the soft ears. Wellan grinned, eyes still closed.

Kate waited, then: 'How were you feeling that afternoon?'

His eyelids flickered. 'Fine, fine.' He frowned. 'Wait. No. That's wrong . . .'

'Take your time,' said Kate softly, pen poised.

Wellan nodded. 'I remember now. I'd had a run-in with Henry earlier in the afternoon. One of our regular exchanges. About my "populist leanings", as he called them.'

'How were you feeling about that?'

'Pissed off. But I'd more or less forgotten about it. I was keen to see Troy. I needed to ask if he'd produce something for the exhibition Woolner was planning at the Royal Society the following January. A big chance for him . . .'

'And Troy arrived,' she prompted amid silence.

'Mmm . . .'

'Tell me about that.'

She watched him shrug. 'He was just . . . Troy, you know.'

'Let's go back a little to when he first arrived. What happened?'

'He just came in and . . .'

'He didn't knock?'

'Sorry, yes. I called out for him to come in. He did. He sat down in the chair . . . We talked for a few minutes . . .'

'What about?'

A frown settled on his face. 'It was just general chat . . . I can't recall. I gave him a drink. He took his folder out and . . .'

'Where from?'

'Where—? Oh, I see. His backpack. We discussed what he'd been doing since his last tutorial . . .' His face in the small pool of light showed he was concentrating.

'How did he look?'

He shrugged. 'Fine. Tired, maybe. He took off his coat . . .'

She gave Joe a quick glance. 'Can you describe it?'

'The coat? Black. Like many of the students were wearing back then . . . Some kind of smooth material up here . . .' As he gestured to his own shoulder Kate was back in the storeroom at Hyde Road, recalling the cold feel of a black jacket against her hand.

'How did the tutorial progress?'

He nodded. 'Mostly very well . . . but Troy was distracted. Like he had something on his mind . . . I'd forgotten that . . .'

'Did he say anything to you about it?'

A head-shake. 'No and I didn't ask. The only other thing he mentioned was a trip to London with his father. He showed me the ticket his father had sent him. I was surprised. I'd thought that they didn't get on.' He opened his eyes. 'The impression I got was that Troy didn't want to go.'

Kate absorbed this, keeping to her agenda. 'How did the tutorial end?'

Wellan flexed his arms, rotating his shoulders. 'We fixed another date and he went.'

'Where was he going afterwards?'

He shook his head. 'I don't think he said.'

Kate pushed the point. 'Think about it. The possibilities are finite.'

Wellan was silent for some seconds. He nodded. 'I remember. He was going back to the house he shared. He told me he was expecting something in the post that day, that it hadn't arrived when he left in the morning so he was going to check it had come.'

Something tugged at Kate's own memory. 'What was he expecting?'

Wellan shrugged again. 'No idea. He never said.'

She'd come to her final question. 'When you heard of Troy's disappearance, did you have any idea or suspicion, anything occur to you about what might have happened?'

He hesitated. 'The ticket I just mentioned. I remember that when I was told he'd gone I thought, "That's what he's done. He's left. He's gone to London".' He shrugged in the following silence.

She closed her notebook and smiled. 'Thank you, John. I kept it as brief as I could.'

He straightened on his chair, blinked and looking from her to Joe. 'I'm shattered. Glad it wasn't the full treatment.'

* * *

They walked to where their cars were parked.

'John Wellan's not from around here?' asked Joe.

'He's from north England. Why?'

He shook his head. 'I've never heard the accent before.'

Kate turned to him. 'I'm confused. A state I don't like. All I seem to be doing on this case is adding to my store of questions and getting few answers.' She glanced up at Joe. 'Who was it who said it's better to know some of the questions than all of the answers?'

'James Thurber.'

She opened her car door. 'He got that wrong. I won't be satisfied until we have *all* the answers we need.'

CHAPTER SIXTY-THREE

Kate was in her room at the university, eyes on the squiggled notes she'd made when they were with John Wellan the previous day. Chin on fist in the surrounding quiet she gazed at them, long enough for them to begin wriggling. The cognitive method had produced some detail, a confirmation of Troy wearing a coat at some time during that day. She looked ahead, hands clasped to her mouth, now sure it was the one she'd seen at Hyde Road. She read other words uttered by John Wellan, increasingly aware of a need to speak to Bill Troy. Her desk phone clamoured. 'Kate Hanson.'

Bernie's voice boomed in her ear: 'We've found Stuey Butts.' Kate's heart dropped. More bad news. 'He's in custody.'

* * *

Kate was watching Stuart Butts through one-way glass. He was sitting low on his chair chewing a thumbnail as Bernie and Joe looked at him. A woman Kate didn't know was sitting nearby, still in her coat, waiting. She'd been sent by the Youth Offending Team to act as the 'appropriate adult'.

The teenager studied the thumbnail. 'I'm saying nothing.'

Bernie frowned at him. 'That's another mistake you're making, lad. You're in bigger trouble now than you've ever been in your life. Like I said, your DNA's on that torch and we've got your palm print at a house break-in.'

'Don't know anything about a break-in but I can tell you about that torch. When I was in that lake house place something stuck in my finger. See?' He held up an index finger. Bernie gave the fingers and chewed-to-nothing nails a cursory glance, seeing no sign of injury. 'There wasn't a real fight. Just messing. I didn't do anything to Harper. That's all I'm saying. Like I said, I'm not talking.' He pushed himself further down on his chair and folded his arms, the down jacket collar riding up to his ears.

'You've had time to think of that story and now it's time we talked about keeping you in custody.'

Stuey looked up at him, a calculating expression on his face. 'Tell you what. I'll talk to that woman.'

Bernie glanced at the appropriate adult. 'What woman?'

Stuey gave a dismissive look. 'Not her. The other one. Got red hair and works with you two.' Kate's head shot up. She gave him a close look through the glass as Bernie nodded agreement for her benefit. A minute later she was sitting opposite the teenager, Joe and Bernie having taken her place next door. Stuart Butts gave her an unblinking stare. 'I know they're watching us. I don't like the blues 'n' twos. You're *not* one, are you?' She shook her head. He pushed further down on his chair. 'There's too many people think they know *all* about me — social workers, probation officers, teachers.' His eyes slid to the one-way glass. 'That fat bloke you work with. All watching me, thinking they know me. Deciding what I am and what should happen to me. They're all tossers.'

The appropriate adult spoke. 'Stuart, these accusations against you are serious and you need to answer the questions being asked of you. I'm here to look after your interests and see that—'

His eyes rolled. 'Yeah, course you are.'

Kate looked at him, nodding at the woman's words. 'DS Watts is also right. You need to talk. Give us any information you have for your own safety.'

The finger probing a back tooth stopped. He took it out of his mouth. 'I can take care of myself. Been doing it for years.' He looked at Kate. 'There's nothing that can happen to me that I can't sort out.'

She watched his face. 'What about your family? Your parents?'

He sent her a dismissive look. '*Them*? They've never done anything for me.' He frowned at the table top, feet jiggling, then looked up again. 'Listen to this, right? I don't want to go home. I'm *not* going home. It's not home. I haven't even got a proper room there. The spare room's full of stuff my old man's robbed.'

Kate frowned. 'Where do you sleep?'

He shrugged. 'Sofa, if the old man's not on it already after having a few too many. Otherwise it's a chair . . . or other places. I'd rather be in Secure than there.'

She thought of a future possibility. 'What if you were just living with your mother? Would that be any better?'

He erupted into raucous laugh. 'You out of your mind? She doesn't do anything without his say-so. There were times she could've done stuff but she didn't.' Kate stayed silent as his eyes became unfocused, his face losing the tight look. 'When I was a kid my old man robbed this game and she gave it to me. I don't know what game it was. I only looked at the picture on the box. *Really* looked. For ages. It was like a painting of these two kids and they were somewhere in the country. Fields and that. It was done in bright colours: red for the boy's jumper, bright green grass and bright blue sky going paler blue as it went higher with these little white clouds in it . . . and the two kids looked happy. I used to wonder where that place was where they lived . . . what it was like to be in a place like that, where there were all these colours and kids were happy.' He sat up. 'He came home one night, took it off me and I never saw it again.' He gave Kate another direct look. 'This is where you ask me to tell you all about what happens at home. That's what the Social does.'

'Do you tell them?'

He looked scornful. 'What do you think! I don't tell them anything.'

'It's up to you what you tell me.' Watching him, she knew he was dishonest, capable of meanness and cruelty. He hadn't started out like that.

The finger was probing again. Removing it he wiped it on his jacket. 'Can I go to Secure if I tell you something? If you get rid of them next door I'll tell you and you can keep it to yourself but make sure I get a place.'

'I don't make those decisions and I can't keep secrets. If you have a reason for not wanting to go home and you tell us, my guess is you won't have to.' She glanced at the appropriate adult who gave an imperceptible nod.

He pushed himself upright on the chair. 'Okay, right. My dad's too handy with his fists, yeah? And the belt.' He pulled back the ski jacket and moved the collar of his shirt to one side. Kate saw an area of blue-yellow bruising on one side of his neck, disappearing under the clothes. He covered it. 'I got that for putting the telly on and waking him up. Like I said, I want out.' One of his feet had now set up an intense jiggle. She saw it, knowing he was about to divulge something distressing. She waited. 'But I know a worse bastard than him. Somebody who's done worse stuff to me than my bastard of a dad ever has. For years. From when I was, like, about thirteen. Not just me, neither.'

'Tell me.'

'I'm not saying any details about what he did.' The words rushed from his mouth, his eyes on hers, unblinking. 'But get this. I'm no gay-boy, right? That's it.' He looked at her then away. 'I'm not rubbish.'

'No. You're not. Who did those things?'

'It was on the news. He's dead but that changes nothing. I *still* hate him. Even more now, because he's got away with it, yeah? I wanted to kill him when he was alive. I wish I had. His name's Henry. Henry Levitte.'

Seconds ticked by. Kate knew she had to say it: 'If you'd told someone—'

'I did.' He dropped his head back, eyes closed, then straightened to stare at her. 'I think I was still about thirteen. They took no notice.'

Kate returned the stare. '*Who* didn't?'

'The cops.' He watched her face. 'No. Not here. This was down at the local cop shop but they already knew me, see. I'd had trouble with them before. When I said that old bastard's name and where he lived they looked at each other, like "Yeah, right". They even wrote down what I'd said but the way they looked at me, I knew nothing would happen. Never even asked me to give a statement. They thought I was a liar. Levitte was this posh git.' He shrugged and began chewing on his thumb again.

* * *

Bernie had left them on hearing Stuart Butts's words. Kate and Joe walked the corridor away from the interview room to UCU. She shook her head. 'Henry Levitte: intrafamilial sexual abuser, frotteur, sexual assaulter, paedophile.'

Joe looked down at her. 'You were right. So who killed him? Stuart wanted to. He's wiry and young but I can't see him having the strength to strangle Levitte and hoist the body, even though Levitte was frail, can you?'

'No I can't. And how would he have got inside the gallery to do that anyway?'

As they walked inside, Bernie's voice drifted over to them from where he was standing beside the computer. 'There's no record of any allegation against Henry Levitte on the system by Butts or anybody else.' He straightened and looked at them. 'With Butts's past form we have to consider that he could be lying.'

'Do you know anybody at his local police station?' asked Kate. She watched him make his way to the phone and took a seat opposite. 'You know, for most of his life Stuart Butts has had a bad deal: starting with parents who don't give a damn. I've seen his mother. Timid. Under-assertive. From what he's said to me there's a critical, overbearing, violent male in the mix as well.'

He shook his head. 'Keep your eye on the ball, Doc. Don't ignore what we know about Stuey Butts. You forgot already that he broke into your house?' He dialled a number and waited, spoke a few words into the phone, waited, then hung up. 'Nothing on the local station's records either. Like I said, you can't rely on what Butts says.'

Kate stood and went to the glass screen. 'From what he said, Stuart believes there's a whole audience of people who watch, disapprove and denigrate him.'

'He's probably right!' muttered Bernie. 'Nobody in their right minds would trust him an inch.'

She was writing. 'He's sixteen and he already has his own biography written in which he's strong, streetwise, able to look out for himself.' She sighed, eyes on the glass. 'His personal myth which will continue to lead him into dangerous situations where he can't take care of and protect himself, regardless of how streetwise he believes he is and no matter how manipulative and nasty other people judge him to be. To have any kind of chance he needs at least one adult in his life who cares about what happens to him.'

Bernie looked at her as he reached for the phone. 'Who's told you all this?'

Kate stood, collected her coat and bag and walked to the door, her words drifting back to them. 'Piaget told me.'

'Who's he when he's at home? If he's one of your university cronies, how about we get him in when we interview Butts again? He might get Butts to talk some more.'

She heard Joe's response as she walked away. 'Piaget was this Swiss guy. Developmental psychologist. Had a lot of theories about how kids think. Died more than twenty years ago.'

'Bloody *great*.'

* * *

Furman was coming towards Kate as she headed for reception, his eyes on her as they neared each other. They stopped in the confines of the narrow corridor. She waited, returning his gaze, knowing there was much on his mind, not all of it to do with the case. 'You've got the rent boy in. What's he said?'

She kept her voice even. 'Nothing I'll repeat until it's been checked and we know how reliable it is.' She waited. He stayed where he was, his eyes roaming over her face and down. 'Move out of my way — *now*.'

After a few seconds he moved aside, watching her as she passed him, then calling after her, 'You and I need to have a really important meeting when you think you can find the time. About a little matter of unauthorised access to medical records.'

CHAPTER SIXTY-FOUR

They were in UCU. 'Mother Levitte's on her way and she knows we've got no concrete evidence.' Delivering this, Bernie glanced across the table to Kate. She'd not long returned from the university and much of her attention had been on her phone since then, hoping to learn that Cassandra had been located. 'Pity you never challenged her when you was at the house.'

Kate's head shot up. 'What are you talking about? We know she destroyed the evidence. Do you have any idea how terrifying it was in that house and her spiking around just beyond that door?'

'Simmer down. All I'm saying is it might have helped. We've got three murders: Troy, Harper and now Levitte, and no physical evidence now which might have linked them. *Plus* there's whoever's been found down at the park. We're still waiting on Connie for answers on that.'

She covered her face with her hands. 'I can't do this.'

Bernie looked at Joe then back again. 'What you on about now?'

Dropping her hands, she said, 'The way you, the police, work! No matter how much we know, it's never enough. I *saw* all the trappings of organised paedophilia in that house. I *saw* Nathan Troy's coat.'

'So you say but *we* haven't got 'em. The CPS likes good odds when it sends cases to court. Good odds means facts plus physical evidence.' There was silence. 'I get how you feel, Doc, but you need to get something as well: strong cases get to court. Weak cases? Forget 'em. Or they fail when they get there.'

'How about the CPS consider going to trial with less and trusting the jury system,' she snapped.

'In this kind of case, with this sex stuff, solid evidence helps people to understand what they're being told. I'm talking about juries here. They're not like you, Doc. It's your world and you're up to your armpits in it.'

She dropped back on her chair, eyes closed. *This* didn't have to be her world. She could turn her back on the pressure, unfairness and injustice of it all and apply for the professorship at the university. No more cold cases, no more bodies, no more contact with Furman.

'As far as the law is concerned all it hears is what you *say* you seen at Hyde Road,' Bernie continued.

'What I *did* see.'

Bernie looked at Joe then back to Kate, holding annoyance in check. 'Put yourself in the place of one of these jury people. Not only are they being told about organised sex stuff involving under-age kids but they see who's in the frame before somebody done him in? A well-known, well-thought-of college professor who's been on the telly a couple of times, who's waiting to get a gong from Buck House.' Kate opened her mouth but he rolled on. 'And who's your star witness? Stuey Butts. You know as well as me what a defence barrister like your ex would be saying about him: "unreliable young thug who makes a bundle from sex".'

She leaned against her chair, eyes on her phone then on Bernie's face. 'I know that. It's still not right. It's still not fair. We look at Stuart Butts and see only what *he's* done, not what people have done to *him.* He's a victim as much as Nathan Troy.'

In the quiet of UCU Kate's thoughts drifting to Stuart Butts's interview. She sat up. 'How did he know I work with you two?' Bernie and Joe looked at each other then at her. 'Stuart Butts. He asked to speak to me — referred to me as a female colleague of yours with red hair.'

Bernie shrugged. 'He'd been here before and he knew you were part of UCU.'

Kate shook her head. 'No, no. *Think*. During the time you two interviewed him that first time I wasn't present. I observed the whole time. He never saw me. I only came into the interview room when he'd left.' There was a short silence. 'How could he know I worked here and what I looked like?'

She got up and walked to the glass screen. 'See this?' She pointed at the note she'd written there. 'When I saw him at the lake he was on his phone.' Turning to look at them she tapped the glass. 'Whoever was on the other end of that call told him who I was. Stuart was speaking to someone who knew *me*. At least by sight.'

Seizing the screen marker she began a list of names, talking as she went. 'These are all the players in our case whom I've had direct contact with: Nathan Troy's parents. Bradley Harper's family. Stuart Butts. Alastair Buchanan, Matthew Johnson, John Wellan, Henry and Theda Levitte, and the three Levitte children: Cassandra, Miranda and Roderick.'

Bernie stared at her. 'You're not suggesting one of the parents is involved in all of this and how does it help us sort this mess? Nathan Troy's murder is our case. Philip Noonan might have killed him. Old man Levitte who was our prime is dead. I don't like Buchanan but there's no evidence to link him to killing anybody. That whole Levitte tribe is off the wall, far as I'm concerned. Bradley Harper's in a fridge downstairs and we're still waiting to hear who it is that's been found down at the park. Noonan could be in the frame for that as well. In short, it's a *mess*.' He turned away then back on an afterthought. 'And examining every word people say under a microscope isn't helping us identify Troy's killer, which is our priority.'

Kate wasn't listening. She was examining the names she'd written, thinking of a Mercedes engine and the thrum of a car at the lake. 'I think we can reduce the list of possibles.' Joe stood and walked to the screen, his eyes on the names then on Kate. 'I heard Theda Levitte's Mercedes when I was inside that house.'

'Let me guess,' said Joe. 'You'd heard it before, when you saw Stuart at the lake.'

She nodded, pointing to the names. 'From all of those listed, which ones are at all likely to have had access to the Mercedes and—'

UCU's phone shrilled. Kate listened as Bernie lifted then replaced it with a muted word of thanks. 'The remains at the park. Connie's ready.'

* * *

Connie looked up as Igor let them into the post-mortem suite and waited as they came to the stainless steel examination table on which lay the remains recovered from the park. Kate gave them a few seconds' close attention then looked to Connie who went straight to the facts. 'Young and male. He was strangled.' Bernie groaned and Kate closed her eyes. *Noonan*. 'And as you thrive on detail I can tell you that he was five-eight in height and in his early- to mid-thirties when he was killed.'

Kate's eyes flew open. 'When you said young . . .'

Connie gave her a look. 'Anybody under forty gets my "young" description.'

'Method of strangling?' asked Joe, as Kate held her breath.

'Ligature. Have a look.' She turned from a nearby table holding aloft a plastic evidence bag inside which was a length of cord very similar to the one she'd previously indicated among her samples, this one soiled, filthy. 'White, once upon a time. You can see, if you look inside the weave.'

Kate did, then looked at Connie. 'Anything else? Any other findings such as DNA or—'

She gave her a mild glance. 'Plenty, if you allow me to tell you, although not of the kind which will satisfy what sounds like a sudden obsession with physical evidence.'

'Sorry,' said Kate, giving Bernie an irritable glance.

'I checked his DNA on the system. He was a MISPER named Joel Smythe.' Bernie's mouth opened, but Connie silenced him with a look. '*Don't* start with the questions again. I'll get to them.' They stood in silence. 'His clothes are over there.' Connie pointed to the examination table, lifting a clipboard to read listed items: 'One short-sleeved cotton shirt, originally white, one pair of buff-coloured chinos, sandals, no socks, low-rise briefs. That's it. All well-worn.' She pointed to a separate area of the table. 'And also *that*.' They looked to where Connie was pointing to a fluffed mass. The fair hair the breeze had ruffled when they were at the park.

Kate had absorbed the information. 'He was killed in the summer — or at least when it was warm?'

Connie nodded. 'Reasonable conclusion to draw and strengthened by what I found in his trouser turn-ups: remains of tiny flowering plants, specifically . . .' She consulted the list again. '*Vicia sativa*, also known as common vetch, and *ranunculus acris* — that's meadow buttercup to you and me. They flower in the summer months up to September so alongside his clothing they're a good indication of the time of year he died.'

Joe looked as if he had something on his mind. 'He wasn't carrying anything? A bag, keys, a billfold?'

'If he was we don't have it.'

Bernie's hands were deep inside his jacket pockets, his focus beyond the remains, considering all that Connie had told them. 'So nothing on him like bits and pieces in his pockets.'

Connie raised her brows. 'Did I say that?' she asked mildly, turning to the table where the clothes lay to pick up a single item inside protective plastic. 'Whoever took his belongings missed this.'

They pressed closer to the table to look. 'Major fail,' murmured Joe. 'Killer in a rush.'

Connie gave a quick nod as she placed it near its owner's bones. 'Initially I wasn't able to say it *was* his. It's the old photo-less kind of licence issued prior to 1998. He got it the previous year. The address on it is his own home, not the parental home, and he appears to have remained living there until he disappeared, which is why he still had it. I put the licence number into the system and got a second confirmation of the holder's name: Joel Smythe. The licence itself indicated two endorsements, one in 2001 and the other in 2004.'

Kate looked at the driving licence then at the remains. 'So there's incontrovertible proof that this *is* Joel Smythe?'

Connie beamed. 'I commend your evidence-mindedness, Kate.' This got a huff from Bernie. 'Yes, because the DNA match was clear, yes, because the licence fits with the identification, but also because I spoke to Joel Smythe's father who told me that Joel broke his right arm on a skiing holiday with his school when he was sixteen.' She pointed to the right arm of the remains. 'I X-rayed it. Found a clear indication of an old radioulnar fracture consistent with the fall his father described. If that isn't enough to satisfy everybody, his second arrest for drink-driving included the taking of his DNA. This *is* Joel Smythe.'

Kate walked the length of the table, stopping at its foot to muse. 'Two young men came to Woolner College. One never left. The other did — but he came back again, years later.' She stood, eyes on all there was now of Joel Smythe. It was clear that his life had not gone smoothly after he left Woolner. *What brought you back, Joel?* The pulsing of the extractor fan drifted into Kate's head, setting up a rhythm: *Where's Cassandra–Where's Cassandra–Where's—*

Bernie's phone shrilled into the silence. 'Yeah? . . . Right.' He cut the call. 'Mother Levitte is here.'

CHAPTER SIXTY-FIVE

Theda Levitte turned on her chair, fat knees parted, face furious. 'Why have I been dragged in here? I want to leave.'

Kate took a seat in one corner as Bernie and Joe sat opposite her, Bernie taking the lead: 'You've been *requested* to attend for interview and this is the deal: you can wait for your own legal representation or agree to the duty solicitor who's here already. What d'you say?' She twisted back to the table, face seething, mouth fixed. Bernie stood. 'Right. We'll transfer you to the custody suite until your own solicitor—'

'Carry on,' she barked. 'I've done nothing and I'm not staying here a minute longer than I have to.' Bernie nodded at the young officer by the door who left the room. They waited amid angry silence until the duty solicitor appeared and took the chair next to her.

Bernie reached to the PACE machine, beginning the scripted words of the caution process and naming those present. 'You do not have to say anything but it may harm your defence if you do not mention when questioned something which you later rely on in court—'

'Go and fuck yourself!'

'—anything you do say will be . . .' He ploughed on, gazing at the wall opposite as the light on the PACE machine glowed. They sat, mute, faces made bleak by the light directly above the table. Duty Solicitor Eunice Wilton looked as if every worry she'd ever had, and a few she'd never considered, had arrived. At Rose Road Eunice went by the soubriquet 'Wet Lettuce'.

Theda Levitte's small black eyes slid to Kate sitting in relative shadow to one side of the room. Bernie was speaking again. 'Due to information obtained by West Midlands Police it is my intention to formally record an interview with you.' She glared at him, leaning back, the plump knees parting again. Kate watched colour surge over Eunice's neck above the neat, white blouse. 'You've been arrested on suspicion of involvement in the murder of Nathan William Troy, aged nineteen, on or around the tenth of November, 1993, and the wilful destruction of evidence pertaining to that murder. This interview is being recorded under caution at Police Headquarters, Rose Road, Harborne, Birmingham. The time is . . .' He continued amid the thick silence. 'Present at this interview are . . .' Her eyes didn't move from his face. 'Would you introduce yourself and confirm that there's no one else—'

'No comment.'

Eunice convulsed on her chair. 'No, no. You have to do what DS Watts—'

'They *know* who I am, you stupid cow.'

Bernie pointed a blunt finger. 'Stop it. We'll wait.' Rigid with anger Theda Levitte supplied the details he'd requested. Kate noticing that rage had thickened the northern accent. Bernie continued. '. . . and anything you do say may be given in evidence—'

'No comment.'

Eunice was having a hard time. 'Shssss! Not yet.'

Kate watched the coarse face. 'Don't shush me.' She glared at Bernie then Joe. 'You've still got Roderick here. What's he said about me?'

Bernie eyed her with distaste. 'You need to listen to the duty solicitor. We're here to get information, not give it.'

Everyone including Kate jumped at Theda Levitte's screeched response. 'He's a liar, whatever he said!'

'Mrs Levitte, *please*.' Eunice cast harried looks across the table.

'You need to start behaving yourself else you'll be downstairs again!' roared Bernie.

'If he's told you I know anything, anything, I deny it.' She turned sideways on the chair, away from Bernie, arms folded beneath the heavy chest.

Kate looked at the duty solicitor whose face was now the colour of two-day-old fish. 'Please, Mrs Levitte. You *must* listen . . .' she bleated.

Turning papers on the desk Bernie found the item he wanted, running his finger down the list Kate had itemised as having seen at Hyde Road. 'Inside your house there were items indicative of activities of a sexual nature between adult males and under-age persons. You destroyed said items because you were aware of an imminent visit by this Force to search your premises. What do you say?' He got no response. Kate watched Bernie's eyes drift over a printout in front of him. 'Let's try this. You worked as a nurse at a psychiatric hospital in Sheffield in the early eighties. Your name was Barr. You left that employment following allegations of mistreatment from patients. You've got priors for theft and fraud in the same name—'

'That's all history,' she snapped.

Bernie gave her a close look. 'Yes. *Yours*. This is your opportunity to help yourself. Tell us what you know about Henry Levitte's sexual activities at your home or I'm stopping this interview on the grounds that you're hostile and uncooperative.' He glared at her. 'Make up your mind.'

Eunice had been giving Theda Levitte harassed glances during Bernie's discourse. 'It's in your interests to do as detective sergeant—'

As if she hadn't spoken Theda Levitte now fixed her eyes on Bernie. 'I can't tell you anything about it because I don't *know* anything.'

Bernie glared at her. 'You were married to Henry Levitte for twenty-odd years. You lived at *that* house with him.'

'So what? I still don't know anything about . . . that side of his life.'

Kate's eyes widened. She turned her full attention to Joe as he spoke. 'For the tape, Lieutenant Corrigan speaking. Mrs Levitte, when you refer to "that side" of your husband's life, does that include his sexual abuse of one or other of his children?' Kate held her breath.

'She was a teenager by the time I met Henry. I knew nothing about it.'

'But you came to know about it,' responded Joe, his eyes on hers.

'I didn't.'

'You would have been aware of Henry Levitte's verbal abuse of his son, Roderick,' Joe continued.

Theda Levitte looked from him to Bernie and back. 'What *is* this? None of this has got nothing to do with *me*. They're not my children.'

Kate caught a nod from Joe to Bernie. Bernie waded in again. 'During the time you and Henry Levitte were married you were aware he was using under-age males for sexual purposes—'

'I know nothing about that. You've got nothing on me because I was never there.' Kate watched the small black eyes move from Bernie to Joe and back.

'What're you saying? You were *never* at home when something you knew *nothing* about was happening?' Bernie leaned forward. 'Stop messing us about. *Tell* us.'

Kate and her two colleagues waited as a calculating look crossed Theda Levitte's face. She'd come to a decision. 'I met Henry when he was doing some work at a gallery in Sheffield.' Her mouth twisted. 'It was no big romance and it didn't take me long to work out what he was really about: sex. Which was okay with me because I *really* like money.'

Kate was scarcely breathing as Bernie lowered his hands from his mouth and spoke. 'You're saying you knew what he was up to?'

Theda Levitte's head gave a vehement shake. 'No. I *didn't* know. I didn't *want* to know.' She saw the disbelief on their faces. 'Think what I got from marrying him: a big house, money, a nice car.' She shrugged plump shoulders. 'I wasn't interested in anything else. It was *none* of my *business*.' In the heavy silence she continued. 'We had this arrangement. He'd give me dates when he wanted the house to himself. It worked out at a couple of days once, maybe twice a month. I'd leave him to it for those days and book a hotel room in Birmingham, have some "me" time, some pampering. I can give you details, bills from the hotels, so you can check I was there.' She gazed across the table at them. 'I was never at the house on those dates. He never gave me any explanation as to what happened and I never asked.'

Joe looked her in the eye. 'You knew there was a room upstairs in your house which was used for organised sexual activity, and another room where the items DS Watts described were stored.'

She stared back at him. 'That upstairs room was always kept locked. I never had a key. As for "items" I've got no idea what you're talking about.'

'Who killed Nathan Troy?' Kate's voice drifted across the room. The small eyes turned on her.

'How should I know? It wasn't *me*. Why would I kill him? Or anybody else?'

Kate stood and walked to the door. She hadn't denied that Nathan Troy was at her home. Theda Levitte had as good as confirmed for Kate what Nathan's coat hanging in that secret room had already told her: that Nathan Troy's journey to death had begun at Hyde Road. She reached the door then turned. 'Where is Cassandra?'

Theda Levitte rolled her eyes. 'Could be anywhere, spending money, picking up men. Who knows?'

Kate walked through the door. Joe watched her go as Bernie started again. 'For the tape, Dr Hanson leaving the room. Theda Levitte, I'm now formally charging you with destruction of evidence relevant to the investigation of the death of Nathan William Troy . . .'

* * *

Kate replaced the marker on the ledge below the glass screen then sat on the table staring at what she'd written, the names she'd crossed out. Words they'd had said to them during the investigation which described Henry Levitte. Renowned artist. Venerable. A great bloke. Devoted father. Old tart. Vain. Self-centred. She recalled her own experience of him: theatrical to the point of foppishness, reliant on his wife's practical strength and capability. She recalled him calmly painting at the gallery whilst his Retrospective grew around him. Kate's eyes moved across the glass. No one had described Henry Levitte as an idler but that's what he was. He hadn't organised his own Retrospective. He'd put that responsibility onto Roderick, knowing what a poor choice he was. *Always the dogsbody*. Whenever Roderick failed he relied on John Wellan to pick up the pieces. She was too tired to think any more. Time to go home.

* * *

Rotating his shoulders to reduce tension, Joe studied the stocky, harsh-faced woman sitting opposite them. 'Henry Levitte was holding parties at your home. Sexual activity with minors was on offer. You just told us he had a "wide circle" of associates. I'm taking that to be a reference to other males involved in that sexual activity.' He looked her in the eye. 'Which meant a hell of a lot of organising: letting attendees know dates, ensuring there'd be sufficient "attractions" for them.' He stared at her with dislike. 'Somehow I don't see Henry Levitte doing all of that. You're saying you didn't do it. Which means there had to have been a "fixer". Who was it?'

Watching her face he knew his words had struck home. She recovered with a shrug. 'I'm not helping you do your jobs . . . and there wasn't anybody.'

'Yes there was. I think there still is. Someone you know *real* well.' The frown between her thick brows deepened as she watched him stand, give a brief nod to Bernie and head for the door and the corridor leading to UCU.

* * *

In the forty-five minutes that Kate had been home she'd organised dinner with Maisie's help. Now she sat at the dining table moving food around her plate with a fork. 'Your mother's off-world, Mouse.'

'Mom?'

Kate looked up, disorientated at being pulled from deep thoughts of Theda Levitte's voice in the interview. 'What? Sorry, I—'

'Daddy's just offered to get me a ticket for—'

Voices. Ticket! The fork clattered to the plate. She was out of the kitchen and inside her study, searching her bag for her phone, tapping in the number from memory. Her call was picked up almost immediately. 'Hello, is that Bill Troy?'

'Yes . . . Dr Hanson?'

'I'm sorry to have to ring you, Mr Troy, but there's something I *must* know. When Lieutenant Corrigan and I came to see you, you told us that you bought the train tickets for the journey to London with Nathan and sent his to him by post.'

His reply drifted down the line. 'That's right.'

Kate steadied her voice. 'Can you remember any details about posting them?'

There was a short silence on the line, then: 'I remember it all. It turned out to be the very last thing I did for my son.' She bit her lip, waiting as a few seconds of nothing came down the line. 'I phoned him and told him I was sending him his tickets. I posted them to him on the ninth of November, first class, and I phoned the next day to check the envelope had arrived.'

'And he told you it had?' asked Kate.

'No. Nathan wasn't there. He was at college but one of the other students answered the phone and said it had come that morning and it was still there in the hall, for when Nathan got back. I'd put my name and address on the back.'

Kate stood, a hand on her forehead. 'Who did you speak to?'

'Sorry, I don't know which one it was.'

'Thank you, Mr — *No*, wait. What time was it when you phoned the house?'

'In the late afternoon. I think it was gone four.'

'Thank you,' said Kate softly as she ended the call.

She had to be sure. Dragging her notebook from her bag she switched on the desk lamp and flicked pages, leaning into the light. Here it was. The cognitive interview. She frowned. What she'd written made no sense at all.

Coat on, she returned to the kitchen to find Kevin slicing cheese, Maisie nowhere in sight but a heavy bass beat had started on the upper floor. 'I'm going out.'

Kevin's voice followed her: 'Out? Where? So, I'm just the babysitter now?'

CHAPTER SIXTY-SIX

The small campus was deserted, the darkened main building outlined against a backdrop of lowering sky and stark trees. Kate glanced at her watch as news slid from the radio. '. . . *thousands of children in the UK are being groomed and sexually exploited by gangs, according to a study released today . . .*'

Hand to her forehead she stared ahead knowing that mean streets and fast-food outlets weren't the only fertile ground for depravity and exploitation. It was no secret that the renowned, the prominent, the moneyed, could be equally corrupt, historically and now: the House of Borgia. The House of Levitte. She leaned against the headrest. What was a gang if it wasn't a group? Both need similar things to operate: organisation, a leader.

She closed her eyes. She'd had to come here. Because three of the victims had had a shared history in this lovely place. Nathan Troy. Joel Smythe. Cassandra Levitte. *Where are you, Cassandra?* She felt the familiar tightening of her head which now happened every time she asked the question. Looking beyond the windows of the car she scanned the surrounding campus, taking several breaths to quell the tide of anxiety.

Head full of tension Kate released her seat belt, got out of the car and started towards Woolner. Nearing the entrance she looked beyond it. A dark-coloured Volvo was parked there. *What's Joe doing here?*

She'd reached the top step when it came. A single-note discord, faint, now growing in strength, a series of repetitive bell-clangs. Knowing its source she turned towards the beautiful old building on the other side of the campus, its copper-domed cupola shielding the multiple carillon. She'd heard it played on a summer evening, its multiple chimes drifting across Bournville village green. But not like this. The clanging discord filled Kate's head as she ran down the steps, across frigid grass and through a screen of trees to the building's entrance. The door was closed. Guessing who was inside she ran to it and pushed. It was locked.

Scanning the immediate area she ran back to a small area of low shrubbery edged with hefty chunks of stone. Lifting the largest she carried it to the door, raised it in both hands and brought it down on the handle. It broke, fell to the ground, other pieces following it as Kate dropped the stone and pushed at the door, her whole being on alert as more clamouring discord hit the air and reverberated around her. She burst through the door into the tumult and stood, chest heaving.

Cassandra was at the carillon, working it with her hands and feet, her long pale hair falling either side of her face. As Kate watched, she grew still. The discord stopped and Cassandra's bare white arms fell to her sides. Kate remained where she was, silent, weak with relief, eyes on the white face illuminated by street light seeping inside. Her face turned to Kate's, eyes huge, empty. 'Do you know?' she whispered. 'Have you got the answer?'

Kate took measured steps forward, keeping her voice low. 'It's why I'm here. I've come to see John Wellan. I've been very worried about you.'

The pale hair swayed as Cassandra's head bowed again. 'I tried to ring you but . . . I lost the number. Give him this. I don't want it any more. I thought he was my friend. He wasn't. He locked me in here. He made me kill my baby.'

Kate gazed at the elegant claret and gold Montegrappa lying across the outstretched palm. Taking it she put it inside her trouser pocket then removed her coat and placed it around the thin shoulders. 'Cassandra, I want you to stay here. Will you do that? *Please.* My friend Joe who you met, remember? He's here and I'm going to find him. We'll come back for you, I promise. Until we do, you *must* stay inside? *Please?*' Getting a small nod Kate turned and left the room, pulling the outer door against its frame then ran back the way she'd come.

CHAPTER SIXTY-SEVEN

Kate sped up the college steps and inside. The huge expanse of entrance hall was deserted but she saw a seam of light showing under the door bearing the name: *Professor Matthew Johnson*. Should she demand answers from him? No. There was someone else she had to see.

Kate was halfway up the main stairs, ears straining for sound where there was none. She frowned. Where was John Wellan? Where was Joe? Did he know what she knew? A low moan sent Kate's heart into freefall as adrenalin surged and fear prickled her shoulders. It came again. This time she recognised it. A low whine-turned-howl.

She stood on the uppermost stair, thinking how effectively he had controlled, silenced, an unstable young woman. Kate heard Cassandra's voice in her head: 'Am-u-let.' Like a child repeating the word of a teacher. Which is exactly what he was. Kate now saw that she'd been too ready to accept his self-presentation. It made no sense that someone who liked and bought finely wrought material possessions would not have noticed, nor coveted Henry Levitte's watch. And the return train ticket? Nathan Troy couldn't have shown them to anyone on the afternoon of his tutorial. He didn't have them. He'd left the house before they arrived that morning. They were still at the student house, waiting for him, sent there first class by his father. Kate's mind sped on. For someone to describe the unlikelihood of Stuart Butts gaining entry to the Retrospective using the words he had, he would have to *know* Stuart. Know how 'well turned out' he could be, know that Stuart had the money to buy expensive clothes. She thought of the reception at the White Box Gallery. Why kill Henry Levitte? Because he was beginning to talk, becoming careless, his behaviour unreliable, threatening the whole awful, crafted structure of organised abuse and everyone who participated in it. He'd had to get to Levitte before Kate and her colleagues did.

She looked along the corridor. His name had been among those she'd listed, who knew of her connection to UCU. She'd crossed out all those named who would have had no access to the Levittes' Mercedes. His name and a few others had remained. Once she'd re-examined all she'd learned about him, all he'd said, she knew it was *him* on the phone to Stuart at the park. The watch. The pen. The car. It was about money and abuse on a scale which *had* to be organised. So it needed something else: an Enabler. *Him.*

Hearing another howl Kate walked the corridor then pushed open the door. The studio was dark. Coming further inside, eyes adjusting to the meagre light from the lantern roof, she saw Rupe several feet away, worrying at something on the floor. Eyes widening as she drew nearer she recognised what it was that was causing the dog's distress.

Heart rolling over she ran to where he was lying on his side, face towards her and the door. '*Joe.* Joe!' She was on her knees, thighs pressed against his back, bending low, searching his face, running her hand over the dark hair. It felt cold. Her hand came away wet. With her other hand she touched his face. It felt clammy and cool. The one thought in her head was that he mustn't be moved.

Rupe whined again and licked her face. She pushed him away, feeling a sudden draught of cold air. She heard soft footfalls on wood as he came inside. She knelt, immobilised, her head now full of her life and Maisie. She looked down at

Joe. She had no choice. She had to put up a fight. Reaching inside the soft overcoat she moved her hand over his chest then stopped. She'd made contact with the sturdy leather strap harnessing the holster beneath his arm. *Joe knew.* He'd come here anticipating trouble. She moved her hand along the smooth leather, straining to recall what he'd told her, what he'd shown her weeks before.

Knowing from Rupe's excited bark that he was near Kate tensed, sensing more whispered footfalls across the floor, the Vans obscuring any real sound. She guessed the Adidas were long gone. Now came the light-head-dry-mouth signs of panic at what she was about to do. *No choice.* She heard his voice above her, the feigned puzzlement. 'What are you doing here, Kate? What's happened?' The realisation rushed her head that she loathed him. For what he was and what he'd done to so many people. To Joe. She was outside herself, knowing what she had to do. He was close now. He was coming. For her.

In an instant Kate was on her knees, her body's central core taut, eyes on their target, her hands joined, both arms outstretched as Joe had shown her, the weight of metal causing them to dip and waver. She'd *never* leave Maisie and he'd hurt Joe and she was ready. Thigh muscles braced, arms rigid, she shouted the single-word warning, just like he'd taught her: '*Stop!*'

He gave a low laugh, still moving towards her. 'Oh come *on*, Kate.'

Eyes on him, retracting her index finger, she fired. He spun and dropped.

Thrown to the floor by the gun's recoil and her own unpractised stance, Kate pulled herself upright, ears full of blast and distant hysterical barks, moans, shouts and heavy feet on stairs, followed by Bernie's voice and that of Matthew Johnson as they came through the door. She moved to Joe, laid her face against his shoulder and wept.

* * *

Joe had been taken away. Wellan had also gone under police escort. Cassandra was on her way back to the Hawthornes and Kate was inside a paramedic car with Bernie. She heard a voice she did not know and then Bernie's: 'Yeah, the three of us work together. He's an American police officer. She's a psychologist. We've got this big case on and . . . it looks like we each got the answer in our own way.' There was a brief silence then, 'What d'you think? Will he be okay?'

The paramedic's reply was vague, non-committal. She gathered what focus she could: 'They need to know.'

Bernie's voice came again. 'Who?'

'Joe's family. In America. We need to tell them what's happened . . . to . . .' She stopped, an ache in her throat as big as the world.

* * *

They had followed him to the hospital. After an hour they were told Joe was still unconscious from the severe blow to his head.

Bernie turned to watch the driving rain now hitting the window as Kate pressed a hand to the glass that separated them from Joe. *Why is it I've chosen the wrong men? Until now. Don't go.*

After another fifteen minutes they were encouraged to leave. Kate arrived home to a sleeping household. She'd climbed the stairs like an automaton, undressed and lay down. Within minutes she was downstairs again.

From a corner of the sofa she watched the sun come up.

CHAPTER SIXTY-EIGHT

Early Friday morning a white-faced Kate was in UCU, eyes unfocused as Bernie returned from the custody suite. 'He's refusing to talk to us till he's seen you. You don't have to do it. I say let the bastard stew.' He looked at her, her face turned towards the rain beating against the windows. The phone rang. She leapt, eyes wide, as Bernie lifted it, watching her as he spoke. 'Bernie W — Yeah, yeah . . . Good. Right, thanks for telling us, love. We'll be in.' Kate's eyes were on him as he put down the phone. 'Joe's conscious. We can go and see him tonight.'

Relief surging, Kate closed her eyes, then stood and went to the glass screen to read the words in Joe's handwriting about two voices he'd heard and linked together. Looking up at Bernie she said, 'You saw this? You understood?' He nodded. She straightened, trying to breathe normally. She hadn't been able to in what seemed like hours. 'I'm going to see him. I want him to talk.'

* * *

The duty sergeant led Kate inside the custody suite's interview room then walked to one side of the door, turned and assumed a waiting stance. Wellan was already there. Kate went to where he was sitting, his left arm in a sling, and sat opposite him. He looked at her as he touched it. 'Thanks a lot.'

She returned his look, knowing that he'd sustained little more than a graze. 'What do you want?'

His face assumed a mock-sad look. 'Don't say we're no longer "pals-in-Academe".' She was on her feet as he raised his good arm. '*Wait.*'

'What do you want?' she repeated.

'Sit down. I want you to do something for me—'

'How—' She pressed her mouth closed, eyes on his face, studying him. '*I* want answers.'

He shook his head. 'I've got no answers for you. I'm saying nothing until I'm interviewed.'

She looked into his face, intent. 'In that case, I'll go with my own answers, as did Bernie — and Joe.' He studied her as she sat back ready to tell him. 'Nathan was angry when he came for his tutorial, wasn't he? Because of what Cassandra had told him. About what her father had done to her.' He sat without moving. 'Nathan arrived at your studio with a plan. To go to Hyde Road and have it out with Henry. Threaten him with the police.' She sat forward, her voice dropping. 'And when *you* heard that, you *had* to stop him.' She sat back again. 'What was it? A lot of lithium in hot chocolate so he wouldn't taste it? So that he would be a little sleepy? Easier to control? Once at Hyde Road, you tried to persuade him not to tell the police.' Kate looked at him with disgust. 'And when he wouldn't cooperate, you struggled with him, subdued him, got Henry to help you get him into the car.' She shook her head. 'It wouldn't have taken much effort by then, the lithium plus any alcohol you managed to get inside him.'

Wellan was staring at the ceiling, looking relaxed. He transferred the stare to her. 'When he left his tutorial with me he was fine.'

Kate sat forward, so quickly that she had the pleasure of seeing him flinch. 'Except for the lithium that's probably true *but* if you didn't murder him why lie to us? At the end of his tutorial did he tell you that he was going back to the student house to check that something his father sent him had arrived?' Wellan looked at her and she could see him trying to work out how she knew. 'Before you drove him to Hyde Road, you offered to take him back to the house to see if it had arrived. It *had*. He put it in a wallet, left it in his room, got back into your car. He never told you what it was, did he?' She now had Wellan's undivided attention. 'It was a return train ticket, the one *you* told us he showed you that afternoon during the tutorial.' She watched his mouth tighten, shaking her head. 'Impossible. He didn't yet have it.'

He placed both hands on his face, gave it vigorous rub then let his hands drop where they quivered on the table; she guessed he needed a cigarette. He looked across at her. 'Now let me tell you what I want—'

'No. One of the most important factors in all of this is that Nathan Troy had a strong sense of right and wrong. You responded to that by destroying him. And then you did the same to a boy I suspect you didn't even know. The only reason Bradley Harper had to die was because he had something of Henry's and you couldn't find it.'

'I knew nothing about Henry Levitte, nor his interests.'

Hearing the smooth words she nodded at him. 'That's the line you'll be taking in interview? That was something else I couldn't understand. How it was that you appeared to know almost nothing about Henry Levitte, despite the fact that you'd been colleagues for years.' She gazed into his face as she brought the plain item with black leather straps from her pocket, holding it up. 'And how it was that someone who evidently liked to own expensive things claimed not to have noticed that Henry Levitte wore an IWC.' He'd turned his face away from her, shoulders hunched. 'I asked you about his wearing a "ring or a watch" and you told me you didn't recall a "watch or a ring".'

Turning to her he frowned. '*So*?'

Kate considered him. 'That change of word order indicated to me which of those two items was the most salient for you: the *watch*. The one *you* were wearing when you put Nathan Troy under the lake house floor.'

Wellan looked beyond Kate to the attending officer. 'I'm finished here.' He stood as the officer approached.

'You said you wanted me to do something?' said Kate. 'Whatever it is, it's probably not going to happen but I can *guarantee* it won't if you leave this room right now.' He stared down at her in silence then sat, looking away.

'Good,' she said quietly. 'Because now I'm getting to Cassandra.' He dropped his head back, sighed then looked beyond her. 'Once you'd arrived at Woolner it didn't take you long to realise the set-up there, recognise Cassandra's vulnerability and the potential of it all for *you*. Your motivation in all of it was money but you weren't averse to using her. When she got pregnant you told her to name Johnson as the father then forced a termination.' He turned to Kate, mouth opening and she glared at him. 'Don't deny it! She's told us. Cassandra has talked and we've *listened*. We know how you used the Eye to control and frighten her so that she wouldn't talk to anyone about what she knew. Thanks to *you* she's now a textbook case of Post-Traumatic Stress Disorder.' Kate stopped, feeling her grip on her anger slipping.

'You can't *know* all of this. I don't believe Cassandra said any of it.'

'Yes, she did.' She reached into her pocket again and brought out another item which she slammed onto the table. He stared at the Montegrappa. 'She asked me to give you this. She's free of you.' Before he could reach for it she took the pen and slid it back inside her pocket, looking at him. 'Johnson and Buchanan have also talked. They always suspected that Henry Levitte was up to no good but like many people they ignored that aspect of him because of another from which they benefited: Levitte liked to wield power. He enjoyed the esteem in which he was regarded when he "helped" people, bestowed favours. Both Buchanan and Johnson took what was on offer: a smooth career path to a good business opportunity for Buchanan and a quick rise through Woolner's faculty for Johnson. Buchanan's good fortune was dependent on his doing something when he was still a student — giving a false sighting of Nathan to establish that he was alive and well days after you killed him. As a person with his focus on the main chance he agreed, although he probably didn't fully realise what he was agreeing to. Johnson made himself useful by monitoring Cassandra back then. He may or may not have realised the purpose: watching Cassandra wasn't about protecting her. It was to ensure that she didn't form any real connection with anyone to whom she might talk, someone who might *listen*. Levitte chose Johnson because there was no risk that he would form a sexual relationship with her.' Wellan's attention was fixed on the floor as Kate watched his face. 'Buchanan's and Johnson's final act of "repayment" was to be uncooperative with our investigation.'

'*Those* two,' sneered Wellan. 'Useless takers, both of them, and Roderick. Don't tell me he's getting away without any charge?'

'He's been charged with sexual assault of Bradley Harper.'

He looked away from her, quivering hand over his mouth. She guessed his thoughts were on his coming interview. 'So that's all you've got?'

She shook her head. 'Oh, no. We've got *you*. You seem interested in what's happening to other people in this. Don't you want to know what's happening to *your* sibling?'

'No thanks. Not interested.'

He was looking increasingly restless and Kate guessed that his need for tobacco was now pressing. '*You* didn't work out unaided what was happening at Woolner. You were helped. Pointed in the direction. By someone who wasn't directly involved but who *must* have suspected what was going on. Lieutenant Corrigan wrote something on the glass screen upstairs before he went to Woolner to see *you*.'

'This is relevant to me?' he asked, tone weary.

'Very much. There's something you don't know about Joe Corrigan. He's a musician as well as a police officer. He has an "ear".' She leaned forward. 'It took someone with a good foreign ear like his to really *hear* the sounds of your and Theda's voices, and he wrote a question: "From the same place?"' She sat back looking at him. 'He guessed the connection.'

'Now let's get to what I want—'

'Not until you tell me why Joel Smythe had to die. We think Troy told him what Henry Levitte had done to Cassandra.'

Wellan's face suffused. 'That's the trouble with sanctimonious people like *Troy*! They talk here, talk there and they *never* stop to *think* of the unintended effect of what they're saying.' He stopped, wiping his mouth with the back of his hand. She saw caution in his eyes as she caught up with her own merging ideas.

She nodded. 'I get it. Troy told Joel what he knew and . . . he didn't realise the effect it had on him?' Wellan said nothing. 'Maybe Joel experienced something similar in his own childhood and Troy's words had a significant impact on him?' Kate knew she'd get no confirmation but she also knew it was a likely explanation for the unexpected downward turn taken by Joel Smythe's life.

She wanted to be gone but there was one more fact she had to share. 'Stuart Butts has told—'

'Stuart Butts is a liar who'd kill his own mother if he thought he could get away with it!' He glared at her, furious. 'He'll run, long before any court proceedings start. *If* they do.'

'He's not running at the moment. He's been placed with people who want to do the right thing for him.'

He gave a harsh laugh. 'Oh, *right*. That'll put the little bastard on the road to good citizenship, I *don't* think. Did he tell you *he* recruited younger kids?'

'He told us about *you*. You fixed everything for Henry Levitte. You enabled him to do what he did. *You* procured under-age children from community centres, drew them in by offering them an art class, then drugs, then money.'

She watched Wellan get up from his chair. She was finished with him and never wanted to see him again. She watched as he walked across the room, forgotten words coming into her head. 'What did you mean when you said you needed a couple more years at Woolner? For what?' He stopped but didn't turn. She frowned at his back. 'You want more money? After all that you'd made through Levitte, plus extortion from the "guests" at the Hyde Road parties — whom we'll be contacting — it wasn't *enough*?' She stopped as he turned to her. 'Where is it? Where's all the money?'

'You'll get nothing from me.'

Kate sat forward, eyes on his face, details of a portrait in his studio of an olive-skinned young woman and an infant slipping into her head. She doubted his explanation that one of his students painted it. 'Two more years . . . and you were planning to relocate. To a new life.'

Wellan's face darkened. 'I've got a team of good lawyers on my side, fighting my case for me.'

'Then think on this,' said Kate, rising from her chair. 'If there is someone waiting for you, a woman, a wife in Greece — or Italy? — she's going to know about this case very soon and when she does she'll be taking all of your money and whatever else you have and disappearing.' She looked into his rigid face. 'When your money's gone will your lawyers still be fighting your corner?'

Kate walked across the room to the door. He watched as she opened it. 'I said I want you to do something for me, remember?'

'Go to hell,' she said, still moving as the custody officer moved towards Wellan and took his arm.

'It's not for *me*. Will you? *Kate*!'

* * *

Looking up as Kate came through the door Bernie got to his feet and went to switch on the kettle, keeping an eye on her as she sat, elbows on the table, both hands at her mouth. He returned with a mug of tea and placed it in front of her. She sipped it, eyes downcast.

'You all right, Doc?' She nodded. 'What was Wellan after?'

She leaned back on her chair. 'He's very concerned. About the future welfare of his dog.'

There was a short period of silence, broken by Bernie. 'Want to come with me or have you got to get home?'

She glanced at her watch. 'Kevin's there with Maisie.' She looked up at him. 'Where?'

'To see the Troys to tell them what's happening and then to see Debbie Harper. After which it'll be coming up to the time we can visit Joe.' She fetched her coat.

CHAPTER SIXTY-NINE

Bill and Rachel Troy listened as Bernie described in limited terms the developments of the case. Bernie stopped talking and Bill and Rachel Troy gave Kate an expectant look. 'The box you've let us borrow has been such a help to us. We need to keep it a little longer.' They nodded as Kate continued. 'We're not able to talk as freely as we'd like because of future court hearings but there is something we want to say. We appreciate the help you gave on our visit here and you, Bill, when I phoned.' She looked back at Rachel. 'You told us something very important about Nathan, about an aspect of his character and how it impacted on the way he lived his life. It helped us understand him. It led us to the reason he died.' She stopped to get her voice under control. 'You said that Nathan was a moral person. You were right. He was.'

In the following silence Rachel Troy looked at her husband, smiled, then looked back to Kate. 'We knew our son. He and I had a strong bond. He would never have stayed quiet about anything he believed was wrong.'

* * *

Twenty minutes later they were inside Debbie Harper's tidy house, being introduced to her sister. 'She's been stopping here on and off, helping me get organised, cleaning the place up.' She'd listened to what they were able to tell her about Bradley, her sister at her side. Now she wept, her sister's hand on her shoulder. After a short silence she rallied. 'Thanks for letting me know. My Bradley was a good lad. I'll have to ring his dad and let him know what's happening.' She looked at each of them. 'You know, I don't think I'll bother. He doesn't come round here any more.'

Bernie and Kate stood and she got up to show them out. 'I'm grateful for what you've done. That other one you work with, the American, after he phoned the social worker to come here that day, she had a meeting at her office. I've got a social worker of my own now. She's helped a lot. Helped me and the kids' dad sort out contact between us. She's got the lads into an after-school club for football and stuff like that and Amber's going to a drama group. The babby's starting at nursery next Monday, five mornings a week. They've said I can stop there as well and help out.' She nodded. 'I'll enjoy that.'

She led them to the door and out. The garden was clear of rubbish. 'Looks better, yeah?'

Bernie turned to her, brows raised. 'Whose handiwork's this?'

Arms folded against the cold she gave him a look. 'Done it all myself.'

* * *

They were both exhausted but Kate prevailed and they went to the Hawthornes. Leila Jones's attitude was still one of disapproval towards Kate because of her unauthorised entry into the medical records but she warmed on learning of Kate's role in finding Cassandra. 'In the short time she's been here she's more or less stabilised. We'll be working with her on historical and recent events within her family. We're starting that process tomorrow at her sister's house. Miranda Levitte has offered Cassandra a home and the Hawthornes will maintain its involvement in her future care.'

Kate wondered how receptive Leila Jones might be to her professional opinion of Cassandra's difficulties then gave an inward shrug. That was for her to decide. 'She's likely to cope better with her mood disorder if she also gets help for post-traumatic stress and a chance to talk about her termination. That is, if she wants to.'

The manager nodded. 'We'll provide whatever she needs.'

CHAPTER SEVENTY

Late on Monday afternoon Kate was staring at rain coursing down the windows of her room at the university. She and Bernie had visited Joe earlier at the Queen Elizabeth Hospital. He was making good progress and would be released in the next couple of days if it continued. She'd watched him as he rested until Bernie touched her arm and they'd walked away, out of the massive building into searing cold.

Wellan had been charged with three murders. Theda Levitte had been charged as an accessory to the organised sex ring operating at her home on the basis that she was aware of it but did nothing to stop it. The Crown Prosecution Service had already indicated its misgivings about Stuart Butts as a reliable witness. Kate sighed. *Why is it that once the Criminal Justice System grinds into action, justice is at risk of falling by the wayside?* The sound of her office door being opened and Crystal's muted voice brought her back. 'Is it urgent? Dr Hanson has a lot to do and she's—'

'Who is it, Crystal?'

She turned from the door. 'One of your student group. Ashley Jenner.'

'Ask her in, please.' Kate looked across the room as the young student appeared. 'Hi, Ashley. What can I do for you?'

The young woman's face was troubled. 'We heard about Lieutenant Corrigan. We got this for him.' She handed a large square envelope across the desk to Kate. 'Is he okay?'

Kate took the envelope. 'That's really kind. Thank you. He's recovering well so he'll be pleased to get this.'

The young face broadened into a smile. 'I've brought something to show you. That's if you've got time?' At a quick nod from Kate she lifted the plastic carrier bag she was holding and placed it carefully on the desk. 'I got this for my mother for her birthday. It's *so* cool. I'll show you.' She lifted out two items, removed layers of tissue and passed them to Kate, watching her as she took them, one in each hand, turning them. 'Remember what you said a while ago, Dr Hanson? That perception depends on how we see something?'

Kate gazed down at enigmatic black markings printed on the white saucer. Frowning, she transferred her attention to the silvered, reflective surface of the cup. Placing it gently onto the saucer she saw seemingly haphazard black strokes transformed into a message reflected onto the cup's curved, glossy side: *Drink me!* She smiled, recalling the lecture she'd given on perception and the old painting she'd used to illustrate her point. She couldn't exactly recall her own words but Ashley had got it about right: *Understanding is all about how we look at things.* She handed the cup and saucer back to her. 'That's really great. I'm sure your mother will love it.'

Ashley had left and Kate was standing at the window, gazing out on the rain-drenched campus, thinking of the cup's curved, shiny surface and how it had yielded the saucer's secret when it was placed just *so*, a fun example of a particular kind of deception: anamorphosis.

Still feeling detached from herself she crossed the room, lifted down her coat and went to the door. 'Crystal. I'm going home,' she called. 'There's something I have to do.'

'Okay, Kate. Have a good rest. Give Lieutenant Corrigan our best when you see him.'

* * *

She let herself into the house. Low light was seeping from the half-open door of her study. Opening the door further she stood, looking inside. Kevin was lying on the sofa, eyes closed, headphones clamped to his ears, one finger keeping time. She walked further inside to the corner of the room, to gaze up at *Sun on Land*. Her detachment evaporated and cold anger rose. She lifted it down, holding it away from her as she carried it across the room. Leaning it against the desk she went to Nathan's box on a nearby chair. Removing the lid she reached inside, felt coolness against her fingers and lifted out the shiny chrome cylinder. Now she understood it all.

With one sweep of her arm she cleared the desk of textbooks, papers, everything, and laid the painting on it. Kevin reared in the ensuing crash and clatter. '. . . Maisie? What're you up to? . . . *Kate?*'

She crossed to the main switch, turned on the light and went back to the painting. Bewildered, Kevin watched her as she placed the shiny chrome tube upright on the disc of broiling sun then lower her head for a sideways gaze along the chrome's smooth, reflective surface. Her eyes travelled slowly upwards, over the image depicted in smooth, cold metal: the small, delicate feet, the long slim legs, the pre-pubescent hips and promise of breasts to the elfin face. Androgynous. Recognisable. Cassandra Levitte.

She straightened, letting the chrome cylinder fall and roll away across the floor. She watched it go, recalling ones she'd seen just like it. In Wellan's studio. In the sitting room at the Levitte house. Had Nathan also seen them? Had Cassandra understood their use and told him what they were? A simple tool for the enjoyment of secret child pornography embedded in Henry Levitte's 'art'.

'Kate?'

Grasping the painting she left the study, went through the kitchen, pausing to drop an item into her pocket, pulled at one of the bolts and threw the door wide into freezing rain and darkness. Outside she dropped the painting into a nearby wheelbarrow, hearing Kevin's voice. 'What the *hell's* going on?' She went to the barbecue, opened it, took out the small tin, removed the cap and took it to the picture, watching liquid hit and slide. She was about to destroy evidence. It didn't matter. Now she understood she would lead her colleagues to other, similar pictures.

Kevin had now made it to the door, in time to see her reach into her pocket for the box and remove a single, long match. '*Jesus!*' He clutched his head, watched her from the door, face aghast. Whatever else he was Kevin was quick on his intellectual feet. He dropped his voice. 'Okay . . . okay . . . Something's happened and . . . you don't like the picture any more?' He followed her movements. 'No, *no*. Wait. You don't like it? No problem. *I'll* take it. You won't ever have to see it again. That's a promise. It's half mine anyway, remember?' He hobbled through the door as the match flared between her fingers. 'No, *Kate*! *Wait* — let *me* take the picture.'

She turned her cool face to him. 'And disseminate pornography?' She released the match. 'No.' Kevin watched, helpless, as it drifted downwards and reached its destination.

Whooosshhh.

Kate watched canvas bubble and curl. When *Sun on Land* was entirely consumed she walked past him and back inside her house.

CHAPTER SEVENTY-ONE

Gander was in UCU, congratulating them on the work they'd done. He nodded to Bernie and Kate then looked at Joe, the stitches in his head almost concealed by the thick hair. 'Sure you're up to coming back today?'

'Yes, sir. DS Watts and I still have a lot to do on the case.'

Gander nodded, sending them and Kate a benign glance. 'First-rate job! First rate. Over the next couple of days I want you to think about something UCU needs.'

Julian looked excited. 'A new glass screen. One of those massive ones with an interactive touch-screen panel and—'

The chief superintendent held up a cautioning hand as Furman looked on, face wooden. 'There's not a lot of money about just now. Tell them how much is available, Roger.'

Furman's lip curled as he read from the sheet of figures in front of him. 'There's . . . let's see . . . one hundred pounds, *maximum*.' His eyes snagged on Kate's and she knew he was relishing the meagreness of the sum.

Gander nodded to them again. 'Not much, I know, but give it some thought. I've also given thought to extra help for you if you need it on future cases. A few extra man-hours?' He glanced at Kate's facial expression and frowned at his own words then guessed there was probably something on her mind, other than his phrasing. 'I'm thinking of giving you Whittaker during your next busy period. Good young officer. A bit . . . overactive. Needs channelling. You can use him, as and when.'

Julian nodded to the chief inspector. 'Whittaker will be pleased. He's wanted to be in UCU for months.'

Kate looked at her student helper, realising that she'd never heard a first name for the young constable. 'What do you call him when you all socialise?'

Julian's eyes flicked round the table and back to Kate. '. . . Whittaker?'

Gander cleared his throat and gave her a direct look. 'There'll be an investigation into Wellan's shooting.' Kate flinched. 'But don't let that trouble you. We know he was coming for you and . . . er, the matter of the medical records. The manager of the nursing home has agreed to . . . let that go.' He paused, eyes still on her face, knowing that she blamed herself for loss of evidence. 'We do what we can to get justice, Kate, we follow the *rules*, then we leave it.' He gave her a direct look. 'Words to the wise: let it be.'

Kate felt tension start to ebb away. Kevin had left and she had some space in which to adjust to all that had happened. She knew she wouldn't apply for either of the available professorships. Not if it meant never coming here to Rose Road and UCU. She looked across the table to Bernie. He wasn't on the 'Human Remains' list for redundancy. They would work together and annoy each other again. A synaptic blip inside her head brought back Maisie's civil rights project and the speech she'd seen. She looked at Gander. 'There is something I'd like for UCU and it won't cost much but we have to discuss it before we decide.'

As soon as Gander and Furman left she told them what she wanted then looked around the table, seeing Julian give her a bright-eyed nod, getting a wink from Bernie. She looked to Joe resting back his head, an easy grin on his face. She reached for the phone.

CHAPTER SEVENTY-TWO

They were walking the frigid Clent hills nodding to other brave souls taking a Sunday walk. That should be 'foolhardy' thought Kate, shielding her eyes from the blinding sun. Now she could see Maisie racing ahead, chasing for all she was worth, hair and coat flying. She hadn't yet told Maisie about firing a gun at Woolner and the Force had contained the details. She needed to think about how to explain it. *If* she told her, that is. Secrets. She shook her head. She had to tell her. She turned to Joe. 'Bend your head forward so I can see how it is in daylight.' He did as she asked and she put a gentle hand on each of his arms and studied the semicircle of healing injury now barely visible within his hair. 'Mmm . . . It's improving. You were very lucky, you know. He hit you hard.'

He grinned down at her. 'Heavy duty Boston-Irish skull.' They looked up to see Maisie running towards them. 'Getting back to what I was saying: Rupe and I have a lot in common. We're both alone here and we need somebody to care.'

She gave him a sideways glance. 'And now you've found what you need, apparently. Each other. Did I tell you you're a *complete* pushover?'

He nodded. 'I think you mentioned that.'

They walked on. 'How long will you be staying with Bernie now that you've given up the apartment?'

His attention was on the rolling hills ahead of them. 'The building work on Regent Road should be finished in less than three months. I'll stay until then.'

'Sounds like a treat.' She laughed.

He did the same. 'Julian's settled in.' Kate knew that Julian had escaped from his room at halls because of Bernie's offer of a room at his house at reasonable rent. 'And Connie dropped in last—'

Kate put a hand on his arm again, giving him a look. 'Hang on! Is that last bit a joke?'

'Would I—'

'Yes, you *would*.'

Joe bent to stroke the hound's head as Maisie reached them, cheeks flaming, breathless, scarcely able to get the words out. 'He's . . . hardly got . . . legs but he . . . *goes*.'

She handed the red lead to Joe and he clipped it onto Rupe's leather collar. 'Come on, boy.' He lowered his voice. 'Listen, don't worry. I'll be pitching for both of us and doing a darn' good job.' He straightened.

'Dream on, Corrigan,' said Kate, voice also low.

He lowered dark brows. 'You said it.'

Grinning, she walked alongside him then glanced up, keeping her tone casual. 'Do you remember *anything* from the time you were unconscious?'

'Not a thing. *Except*,' Kate's heart missed a beat. 'I remember feeling rain on my face.'

She frowned and shook her head. 'It didn't rain until you were in the hospital.'

He watched her as she ran ahead to join Maisie, their red hair lifting and flying, the dog circling them, ears flapping in the cold wind. He called after her: 'It did, Red, I felt it . . .' the wind taking his words.

* * *

The evening's rota of cleaning staff was busy inside Rose Road. The door of the Unsolved Crime Unit swung open and one of them came inside dragging a vacuum cleaner. He applied it to the carpets then dusted the surfaces and immersed a couple of china mugs in hot water. After fifteen minutes he collected his cleaning materials and took a last look around the large, square room, something pulling his attention to the wall opposite the door, where the wide windows looked out onto smart little terraced houses opposite.

His eyes drifted upwards to the wall above. *That* hadn't been there yesterday. He stared at the large black script letters, his mouth moving:

Let Justice Roll Down.

THE END

ACKNOWLEDGEMENTS

My grateful thanks to the following for their generously shared expertise and their patience: Chief Inspector Keith Fackrell, West Midlands Police (Retired); Dr Jamie K. Pringle, Lecturer in Engineering & Environmental Geoscience, Keele University; Jason Spencer, FGA, DGA, RJ Dip., Manager, retail jewellers, Birmingham; Ben Steele, IT Adviser; Dr Adrian Yoong, Consultant Pathologist, Birmingham. Each one is a star and any technical errors in this book are totally mine.

Deepest thanks are due to two people who have also provided professional insight, plus unfailing encouragement and support: my editor at Orion, Jemima Forrester, and my agent Camilla Wray at Darley Anderson. I'm indebted to both.

Finally, thank you to my family for its continuing encouragement, likewise to my friends, all of them 'radiators' — you know who you are.

THE JOFFE BOOKS STORY

We began in 2014 when Jasper agreed to publish his mum's much-rejected romance novel and it became a bestseller.

Since then we've grown into the largest independent publisher in the UK. We're extremely proud to publish some of the very best writers in the world, including Joy Ellis, Faith Martin, Caro Ramsay, Helen Forrester, Simon Brett and Robert Goddard. Everyone at Joffe Books loves reading and we never forget that it all begins with the magic of an author telling a story.

We are proud to publish talented first-time authors, as well as established writers whose books we love introducing to a new generation of readers.

We have been shortlisted for Independent Publisher of the Year at the British Book Awards three times, in 2020, 2021 and 2022, and for the Diversity and Inclusivity Award at the Independent Publishing Awards in 2022.

We built this company with your help, and we love to hear from you, so please email us about absolutely anything bookish at feedback@joffebooks.com

If you want to receive free books every Friday and hear about all our new releases, join our mailing list: www.joffebooks.com/contact

And when you tell your friends about us, just remember: it's pronounced Joffe as in coffee or toffee!

ALSO BY A.J. CROSS

DR KATE HANSON MYSTERIES
Book 1: THE COLDEST CASE
Book 2: THE COLDEST CLUES

Printed in Great Britain
by Amazon

52200468R00239